D1121832

AUG   2016

THE WILD ONES

THE WILD ONES

A WESTERN DUO FEATURING SHERIFF BEN STILLMAN AND YAKIMA HENRY

PETER BRANDVOLD
AND FRANK LESLIE

FIVE STAR
A part of Gale, Cengage Learning

GALE
CENGAGE Learning®

Farmington Hills, Mich • San Francisco • New York • Waterville, Maine
Meriden, Conn • Mason, Ohio • Chicago

GALE
CENGAGE Learning®

LIBRARY OF CONGRESS CATALOGING-IN-PUBLICATION DATA

Names: Brandvold, Peter, author.
Title: The wild ones : a western duo featuring Sheriff Ben Stillman and Yakima Henry / by Peter Brandvold and Frank Leslie.
Description: First edition. | Waterville, Maine : Five Star Publishing, a part of Gale, Cengage Learning, [2016]
Identifiers: LCCN 2015037305 | ISBN 9781432831349 (hardcover) | ISBN 1432831348 (hardcover)
Subjects: LCSH: Sheriffs—Fiction. | Racially mixed people—Fiction. | BISAC: FICTION / Action & Adventure. | FICTION / Westerns. | GSAFD: Western stories.
Classification: LCC PS3552.R3236 W554 2016 | DDC 813/.54—dc23
LC record available at http://lccn.loc.gov/2015037305

First Edition. First Printing: February 2016
Find us on Facebook– https://www.facebook.com/FiveStarCengage
Visit our website– http://www.gale.cengage.com/fivestar/
Contact Five Star™ Publishing at FiveStar@cengage.com

Printed in the United States of America
1 2 3 4 5 6 7 20 19 18 17 16

CONTENTS

★ ★ ★ ★ ★

STILLMAN'S WAR
BY PETER BRANDVOLD

★ ★ ★ ★ ★

CHAPTER 1

Ben Stillman, sheriff of Hill County in the vast northern Montana Territory, slipped his ivory-gripped Colt revolver from its soft leather California holster angled for the cross draw on his left hip, and checked the loads. He plucked a .44-caliber bullet from his shell belt and slid it through the open loading gate, filling the one empty chamber that had been resting beneath the hammer.

Now all six chambers showed brass.

Stillman flicked the loading gate closed with his gloved right thumb, and spun the cylinder.

"How you wanna play it, Ben?" asked his deputy, Leon McMannigle, who sat his steel-dust gelding to Stillman's right.

Their breaths plumed in the chill night air.

October had come to the Two-Bear Mountains, a northern Montana "island" range sitting in isolation from the high, massive ridges of the Rocky Mountain spine jutting farther west. Dead leaves occasionally fell from the cottonwoods, aspens, and box elders lining Loco Jack Creek, which ran through the trees and brush to the left of the lawmen. The creek gurgled and tittered over rocks edged with thin shards of starlight-reflecting ice. The falling leaves made a soft ratcheting sound as they landed.

The cold air was stitched with the smell of burning cottonwood.

"Oh, I don't know," Stillman said lazily. "How 'bout like we always do? I take the front and you take the back?"

"You know, Ben, sometime I'd like to try the front door for a change."

"Front door's usually hotter." Stillman swung down from his saddle and slid his Henry repeater from its scabbard. "But, hell, if you feel slighted, you can go in the front door . . . and I'll take the back."

He arched a salt-and-pepper brow at his friend and deputy.

Leon stared off through the trees, in the direction from which the wood smoke was emanating. "Ah, hell," he said finally, running a black-gloved hand down his cheek of the same color. "I reckon I'm just romanticizin' a front door entrance. And since I'm so used to the back door, might as well not fix what works."

He reached back and down to slide his Winchester carbine from his own saddle boot jutting over left saddlebag pouch. "What time you want to do-si-do in the kitchen?"

Stillman slipped his Ingersoll watch from his pocket, and flipped the lid. "It's about ten forty-five. How about eleven-fifteen? Give us plenty of time to get situated."

Leon reached inside his blue-and-black plaid wool mackinaw and fished his old, battered railroad turnip from the breast pocket of his hickory shirt. He flipped the lid. "Ten forty-five it is." He adjusted his own watch, and dropped the turnip back into his pocket.

Stillman quietly pumped a cartridge into his Henry's action. "You sure you don't want the front door? I don't want you to feel insulted or anything. Back door sounds fine as frog hair to me."

Leon showed the whites of his eyes in the darkness. "Nah, nah. Now that I think on it, I've always been a back door sorta fella, anyways. Just shy, I reckon. Yep, I'm more comfortable enterin' the back door than the front. Besides, you're the sheriff and I'm your deputy, and shame on me for questioning your methods, Ben!"

Leon jerked his black, broad-brimmed hat down low over his eyes, reined his steel-dust gelding around, and trotted the horse off in the darkness, following the slow curve of the creek.

Stillman gave a wry snort as he watched the former buffalo soldier disappear in the darkness, the creek glittering like a black snakeskin in its sheath of brush and trees. When McMannigle's soft hoof thuds had dwindled to silence, Stillman led his fine, broad-barreled bay, Sweets, over to a dead tree and tossed the reins over a spidery limb.

"Stay, boy," he said, patting the horse's long, sleek neck. "You stay and don't let anyone sneak up on us from behind, all right? Okay, then . . ."

Sweets gave a low whicker and sniffed Stillman's high-crowned ten Stetson. The stallion obviously knew what was happening. He'd been through it all before many times—him waiting while his rider ran down border toughs and owl hoots. Usually after a considerable amount of shooting. Stillman wondered if the horse ever anticipated a time when, after the shooting, Stillman did not return and Sweets was left on his own.

Stillman himself did. There had been a time when he did not think about such things, like back when he was a young, hotheaded, hard-pounding deputy US marshal running down federal criminals throughout the territory from the Milk River in the north to the Powder in the south, from the towering peaks of the Rockies in the west to the sandy bluffs and wide, muddy streams in the east.

Now, though, pushing fifty and married and with a bun in his wife Faith's oven, he probably thought about it too much. That was the problem with getting old. You started to think about what you had to lose. At least you did if you'd acquired such things as a loving wife and the promise of a family.

Things you sure as hell didn't want to lose.

A fear of mortality was not always a lawman's friend. It made you overly cautious and thoughtful at times when it was best for your instincts to guide you. Fear . . . and the thinking that resulted from it . . . could get you killed.

Stillman shoved all that mind rot aside. At least as far to one side as possible given his unbridled delight at the thought that he'd soon have either a son or a daughter and his fear of missing out on that experience. That he and Faith, his young and beautiful French wife born and raised in the Powder River country, would have a boy to raise on their humble little chicken ranch on the bluffs north of Clantick.

The big, broad-shouldered sheriff clad in a buckskin mackinaw and with a knit green scarf wrapped around his neck, inside his coat, moved off into the brush and stopped just inside the dark columns of the trees at the edge of the creek. He brushed his hand across his nose and brushy, salt-and-pepper mustache, and stared beyond the creek, listening hard. His breath plumed in gray puffs around his head.

The old Turner cabin was about fifty yards beyond the rippling, glinting water. That's where he and McMannigle had decided the four or five rustlers who'd been preying on the northern Two-Bears for the past three months had been holing up when they weren't driving small herds of stolen beeves up to Canada. Stillman and Leon had come upon the place when the rustlers hadn't been here though there'd been plenty of cow tracks around the place, and they'd found fresh food leavings and split firewood inside the ramshackle cabin. They'd also found two running irons and a carbine.

Running irons were what long-loopers used to touch up the brands on the cattle they stole.

Now, tonight, it was time to put the rustlers out of commission.

Stillman found a rocky ford just upstream and crossed the creek, barely getting his boots wet. He moved quietly through the woods, weaving around black tree columns and avoiding thick clumps of brush. His nose was filled with the cool, loamy tang of the forest. Occasionally, he scented the smoke from the cabin. His boots crackled softly on the soft forest floor. Often, especially at times like these, he wished he could move as quietly as an Indian and wondered how in hell they did that.

He'd just spied the flickering lights of the cabin windows when a warbling, windy sound rose before him, growing quickly louder. Instinctively, he ducked sharply, dropped to one knee, and felt the brush of displaced air against the crown of his hat a moment before something thudded into the broad elm tree he'd just stepped around. He glanced over his shoulder and up to see the handle of the ax embedded in the tree still quivering.

He whipped his head forward. Boots crunched and thudded. A shadow darted between him and the windows of the shake-shingled cabin crouching in the darkness fifty feet away, in a small clearing. Twenty feet ahead of Stillman was a chopping block and a small pile of freshly split stove wood.

The man sprinting toward the cabin shouted, "Law trouble, boys! *Law trouble!* Grab your guns and start *shootin'!*"

The shrill voice echoed around the clearing, pitched with a mixture of anxiousness and cocky amusement. The shadow stopped suddenly between Stillman and a window. The man reached for a rifle that had been leaning against the cabin's front porch, and, quickly pumping a cartridge into the chamber, wheeled toward Stillman.

The sheriff shouted, "*Law!* Throw the gun down!"

The announcement and admonition were perfunctory. Stillman knew the rustler wasn't going to heed the warning. That's why the lawman had already pressed his Henry's brass butt plate to his shoulder and was squeezing the trigger before "down!" had even left his lips.

The Henry thundered loudly, smoke and flames lapping toward the cabin. The rustler gave a choked, *"Ohh!"* and stumbled back toward the porch, firing his own rifle into the air. He fell backward and smacked his head with a resolute thud against the front of the porch and rolled sideways onto his belly, giving strangled wails.

Shouts and the loud thumps of stomping boots rose from the cabin. Shadows jostled behind lamp-lit windows.

Stillman took about one second to reconsider his strategy and then, ejecting the spent, smoking shell casing from his Henry's breech, and levering a live one into the action, bounded off his heels and started running toward the cabin.

"Leon, I'm goin' in nowww!" he shouted, lifting his knees high to avoid tripping over unseen obstacle in the darkness, holding the Henry high across his chest.

The door burst open and a shadow edged in lamplight lurched out onto the porch. There was the raking, metallic rasp of a rifle being cocked, and then lamplight winked off the barrel as the man on the porch raised his rifle to his shoulder.

Stillman stopped, dropped to a knee, shouted "Hold it!" again perfunctorily, and squeezed the Henry's trigger even as he yelled it. The man on the porch grunted. His own rifle barked and flashed, sending a round screeching two feet to Stillman's right and loudly hammering a tree behind him, flinging bark in all directions.

The rustler gave a croaking sound as he bounced off the doorframe, and, dropping his rifle, twisted around and fell just inside the cabin's open door. Even before he hit, Stillman was off running, wincing a little at a stitch in his right knee—he wasn't as young as he used to be and he'd never been light on his feet—and gained the porch in one leaping stride.

There was much shouting and screaming and boot pounding inside the cabin. As the big sheriff crossed the porch, there was the screech of shattering glass as someone broke out a window to his left.

As two rifles began barking inside the cabin, Stillman hurled himself through the open door, leaping the stocky dead man still quivering over the doorjamb. Stillman hit the puncheon floor on his right shoulder, raising the cocked Henry.

A man was just then turning from the front window. Another was turning from a window beyond him, on the cabin's far side, where that man had been crouching over a rickety rocking chair.

The first man cursed and fired his Winchester carbine, but the bullet merely blew slivers off the edge of the table strewn with bottles, plates, glasses, and food leavings and that offered Stillman partial cover. Stillman fired from his right hip but because his momentum was still sliding him across the floor toward the dark mouth of a narrow stairs rising to the second story, his bullet flew wide of its mark.

"You son of a bitch!" the tall, gangly man with a colorless goat beard bellowed as he snapped off another shot.

The bullet hammered into the wall as Stillman gained a heel and threw himself behind the sheet-iron stove, on top of which a cast-iron pot bubbled bean juice up around its rattling lid. He raised his Henry over the top of the stove, fired, and evoked a resounding yelp from the man on the other side of the table.

Seeing the other man, harder to Stillman's right now, aim his own rifle at him, Stillman jerked his head back behind the stove's broad, tin chimney. The second shooter's bullet blew the pot of beans off the stove and onto the floor over the sheriff's left shoulder. The man's second bullet clanked loudly off the front of the iron stove. The man on the other side of the table yelped again as the ricochet plunked into his belly with a dull thump.

"Oh!" he screamed, lowering his arms and dropping his chin to look at the blood oozing out of the hole in his checked wool shirt, between the flaps of his cracked, black leather vest. His dark eyes were wide and bright with horror.

"Oh, now! Ohhh! *Ohhhhh!*"

His caterwauling distracted the second shooter—a tall man with very long, dark-brown hair hanging over a beaded elk-hide tunic. He wore a tall, bullet-crowned black hat. Stillman raised his Henry and sent the man hurling backward through the window at that end of the cabin. He sort of folded up like a jackknife and took his leave of the hovel in a screech of breaking glass.

He landed with a deep thud outside the cabin, and Stillman heard him expel a muffled grunt even beneath what the lawman now realized were a girl's hysterical screams emanating from the cabin's second story.

Chapter 2

Stillman removed his hat and edged a look around the door to the stairwell.

He peered up the steep, short wooden stairs to see a pale, naked, bearded man aiming two pistols at him from the top of the steps. The armed man angled both revolvers down over the stairs, both hammers cocked.

Stillman jerked his head back as both pistols barked and tore two large divots of wood from the casing, one sliver pricking Stillman's right cheek. The girl continued screaming at the tops of her lungs behind the naked, bearded shooter.

"Come on out, lawman," the naked gunman shouted. "Or I'll kill this little whore up here!"

Whore?

Stillman hadn't realized they had a girl until he'd heard the screams.

He set his Henry aside and yelled, "Hold on, hold on, for chrissakes! Who's the girl?"

He slipped his Colt from its holster, clicked the hammer back.

"Nothin' more'n a side of purty beef if you don't throw your guns down and get out here where I can see you!"

The girl screamed louder.

"All right, all right!" Stillman snaked his pistol around the side of the door casing, keeping the barrel nudged up taut against the wood. He glanced around the casing to get his bearings and then pulled his head back and triggered his Colt once, twice, three times, shouting, "Here you go, you son of a bitch!"

The shooter triggered both his own pistols once more after Stillman's second shot, the two bullets tearing into the floor at the bottom of the stairs. Stillman heard him groan.

As the sheriff pulled his revolver back away from the door casing, there were a full two seconds of silence before he heard the thunder of a body rolling violently down the stairs. He glanced to his left to see the naked shooter come tumbling out of the doorway and turning a forward somersault into the kitchen, where he lay flat on his back, spread-eagle, eyes open.

His mouth opened and closed inside his beard, like a fish's. Blood trickled out one corner of it to stain the dark red hair on his chin. Blood also oozed from the three holes in his pale, bony torso.

He gave a jerk, sighed, and lay still.

Stillman slid his head halfway around the casing again, cocking the Colt and aiming it up the stairs—at nothing but a low stretch of scarred, wooden ceiling across which dull, umber lamplight wavered from somewhere ahead and to the right. He could hear someone stumbling around up there, breathing hard.

The girl had stopped screaming and was now only whimpering loudly in the close quarters that smelled of sour sweat, a kerosene lamp, and a charcoal brazier.

"Shut up, you crazy bitch!" a man's voice barked.

The girl mewled.

Stillman climbed the stairs slowly, stretched his gaze over the top in time to see a half-dressed man climb out a window ahead and on his right, near a bed covered in pelts and atop which a pale, sandy-haired girl sat with her back against a wall, naked, her head resting in her arms atop her upraised knees.

"Stop, or I'll blow you to hell!" Stillman shouted.

The half-dressed man swung around toward Stillman, a pistol

in his hand. His free arm was loaded down with clothes and a pair of saddlebags. He was wearing a hat, which shaded the top half of his face. His pistol flashed and barked.

Stillman pulled his head down below the top of the stairs as the slug chewed into the floor two feet ahead of him. When he looked up the stairs again, the man was gone. Stillman heard a crunching thud, felt the slight reverberation beneath his boots on the stairs. Apparently, the man had leaped onto a lower outside roof.

Stillman bolted up the stairs. Halfway to the window, he heard Leon shout, "Stop right there or you're a dead man, amigo!"

There were two quick reports, one practically on top of the other one. There was a muffled grunt. Stillman crouched to peer through the window, saw a shadow dash off into the woods behind the cabin.

"Leon!"

"Ben, you all right?" the deputy called up from somewhere unseen in the dark yard below.

"Unhurt. How 'bout yourself?"

"Fine as frog hair. I think I pinked that son of a bitch. All clear in there?"

"Yeah."

Stillman pulled his head in from the window and turned to the girl, who was staring at him with a combination of terror and relief over the tops of her upraised knees. She was naked and pale, and she was clamping one arm across her left breast, cupping her right breast in that hand. A tuft of hair and a swell of fleshy pink shone between her legs, down low against the pelt she was sitting on.

Stillman looked quickly away from it, shame briefly warming his ears.

Frowning, he said, "What's your name, miss?"

"Orlean Hollister," she said in a little girl's pain- and horror-pinched voice, tears dribbling down her pretty, pale cheeks. "Those men . . . they . . . they kidnapped me from my father's ranch!"

Stillman moved over to her, lowering his smoking Colt. "Watt Hollister's daughter?" Hollister was one of the largest, most respected ranchers in Hill County, his vast holdings spilling down the Two-Bear Mountains' western flanks toward the breaks of the Missouri River. His gaze encompassed nearly ten thousand acres, and, depending on the time of year, he had anywhere between twenty and thirty riders on his payroll.

The girl nodded, lowered her face again to her knees, and sobbed. "Oh, god—what they did to me! Over and over! I'm so *ashamed*!"

Stillman patted the girl's shoulder. The warm room reeked of coal, man-sweat, musty pelts, whiskey, and sex—if you could call it that. "It'll be all right. We'll get you back home."

Boots thudded below and a voice called up the stairs, "Ben?"

"I'll be right down." Stillman squeezed one of the girl's hands. "It'll be all right. Why don't you go ahead and get dressed and we'll get you on the trail back to Clantick? Should be there by morning."

The girl lifted her tear-streaked face and pinched her pain-racked, light-brown eyes. She had about five freckles on the nubs of her pale, plump cheeks and a thumb-shaped birthmark on her neck. She sniffed and said beseechingly, "I couldn't help what they done . . . made me do." She clamped Stillman's hand desperately in her own. "They said they'd kill me and send me back in pieces to the ranch. I didn't want . . . I couldn't let my mother and father go through that!"

"It's all right," Stillman repeated, placing a comforting hand on the back of the girl's head. "No one will blame you for this. Your folks will understand."

Staring at him, the girl drew her lips into her mouth and tried a smile.

"Go ahead and get dressed," Stillman said, giving her back a couple of soft, reassuring pats.

As Stillman turned away from the bed, he heard the stairs creak and a spur ching.

"Everything all right up here?" Leon said.

The deputy's black hat and dark face rose up into Stillman's view from the dark stairwell.

Stillman stopped in front of the stairs, and sighed. "Well, sort of." He glanced over his shoulder.

With his boots planted halfway up the stairs, Leon glanced around the cluttered, smelly, dimly lit half-story room, frowning. "The back door was blocked by firewood, Ben," he said absently.

Stillman gave an ironic chuff. "Yeah, I considered that possibility . . . when I was halfway to the cabin."

Leon's eyes settled on the girl, and then he looked at Stillman, wrinkling the skin above the bridge of his nose. "Who . . . ?"

"Watt Hollister's daughter."

Stillman took one step down the stairs. Leon had started to turn and start down himself when, glancing around once more, his wide, molasses-dark eyes widened until they were nearly all whites, and he shouted, "Ben, *down!*"

Stillman threw himself forward and sideways. Behind him, a gun crashed loudly. As Stillman hit the floor to the right of the stairwell, he saw Leon snap up his Schofield .44, extending it straight out from his shoulder. The Remy flashed and roared as the gun behind Stillman barked once more.

At the same time, the girl screamed.

Lying prone, Stillman turned his head, whipping his longish, salt-and-pepper hair from his eyes to see the girl fly back onto the bed, dropping a small, smoking pistol onto the floor with a dull thud. She lay back on the bed, still naked. Her pale, slender legs dangled toward the floor, twitching.

Stillman stared, his lower jaw hanging in shock. "I'll be . . . goddamned . . . !"

Leon stared wide-eyed over the smoking barrel of his still-extended Schofield. Very slowly, he started to lower the gun. In a low, bewildered rasp, he muttered, "She was . . . she was . . ."

He let his voice trail off.

Silence filled the half-story space cluttered with old, moldering tack and mining supplies left over from the place's previous owner and the occasional outlaw gangs who holed up in the place from time to time, usually on their way from some holdup farther south and on their way to Canada.

Stillman slowly gained his feet. Leaving Leon standing statue-still in the stairwell, he walked over to where the girl lay slumped on the bed. She sat on her butt, her torso twisted onto one shoulder, feet dangling about six inches above the floor. Her feet were small and pale and slender. She wasn't a very big girl. Stillman guessed she didn't weight quite a hundred pounds. He'd heard that Hollister had a daughter, but he'd never met the girl. He'd met Hollister's three sons but never the girl. Hollister and his wife, Virginia, both native Texans, were known to keep the girl close to home. Virginia, nearly twenty years Watt's junior but as persnickety as a woman twice her age, was known to be devout.

Stillman placed his left hand on the girl's right shoulder and gently rolled her onto her back. Her small, pointed, pink-tipped breasts flattened out against her chest. They were white as marble, with fine blue veins just beneath the surface. Blood trickled through the shallow valley between them from the neat, round dimple in the middle of her chest, just above her breast-bone.

The girl's eyes were wide open and staring, the flickering, umber lamplight wavering over them like light on a frozen pond. Her chest lay still. She was dead.

Watt Hollister's daughter was dead.

Floorboards creaked behind Stillman. McMannigle's spurs rattled faintly. "She was . . . she was . . ."

"I know," Stillman said, seeing the deputy's shadow elongate across the bed to the sheriff's left. "She was going to back shoot me."

Stillman gave an inward shudder. He'd been back shot before. By mistake by a drunk whore. He cringed at the thought of it happening again. That bullet, still in his back, had closed the book on his career as a deputy United States marshal.

"Why?" Leon asked in dull exasperation as he stood beside Stillman.

Staring down at the girl, his ears ringing from confusion and all the gunfire in the tight confines, Stillman said, "She would have shot us both, if she'd had her way."

"But, *why*?"

"Maybe she wasn't as unhappy as she let on. About bein' a hostage."

"You think she went willingly with them rustlers?"

"I don't know. Maybe her father can help fill in the gaps. We'll get her back to the Triple H Connected, hear what he has to say."

"Holy shit in the nun's privy—I know what he's gonna have to say about me killin' his daughter!"

"Like I said, she would have killed us both—you after me. *Why* is what we have to find out." Stillman started to reach for the girl.

McMannigle nudged him, said, "Let me, Ben. I shot her."

Leon wrapped the girl in a large deerskin blanket, tucking both ends so that none of her pale, fragile-looking body was exposed, not even her hair. When he had picked the bundle up in his arms, he followed Stillman down the steps to the first floor where the three dead men lay.

McMannigle took the girl out onto the porch while Stillman looked around. Blood was liberally splattered over the kitchen area of the cabin. A pair of saddlebags hung from a chair back near where the man who'd fired out the window lay slumped on his side against the front wall.

Stillman opened the flap of one of the bags, reached in, and pulled out several packets of greenbacks and silver certificates. He opened the flap on the other bag, and pulled out several more pouches.

"What you got there?" McMannigle asked as he stepped back into the cabin.

"The reason the Hollister girl wanted to fill us full o' lead," the sheriff said.

CHAPTER 3

Stillman drew a puff from his cigarette and blew the smoke up toward the rusty Rochester lamp hanging over the table by an equally rusty wire. The smoke hit the lamp and fanned out in a large, luminous cloud.

Stillman and McMannigle had dragged the dead rustlers off into the corral flanking the cabin, excepting the dead Hollister girl, who lay on a pallet in the rundown parlor. The lawmen didn't want wildcats or coyotes getting to her during the night. They didn't want to take a mangled corpse back to the Hollister ranch. They'd decided to catch forty winks here in the cabin and get a fresh start back to Clantick in the morning.

The sheriff was counting the money he'd found in the saddlebags. He tossed the last of the bills onto a stack on the table before him. "Eleven thousand four hundred and twenty . . . thirty . . . forty . . . fifty . . . six and one more dollar makes eleven thousand four hundred and fifty-seven dollars. They really raked in the money, sellin' stolen stock up in Canada. I'm gonna have to ride up there one of these days and have a talk with the Mounties in Moose Jaw. See if they know who's buyin' long-looped Montana beef."

"Sizable chunk of change," Leon said, splashing more whiskey into the tin cup before him, a half-smoked cheroot smoldering in his gloved hand. "But mere chump change to the Hollisters."

The deputy splashed more whiskey into Stillman's cup and set the half-empty bottle down on the table. Stillman took another drag from his quirley and ran a hand through his thick, wavy hair, blowing smoke up at the lamp again. He took a sip of the whiskey, the comforting burn of which helped stave off the cold pushing through the broken window and shuttling a draft around the cabin despite the stove the lawmen had stoked.

"Yeah, it's odd for a rich girl to take up with raggedy-heeled owl hoots," Stillman said. "But I've seen crazier things in the half a lifetime I've lived so far."

McMannigle looked at the long, deerskin bundle lying on the floor near the small stone hearth in the parlor side of the cabin. They hadn't built a fire in the fireplace because, judging by the leaves and cobwebs in it, the chimney was likely blocked by birds' nests or leaf snags.

The Stanley place hadn't been a permanent home in several years, since Indians had driven the Stanleys out of this valley before Stillman had come out of retirement to become Hill County sheriff. The land had since been bought by a neighboring rancher, but no one had moved back onto the headquarters—except itinerant bands of owl hoots, that was. Despite Stillman's best efforts, such curly wolves were still fairly common in this vast, remote northern part of a still wild and woolly territory.

"You suppose she took up with 'em because she was in love with one of 'em?" Leon asked as he stared forlornly at the bundle.

"There were two upstairs with her."

McMannigle turned to Leon, glowering. "Two?"

"Two."

"That delicate little girl was taking two men at the same time?"

"Maybe she wasn't as delicate as she looks."

"Well, I'll be." Leon looked at the girl again and shook his head. "I wonder what old Watt Hollister would say about that."

"I'd heard old Hollister and his wife were right protective of the girl. Sometimes that'll turn a girl . . . or a boy . . . as wild as a young coyote with the springtime itch. I'm bettin' that's what happened here. I don't know. We'll talk to the old man, get his side of it, try to get to the bottom of it."

"Could be these men rode for Hollister," Leon said.

"Could be."

"Maybe that's how they come to know little Miss."

"Could be."

McMannigle stared at the girl for a time and then slid his gaze back to Stillman. "You know her name, Ben?"

"She said it was Orlean. Orlean Hollister."

"Orlean?"

"That's what she told me. I heard Virginia Hollister's family was originally from New Orleans."

Leon drew a deep, ragged breath and shook his head again. "Sure wish I hadn't had to shoot her."

"Well, you did have to." Stillman stretched his back with a wince, splashed more whiskey into his deputy's tin cup, and used the bottleneck to nudge the cup toward him encouragingly. "If you hadn't, you'd have my wife to contend with, and when she gets that French blood of hers up, you'd rather tangle with two hydrophobic wildcats in a Dougherty wagon."

McMannigle lowered his head and chuckled.

"Besides, she'd likely have drilled your ass, too. So call it self-preservation as opposed to suicide."

The deputy sighed, lowered his head again, and ran a hand over his close-cropped, wooly, black pate. "I just got a big problem with shootin' women, Ben. Especially young women. Especially young *white* women. You'd understand if you was black."

"You think *I* like shooting young white women?" Stillman

grinned and mashed his quirley out on the table. "Drink up and let's get some sleep. Sun'll be up in a couple hours."

Stillman and McMannigle were up at first light.

They brewed a pot of coffee on the cabin's sheet-iron stove and breakfasted on the hot, black coffee, elk jerky they'd packed, and a can of tomatoes they found on a shelf in the cabin. Afterwards, they both smoked a cigarette out on the front porch, watching the sky turn green over the low, forested western ridges.

As they did, Stillman laid out his plan for the morning.

"You go ahead and start back to town with the girl and what's left of those owl hoots in the stable," he told Leon. "We'll throw them over their horses' backs and give Auld a few bucks to bury them if no one claims them, which I doubt anyone will."

"You're goin' after the man I wounded?"

Stillman nodded. "How bad did you wound him?"

"Couldn't tell, but I heard him give a yelp. I got him, all right. Might be layin' up there, waitin' for us to pull out and see if he can't get a hoss." McMannigle blew cigarette smoke out into the still-dark yard in which birds were chirping almost maniacally. The chirps seemed to be increasing as the light intensified in the arching sky. "Might be dead, far as that goes."

"I'll check it out. Either way, I'll find him. And we won't be leavin' him any horses. All the horses will go with you. When I find him, I'll catch up with you."

"What about the girl?"

"We'll have Auld put her in a box, and I'll haul her out to the Triple H Connected, turn her over to her folks."

"I oughta do that. Explain it to her old man. I shot her."

"I'm the sheriff," Stillman said, giving his deputy a commanding look from beneath the brim of his broad tan Stetson, blowing cigarette smoke out his nostrils. "It's my job. You shot her in the line of duty, in self-defense, and that's enough of *that* conversation."

"Well, I oughta ride with you, anyway, Ben."

"We're the only two lawmen in this whole damn county, Leon. And we have tracklayers from the railroad in town. You know what kind of a ruckus they can raise. It don't make sense for both of us to haul one dead girl way out to the backside of the Bear Paws. That's a two-day wagon ride, round-trip."

Stillman shook his head and flicked his quirley into the yard. "No, I can't justify us both leavin' the office unattended after we already both been gone for two days. I'm goin' alone and, like I said, that's the end of *that* conversation."

He tossed the dregs of his coffee into the yard, adjusted his hat, set his cup on the porch rail, and moved down the porch steps to head for the corral and stable.

When the lawmen had gotten the dead men's horses saddled and the bodies tied over the saddles of their fidgety mounts, who didn't care for the smell of blood, they led the pack string, tied tail to tail, back to the cabin. They tied the dead Hollister girl over a blue roan, and Leon mounted his steel-dust gelding with the roan's bridle reins in his hand.

"I'm hoping to catch up to you before you get to Clantick," Stillman said.

"All right, then."

"Leon?"

McMannigle was still getting seated. "Yeah?"

Stillman glanced at the deerskin shrouding the dead Hollister girl. "Nothin'."

There was nothing he could say to ease his deputy's pain. Stillman would have felt the same way over shooting a girl, even one he'd been fully justified in shooting. Well, not the same way, exactly. Leon had the added complication of his having killed a white girl. Stillman knew he could never fully understand that part of it. He'd hold his tongue.

"You be careful, Ben. You know—a wounded wildcat, and all that." Leon pinched his hat brim.

The deputy turned forward in his saddle and touched spurs to the flanks of his steel-dust gelding. The horse started off down a brushy two-track trail that curled west through the aspen and box-elder woods and toward a bend in the quietly chuckling creek that skirted the ranch yard. The six horses with their grisly cargoes lurched forward and eased into walks, leaving the yard as they passed a squat log shed with many holes in its roof, before McMannigle spurred his own mount into a spanking trot, and the packhorses, tied tail to tail, begrudgingly followed suit.

Stillman watched the horses drift off along the trail through the woods then went back to the stable to saddle Sweets. He left the bay tied outside the dilapidated, peeled-pole corral while he looked around. He found some light blood splatters just behind a low-slung rear addition to the cabin. The addition was abutted by a long, high stack of freshly split firewood, as though the rustlers had planned to lay up here for a while.

Some of the logs were strewn about the base of the stack. The man who'd leaped out the window had apparently jumped onto the stack and then to the ground, where he'd encountered Leon and had taken a bullet from the deputy's Schofield. The ground was fairly hard-packed and littered with bits of old hay, oats, and straw, but Stillman managed to pick up the man's boot tracks and follow them to where he'd run around the west side of the corral and into the woods north of the ranch yard.

Stillman lost the boot prints in the trees but kept moving north until he found another streak of blood on a deadfall aspen. He kept walking north until the woods gave way to open ground—a brief stretch of blond prairie grass that rose gently toward the creek and its slim sheathing of autumn crimson chokecherries and sumacs and yellow river willows. The creek was shallow, so Stillman crossed it easily. After he'd gained the other side and had continued walking forty yards from the stream, looking for more tracks and more blood, he began feeling the burn of frustration.

He'd seen nothing since he'd left the creek.

He climbed to the top of the rise and looked down into a shallow valley with what appeared to be an arroyo running down the middle of it, parallel with the ridge Stillman was on. The ridges on either side of it were stippled with piñon pines, with a large, old, lightning-topped cottonwood standing farther down near the rocky streambed. A raptor of some kind—it looked like a golden eagle—sat hunched in its deep feathers on one of the charred limbs. The arroyo jogged down to Stillman's right for a hundred yards and then meandered away from him, toward the southeast and a swell of low, brown hills.

The arroyo would be a good, sheltered place for a wounded rustler to hole up in. Possibly die in. That eagle might be waiting to dine.

Stillman spat to one side, doffed his hat, and ran his hand through his hair that was sweaty now, as the day was heating up as the sun inched farther above the horizon. He had to recon the arroyo. He didn't want to, because he wanted to get back to Clantick and deal with the dead Hollister girl. Something told him that Leon might go against orders and take the girl back to the Triple H Connected on his own.

McMannigle was a loyal, invaluable deputy, and while he rarely went against Stillman's orders—in fact, the sheriff couldn't recollect when he ever had—Leon was pretty torn up about the girl. He felt the need to take responsibility for her death, to explain the matter to her folks. Maybe, in a roundabout way, he was seeking forgiveness. An admirable attitude, of course. But also one that might get him killed.

Stillman just now realized that part of his reluctance about having his deputy ride out to the Hollister place was due to his fear of how Leon might be received.

A black man hauling the body of the white girl he'd killed back to her own people. Especially Southern people . . .

Still, the sheriff felt a strong obligation to investigate the arroyo. He didn't want to leave one of the rustlers at large and risk him getting away and possibly forming another bunch or seeking revenge for his dead accomplices. That would be like leaving a keg of dynamite out here with the fuse attached.

Stillman cursed, spat again, and tramped back down the rise and across the creek. He retrieved his bay stallion from the ranch yard, and, mounted, rode up and down the arroyo and along both of its brushy banks several times, looking for the wounded rustler. He rode for nearly ninety minutes and as far as a mile out along the streambed's southeast jog, and found nothing more interesting than a moldering, wheelless wagon rotting among the brush and rocks, and the bleached bones of several cows and one horse.

No blood. No footprints. No body.

Nothing.

Confounded, he rode straight south and investigated a coulee and another, shorter canyon. He found one sock, but it was so badly sun-faded and torn that, while it might have belonged to his quarry, he doubted it. It wasn't enough evidence to keep him out here any longer.

Cursing under his breath, Stillman turned Sweets toward home.

A vague apprehension had been eating at him for the past two hours. Suddenly, he was more worried about McMannigle than he was about finding the wounded rustler.

He hoped like hell that saving Stillman's life wouldn't get Leon killed.

CHAPTER 4

Several hours later, well past midday, Stillman pushed Sweets on into Clantick.

The little town, which was the seat of Hill County, sat amid chalky, sage- and yucca-spiked buttes lining the Milk River, which meandered only a quarter mile north. It was near the river that Stillman's own small chicken ranch perched on the shoulder of a flat-topped butte overlooking the dusty settlement that around twenty-five years ago had started out as a hide hunter's camp but had gradually been transformed into a ranch supply hub—one that would soon be connected by Northern Pacific rails not only to Chicago and points east, but to the West Coast, as well.

Still, it remained a humble little village and home to only around a thousand or so souls—most of them good, hard-working souls, though there were a few sour apples in every barrel. The business buildings—mostly log but some adobe—pushed up around Stillman now as he slowed his hard-ridden but stalwart bay to a walk, signs announcing the various businesses reaching into the street upon skinned pine poles.

Fallen cottonwood leaves skidded across the street, as did the occasional tumbleweed or newspaper torn from a trash heap.

There was a lot of horse and wagon traffic, and Stillman returned the greetings of several men he knew standing around outside of the harness shop, feed supply shop, Verne Gandy's Mercantile, and the town's several saloons. No fewer than a dozen saddle horses were tied to hitch racks fronting the two main watering holes, the Milk River Saloon and the Drover's. The din of loud conversation, laughter, and the patter of piano music swelled out over the saloons' louvered doors. There were the clinks of coins and the clatter of roulette wheels, which meant that the money the cowpunchers had made from the various fall roundups was burning holes in the boys' pockets and was just now switching hands mighty quickly.

A girl's scream sounded from a Milk River Saloon second-floor window, causing Stillman to jerk back on his horse's reins.

"Goddamn you, Pike," shouted the girl. "I told you no free feels! You wanna squeeze my titties, you pay downstairs *first,* or get the hell *out!*"

A man's drunken voice gave a simpering retort, and Stillman booted Sweets on down the street. He'd recognized the voice of an aging whore named Starr Brightly—she claimed it was her actual name—and the sheriff was confident that Miss Starr was capable of taking care of herself. In fact, Stillman was worried more about the man who'd tried to cop a free feel than he was about Starr, who carried twin derringers in sheaths strapped to her garter belts and wasn't afraid to use them.

Stillman wove Sweets through the traffic and stopped the horse in front of the two large, open doors of Auld's Livery & Feed Barn, which is where Leon customarily stabled his horse and which was where he'd likely deposited the bodies he'd ridden into town with. Auld served as the town's liveryman, water-witcher, well digger, gravedigger, wheelwright, and undertaker, which mainly consisted of hammering together simple pine coffins, or wooden overcoats, as Auld called them, and depositing the bodies of the deceased in same.

Auld usually hired whores to bathe and dress the bodies. That is, when such niceties were called for, which wasn't all that often.

Stillman dropped Sweets's reins in the broad patch of hay-flecked shade fronting the barn and stepped between the doors, peering into the place's deep shadows. "Auld?"

"Ah, Christ! You damn near scared me into a heart stroke, Sheriff!"

Stillman hadn't seen him at first because of the heavy purple shadows, but now as his eyes adjusted from the brassy sunlight, he saw the burly, bearded liveryman in pinstriped overalls and floppy canvas hat standing near an open storage room door about halfway down the barn's central alley. Auld was holding a couple of long pine planks in his arms, and he was scowling at Stillman, red-faced behind his bushy, gray-brown beard that climbed his cheeks to nearly his angry blue eyes.

Beyond him, the barn's rear doors were open. Stillman could see that Auld had the bodies of five men laid out on sheets of plywood propped on sawhorses. Auld's fat tabby cat, Gustave, was sitting on one of the planks, beside one of the dead men. The cat's tail was curled forward around its fat body, and Gustave was blinking slowly and with typical cat-like insouciance as he stared toward his master and Stillman.

"I see Leon made it back with the dead men," Stillman said.

"*Ja*, he made it back, all right." The liveryman raised a large, gloved, roast-sized fist threateningly. "And that goddamned city council better pay me for my work here, because the last time those tight bastards made me wait until—"

"I'll see you're paid before you get them cadavers in the ground up on Boot Hill," Stillman said, cutting off the big, beer-bellied German before he could launch himself too deeply in one of his typical tirades. In more civilized places, a coroner's jury would have investigated the deaths, but this far off the beaten path, Stillman unofficially assumed the job as county coroner. In a pinch, a real coroner was brought in from Helena, but only when there was a real question as to the cause of someone's death.

Stillman usually just filled out an affidavit, had it witnessed by Leon or Elmer Burke, who owned the Drover's, and filed it with the circuit judge, who did only God knew what with it.

"Do you have the girl, too?" Stillman asked.

"That's what you said last time!"

"I said what last time?"

"That you'd see I was paid promptly but those skinflint bastards said they had to wait to see what that crooked banker said about—!"

"Auld!"

"What?"

"Do you have the girl back there, too?"

"No, I don't have the girl! I gave your deputy my last wooden overcoat and rented him a buckboard, and he took off for the Triple H Connected! And he didn't pay me one dime for that box! Not one dime! Each box is two dollars, and that barely covers the materials to say nothing about—!"

"Goddamnit!"

"Goddamnit is right. You know what I think those city council fellas do with our hard-earned tax money? I think they—!"

"Auld!"

"*What?*"

"Shut your piehole and saddle me your fastest mount! Then you can unsaddle Sweets and—!"

"Ben!"

The girl's scream had risen from behind Stillman and back down the street in the direction from which he'd come. The waitress from Sam Wa's Café was running toward him, taking care not to get run over by the horsebackers and farm and ranch wagons hammering up and down the usually quiet street. Fall was always a busy time of the year in Clantick, but the Northern Pacific's push just west of here was making it busier.

Evelyn Vincent was holding the skirts of her cream-and-salmon Mother Hubbard dress above her black leather shoes, as she gained Stillman's side of the street. Her sandy-blonde hair had tumbled half out of the neat chignon she usually wore behind her head when she was working, and her heart-shaped face was red from anxiety.

"What is it, Evelyn?" Stillman asked, walking down the street to meet her.

Just then he heard shouts rising from the far side of the street and down a ways. They seemed to be coming from Sam Wa's place.

"Ben—please, help!" Evelyn cried, grabbing his right wrist and tugging him along behind her. "It's Sam and one of the customers! They're fighting. With knives!"

Stillman started to follow the girl back across the street at a slant, adjusting his big Colt .44 on his left hip and sliding his gaze this way and that, negotiating the traffic. He held his arm out to stop a ranch wagon moving toward him from the left, evoking an indignant bray from one of the mules in the wagon's traces, and then he and Evelyn gained the street's opposite side.

Evelyn was walking slightly ahead of Stillman, nearly running and glancing over her shoulder to say, "He's fighting with one of the customers. The man's a horror. He pulled me onto his lap and kissed me and . . . and he put his hands where . . . well, where no man should put his hands unless he's given permission!" The young blonde paused, breathing hard as she hopped up onto the small, wooden veranda sagging off the front of the small log shack that housed Sam Wa's Café. The smell of fried chicken and steaks and rich gravy mingled with the smell of the blue-tinged wood smoke hovering over and around the shack.

"Wait out here," Stillman told the girl, grabbing her right arm to stop her.

A couple of men dressed in the shabby checked suits of drummers were milling near the front screen door, peering anxiously inside.

"You pay or you go to jail, like everyone else!" Sam Wa was shouting inside the place. His Chinese accent had grown less severe over the several years he'd been living and slinging hash in Clantick. "You pay now and then you go—get the hell out of Sam's place, and never . . . !"

Dressed in a purple smock and fringed deerskin trousers over which he wore a soiled, green apron, the rotund Chinaman saw Stillman, and his almond-shaped black eyes brightened. Sam curled a shrewd smile that was framed by his long, gray-brown, mare's-tail mustaches that hung several inches down below his lower jaw.

"Sheff, Sheff!" he called, still unable to pronounce "Sheriff" correctly. "Arrest this man. Get him out of here before I gut him like feesh!"

He very easily could have gutted the man with the large, wooden-handled meat cleaver he was holding in his large, pudgy left fist. Sam and his troublesome customer were both crouched like pugilists in the middle of the restaurant, in a sizeable gap between oilcloth-covered tables.

The customer was Sam's size. He was a sinister-looking cuss with long, coarse, yellow-blond hair hanging past his shoulders, and a thick beard two shades darker than his hair. He wore a ragged buffalo-skin vest and checked orange trousers with hide-patched knees, the cuffs stuffed into high-topped, fur-trimmed moccasins. An empty knife sheath jutted from one of the moccasins. The knife was in the man's right hand, and he was holding it up between him and Sam as the two men scuffled around in the gap between the tables, the blond gent grinning menacingly while Sam was prattling in what Stillman assumed was Chinese.

Stillman had seen the blond cuss before. He'd been in town a lot recently, drinking and gambling. The sheriff had heard he was a market hunter for the railroad crew working west of here . . . when they weren't in town raising a ruckus, that was.

"Stay out of this, Sheriff!" the blond gent said, glancing at Stillman and letting his eye flick to the five-pointed star pinned to Stillman's blue, white-pinstriped shirt, near his left brown leather suspender. "This Chinaman's cussin' me out though he does it in dog-talk so I can't figure it out, but no Chinaman's gonna talk to Seymore M. Scudder that way!"

"Throw those blades down!" Stillman ordered, moving quickly.

"He's nothin' but a goddamn Chinaman, and he done accused me of not payin' for my meal!" Scudder slashed his big bowie knife at Sam Wa's bulging belly. Sam had been a Chinaman in the American West long enough to have learned how to handle a knife-wielding hooplehead. He expertly feinted, shuffling his slippered feet with uncommon grace while showing his sharp, yellow teeth the way a mountain lion bares its fangs, and growling.

"I gut him, Sheff!" Sam shouted warningly, making slashing motions with the blood-crusted meat cleaver. "I gut him now! Sam's gonna carve dis bastard up and feed him to my hogs!"

Stillman pushed one of the onlookers aside. There were five or six men standing around, some placing bets, all yelling encouragement to either Sam or his bearded opponent. Stillman was close enough now he could smell the alcohol stench oozing from Scudder's pores. He was glassy-eyed and stockyard mean from drink.

"Scudder, I told you to throw that knife down!"

The market hunter spun suddenly toward Stillman, pale blue eyes flashing yellow as he said, "Sheriff, if you're sidin' this heathen, I'll gut you same as him!" He thrust the Bowie toward Stillman. The sheriff lurched back just in time to keep himself from being gored by the savagely curled tip of the razor-edged Bowie.

Rage burned through Stillman.

He, too, had danced with knife-wielding hoopleheads.

Bounding forward without hesitation, he slammed his right fist into Scudder's face before the hunter could bring the knife back again. Scudder grunted and stumbled backward. Stillman stayed on him, grabbing the blond market hunter's knife wrist with his own right hand and smashing his left fist into Scudder's face—three quick, brutal jabs that turned the market hunter's nose and lips the deep red of tomato sauce.

As Scudder fell straight backward, screaming and clamping both hands over his ruined face, a man behind Stillman yelled, "I had money on him, you tin-starred son of a bitch!"

Stillman wheeled in time to see one of the onlookers—a barrel-shaped, freckle-faced gent in a rabbit-fur hat and rabbit-skin vest—begin hauling up a Russian .44 from a holster thonged on his right thigh. Stillman brought his own revolver up first, and fired a half second before the freckle-faced gent's Russian roared.

In the doorway, Evelyn Vincent screamed and clamped her hands over her mouth.

The freckle-faced gent's slug tore into an oilcloth-covered table several feet to Stillman's left while the shooter twisted around to face the door and dropped his gun as he clamped a hand over the bloody hole in his right arm. He fell to both knees, lifted his head, and spewed hoarse epithets at the ceiling.

He glared, crimson-faced, over his shoulder at the sheriff. "You're gonna die! Oh, Stillman, you're gonna die for that—if it's the last thing I do!"

Stillman sighed and let his pistol hang down along his right thigh. He looked at the man with the ruined face, who was lying supine on the floor, rolling this way and that, clamping his hands to his face and sobbing.

He looked at the barrel-shaped, freckle-faced gent he'd just pinked, and cursed.

If there'd been any doubt before in his ability to leave town, there was none now. Now, he had two prisoners to look after and a wild dog of a town to leash.

His deputy was on his own.

CHAPTER 5

As the buckboard wagon crested a steep hill, its iron-shod wheels squawking, Deputy McMannigle drew back on the reins of the rangy piebald in the traces. The horse stopped and shook its head as though sensing the wagon driver's own apprehension.

"What you so edgy about?" Leon griped to the horse. "You didn't shoot the stupid little . . ." He let his voice trail off. He knew better than to speak ill of the dead.

He gave a fateful sigh, poked his hat brim up off his forehead and stared across a creek that ran between hills below him, toward the headquarters of the Triple H Connected Ranch, which sprawled across a tabletop bluff beyond. Cattle grazed along the slope of the bluff, some standing in the creek and staring with dim-witted curiosity up toward McMannigle, water dripping from weeds clinging to their jaws.

A dog's angry barks lured the deputy's gaze up the bluff to where the dog stood under the wooden ranch portal, with the Triple H Connected brand burned into the crossbeam. The dog was a shaggy, tricolor collie or shepherd, and it jerked its snout up with each bark. After every three or four barks it glanced over its left shoulder toward the big house standing on the top of the bluff beyond it, as though looking to see if its warning was being heeded or if it was wasting its time out here.

It was almost dusk. Shadows were growing long and purple with salmon-gold trim.

Purple smoke curled from the large, fieldstone chimney that jutted up from the house's right end. The log house was two and a half stories, and it looked like a barn except for the front porch and the rows of shutter-outfitted windows running along all three stories—and the chimney, of course. A log bunkhouse sat to the left of the house. Two barns of different sizes, several corrals, and sundry outbuildings sat forward and to the right.

McMannigle had been out here twice before with Stillman, when Hollister had complained of nesters—small ranchers staking claim to what he considered his own graze. Hollister did not tolerate interlopers of any kind. He'd told the lawmen so when they'd ridden out here. He tolerated neither nesters nor rustlers, and if Stillman and McMannigle didn't deal with the problem, he'd deal with it himself.

With long riatas outfitted with a hangman's noose.

He told the lawmen that much, as well. The lawmen knew that Hollister would have preferred to handle the matter himself, and had certainly done so in the past, but was trying to change with these more lawful times.

Now, shaking the reins over the piebald's back and clucking to the horse, starting down the hill, McMannigle wondered how old Hollister would feel about a black man who'd killed his daughter. As he wondered about that, he half-consciously patted his Schofield revolver holstered on his right thigh, and glanced at his sheathed Winchester lying under the wagon seat. He'd made sure both weapons were fully loaded, just in case.

Probably crazy, riding out here alone. Not only crazy, he deserved to be fired for it. He'd gone against the wishes of his boss, a man he respected. But something hard and stubborn in the deputy had compelled him to ride out here with the intention of explaining himself. Any man with an ounce of integrity would want to do the same thing. Leon didn't want to hide behind Ben's badge.

What he'd had to do was tragic, but it was justified. If he'd ridden out here with Stillman, and let Ben explain it, it might have looked as though something weren't right about what Leon had been forced to do.

The deputy crossed the creek at the bottom of the hill via a stout log bridge, blackbirds cawing in the cattails lining the rippling water that flashed salmon green over white stones. The dog kept barking more and more angrily as the stranger started up the side of the bluff in the wagon. A high, short whistle silenced the dog, who turned and disappeared over the brow of the bluff.

The dog's place was taken by a rider on a brown-and-white pinto pony. The rider held a carbine straight up from his right thigh. He wore a funnel-brimmed Stetson, a sheepskin vest over a brown shirt, and from what Leon could see of his face from a hundred yards away, it looked flat and blandly belligerent. He sat the pinto giving Leon the hairy eyeball as the wagon clattered on up the gradual incline.

The pinto whinnied a greeting, shifting its front hooves, and the skewbald pulling the wagon shook its head and whickered.

As the wagon climbed, the ranch yard spread out in front of McMannigle. It was larger and with more space between buildings than it had appeared from the opposite hill. The main lodge sat back on the far side of the bluff. A tall, lean, gray-haired gent in dark trousers and suspenders stood on the front veranda.

He appeared to be wearing a bib, and he was chewing. The dog sat beside him, staring intently toward Leon, occasionally shifting its front paws. In the funeral silence now at dusk, the deputy could hear the dog giving soft, throaty mewls and restrained yips.

As McMannigle approached the rider with the rifle, two more men with rifles walked out away from the bunkhouse on the yard's left side. They moved with slow, menacing ease, holding the barrels of their long guns on their shoulders. One was nibbling what appeared to be a baking-powder biscuit.

The deputy had interrupted supper here at the Triple H Connected.

As he halted the wagon in front of the horseback rider, who had canted his head slightly to one side and was giving Leon the stink eye from beneath the brim of his funneled brim hat, which was festooned with a band of small silver conchos, Mc-Mannigle saw a curtain move in a lower-story window of the house, just right of the half-open door and near the tall, lean, gray-haired gent standing there beside the dog. The lean gent would be Watt Hollister himself.

A pale shape moved in the window in which the curtain had jostled.

The door opened wider behind Hollister and three younger men filed out to stand to the right of the old man but giving themselves a respectful separation from him. They might have been standing slightly farther back on the veranda, as well. Two of roughly the same height were attired in rough range gear, like the waddies now facing and approaching the deputy. The third, taller younger man on the veranda was clad a little more dapperly in gray whipcord trousers, a nice shirt with fancy piping over the shoulders, and a string tie.

He was the oldest boy—Nash Hollister. The other two would be Zebulon and Samuel.

A woman stepped out of the door, now, as well. This would be Mrs. Hollister. Virginia, Leon believed her name was. She had a dark, knit shawl wrapped over her shoulders, her dark-brown hair coiled in two buns atop her severely shaped head with a pale, oval face cleaved by a long nose hooked and crooked as an arthritic witch's finger. She'd been the one in the window. She stepped to the opposite side of Hollister from the sons, also giving some separation, and opened the book she held in her hands and started right in, reciting the Lord's Prayer.

There was no doubting what it was. She was reciting it from the Good Book loud and clear, not looking down at the book but staring toward the black stranger and the wagon carrying what everyone could probably see was a casket, for the sides of the buckboard were less than a foot high. Her voice rang crisp and clear and without emotion.

". . . Thy will be done in earth, as it in Heaven. Give us this day our daily bread . . ."

"What you got there, boy?" asked the man sitting the pinto twenty feet in front of Leon.

He had a low, raspy voice, and he lifted his spade-shaped chin slightly to indicate the deputy's cargo. McMannigle thought his name was Westin, the foreman. He and the two hands standing to Westin's right regarded Leon with expressions ranging from incredulity to sneering indignation.

McMannigle stared hard at the men facing him, trying to keep his anger on a leash. Now was not a time for anger. He would be treated poorly here, as he usually was by dim-witted white men, but he had a job to do, and the only way to do that job effectively was to remain even-tempered.

That said, he saw no reason to waste time on underlings.

He shook the reins over the skewbald's back and continued forward.

"Hey!" the foreman groused, sharply reining his horse off to Leon's right to avoid being run over.

The skewbald bulled through the space he'd vacated, and the wagon clattered and rattled and the casket thumped in the box, as the deputy crossed the yard, swerving left around a windmill and stock tank and then pulling up to the lodge's veranda at an angle.

He stopped about fifty feet away. The dog barked once.

Hollister looked down at the dog and then tossed the chicken leg he'd been nibbling into the yard, past the woman who was still reciting the Lord's Prayer and holding the open Bible as though for extra comfort. The dog dashed into the yard and attacked the bone as it would a rabbit.

The old man turned to his three sons staring glumly toward the wagon, muttered something McMannigle couldn't hear, then ripped the bib from around his neck, wiped his mouth and walrus mustache with it, and tossed it onto the veranda floor. He moved down the veranda steps and into the yard while the woman continued reciting the Lord's Prayer crisply behind him, staring off into the distance over Leon's right shoulder.

The deputy had recited the words in his head, so he felt he had to say them:

"Mr. Hollister, I'm sorry I have to inform you of this, but there's been an unfortunate turn of events. Last night . . ."

He let his voice trail off. The old man didn't seem to be listening. Watt Hollister moved over to the wagon box and stared grimly down at the simple pine box that had shifted around a little to sit at an angle in the wagon bed. Leon saw that the lid had popped up slightly on one side though the gap was not wide enough to reveal the coffin's contents.

The old man was stooped over slightly, and broomstick-lean—a gray-headed, gray-mustached scarecrow losing its straw. He appeared as though the simple movement of walking might cause his hips and shoulders to slip from their sockets. His forehead and cheeks, across which his thin, ruddy skin was drawn so taut it appeared as transparent as wax paper, were a mass of liver-colored spots and moles and crimson blemishes.

His sunken, bony jaws and pointed chin resembled a plow blade. His knob-like shoulders were shaking inside his flannel shirt, as was his wing-like arm as he lifted it to set an arthritis-gnarled hand atop the coffin lid.

Leon silently opined that Watt Hollister was not shaking from emotion but from the palsy.

Staring down at the unvarnished box with a look of heartrending bereavement, old Hollister said raspily, "My daughter in there?"

"Yessir, she is."

With that, Mrs. Hollister's voice suddenly broke away from the prayer and she raked in an ululating breath. It was a gasp, but it resembled the shrill warbling of a whippoorwill. The woman dropped to her knees with a dull thud. The Bible fell with another thud and a windy flutter of its pages.

Without turning his head, Watt Hollister said quietly, "Zeb, take your mother inside."

The youngest-looking of the Hollister sons moved over to the woman now sobbing with her head down, and gently pulled her to her feet. "Come on, Ma," he said quietly, the breeze playing with his sandy hair that rose to a cowlick in back.

Hollister turned his rheumy brown eyes to Leon and shifted his fragile jaws around as though grinding his teeth, and his long, broad, pitted nose reddened. "How?"

Leon blinked, studied on his answer. He'd been going to tell it just like it had happened. But the old man was so palsied and old and dried up and ready for the grave, that he didn't have the heart to tell it like that. He did not have the heart to tell the truth.

"I shot her by accident," McMannigle said in a low, dull voice, leveling his own gaze on that of the old man glaring back at him. "Sheriff Stillman and I were after rustlers holed up in a cabin on Loco Jack Creek. You probably know the ones I'm talkin' about. They were . . ."

"Yeah, I know—they was rustlin' over here in my country. Led up by a young firebrand who used to work fer me. Tommy Dilloughboy. Stinkin' half-breed Injun, Dilloughboy. Cree from

Canada. Never shoulda hired his like in the first place. I run him and the others off after my foreman got suspicious. Stretched hemp on two of 'em. I heard they drifted over to the eastern side of the Two-Bears. So, you and Stillman finally caught up to 'em . . . and killed my girl in the bargain."

He flared his right nostril at that and continued to grind his jaws around like a milk cow chewing hay.

"That's right, Mr. Hollister. We didn't know she was with those men. They were led by Tommy Dilloughboy, you say?" McMannigle hesitated, wishing that the old man would clarify the girl's presence in the cabin with the rustlers for him.

When no explanation appeared imminent, but the old man only continued to stare at the deputy with red-nosed, smoldering-eyed wrath, Leon cleared his throat and admonished himself to tread carefully. No point in making things worse than they already were. "What I mean to say is—we didn't know they had her. She was near one of 'em in the cabin, and my bullet, intended for one of the rustlers, struck your daughter."

"You killed her."

"That's right, sir. By accident. And for that, I truly apologize."

"Did you kill all them long-loopers?"

"Yes. Or . . . almost all. One got away but he was wounded. The sheriff went after him, probably found him by now."

Old Hollister sucked another rattling breath and then let his quivering hand flutter atop the coffin lid. Stepping back away from the wagon, he said, "Boys, come on out here and take your sister into the house so we can dress her for a proper burial."

Nash and Samuel Hollister walked down the porch steps and into the yard. Nash was tall and lean like his father, but he was a square-shouldered young man. Not so young anymore. He appeared at least thirty. A younger, sturdier version of the old man. He kept his arrogant, gray-eyed gaze on McMannigle as he led his younger brother, who was a good six inches shorter than Nash, out into the yard.

"The darkie killed her, eh, Pa?" Nash said as though Leon couldn't speak for himself.

The older Hollister just jerked his bony hand, thumb extended, over his shoulder toward the house. "Just haul her in there and keep your goddamn mouth shut till I tell you to open it!"

Silently, the two brothers slid the coffin out of the wagon and, each taking an end, carried it up the veranda steps and inside the house. The deputy could hear their boots thumping on the floorboards. A shrill cry rose from somewhere inside the house. It rose in volume and began ululating again. McMannigle could hear it reverberating in there.

It lifted chicken flesh across his shoulder blades.

Watt Hollister turned to Leon. "You've come a long way. I'd offer you a bait of food, but you'd have to eat it out here. I only allow white folks inside the house. Your badge doesn't mean anything to me."

He'd said it as though without acrimony, as though it were a perfectly reasonable stipulation. That was all right. The deputy had been as casually relegated to the level of vermin before, and far worse. Under the circumstances, he tried not to let it bother him.

"Obliged, but I best be headin' on back to town."

Leon pinched his hat brim to the man and then shook the ribbons over the skewbald's back. He didn't feel obligated to apologize to the man again. He'd done that. He'd even taken sole responsibility for the girl's death. He'd done enough. He was sorry the girl was dead, but his guilt was assuaged.

He was sorry he'd had to go against Ben's orders, but he was glad he'd come.

Hearing the woman's squeals in the house behind him, and

the dog's halfhearted barks, the deputy aimed the wagon for the portal at the edge of the yard. The horseback rider with the funnel-brimmed hat was still sitting his pinto there, the horse's white spots glowing in the darkness.

The other three men with rifles were lined out beside Westin, standing slackly, thumbs in their pockets, heads canted to one side. It had gotten darker since Leon had ridden into the yard, and the men were standing in menacing silhouette against the cloud-scalloped, salmon-streaked western sky. More men were standing around outside the lamp-lit windows of the bunkhouse. Smoke from their cigarettes or cigars wafted grayly in the purple shadows.

None of the punchers said anything as Leon put the horse and wagon under the portal and started on down the hill toward Clantick.

The old man walked a little unsteadily across the veranda and into the house. The dog was behind him, mewling.

Nash was waiting in the kitchen lit by a bracket lamp, leaning his big frame against one wall near a loudly ticking casement clock. Hollister's oldest was smoking a cigarette.

The old man stopped just inside the door and turned to stare back outside at where the wagon was a fading gray blur in the darkness at the edge of the yard. Its clattering was drowned by the howling of Virginia from upstairs, where the boys had deposited the coffin of their dead sister in her room.

"I don't want that man to make it back to town, Nash."

The son chuckled softly, incredulously. "You sure, Pa? He is a lawman. Stillman's deputy. You sure you wanna go up against Still—?"

"You heard me," the old man said, so low and brittle as to be nearly inaudible. "I want him dead. I don't want there to be any sign of him. The man, the horse, the wagon—I don't want

51

anyone to find them. I don't want a trace of that man to ever be found." He glanced over his shoulder. "You hear me? He killed your sister. A black man. I want it like he was never even alive."

Nash stared at the old man, blinked once slowly, sighed, and shrugged his left stout shoulder. "All right."

"Wait till he's off the Triple H Connected and then get rid of him. I don't want him goin' back to Clantick and talkin' about your sister."

"All right, Pa," Nash said, brushing past the frail old man and casually strolling outside, blowing cigarette smoke out his nostrils. "It ain't gonna change what become of Orlean, but I reckon you're the boss."

CHAPTER 6

"Give no quarter," Sam Wa was saying now at the end of the night in the kitchen of his restaurant. "Give no quarter to rabid dogs or men who don't pay!" He slapped a pudgy hand down on the food preparation table before him. "Ha! No quarter to rabid dogs or men who don't pay!"

Sam sat at the stout, scarred wooden table, sitting back in his chair with a sharp-eyed look, puffing his opium pipe, which was the fanciest pipe Evelyn Vincent had ever seen, carved as it was with tiny green dragons spewing red flames down the pipe's stem to the broad, porcelain bowl.

It was midnight and they'd finally closed. They'd finished cleaning up, and Evelyn was pouring a wooden bucket containing the last of the night's food scraps—steak bones, bread crusts, eggshells, coffee grounds, leftover potatoes, and rice and whatnot—into a large, corrugated tin tub.

"That's right, Sam," she said, straightening and blowing a vagrant lock of sandy-blonde hair from her blue right eye. "Give no quarter!"

"Give no quarter. Ha!"

"That's right—give no quarter to men who don't pay."

"No quarter. That means when they don't pay I do just what I did today—I take a cleaver after them." The round-faced Chinamen laughed around the pipe stem, puffing the cloying, sweet-smelling smoke into the air of the kitchen still rife with the smell of cooked food and scorched lard and steak grease. "Did you see me with the cleaver, Evan?" While his English was pretty good, there were some names, including hers, he could not pronounce.

"I saw you and your cleaver, Sam," Evelyn said, dragging the big tin washtub over to the kitchen's rear door that faced the alley behind the café as well as Sam's little log shanty and his hog pen and chicken coop. "I just wish I would have seen both of you a little earlier, when that drunken renegade was grabbing me in places respectable men just don't grab respectable young women. Without permission, that is!"

Evelyn was thinking that she wouldn't mind being grabbed in those places by someone nice, someone she liked. She was well into her twenties, and it was about time she was grabbed like that again. It had been a while since the last time. At least, it had been a while since the last time she'd been grabbed and touched and fondled by someone she was fond of. Since she'd been gently kissed. If she wasn't careful, she was going to end up an old maid emptying Sam Wa's slop buckets while the pie-eyed Chinaman sat back in his chair getting loopy on that pretty pipe of his when she was ninety years old—all stooped over and pinched-face, dried up, and mean from lack of love in her life.

Doc Evans's intellectually handsome face passed across her mind's eye, and she physically shook it away. That was silly. She had to admit feeling an attraction to the man, but he was a good fifteen years older than she, much better educated—why, he'd probably read nearly every book that had been written since the Bible—and, besides, he was spoken for. Sometime soon, he'd marry his sometimes helper, Katherine Kemmett, who, traveling clear across Hill County as a nursemaid and midwife, had interests similar to the doc's. Everyone in town knew the two were meant for each other and would soon be married, though Evelyn didn't think they'd set a date yet.

The doc, a bachelor for so long, was dragging his feet on the matter. That's why, Evelyn supposed, she still held out a glimmer of hope that maybe . . .

She chuffed at her silliness and, pulling on her striped wool blanket coat, returned her attention to Sam Wa. "Like I was sayin', I'd appreciate it, Sam, if you and your meat cleaver would . . ."

Evelyn let her voice trail off, turning her mouth corners down. There was no point. Sam was staring dreamily through the heavy smoke wafting around his head, his black eyes reflecting the light of the Rochester light hanging over the table before him. He was busy reliving his prowess with the meat cleaver and his admirable unwillingness to give quarter to men who don't pay their bills.

Despite that, it was thanks to Ben Stillman's intervention that he didn't end up getting himself gutted like a fish, Evelyn thought with an inward chuckle as she opened the door and dragged the heavy washtub outside into the dark, windy alley. She dragged the tub over to the wooden wheelbarrow, looked down at the slop-filled tub, and then moved back over to the door and poked her head inside.

"Hey, Sam, how 'bout . . . ?"

Sam was holding the cleaver up in front of his chin and chuckling through his long, yellow teeth as he flicked his thumb across the blade, thoroughly smitten with himself. Evelyn knew by the pulsating, yellow light in the man's muddy eyes that he was lost in an opium fog. Soon, he'd amble over to his cabin—if he didn't fall asleep on a straw pallet he kept in his office part of the café kitchen, that was—and be sound asleep until an hour after Evelyn had returned in the morning to start serving breakfast.

Evelyn gave a disgusted chuff and closed the door. She went over to the tub and had little trouble wrestling it onto the wheelbarrow. She'd wrestled that tub onto the wheelbarrow twice a day for the past two years that she'd been working for Sam. Evelyn wasn't a big girl, but the backs of her thighs and her arms and her back were strong. She'd make a good wife one day, Sam had told her when he'd come upon her making the maneuver.

"Fat chance," Evelyn said now as the cool, autumn breeze spiced with the smell of wood fires blew her hair around her face.

She grabbed the barrow's handles and gave a grunt as she began pushing it along the well-worn path behind the café, curving around Sam's stone-and-wood keeper shed and root cellar and the privy and across a trash-strewn lot to where Sam's shake-shingled cabin sat among several cottonwood trees and lilac bushes, all of which now had nearly finished shedding their leaves.

She pushed the wheelbarrow and the stinky washtub around behind Sam's shack, dark and silent in the cool, breezy, starry night, and over to the shed and large stable. To the right of the stable were Sam's chickens, which Evelyn had locked up in their coop several hours ago, so a weasel or mink wouldn't slip through the chicken-wire fence and go on a slaughtering tear. Sam relied on his chickens, just as he did his hogs, over at the café. One of his specialties was chicken and dumplings. Another was well-seasoned pork chops, and his bacon was regarded as second to none on the Hi-Line.

Evelyn aimed the wheelbarrow for the hog pen that sat on the stable's left side. Behind the hog pen and the chicken coop was the paddock housing Sam's mule.

In the corner of Evelyn's left eye, a shadow moved.

Evelyn gasped as she stopped pushing the wheelbarrow and released the handles. "Who's there?"

She stared toward the back of Sam's leaning shack. Starlight limned the spidery shrubs that abutted the stone foundation, near a large pile of logs that Sam would hire one of the town's odd-job men, likely Olaf Weisinger, to split for him before the first snow flew.

Evelyn could pick out nothing but the breeze-jostled shrubs and the firewood.

"Is someone there?" she called, lifting her hand to slide a lock of wayward hair behind her left eye.

Her heart thudded. She'd seen something move over there, near Sam's shack. But now she could see nothing but the shack itself and the bushes. She must have only seen the movement of the bushes in the breeze. Or perhaps one of the town's many stray cats had leaped down from Sam's low roof and scuttled off in the brush.

It was dark out here, and the only sound was the breeze though in the distance she could hear the hammering of a piano in one of the saloons. She recognized the playing of Merle Stroud, a retired cowboy who played at the Drover's every weekend. This was Friday night. Or Saturday morning, more like. Folks were having fun. At least, it seemed everyone was having fun except poor, lonely, overworked Evelyn Vincent.

She had no family. No beau. Few friends. She had to work so darned much to keep herself fed and housed over at Ma Latham's boardinghouse that she didn't have time for friends. The chicken flesh that had risen all up and down Evelyn's back retreated. Now it was replaced by the hollow ache of loneliness and the nagging disenchantment of a young woman's stymied life. The distant patter of the piano and the occasional whooping and hollering of Friday night revelers mocked her.

"Oh, hell," she said, sort of enjoying the raw ache of self-pity. A girl had a right to indulge herself now and then.

Slumped like a martyr, she continued pushing the wheelbarrow over to where Sam's half dozen hogs slumbered in piles of straw beneath the stable's overhang. She wrinkled her nose against the fetor, and then lifted the wash bucket by the handles on each end, and heaved it over the top rail with a grunt.

Splat!

A couple of the hogs heard and smelled the fresh delivery, and grunted as they climbed to their feet and came thumping over, hanging their heads low to the ground and oinking hungrily.

"Enjoy, boys," Evelyn said.

She'd just started to turn back to the wheelbarrow when she heard the crunch of footsteps in the coarse weeds and gravel behind her. An arm was thrust around her head from behind and a large, rough hand closed over her mouth, muffling Evelyn's startled yelp.

The hand pulled her back against a man's rising and falling chest—she could feel the desperate heat of him behind her—and then she saw a face slide up close to her left cheek. It was a dark, ruddy face framed with thick, dark hair.

"*Shhh!* Evelyn, don't scream, okay? It's me, Tommy. Tommy Dilloughboy!"

That froze her. She slid her eyes far to the right. Sure enough, it was Tommy. She could see his dark-tan, handsome, brown-eyed face in the darkness.

Slowly, he took his hand away, holding it up in front of her face for a few seconds, in case he should need it again. Then, when she didn't scream but only continued to stare at him in wide-eyed surprise, he grinned, showing all his solid, white teeth including the front one that was chipped a little and which somehow only added to the young man's boyish handsomeness. Tommy's thick, wavy hair blew around beneath his hat in the breeze.

"Tommy, what are you doing here?" Evelyn said.

"Shh," he said, placing a finger against his full, well-formed lips. He smiled again to put her at ease, his cheeks dimpling.

"Don't exactly wanna advertise the fact. It bein' so late and all, I mean. Might wake the neighbors."

"I thought you were working out at the Triple H Connected," Evelyn said, keeping her voice down.

"Yeah, well, I was, but . . . you know, after roundup, over half the crew got cut. I reckon you could say I'm sorta ridin' the grub line." Tommy grinned and wrapped his arms around her. "Sure is good seein' you again, Evelyn. I swear, I was thinkin' about you all summer till I was fit to be tied. I wasn't all that unhappy when old Hollister cut me." He pulled her closer, held her tighter. "Gave me the chance to come callin' on you, see your purty eyes again."

"Oh, Tommy." Evelyn gazed up at him, slid a lock of hair away from his right eye.

It had been several months since she'd last seen him after they'd spent four blissful weeks in the spring, riding in the country together and taking walks around town and along the river. They'd first met at Sam Wa's, and he'd asked her out the very first time they spoke. She hardly knew the boy, but Evelyn had found herself pining for him to distraction after he'd had to leave and accept a summer job, punching cattle out at the Hollister ranch.

He'd gotten into some trouble in town. Nothing serious. Just the usual stuff hot-blooded young men get into, and that had been another reason he'd felt the need to leave town for a while. To give Sheriff Stillman and Deputy McMannigle time to forget about him.

"You come back to town to find work?" Evelyn asked him, still gazing up at those big, round eyes of his. She swore that Tommy Dilloughboy was like peppermint candy that melted in a girl's mouth the second it touched her tongue.

"Well sorta. And . . . well, I sorta got a problem, Evelyn."

"What is it, Tommy? What happened?"

The young man winced, grunted. He placed his hand on his side. There was a bulge beneath his shirt. Over the bulge the young man's blue-and-red-plaid shirt glistened faintly in the starlight. Evelyn gently placed her hand over the bandage, felt the cool, oily substance soaking his shirt and which could only be blood oozing from a wound in his side.

Evelyn sucked a sharp breath. "Oh, Tommy!"

CHAPTER 7

Leon McMannigle hauled back on the skewbald's reins.

The wagon clattered to a stop on the pale two-track trail curling through a shallow canyon somewhere west of the Triple H Connected. The horse blew, breath frosting in the cool night air.

The deputy turned to look over his right shoulder, narrowing his eyes to probe the darkness along his back trail.

"What the hell was that?" he muttered.

He'd heard something. He wasn't sure what that something was. Possibly a shod hoof ringing off a stone. About fifty yards back he'd had to swing the wagon around rocks that had apparently rolled down from the low but steep, southern ridge to litter the trail. If he had horseback riders following him, one of their horses might have kicked one of those stones.

Leon stared along his night-cloaked back trail. The southern ridge was steeper than the northern one, and it was butterscotch colored in the darkness. The northern ridge was darker with foliage, piñon and ponderosa pines and Douglas firs climbing the gentler but higher ridge toward the star-shot sky. Now as McMannigle stared up that long, dark ridge stretching toward the firmament, there was a soft, muffled thud, like that of a pinecone tumbling to the ground. At least, that's what it had *sounded* like.

Could have been a footfall. There was another sound on its heels. A man's grunt?

Apprehension tightened the muscles across the lawman's back.

Were men up there?

Leon hadn't liked the way his visit to the Hollister place had gone. Of course, he hadn't expected the old man to shake his hand and invite him inside for a glass of brandy and a Havana cigar. But he hadn't expected such menace, either. The old man had not been openly hostile, but his eyes set deep in leathery sockets had fairly glowed with fury when he'd learned that his daughter had been residing in Auld's wooden overcoat.

Had that fury compelled Watt Hollister to send his men after McMannigle?

Could the old rancher be so incensed by his daughter's death that he'd actually try to murder the lawman who'd killed her?

Leon vaguely wished he had gone ahead and told the old man the truth: That the little fool had had that bullet coming to her. Maybe that would have clarified things for old Hollister, made the old man realize the shooting really hadn't been Mc-Mannigle's fault at all. It had been Miss Orlean's fault entirely.

Hollister's sending men after him would be what the deputy deserved for trying to soften to the old man's blow. A mistake, he'd told him. An errant shot. McMannigle's ass it was!

Leon looked around. Suddenly, the night was quiet. No more hoof thuds, no more falling pinecones or grunts. Maybe his imagination had been playing tricks on him. Maybe no men were skulking around behind and around him, after all. Old Hollister was a respected Hi-Line rancher. Yeah, he was known to hire cold steel artists to protect his land and his herds from interlopers and long-loopers, but most ranchers did that, especially those operating as remotely as Hollister was.

Mostly—at least as far as Leon *knew,* and aside from hanging a rustler now and then—the old man and his boys were law-abiding citizens. True, they were obviously broken up by the death of their daughter and sister, but they wouldn't be stupid or criminal enough to try to kill the deputy county sheriff who'd shot her and taken responsibility for it.

Would they?

No. Leon's imagination had gotten away from him, that's all. None of the Hollisters were cold-blooded murderers.

Feeling a little easier, Leon looked around again, but this time in hopes of finding a place to camp for the night. He shivered inside his plaid wool coat and lifted the fleece-lined collar against the chill. Damned cold out here. Had to be below freezing. There was no moon, so it was good and dark. The stars helped a little, but McMannigle didn't want the skewbald to trip over a rock like those behind him, and fall and break a leg or even just throw a shoe. They were still a good two, maybe three hours from Clantick, and he didn't want to get stranded way out here afoot. Ranches out this way were literally few and far between. He wouldn't find help for days.

He needed a protected place somewhere off the trail a ways. Not seeing what he wanted anywhere near, he clucked the skewbald ahead. The wagon rattled and barked along the canyon trail. The din it was lifting caused Leon to grind his teeth. If there *was* anyone stalking him, they'd have no trouble finding him, with all the noise the wagon was making.

He crossed a low divide and dropped into another, broader valley. A stream prattled along the base of the high, forested slope on his right. He spotted a horseshoe clearing in the forest that ran down onto the valley floor, and turned the skewbald off the trail, drawing up to the edge of the clearing a minute later. He inspected the prospective bivouac, deeming it suitable, and then parked the wagon against the west side of the notch forming the clearing, which was backed up by the forested slope and the creek.

Leon thought the creek was one of several forks of Cavalry

Creek, so named for a cavalry patrol ambushed here by Crow Indians a dozen years ago. Here at the west side of the clearing, the wagon would be somewhat concealed by the shadow of a steep escarpment to the west, which sprouted like a large, gray flower from the top of the gradual, forested slope, blotting out a small portion of the stars.

Quickly, McMannigle unharnessed and tended the horse, picketing the tired beast to a pine near the rippling water. He rubbed the horse down with a scrap of burlap, fed it a bait of oats from a feed sack he'd outfitted the wagon with, and then gathered wood.

Soon, he had a small fire dancing and smoking in a pit he'd dug near the stream. It was in a low point of the clearing, but he did not delude himself into thinking the flames could not be seen from the main trail only a couple of hundred yards to the north. If it had been warmer, under similar circumstances he would have cold camped. But it was too damned cold to camp out here without a fire, especially since he doubted Hollister was on his trail.

The more he thought about it, the more absurd it seemed. Hollister had not lived to push seventy years old, having built up a prosperous cattle ranch—one of the most prosperous not only in the Two-Bears but in northern Montana Territory, in fact—to turn killer late in life. He might be madder'n an old wet hen, and he might be grieving the loss of his daughter, but he was not a killer.

Just the same, Leon kept his Winchester carbine near as he brewed a pot of Arbuckle's and nibbled the deer jerky and biscuits he'd shoved into his saddlebags before he'd lit out from Clantick. While the coffee brewed, he spread his hot roll near a grassy thumb of turf that, in lieu of his saddle, which he had not brought, would have to serve as a pillow.

He hauled his makings sack out of his coat pocket and rolled a smoke. By the time he'd sealed the quirley, his coffee water was boiling, so he added a small handful from his Arbuckle's pouch, gave the water a minute to return to a boil, removed it from the fire, and added a little cool water from his canteen, which he'd filled from the creek, to settle the grounds.

He poured the hot, black brew into his old, battered, speckled-black tin cup that he'd been using in camps since he'd been a buffalo soldier, fighting the Apaches down in the Southwest just after the war. The cup was half rusted where it was badly dented, and the handle was loose, but the cup and the man had been through too much together for the man to cast the storied, old vessel aside just yet.

The cup was beaten up, but it still held coffee. Even kept it hot on cold nights like this one here. It was an old, familiar companion when no other friends were near.

The cup smoking beautifully, tendrils of steam curling toward the stars, McMannigle sat back against a rock near the fire. He'd intended to smoke and drink the coffee leisurely, taking his time and enjoying himself. But his keen ears had been picking up muffled sounds since just after he'd started to roll the quirley, before his coffeepot had begun boiling, dribbling water down its spout. It hadn't been easy, rolling the quirley as though nothing were bothering him, but his experience in *Apacheria* had taught him to remain calm when the chips were down.

To be patient.

Men—at least five but maybe six or even seven men—were trying to sneak around him in the darkness. His imagination had not been playing tricks on him, after all. They could be your average owl hoots looking to rob a lone rider of his horse and guns and anything else they could find of value on his person, but he didn't think so.

He was beginning to think his initial apprehension about old Watt Hollister had been right, after all.

The horse whickered softly. It was an older horse, its senses dull, or it likely would have picked up the stalkers earlier. Even now, it looked around only briefly before lowering its head to crop the buffalo grass growing around the aspens lining the creek.

Leon's ears were pricked, listening intently. It was hard to pick out the sounds of furtive footsteps above the chuckling of the creek, but he could do it. He could hear the occasional crunch of grass and the muffled snap of a small twig. Meanwhile, shifting his eyes from side to side while keeping his head pointed at the fire without moving it overmuch, he pretended to casually enjoy his coffee and his cigarette. Inside his chest, his heart was beating slowly but heavily, like a war drum during a pow-wow the night before an attack.

Leon feigned a yawn, blew cigarette smoke into the darkness to his left, using the opportunity to scan the slope rising not ten feet away from him. The horse was on that side but behind him, the wagon on that side, as well, but several yards in front of him. Now, as he began to turn his head back forward, he saw a shadow slip out of the trees about twenty feet up the slope.

He held his head forward and continued to sip his coffee and smoke the quirley. As he did, he watched the stalker on the slope out the corner of his left eye. Meanwhile, men were moving toward him from both sides of the horseshoe-shaped clearing. He could see their shadows. At times, he could even see starlight winking off the rifles they were carrying.

Hastily counting the shadows, he came up with seven men, including the gent now crabbing toward him down the slope.

As long as the man was moving, Leon would hold his position.

In the corner of his left eye, the man stopped. McMannigle saw him raise a rifle. The deputy slung his coffee cup away, and, tucking the quirley into a corner of his mouth, he grabbed his carbine and threw himself sharply left as the rifle of the stalker on the western rise flashed and cracked. The slug plunked into the deputy's nearly full coffeepot, and spilled coffee sizzled and steamed on the leaping flames, smelling like pine tar.

Leon rolled and rose to one knee, cocking and raising his carbine to his shoulder, quickly aiming and firing.

The man on the slope gave a high-pitched screech, dropping his rifle and making a face as he grabbed his left knee with both hands.

The wounded shooter screamed again, "I'm hit!" and lost his footing. He rolled down the slope to pile up at the base of it, writhing and yelping like a gut-shot coyote. "I'm hit! I'm hit! Oh, god, I'm *hit!*"

A brief glimpse at the sandy-haired kid in a blue wool coat clutching his bloody knee and writhing at the edge of the firelight told Leon he'd just shattered the knee of Hollister's youngest, Zebulon.

The skewbald loosed a shrill whinny, bucking and pulling at its tether rope.

Rifles began barking in the darkness of the clearing, red-blue flames lashing toward Leon, who dropped again and rolled and came up running wildly, splashing across Cavalry Creek and desperately climbing the slope into the pines while men shouted and rifles barked and bullets chewed into the slope at his heels and into the trees around him—tearing the night wide open at its seams.

CHAPTER 8

"Whoa," said Tommy Three-Hawks, stumbling into Evelyn's arms.

"Tommy!"

"Shhh," Tommy said. "No one'd best know I'm in town, Evelyn. Stillman finds out . . . sees me with a bullet hole . . . he's liable to come to the wrong conclusion. An understandable conclusion, given my less than respectable history here in Clantick, but the wrong conclusion just the same."

Evelyn couldn't hold him. He slipped out of her grasp and dropped to one knee, groaning and clamping a hand over the blood staining the left side of his shirt, a few inches above his cartridge belt.

"Tommy, don't die," Evelyn said, dropping to a knee beside him and staring anxiously into his handsome face. She'd thought she'd forgotten about him but now, seeing him again—especially seeing him again injured—made her realize that she'd only been suppressing thoughts about the wild, handsome young half-breed with the devil-may-care glint in his dark-brown eyes.

He drew a raking breath, swallowed, winced, and shook his head. "Ah, it's only a flesh wound."

"We gotta get you to Doc Evans."

"No!"

"*No?* Tommy, you need a doctor. Only Doc Evans can get that bullet out of your side!"

"The bullet ain't in there. It just pinched my side's all. I just need to get it cleaned out, need a place I can lie down for a spell. Sleep. Maybe get some vittles down my throat."

Evelyn slid his hair back from the side of his face and touched his left cheek and forehead. His skin was sweat-beaded, clammy. "Tommy, you're burnin' up!"

He looked at her desperately. "Really, Evelyn—I just need a place I can hole up for a day or two. You must know a place, don't you? Nobody knows this town like you do."

Evelyn gazed at him skeptically. What was he up to?

"Tommy, how did this happen?"

He turned his head away, spat in disgust. "Ah, hell—you won't believe me if I told you."

Irritation spiked through the young woman. She straightened and stepped back away from the handsome firebrand, crossing her arms on her chest. "Tommy Dilloughboy, if you expect me to help you, you'd better be straight up with me!"

"Evelyn, *shhhh!*"

Raising her hard-edged voice, she said, "And you can stop shushin' me right now! Are you playin' me for a fool? You know what I think? I think you got yourself into trouble again, threw in with the wrong curly wolves just like you did last summer, and got shot holding up a bank or a stagecoach."

Tommy stared up at her, his eyes wide and round with exasperation. Gradually, he turned his mouth corners down and looked away from her. "Ah, hell—I can't blame you for believin' that. Not after what happened last summer."

He'd thrown in with two other young men and raised hell in a couple of the saloons in Clantick and over in Big Sandy. Considering themselves the next James gang, Evelyn supposed, they'd concocted a plan to rob the Drover's Saloon in broad daylight. Thank goodness the liveryman, Emil Auld, had overheard them talking behind his barn one morning, and informed Ben Stillman.

Ben had intervened before the trio of would-be tough nuts could follow through with their devious scheme and ruin the whole rest of their lives. The sheriff had thrown Tommy and his cohorts into jail for a week, so they could take stock and reconsider the path their lives were taking. Only when they'd promised to follow the straight and narrow from then on as well as vowed to not show themselves in Clantick for the next year, Ben released them.

That was the last that Evelyn had seen of Tommy until now.

"Of course you can't blame me for believing that," Evelyn said. "My old man always said a zebra can't change his stripes."

"Ah, come on, Evelyn. I ain't no zebra. And I ain't no curly wolf, neither."

"What are you, then? How did you get yourself shot?"

He gazed up at her, his dark eyes even rounder than before. Those eyes and those looks he gave her sent a warm hand sliding down her belly and made it hard for her to keep her dander up. But she would, by god, until she was sure he'd told her the truth about his current situation.

Evelyn Vincent might be many things, but she would not allow a boy to make a fool of her more than once!

She kept her gaze hard and uncompromising, her face set grimly, skeptically, as she stared down at the young man where he knelt before her, the starlight flashing in his liquid-brown eyes.

"I didn't get myself shot," he said, sheepishly indignant. "Someone took a pot shot at me after I'd left Triple H Connected. I was headin' over to the Chinook country, hopin' to get more ranch work or maybe livery barn work for the winter. Bad luck was doggin' my heels, I reckon. Just like it's done my whole doggone life. Some no-account I never even seen was out to rob me. He or they—I don't even know how many there were—popped this here pill at me, knocked me out of my saddle. I hit my head on a rock. Must've been unconscious for a time, because when I woke up my horse and everything I owned except my coat and my gun was gone! I got to town by hitchin' a ride in a freight wagon."

He stared up at her, grimly.

Evelyn stared down at him.

"Ah, hell." He turned his head away from her head, and punched the ground with the edge of his fist. "Ouch!" He shook his fist. "Don't worry about it. If someone like me told me such a sad tale, I wouldn't believe him any more than you believe me." He sucked a deep breath and heaved himself unsteadily to his feet. "That's all right, Evelyn. I just thought . . . I just thought after what we meant to each other for a time last spring . . ."

"Tommy, where you going?"

He kept walking off along the rear of Sam's stable, heading away from her. The breeze tousled his thick, brown hair, lifted the hem of his ratty blanket coat to reveal the gun and holster strapped around his right leg. Glancing over his right shoulder, wincing, he said, "Not sure yet. I'll find a place. I'll be all right, Evelyn. I'm sorry to pester you. Good night."

She'd already run over and grabbed his left arm, stopping him. "Tommy, don't be ridiculous. You can't just wander off on this dark and cold night with that hole in your side oozing blood like it is."

"There's probably an old abandoned trapper's or prospector's cabin down by the river I can hole up in."

"But you won't have any wood, and you're in no condition to gather any. Tommy, won't you please let me take you to Doc Evans?"

"He'll just tell ole Stillman. You heard the sheriff. He didn't want to see me in town for a year. He sees me, he'll throw me in the calaboose again, and I ain't goin' back to his calaboose."

"Doc Evans won't tell Ben."

"Sure, he will."

Evelyn shook her head. "No, he won't. Not if I ask him not to. The doc's a good friend of mine."

Tommy cocked a brow. "How good?"

"Oh, stop it! Can you ride a little ways?"

Clamping a hand over his lower left side, the young man stretched his lips back from his teeth. "Not far. I reckon I could ride as far as Evans's place, though, if I had to."

"Well, you have to. You're burnin' up and you've lost a lot of blood. You need a doctor, and Doc Evans is the best. Wait here!"

Evelyn ran around behind the hog pen and into the paddock housing Sam Wa's mule, whom Sam had not named but whom Evelyn called Whiskers because of his brushy muzzle. The mule brayed with a start when he saw Evelyn, and backed away. Recognizing the girl's familiar face, however, he thrashed his tail from side to side, gave a stomp of his front hoof in eager greeting, and brayed again.

"Oh, hush, Whiskers," Evelyn admonished the beast, though she figured that Sam was deep in his opium cups by now and wasn't hearing a thing but only chopping up the kitchen table with his meat cleaver and seeing the face of the man who'd refused to pay his bill.

When Evelyn had wrestled a hackamore over Whiskers's ears, she led the docile mule around to the front of the stable, where Tommy was sitting on the ground, his back to the stable door. His head hung forward, as though he were half asleep.

Evelyn's voice roused him, and he grinned. "For a minute there, I thought you'd run off on me."

"You know I wouldn't do that," Evelyn said in mock disgust, her brusque tone belying the good feeling that had come over her, encountering the charming young half-breed again while the sensible part of her admonished her to tread carefully.

Maybe it was just plain old female instinct, but she felt a warm self-satisfaction in being needed. Especially by a young man she realized she was still very much charmed by if not in love with, which was possible.

How quickly her dour mood and dark outlook had lightened and colored, her loneliness retreated, in only the past ten minutes.

"Can you climb up onto Whiskers's back, Tommy? He's a big son of a buck!"

She helped the young man to his feet.

"I'll make it."

They each used the overturned slop bucket as a step, and swung up onto the mule's back, Evelyn first, and then Tommy seated himself behind her.

"Don't worry, Tommy," Evelyn said into the breeze, which blew her badly mussed hair back behind her shoulders. "Doc Evans will have you back on your feet in no time."

She batted her heels against the mule's flanks. Whiskers brayed and lunged into a trot, heading down an alley that paralleled Clantick's main street, in the direction of Clyde Evans's big, old house perched on a butte on the town's western edge.

"Nash!"

"Zeb!"

"Help me, Nash! Samuel! Oh, Christ—I'm hit bad!"

Nash Hollister stared over the top of his covering boulder and saw the deputy run up the slope beyond the fire and the creek, and disappear in the darkness. The man's horse had broken free of its picket rope and was now galloping off across the clearing, buck-kicking angrily at the fusillade. A couple of the other Triple H Connected men were shooting toward the slope, rifles cracking, powder smoke wafting in the cool air.

"Hold your fire! Hold your fire!" Nash shouted, holding up

his left hand. "Don't waste your bullets!"

Nash looked at his youngest brother, Zebulon, writhing on his back to the right of the deputy's fire that was still steaming from the spilled coffee. The middle Hollister brother, Samuel, was hunkered behind the rock to Nash's right.

"Zeb, hold on—we're comin' for ya!" Samuel looked at Nash. "Holy Christ—it sounds like he's hit bad." His voice had a frightened tremor in it. His long, gray eyes—the same shape and color as their mother's—sparked with worry. Samuel was the weakest of the three brothers. The laziest and the weakest, and he was also the worrier in the family. Tears glistened in his eyes now and began to dribble down his cheeks, resembling small, gold beads in the firelight. "What're we just sittin' here for? Zeb's hurt bad, Nash!"

Nash was aiming his rifle at the slope. His voice was low, raspy. "All right. You go. I'll cover you. Wouldn't put it past the darkie to lay in wait for us up there to get lit by his fire. Go, but be careful, Samuel. Keep your head about your fool self!"

Samuel was up and running, holding his rifle low in his left hand, not even looking toward the slope. "I'm comin', Zeb! Hold on, little brother!"

"Ah, shit—I'm hit *bad,* Samuel!" Zebulon cried, his voice so pinched now as to be almost inaudible.

Nash scrutinized the slope. The fire was dying. That was good. It meant the deputy couldn't see them much better than Nash and his men could see him. Deciding the man had probably run on up the slope—he wasn't fool enough to try to take on six men armed with rifles, men who also had horses when he himself was on foot—Nash slowly rose from behind his rock. Holding his rifle at port arms across his chest, he moved over to where Samuel was kneeling beside the writhing, bawling Zeb, but he kept his eyes on the slope.

"How is he?"

"Ah, Christ, Nash—look at his knee!"

"Bastard done crippled me, Nash!" Zeb sobbed. "*Kill* his black ass for me!"

Nash glanced at Zeb's knee, which was all blood. It looked as though the younker had taken the bullet in the kneecap, shattering it.

"Get him up." Nash glanced at the four other men, who were sort of crouching over their aimed rifles and staring warily up the slope beyond the fire. "You fellas, get after him! I gotta get Zeb back to the ranch. He's hurt bad. You stay after that damn tin star and finish him—hear? There'll be a bonus in it for you."

The four were not the best of Nash's lot, because he hadn't thought he'd need his best for one lone lawman in a wagon. The fewer involved in this the better. The fair-to-middling rawhiders glanced around at each other, silently conferring. Meanwhile, Samuel had wrapped one of Zeb's arms around his neck and was hoisting the howling young man to his feet.

"What is it?" Nash asked the four gunmen whom he and his father had hired to keep nesters off the sprawling Triple H Connected range.

The rawhider who called himself Morgan swallowed, his Adam's apple rising and falling in his long, unshaven neck in the firelight. "It's dark. And he has the high ground. Might be best if we wait till mornin'."

The other three flanking Morgan looked at Nash expectantly, seeming to agree with their spokesman.

"You wait till mornin', you can kiss that bonus good-bye. And you can haul your freight off the Triple H Connected, for all that. Good luck tryin' to find more work this late in the year."

The four glanced around at each other again, darkly. Morgan shrugged. Turning their mouth corners down, they moved around the fire, spread out, crossed the creek, and began climbing the slope, staying about fifteen feet apart. They moved slowly, crouching, aiming their rifles up at the dark columns of the pines above the deputy's bivouac.

Nash helped Samuel get the sobbing, groaning, often-mewling young Zeb started back to where they'd tied their horses. They hadn't gone more than ten feet before a man shouted, "There!"

A rifle cracked loudly. The slug spang shrilly.

Another rifle farther up the slope thundered and flashed amid the gauzy pines. It kept thumping and flashing, the shots echoing hoarsely around the valley and nearly drowning out the screams of the four rawhiders Nash now saw rolling wildly back down the slope through the pines.

They flung away their rifles and lost their hats. Their spurs chimed raucously. One rolled all the way down the slope to splash into the shallow creek beyond the fire.

The rifle fell silent.

The man in the creek arched his back and groaned.

He dropped back down into the creek and lay still.

"Shit," Nash said, and continued helping Samuel lead Zeb back toward their horses. "Maybe that wasn't the best decision, after all."

CHAPTER 9

"You think he's gonna die, Nash?" Samuel asked, trotting his palomino a couple of feet off Nash's right stirrup.

The middle brother was staring fearfully at young Zeb, who rode double with Nash, who had his arms around the youngest Hollister brother so Zeb wouldn't tumble off onto the trail they were following back in the direction of the ranch headquarters. Zeb's horse, as well as the horses of the four dead hands, was trailing along behind Nash and Samuel, tied tail to tail.

Nash hadn't wanted to leave the horses in fear that Stillman's deputy would run one down and head on back to Clantick before Nash could get back after him. He'd been reluctant about going after the lawman and bringing big trouble down on the Triple H Connected, but now he had no choice.

If you're going to make an attempt on a lawman's life, it had better be a successful one or there'd be hell to pay. Besides, Nash was embarrassed. Him and six other men couldn't bring down one man, and they'd pretty much had him dead to rights. They must have underestimated him. Nash had heard that Mc-Mannigle had been an Indian fighter.

Well, he wouldn't underestimate him again.

Zeb had passed out from shock and pain, and he rode bobble-headed, his chin with its little fringe of sandy-colored goatee dipped toward his chest.

"If he dies, Pa's gonna be madder'n he is already!"

"Samuel?"

"What?"

"Kindly shut the fuck up!" Nash shouted, leaning far out from his saddle and nearly getting up in his younger brother's face. He had too much to think about to listen to Samuel's anxious ramblings.

Samuel jerked back in his saddle with a start and stared at his older brother from beneath the brim of his Stetson. Too dumbfounded by the outburst to respond to it, he merely wagged his head once and then stared forward over his horse's twitching ears as they continued up the trail.

They gained the headquarters yard forty-five minutes later, galloping the horses now, heading for the house. Despite the lateness of the hour, Nash saw shadows move in the lit windows of the long, log bunkhouse to his left, heard the door latch click then the hinges squawk as the door came open and several men stepped out onto the gallery, a couple holding rifles. The collie dog, Barney, came barking out from beneath the front porch of the house, the white spots on his coat glowing in the light from the windows bleeding into the otherwise dark yard.

Shadows moved in a few of the house's windows, as well. The front door opened as Nash pulled his chestnut gelding to a halt in front of the veranda, Samuel moving along behind him, jerking the bridle reins of the first of the riderless horses he was trailing.

Much like the dog's white spots, Watt Hollister's gray hair glowed in the darkness as he stepped out onto the broad front porch, pulling the halved-log door closed behind him.

"You get him?"

Nash swung down from the saddle and caught his youngest brother as Zeb rolled toward him out of his saddle. With the unconscious Zeb stirring in his arms, groaning, Nash walked over and deposited his wounded youngest brother into Samuel's arms.

"Get him upstairs. Then send Carlton for Mrs. Wolfram."

Samuel nodded and carried his brother on up the veranda steps. The old man began cursing and when Samuel got Zeb inside, their mother began screaming shrilly. Ignoring the emotional outbursts, Nash turned to stare past Samuel toward the bunkhouse.

"Joseph over there?" he called as his mother's screams retreated deeper into the house.

The several men on the bunkhouse gallery shifted around, muttering. A shadow moved in the window nearest the bunkhouse's open door, and a short but thickset man tramped out onto the veranda, his long, black hair hanging to his broad, rounded shoulders straining the seams of his threadbare underwear shirt.

"How can I help, boss?"

Joseph Triejo's voice was deep, resonate, and thickly accented. The Mexican cowpuncher was the second lieutenant here at the Triple H Connected, behind the foreman, Blaze Westin. Triejo had been many things in his long life on the frontier, including an army tracker—one of the best north of the Platte River—and while it wasn't openly discussed, everyone at the ranch knew he'd also been involved in several range wars down in Wyoming and Colorado.

That's why the xenophobic old man had hired him, why the former regulator was up here now, north of the Missouri River, working on a remote ranch and staying beyond the reach of both federal and territorial arrest warrants. The old man didn't mind hiring criminals as long as said criminals were discreet about their pasts and followed orders.

Joseph Triejo was getting old, pushing fifty. He preferred a quiet life these days. But he was still a hell of a tracker, arm wrestler, boxer—even against men half his age—and he was hell with his ancient, army-issue Spencer carbine. Nash had seen him at work against three rustlers they'd caught doctoring Triple H Connected brands down in the Missouri breaks earlier that summer. Three loud thumps from Triejo's old Spencer, and all three rustlers followed their spilled brains to the ground around their branding fire.

Nash said, "I need my best tracker on the trail of that deputy sheriff. We can't let him get back to town."

"A lawman, boss?"

"You got somethin' against killin' lawmen, Joseph?"

Nash could see only the short, broad-shouldered man's silhouette facing him, but he imagined a smile flicking across the old killer's craggy, pitted face with its mare's tail mustaches hanging beneath his chin. Joseph was known to harbor no soft feelings for any lawmen anywhere. His two younger brothers had been gunned down in cold blood by two deputy sheriffs in New Mexico, and a posse had tried to do the same to Joseph.

He'd outrun those he hadn't killed. He was still running.

"You want me to go tonight, boss?" the tracker asked in his deep, accented voice.

"If anyone can track him at night, it's you. The rest of us'll catch up to you sometime after sunrise. Take the Spearhead Trail to Cavalry Creek—that bend where you cut firewood last summer. He climbed that mountain to the south. He's on foot. I wanna make sure he stays that way until we've run him to ground. Just find him and pin him down till morning. Blaze, you go with him."

The stocky Mexican tracker turned, and his boots thudded, spurs chinging, as he headed back into the bunkhouse to gather his gear. Westin nodded his hatless head, flicked his cigarette into the yard where it bounced with a soft thump and sparked, and then he followed Joseph into the bunkhouse.

Nash turned and climbed the veranda steps. The lodge door opened, and Carlton Ramsay stepped out, donning his hat and wearing his deerskin overcoat. The middle-aged Carlton was the camp cook and housekeeper—an old cowboy too stove up to punch cattle any longer. He was an old friend of Nash's father, one of the first men the old man had hired when he'd built up the Triple H Connected from little more than a one-room cabin and some breeding stock he'd driven up from Texas just before the war.

"That knee don't look good, Nash. Not one bit good. The boy needs me to fetch Doc Evans for him, not Mrs. Wolfram."

"No one goes to town till this is over. No word of this matter leaves the Triple H Connected."

"Nash, your little brother's gonna be a cripple without a good sawbones tendin' that knee."

"He'll likely be a cripple anyways, Carlton. Just fetch Mrs. Wolfram like I told you and quit crowin' about it."

"Well, your old man's crowin' about it." Ramsay raised his sheepskin collar to his hollow, gray-bristled cheeks against the night's chill and ambled toward the veranda steps. He smelled like whiskey, but then he usually smelled like whiskey this time of the night, as did Nash's father. Ramsay could still steer a buggy as far as the Wolfram place, two miles away. "He's crowin' about it plenty!"

Mikhail Wolfram punched cows most of the year for the Triple H Connected, and in return for his many years of service, Watt allowed him and his wife Maggie to have their own cabin and run a few chickens on Triple H Connected range. The old man valued loyalty above all else, and did not hesitate to reward those most loyal to him.

As Carlton Ramsay dropped down the front steps, Nash could hear his father's bellows echoing throughout the house. Nash went inside to see old Watt coming down the stairs straight ahead and right, clinging to the rail as though it were the rail of a ship pitching in high seas. His liver-spotted face was livid.

Spittle spewed from his walrus-mustached lips as he lifted each bony foot deliberately in turn.

". . . only daughter murdered—my dear, sweet Orlean butchered by a blue gum." He was wheezing, breathing hard. "I send my boys out on the simple chore of killin' one worthless coon with a badge—one goddamn deputy county sheriff who killed an innocent girl—and you bring your youngest brother home with a ruined knee! He'll never walk on that knee again if he lives the night, which is doubtful given how much blood he's lost!"

Nash said, "Go ahead and fall and break your neck, you old scudder," as he moved over to the large, black range and removed the coffeepot that remained all day until midnight on the warming rack—when it wasn't brewing a fresh batch.

The old man stopped and, sliding his lower jaw from side to side, glared from the foot of the stairs. "What did you say?"

"You heard me. Do us all a favor. Go on back up there and run down and snap your scrawny, fuckin' neck here on the kitchen floor!" Nash filled a large, white stone mug. He could hear his mother and Samuel talking in the upper story. Zeb was cursing like a gandy dancer on a hopping Friday night when all the half-breed whores were going for half price.

Nash had to hand it to his youngest sibling—Zeb could curse with the best of them. He was a top hand, too. Good with a lariat as well as with a six-shooter, and out here you needed both.

But you had to know when to use the one and not the other. He thought the old man had gotten that wrong tonight. They should have merely threatened the deputy with a lynching, scared hell out of him. That would have been enough, under the circumstances. One of their own had died—the only girl in the family—so someone had to pay *something* or the Hollisters might begin to lose respect across the Hi-Line. But threat of a necktie party would have been enough.

A black man especially would have gotten a clear message he'd done something wrong.

No real laws would have been broken. At least, none that would warrant lawmen sniffing around out here. Now, all hell had broken loose. Now, who knew what was going to happen?

Now, they'd have to deal with Stillman.

The old man moved over to the stove and pulled a pothook from the wood box, raising it over his right shoulder and gritting his teeth, the pupils of both eyes as red as the fire in the range. "I oughta kill you for that, you ungrateful catamount!"

Nash glowered down at the old man, whose chin came up only to the eldest Hollister son's shoulder. "Put it down or I'll gut shoot you, you old bastard!"

"Nash, you stop talkin' to Pa that way!"

Nash looked up and behind the old man to see the curly-headed Samuel standing halfway down the stairs, glaring into the kitchen. His hat was off, his curly hair mussed and hanging in his eyes. "Stop it, you hear? We got enough trouble without you and Pa goin' at it like two bobcats in a cage!"

Nash grinned with menace at old Watt. The old man glanced over his shoulder at Samuel and then, his warty, liver-spotted, hawk-nosed face gaining a sheepish cast, he slowly lowered the pothook and then dropped it back into the wood box.

Nash blew on his smoking mug as he went over and sat down at the long, oilcloth-covered table that seated the whole family and Carlton Ramsay and sometimes the foreman, Blaze Westin, as well. There was a wooden bowl of walnuts and a nutcracker on the table, beside a hurricane lamp with a soot-stained, spruce-green chimney.

Lost in his angry thoughts, Nash sipped his coffee and then cracked a walnut and ate it.

Meanwhile, Samuel came down, quickly removed his coat

and then ladled water from the stove's warm water reservoir into a tin bowl. He set the bowl on the table and started opening and closing cabinet drawers. Old Watt poured himself a cup of coffee, splashed whiskey into it, returned the bottle to its shelf over the dry sink, and then walked into the open parlor, where a small fire blazed in the stone hearth. He was muttering under his breath, talking to himself as he was doing more and more these days, Nash had noted.

As Samuel hurried up the stairs with the steaming bowl and several cloths wrapped over his forearm, the old man scowled at Nash from his worn, torn, bullhorn chair angled near the fire. "Your sister's dead! Doesn't that mean nothin' to you?"

His face was even redder than before.

"No, it don't mean shit to me."

"What?"

"I said it don't mean shit to me!" Nash said, breaking a walnut shell to smithereens that rained in tiny crumbs onto the oilcloth. "It don't mean shit to me because she's been dead a long time. Her soul, anyway. You killed her soul years ago, you dried up old peckerwood!"

Watt punched his chair arm with the edge of his fist. "How in the hell did I kill Orlean's soul?"

"By lockin' her up out here. By makin' sure she didn't go to town alone. Never alone. No boys from town or any of the ranchers could ever come out here and sit and talk to her for longer than fifteen, twenty minutes, and then either you or Ma had to be around to make sure nothin' *improper* happened!"

"That's how a girl is raised, Nash!"

"You didn't raise her, you old fool. You locked her up. Just like a cat from the hills, a girl—or a boy, for that matter—is going to go wild if you lock 'em up. And that's just what she did. I saw it happen just after Ma took that wooden spoon to her backside out in front of the bunkhouse when she caught her 'makin' eyes' at the half-breed, Dilloughboy, who you promptly run off the place. Couldn't you see she was gone for the boy?"

Nash gave a caustic laugh and obliterated another walnut. "And she was gone after that. Took off with him. Gone for good. Even helped him throw a gang together and start stealin' our beef! Hah!"

He shook his head and, chewing the walnut, blew on his coffee. "The girl had sand, I'll give her that. She's cut from the same cloth as me an' Zeb, only she's even tougher, more defiant. She wanted to ruin your withered-up old ass and would have, too, if you didn't have so many pistoleros ridin' for you. Purely fittin'. Watt and Virginia Hollister's own well-brought-up daughter goes wild, throws in with a half-breed Injun from Canada, and tries to ruin her lovin' family!"

Old Watt punched his chair arm again. "Shut up. Shut you, d'you hear?"

"And you want to kill that deputy for killin' her when it's really you who killed her. You and Ma. Ah, shit, I reckon us brothers even had a hand in it. Only, *this* way it makes you feel better. Somebody actually killed her, and you can cover up your part in it—and defend her *honor!*—by goin' hog wild on the poor, badge-totin' sonofabitch who had no idea the bailiwick he was ridin' into when he rode out here with that coffin in his wagon. Gotta admit, I felt the same way when I first seen him. The black bastard killed my sister. I'm a Hollister, and he killed a Hollister, and by god, he *should* pay for that."

"He should, by god. He will, goddamnit, Nash!"

"Yes, he will, Pa. Oh, yes, he will! Hell, what choice do we have now? We done tried to kill him. If we don't finish him off, he'll report tonight's unseemly little events to his boss, Stillman, and then there'd be holy hell to pay. No, no. The fuse has done been lit. Now we gotta watch the whole keg explode and see where the Triple H Connected lands once the smoke clears."

"He killed your sister. He killed my sweet baby girl."

Nash looked at old Watt, who had turned now to the fire, his boots flat on the floor. He rested his arms and the hand holding his whiskey-laced coffee on the chair arms. He had a drawn, sadly pensive look on his ruined, ancient, dull-witted face.

Nash almost fell sorry for the old, half-demented codger. But then he remembered Orlean back when she was younger, and her eyes had danced, and she laughed at the drop of a hat. No more spirited filly had ever lifted dust at the Triple H Connected. Gradually as she matured, though, the fire had left the girl's eyes, and the flush of young womanhood and her innate zest for life was bleached from her cheeks by the invisible walls her parents and even her overly protective brothers had erected around her.

And then she was gone.

And now she was laid out dead in her old bed, in her old room, waiting to be planted on the hill behind the house where Nash's grandmother, Rose, had been buried along with the first Hollister child, stillborn.

"Don't worry, Pa," Nash said, holding his coffee in both hands and looking off at nothing, feeling as used up and dead as the girl upstairs. "He'll die. You'll get your revenge for your *sweet baby girl*. We'll feed his black carcass to the wolves. But I ain't doin' it for you. You keep that straight in your head."

He sipped the coffee again, licked his mustache. "I'm doin' it for the Triple H Connected."

CHAPTER 10

McMannigle hobbled through the pines at the crest of the ridge.

The bullet in his upper-right thigh felt like a hot blade being twisted and turned by some cunning torturer. Ignoring the wound for the moment, sucking sharp, pained breaths through gritted teeth, he dropped to his butt behind a tree and then, holding his carbine in both hands, twisted around to stare down the ridge in the direction from which he'd climbed.

Silence slid up the slope toward him.

There were only the quiet rasps of falling leaves and the faint wheezing of the breeze through the barren branches of the aspens. The glow from his fire was barely visible. It was merely a pinprick of pink light from this distance of a hundred yards or so and through the scattered conifers and deciduous trees stippling the incline.

He held his breath and pricked his ears sharply. Still, nothing. It didn't sound like any more of the Triple H Connected men were moving toward him. They could be trying to get around him from each side, but Leon didn't think so. He'd likely killed the four climbing the slope for him. If he'd counted correctly before the shooting had started, that left only two upright. Two of the three Hollister brothers, most likely. He knew at least two of his ambushers had been Hollisters, so all three boys had likely been along to avenge their sister.

Since Leon had shot their brother, the other two were likely getting young Zeb back to the ranch headquarters.

"Sons o' bitches."

McMannigle leaned his rifle against the tree and shifted his position until starlight shone on his wounded right thigh. The bloody wound glistened darkly halfway between his knee and his right-front denims pocket. Most of that leg was numb. That foot felt heavy, and it was tingling painfully.

"Sons o' bitches," Leon groused again.

Rage seared him to enflame the heat of the wound in his leg. They'd waited until he was a couple of miles from the ranch headquarters, and they'd bushwhacked him. Probably intended to kill him out here in this wild country a good twenty miles southwest of Clantick, where no one would find him.

Murderers.

Cold-blooded murderers.

But he was a fool to have banked on them not taking revenge for his killing the girl. Had he really thought he would have been able to square that with old Watt Hollister and his three sons?

Well, he had thought so. And he'd been three kinds of a fool to think it, too. Hadn't he been alive long enough to know the evil men were capable of?

He might have been a lawman, but that didn't mean much out here where most folks still took the law into their own hands. And then of course his being black had made the attempt on his life all the easier.

Leon groaned as he squeezed his thigh and watched the oily, dark, faintly glistening blood ooze up out of the hole. He'd taken a ricochet. He thought the bullet had ricocheted first off a rock and then off a tree bole. It was hard to tell, but he didn't think it had gone that deep into his flesh.

Groaning and grunting and cursing his foolishness at underestimating the savagery of the Hollisters, he tied his neckerchief around his thigh, just above the wound, to stem the blood flow. Then he slipped his Bowie knife from his belt sheath, and dug a box of stove matches from his shirt pocket where it was snugged down beside his hide makings sack.

He looked around once more to make sure he was alone up here, and then, hunkering down in the tree's thick shadow to be extra cautious, scraped the match to life on his thumbnail. He swiped the flame across the blade of his bowie knife several times until gray smoke curled up from the blade edge and he could smell the tang of hot steel.

"Okay, now," he said, raking breaths in and out of his lungs. "You ain't gonna pass out on me now, are ya, Leon? No, I'll say you ain't gonna pass out, because you done fought Apaches and you're no man to be trifled with. You pass out on me, Deputy, you'll just be provin' you got soft in these past five years, since you moved north out of *Apacheria,* and you oughta just turn your badge in and hang up your shootin' iron and go live by yourself in one o' them empty shacks down by the river. Now, ain't that right, *Deputy?*"

He lowered the still-smoking knife blade and heard himself mewl softly as he tried to widen the hole in his pants leg. That wasn't happening, however. The area was too painful, and he'd only cause himself to pass out before he even started to dig for the bullet.

"Nah, nah, nah," he told himself. "Don't worry about the cloth. Just go in an' probe for that bullet, and pluck the damn thing outta there. You don't, you ain't goin' anywhere, and you'll just sit here on your ass and bleed dry. And then those sons of Hollister bitches—pardon me, Miss Virginia, ma'am, since I know you're such a good Christian woman, an' all—will have accomplished exactly what they set out to do, which was to kill your black ass like you was no more than a calf-killin' coyote! *Ahhh, fuck, that hurts!*"

He tightened his jaws and stared down to watch his right

hand plunge the tip of the knife directly into the wound. Mewling softly and breathing through his teeth, he shifted the knife handle this way and that and forced himself to hold his leg as still as stone.

That wasn't easy, given the searing pain that darted around as he shifted the knife, sending bayonets of hot agony up and down his leg and into his crotch and belly. He bit off his left glove and stuck his left index finger into the wound as well, and immediately felt the little chunk of lead just to the left of the hole. It was about an inch deep. Sighing and groaning deep in his throat, he worked his left finger as well as the knife until he'd rolled up the little chunk of lead that was causing him such a huge, wide world of grief onto the tip of the knife and held it there while he removed it.

"Well, I'll be a sonofabitch," Leon said, grinning, tears of misery rolling down his cheeks and beads of cold sweat popping out on his forehead. He held his bloody right thumb and index finger, between which he was holding the bloody, flattened bullet, up in front of his face. His hand was shaking as though from the ague.

"There you are you little devil! Why, I'll be a monkey's uncle. You ain't much bigger'n a black-eyed pea! Imagine somethin' so small grievin' me *so bad*!"

He tossed the bullet away, sucked another sharp breath, and then untied the neckerchief and moved it down over the wound, to stem the blood, and knotted it again.

"Oh, shit—I sure could do with a drink."

He looked around the tree and down the slope. He could no longer see the pink glow of his fire's coals. The fire had gone out. He had a bottle down there in his saddlebags. Did he dare retrieve it?

He raked a thumbnail down his bristly cheek, thinking it over. He doubted he'd make it back down to the camp and back up here on his bad leg. He'd best stay up here on high ground, from where he not only had the best view of the valley but a good place to hold off any more riders.

He didn't doubt that old Hollister would send more men after him. Probably not till after sunrise, but since he couldn't move well, if at all, the deputy had best stay right where he was. Maybe by morning he'd be feeling better and he could haul his wounded ass down the backside of the mountain and . . .

What?

Hide like a wounded bobcat?

How long could he stay alive out here, wounded and unable to get around, without food and water?

He looked down the slope again. He had both food and water down there. He also had a traveling flask of . . .

His eyes grew round. His lower jaw sagged.

He reached into his left coat pocket and, wrapping his hand around his hide-covered traveling flask, he shaped a delighted grin. He'd forgotten that earlier, just after he'd gathered firewood, he'd removed the flask from his saddlebags and slipped it into his coat pocket for easy access.

He pulled the flask out of the pocket, uncapped it, and took a long pull. Instantly, the fiery liquid spread a balm throughout his belly and tempered, if only slightly, the metronomic throb in his right leg. He sat back against the tree, took another pull, and then another. He shook the flask, judging the amount of remaining firewater, and then capped it and returned it to his coat pocket.

He settled farther back against the tree. Despite the cold night air and the pain in his leg, his eyelids grew heavy, as did his head. He drew a long, raspy breath, crossed his arms on his chest, dropped his chin, and felt sleep close over him like a dark, furry glove.

A voice woke him.

McMannigle opened his eyes and jerked his head up. It took him several seconds to get his bearings and to remember the cause of the heavy, throbbing agony in his right leg. A man's voice rose again behind him, and his heart thudded.

Someone was here.

He scrunched lower against the ground, gritting his teeth against the pain in his leg, and doffed his hat. He looked around the tree to stare down the slope toward the valley. He must have slept for over an hour, for the darkness was softening, the stars fading. Dark shapes shone against the faint gray bleeding into the valley from the east.

Leon shuttled his gaze slowly across the slope dropping away below him, pricking his ears, listening intently. Now he heard nothing except the rasp of the breeze picking up. Had he dreamt the voices?

A twig snapped dully.

McMannigle jerked his head hard left. A man-shaped shadow moved between two piñons, the gray light of the false dawn showing the fleece lining his heavy coat and flashing off the breech of the rifle in his hands. The man stopped, jerked his head up, lifted his rifle, shouting, "He's here!"

Boom!

The man's last word had been drowned by the thunder of McMannigle's rifle. The man's own rifle belched, stabbing flames toward the ground, blowing up dirt and pine needles three feet away from the deputy. The man made hiccupping sounds and his boots raked and thudded as he stumbled back through the pines on his spurs.

Leon sensed someone behind him now, moving toward him from the opposite side of the slope from the man he'd just shot. Using his Winchester as a crutch, he hoisted himself to his feet and, scrunching up his face against the pounding throb in his leg, feeling weak and sick to his stomach, he threw himself forward, dragging his wounded leg down the backside of the slope, pushing through pine branches.

Behind him, a rifle thundered. The slug screeched over his right shoulder and thumped loudly into an aspen bole. Leon scissored his left leg forward, dragging his right boot.

The rifle thundered again.

At the same time, McMannigle tripped over a deadfall, dropped hard, losing his rifle, and began rolling wildly down the bluff's steep back slope. The ground rapped him like a wild man with an ax handle. He had to suck the pain down deep to keep from screaming. Fortunately, he didn't roll far. He landed on a bench-like area, tumbled forward through several evergreen shrubs, and lay on his back, raking air in and out of his lungs like a landed fish.

Stifling a sob, he lifted his head.

His vision swam. Dirt and pine needles coated him. He looked down at his thigh. Blood oozed out around the neckerchief he'd tied over the wound. He looked around for his rifle but didn't see it. He lowered his right hand to his holster. Empty. He'd lost his Schofield revolver, too.

Shit . . .

He lay listening intently. There was no doubt that the second shooter was moving down the slope toward him. No doubt at all. Leon couldn't move, or he'd give away his position. All he could do was lie here, wounded and bleeding and in silently screaming agony, and wait for the rifle-wielding killer to finish him.

CHAPTER 11

Stillman opened his eyes with a start.

He looked to the right, where a window shone with the gray-blue light of dawn.

"Good morning," said a female's warm, intimate, raspy voice above faint raking sounds.

Stillman blinked, squinted, blinked more sleep from his eyes. Faith's image clarified in the bedroom's heavy shadows. His tall, chocolate-haired, brown-eyed wife stood in front of an oval-shaped, wood-framed floor mirror just off the foot of their brass-framed bed, tilting her head and brushing her rich, flowing mane from the inside out.

She wore a flowered satin nightgown that only partly covered her burgeoning, pregnant form. Her belly containing their first child was as round as a large ball, and her two swollen breasts, large as nine-month-old retriever pups, spilled over the top of it, the sides of the magnificent orbs bulging out from behind the skimpy garment that Stillman had given her for their one-year anniversary. The right strap hung down her arm, and that side of the gown hung nearly all the way down the right breast, as well, revealing the tip of the brown areola.

Both breasts jostled as she tilted her head to the other side, and continued brushing, the rich lips of her long mouth quirking a warm smile as she blinked slowly.

"You should sleep some more."

Stillman pushed up to a half-sitting position, propped on his locked arms. He was fully dressed, as he'd only lain down for a nap. He tore his gaze from the beautiful woman before him to the window. "How long I been out?"

"Only two hours. You came in after three. Two hours isn't enough sleep, Ben."

"Wasn't plannin' on sleepin' at all. It's Friday night, and I got two prisoners locked up in the calaboose."

"Leon's probably back, tending them."

"He's another thing I gotta check on. Gotta make sure that jasper's back."

Faith set the silver and tortoiseshell-backed brush on the dresser and walked over to the side of the bed. She did not pull the strap up her arm, but let the nightgown dangle off the tip of her right breast.

"He'll keep." She sat on the side of the bed and leaned across her husband's belly to prop herself on her right arm. "You should sleep another hour, at least."

"I just came home for a cup of coffee and a bite to eat, you vamp. You led me up here, made me lie down, told me you'd wake me in an hour. You're a bad girl, Mrs. Stillman." He was caressing her voluptuous, infernally supple and erotic form with his eyes, and she delighted in it, showing all her fine, white teeth through a sparkling, sexy smile that lifted color in her high, perfectly sculpted cheeks.

"Guilty as charged. I just don't want you to wear yourself out. Soon, you're going to have a child to help me raise."

"His or her mother's likely gonna put me in a wheelchair."

"Oh, I think you can handle it." She leaned down and pressed her soft lips to his forehead. "Really, Ben—I think you should sleep. Leon's probably back from the Triple H Connected by now."

"Yeah, well, if he is, he's had a long night and needs his sleep worse than I do, though he don't deserve it—goin' against orders like he done."

Stillman pushed himself up a little farther and started to roll toward the edge of the bed. Faith placed her hand on his chest, pushing him back down.

"Hold on. If you can't sleep, we can try something else to help you relax, *mon cherie*. Relax and invigorate you, *oui?*" Faith, nearly twenty years younger than Stillman, hailed from a wealthy French ranching family down around the Powder River country, and her earthy, ranch-born-and-bred femininity coupled with her seductive French blood was never more apparent than in the main bedroom of the Stillman house, the bed of which Stillman was sure they'd bust into a pile of jackstraws before they got their second bun in the oven.

Stillman reached up and grabbed her full, supple breasts in his hands, and squeezed. Lowering his hand to caress her large, hard belly, feeling a warmth rising in his loins, he said, "Might not be such a good idea . . . for a woman in your condition, I mean." He looked at her, arching one brow, desire at work in him. "You think?"

Faith blinked once again, slowly, and leaned down to press her lips to his. She prodded his teeth with her tongue and nibbled his mustache as she pulled her head away. She smoothed his thick, gray-brown hair back from his temples, kissed his forehead, and then slid the left strap of her nightgown all the way down her arm.

The dress tumbled over her belly, exposing the succulent breasts with jutting nipples.

She placed his hands on them and held them there, breathing deeply, luxuriating in the masculine warmth of her husband's big paws on her.

"Yes, but you know as well as I do, *mon cherie,* that there are other things we can do." She ran her tongue across her upper lip and then began unbuckling his belt. "I believe *we've* gotten quite good at it, in fact, no?"

Stillman laid his head back on the pillow, and groaned.

A half hour later, Stillman clicked his Colt's hammer back.

"All right, come on out of there before I start loosin' lead. Come on—I see you back there!"

Stillman was sitting his horse at the corner of Gaylord Street and Clantick's main drag, First Street, and he was aiming his revolver across the front of a barbershop on his right, toward the ends of a muffler he could see blowing out of an alley mouth. He'd just ridden down from his and Faith's little ranch on a bluff north of Clantick, when, approaching First Street, he'd glimpsed the shadowy figure dart into the alley between the barber shop and a little tobacco shop just beyond it.

The blowing muffler ends disappeared, as though whoever was standing in the alley had stepped back farther away from the mouth still gauzy with early morning shadows.

"I'm not going to tell you again!" Stillman warned. "Come on out of there *now*!"

Haltingly, a figure emerged from the mouth of the alley. The slender person wore a white knit cloth cap, the muffler, and a long, gray coat. Long, sandy-blonde hair blew around the girl's head in the wind. Sheepishly, she lifted her dimpled chin, and smiled a little too brightly, slapping a hand to her chest. "Oh, Ben—it's you!"

The sun just now rising behind Stillman shone in her pale blue eyes.

"Evelyn?"

"I didn't know it was you. Didn't even recognize your voice with all the trash blowin' in the alley."

Stillman depressed his gun hammer and returned the Colt to its holster. "What're you doin' out here so early, actin' so . . . secretive? You ain't plannin' a holdup, are ya?" He chuckled.

"Oh, no—nothin' like that, Ben." Evelyn looked around, her cheeks flushed with embarrassment, and she appeared to be straining for an explanation before she hooked a nervous thumb over her shoulder and said, "I was . . . I was just comin' from the doc's place."

"The doc's place?"

"Yeah . . . I . . . uh . . . brought him breakfast. You know how he likes Sam's venison liver and onions. We had some left over, so I took 'em up to him."

Stillman canted his head in disbelief. "You tellin' me, little lady, that Doc Evans is up at this hour?" The sawbones was a notorious drunk who between patients was known to either frequent the Clantick whorehouses till late at night or mid-morning of the next day, or to stay home and read the books in his vast classical library and drink brandy till he passed out.

"Yeah, well . . . he was awake, all right." Evelyn smiled, the flush in her cheeks deepening. "I was a little surprised by that myself. Thought I'd have to leave the vittles on his table. Oh, well—I reckon I'd best be heading back to the café now, Ben. I wasn't sure who you were, and it was such a wild Friday night, I thought you might be one of them wild track layers."

She'd stepped out onto the street and was now making her way past the sheriff straddling the big bay. She headed in the direction of Sam Wa's café. "No girl is safe with them in town!"

"No, I reckon not," Stillman said, scowling after her. He'd be damned if she didn't seem odd. He'd seen Evelyn and Evans together quite a bit, usually just having coffee together in the café.

They wouldn't have struck up a dalliance, would they?

Stillman wiped the thought from his mind. Everyone knew that the doc had promised his frequent medical partner, the Widow Kemmett, that they'd be married soon. Not even Evans, whose morals were unquestioned only because everyone pretty much knew he didn't have any, would do something that low-down-scoundrel-dirty and cruel—breaking Katherine Kemmett's heart in favor of a much younger girl.

Of course, Stillman didn't have much room to judge a man harshly for choosing a younger woman though he'd always felt that he hadn't chosen Faith so much as Fate had chosen her for him.

And, of course, he hadn't promised himself to another woman . . .

Ruminating, he clucked Sweets ahead and headed south toward the jailhouse, hoping he'd either find his deputy there or some sign that he'd made it back to town in one piece. As Stillman pulled up to the hitch rack fronting his office, he saw a horse standing in front of Auld's Livery & Feed Barn on the opposite side of the street and a half a block farther west.

The sun had risen enough that the sheriff could see that the horse was a beefy skewbald. It had probably gotten out of Auld's paddock during the night, took a little run around town, and had now returned for breakfast. Auld or his sometimes assistant, Olaf Weisinger, would likely let the horse in when the livery opened for business at eight.

Stillman tied Sweets to the hitch rack, unlocked the office door, and headed on inside to find no sign that McMannigle had returned to town. If he had, he'd surely have built up the fire in the stove that stood in the middle of the rear cell block, which was housing the two troublemakers from Sam Wa's Café—Seymore Scudder and the barrel-shaped, freckle-faced gent, Llewelyn Sweney. Both hard cases were market hunters though they'd be out of a job at least until the circuit judge pulled through Clantick, and tried them, which likely wouldn't be for another week or so.

"How good of you to put in an appearance, Sheriff," griped Scudder from behind the cross-shaped bandage that Doc Evans had placed over his nose and cheekbones and up around his swollen, bloodshot eyes. "If you'd shown up a few minutes later, we'd likely be frozen up stiff as corpses!"

Stillman had just pulled his hand away from the stove, which he'd banked early this morning before he'd gone home, and which was still warm though far from hot. It was a little chilly in the cell block, but his two prisoners had been in no danger of freezing to death.

Sweney sat on the edge of his cot in the cell beside Scudder's, two army blankets draped over his thick shoulders. His right arm, which Stillman had drilled with a .44 round, was in a sling. "We got rights, Sheriff. The right not to freeze to death while we're incarcerated in this rat-infested shack you call a jailhouse!"

"And we'd like coffee and some pancakes and eggs and a big slice of ham!" added Scudder.

"You two got a little uncomfortable this mornin', did you?" Chunking split pine logs through the potbelly stove's open door, Stillman chuckled. "Well, I'm real sorry about that. To think that I'd go and let the fire burn down on two such honorable, upstanding citizens locked up in my jailhouse. That burns me with shame, purely it does."

He chuckled again as he used one of the logs to stir the coals inside the stove.

"Fuck you, Stillman," bellowed Sweney. "My arm hurts somethin' fierce, and it hurts worse when I'm cold and hungry!"

When Stillman had the stove fire burning and the iron stove ticking, he closed the door. "No, Sweney." He grinned without mirth as he stared through strap-iron bands of the cell door at the square-headed, pugnacious, freckle-faced gent. "Fuck you. You, too, Scudder. You'll get fed when I feel like feedin' ya."

Stillman walked back through the cell block and into his office, closing the stout, wooden door on the prisoners' chorus of bellowing curses, and turned the key in the lock.

He was paying no attention to the hard cases' complaints. His mind was on Leon. It wasn't all that odd that his deputy hadn't yet made it back to town, as it had been a dark night and the Triple H Connected was a good twenty-mile ride southwest, over and around some fairly high Two-Bear Mountain ridges. Likely, Leon would have stopped and camped for the night and started back toward town at dawn.

Stillman would likely see him soon. And when he did, he'd give him one hell of a tongue-lashing for disobeying orders, though deep down Stillman understood why he'd done what he'd done. But orders were orders. McMannigle would be expecting the reprimand.

Still, the sheriff felt more than a twinge of uneasiness in his belly.

Instead of building a fire in the main office, he walked out onto the front stoop, looking around at the street over which the sun was sliding purple shadows into alley mouths and up against building fronts. Smoke from breakfast fires wafted in the breeze, rife with the tang of pine and cedar cut in the creek bottoms and mountains. Several shopkeepers were sweeping their porches or arranging merchandise into outdoor displays.

Reaching inside his coat for his makings sack, Stillman glanced along the street to his right. He left the pouch in his pocket. The burly, bearded, overall-clad Emil Auld was standing just outside his open barn doors, appraising the skewbald facing him. Auld had a hand on a rope attached to the horse's hackamore, and he was sort of leaning back and looking down, inspecting the horse's hooves.

"Auld!"

Stillman dropped down into the street and started walking toward the barn, gradually increasing his pace as his heart quickened. As he approached the liveryman, who was raking his

101

faintly perplexed gaze between Stillman and the horse, Auld said, "Deputy McMannigle—he's back?"

"No, he's not back," Stillman said.

"This here is the horse I gave him to pull his wagon."

Stillman stopped in his tracks. "No wagon?"

Auld looked around, pursing his lips and shrugging. "Do you see a wagon?"

"Goddammit!"

Stillman swung around and jogged back to the jail office. He went inside and quickly stuffed some trail supplies and two boxes of .44 shells—one for his revolver, one for his Henry rifle—into a pair of saddlebags, and grabbed his bedroll hanging from a coat hook by a leather thong. Heading back outside, he closed and locked the door behind him, slung the saddlebags behind his cantle, tied the bedroll over them, and stepped into the leather.

He stopped with the horse half-turned away from his office, scratching his chin and scowling.

He needed a deputy . . .

He neck-reined the big bay toward Sam Wa's Café, and spurred the horse into a gallop, hooves drumming in the still-quiet but brightening street, riding through tufts of tangy chimney smoke. At Sam Wa's, he checked the horse down, swung out of the saddle, mounted Sam's little, sun-silvered boardwalk and pushed the door open, causing the cowbell to clatter.

Evelyn was just then pouring coffee for her only two customers at a table along the wall to the right and about halfway down the room.

"Evelyn?"

The young blonde, her hair pinned up, turned to Stillman. Again, her face acquired a flushed, sheepish look, causing the sheriff to half-consciously speculate about what had happened over at the doc's place. "Ben . . . ?" Smoke curled from the spout of the big, black coffeepot she held by a pot holder in her right hand.

"Consider yourself deputized."

"Huh?"

The extroverted, eminently affable and big-hearted girl was well liked throughout the town if not the county. Evelyn was like a receptive bartender in that she knew most everyone's secrets and troubles, she did not flinch at doling out advice based on lessons she'd learned from her own troubled past, and her forthright manner commanded moral authority. Stillman knew that if he could trust anyone to keep the peace when both he and Leon were away, that person was Evelyn Vincent.

"I have to head out to the Two-Bears—"

"Is it Leon?" Evelyn asked, eyes wide with concern.

"Yeah, it's Leon. Anyone causes a ruckus between now and when I get back, beetle your brows at 'em. If that doesn't work, use that bung starter you keep behind the counter. If *that* doesn't work, send Sam and his meat cleaver. Good luck. Be back soon!"

He pinched his hat brim to the girl staring at him with her mouth agape, and went out and closed the door. He mounted Sweets and spurred the horse west at a full gallop, causing a couple of dogs to run after him, nipping at the bay's hocks and barking.

CHAPTER 12

On his back on the side of the mountain, Leon waited.

He seemed to be waiting a long time, his back against the cold ground, blood oozing from the wound in his leg, before he heard the faintest foot tread—the very slight crunch of gravel and pine needles crackling softly under a man's stealthy step. The deputy had begun to wonder if the second stalker—were there only two or were there more closing around him?—was coming for him or was he maybe waiting atop the ridge for him to show himself, so he could shoot him from long distance with the rifle?

He was here. Only a few feet away.

There was another footfall so faint that if it hadn't been so early-morning quiet and the birds had not started chirping yet, the deputy wouldn't have heard it.

Having neither his revolver nor his rifle, he'd slid his bowie knife from his belt sheath. He squeezed it in his right hand up around that ear, the blade pointed straight above his head.

His heart thudded slowly, heavily.

Suddenly, the barrel of a rifle was thrust through the trees screening Leon. The rifle roared, lapping flames. The slugs screeched over Leon and chewed into the trees and spanged off rocks beyond him. Leon lay flat, gritting his teeth and squeezing his eyes closed, waiting for the man to lower his rifle's barrel.

When he did that, that would be the end.

Leon's heart raced. His hand sweated around the handle of

the bowie knife.

As suddenly as it had started, the rifle's rataplan ceased after six shots. McMannigle had been counting the rounds the way a man sealed alive in a coffin counts the nails being hammered through the lid.

The din hadn't died for much over a second before the deputy lifted his head and, with a grunt, flicked the bowie knife two-fingered from beside his right ear. The knife whistled as it tumbled through the air, crunching through the thin screen of branches in front of him.

There was a crunching thud.

A sucked breath. A gasp.

There was a clattering thump as the man dropped his rifle. He stumbled forward through the screen, the piñon branches parting like a tattered curtain. The man was short and thick, with heavy, round shoulders and long, greasy black hair dangling from beneath his black slouch hat with a beaded leather band around the crown. The man's face was massive and hideously ugly, with wide-set eyes, a wedge-shaped nose, and many deep pockmarks in his red-dark skin.

He staggered into the slight clearing in which Leon lay, staring wide-eyed up at the man, who wore a dark wool, three-point capote that hung to his knees. The wooden handle of McMannigle's knife stuck out of the man's upper-left chest. Leon thought he'd missed the man's heart, but frothy blood was bubbling up around the blade, soaking the man's coat. The stuff that didn't soak into the wool dribbled down the front.

The man stared down at Leon blankly at first, but then his oily black eyes flashed, and his mustached mouth curled a wry grin. He lifted his right hand, wrapped it around the knife handle, and made a strained expression, narrowing his eyes, as he tugged at the bowie. Pulling on the handle, he gritted his teeth. His hand quivered as he gave a yelp and, with great effort, pulled the blade out of his chest with a wet sucking sound.

Tears welled in his dark eyes, dribbled down his cheeks.

Blood dripped thickly from the Bowie's wide blade.

The stocky Mexican glared down at McMannigle, took another shambling step toward him, and started to lift the knife threateningly. Before he could get it half raised, he dropped with another yelp to his knees and blinked his eyes as he continued to glare down at Leon, gritting his teeth.

The Mexican's torso sagged forward. McMannigle rolled onto his left shoulder a half second before the big Mexican shooter landed with a heavy thud and a sigh onto the ground Leon had just vacated.

The Mexican's broad, rounded shoulders wobbled. His legs shook, he made a gurgling sound, and lay still.

Leon rolled onto his belly, got his knees under him, and heaved himself up until he was half standing, extending his wounded right leg out to the side, keeping as much weight off it as he could. He tightened the bandage over the wound, breathing hard, groaning, and then looked around, listening. He couldn't hear much above his own heavy, raking breaths, but he thought he must be alone.

If there were others out here, they would have shown themselves by now.

He stared down at the inert Mexican. The sun was nearly up now, and its soft, blue-gray light showed the blood pooling on the gravel and pine needles beneath the dead Mex's chest and belly. Leon groaned again as he picked up his bowie knife, cleaned it on the dead man's coat, and slipped it back into his belt sheath.

He pulled the man's Smith & Wesson and stuffed it into his own holster. His heart beat insistently now, hopefully. These two must have horses tethered somewhere at the foot of the mountain. McMannigle had to get to a mount and get started back to Clantick before he bled dry.

"Easier said than done, hoss," he told himself.

He pushed through the screen of branches and stumbled over the dead Mexican's rifle. Leon picked up the Winchester Yellowboy, made sure there wasn't a shell in the chamber, and then used the rifle as a crutch as he got started back up the steep side of the bluff.

The severe incline winded him quickly. His head pounded and the slope rose and fell around him. He was dizzy from blood loss. But he pushed on, maneuvering sideways up the slope, using the rifle barrel to hoist himself and then sliding the wounded right leg up behind him. It was excruciatingly slow and painful going, and he had to stop several times to rest and let the hammering in his skull subside.

He finally made it, and after a two-minute breather, leaning on the rifle, he started down the front side of the bluff, which was far less steep than most of the back side. He leaned hard on the rifle with every step, but he made fast progress, noting with a scowling disdain a couple of the men he'd killed last night. By the time he reached the bottom of the bluff, the sun was up and warming the frosty air, gilding the leaves slowly tumbling from the aspens lining the sparkling creek. The sky was faultless, cerulean blue.

It would have been a damned fine morning if he wasn't losing blood and strength fast, he vaguely opined as he looked around for his now-dead stalkers' horses.

He shuffled upstream from a man who lay dead in the shallow water, dropped down beside the creek, and, though it aggravated the pulsating burn in his thigh, he lowered his head to the water and drank thirstily. The water was so cold he thought his teeth would crack, but he drank his fill, feeling nourished and ever-so-slightly invigorated.

He looked at the dead man whose limbs bobbled in the current. His faded red neckerchief snaked six inches out in the current. The man's eyes were half open, and his mouth was slack beneath his sandy-brown mustache, giving him a sad, longing look.

"Damn, that's good," Leon jeered, smacking his lips as water dribbled down the corners of his mouth. "A drink of fresh spring water on a purty mountain morning. That's a pleasure you'll never have again, my friend. Should have left this darkie well enough alone!"

McMannigle gave a disdainful chuff then limped across the creek, paused beside the cold, gray remains of his fire, and reached into his saddlebags for several strips of deer jerky. He ate one whole strip standing over the bags, and washed it down with several swigs of whiskey from his flask. Then, chewing another strip, he shuffled out away from the fire ring and into the clearing, chewing and grunting and dragging his right boot across the short grass and gravel, weaving between bristly pine shrubs.

He found the horses near the trail, tied to a single, blowdown pine out of sight from the clearing.

"Oh," Leon said, tears of joy veiling his eyes and running down his cheeks.

He didn't know when last he'd been so happy to see a saddle horse. And here were two—a handsome roan and a short, broad-barreled Appaloosa, which had probably belonged to the stocky Mexican. Their breeze-brushed coats shimmered in the golden light of the rising sun.

Both horses had been standing facing the blowdown pine but now they were staring at the black man shambling toward them, leaning on a rifle and dragging his right leg around which the green neckerchief was tied. They stared darkly, twitching their ears. Suddenly, the roan lifted its head and whickered.

"Easy, fellas," Leon said. "Easy, now, easy."

He looked at the reins tied to separate branches of the blow-down. Neither set appeared to be tied all that tightly. The horses were likely well trained and the tying of the reins had only been a precaution.

Frightened by the stranger shuffling toward him, the roan whinnied and pulled at the reins, which held, but the deputy could see the slipknot loosen a little.

Oh, no.

"Hold on, now," Leon pleaded, panting, keeping his voice down as he slowed his pace. "Hold on. Easy. I'm just gonna take these reins here . . . slip them over the branch . . . like *that*!"

Relief washed over him when he'd grabbed the roan's reins, slick from a fresh greasing. But then the roan jerked its head up sharply and lunged back away from the pine. Leon managed to hold onto the reins but the roan's lunge pulled him sharply forward. He lost his footing, wounded leg barking madly, and fell in a heap. Fire shot up and down his leg. Somehow, he'd managed to hold onto the slick reins, and, dropping the rifle, he closed both his hands around them, wrapping them around his knuckles.

He wouldn't give up the reins if the horse pulled both his arms out of their sockets!

"Oh, now, don't do that, hoss!" Leon ground his teeth together. "Don . . . don't do that, now, you scoun . . . I mean, you fine-lookin', precious animal!"

He let the horse's pressure on the reins help pull him to his feet. He stood still for a time, holding the reins, but neither saying nor doing anything, just letting the horse relax with him present. When the beast had grown relatively calm, Leon limped slowly over to the left stirrup. The horse whickered and backed away. The deputy froze again, stress tightening all the muscles in his back and filling him with dread.

If he could not get himself mounted, he was a goner.

More riders from the Triple H Connected would likely be heading this way soon. He had to get back to town, inform Ben what had happened, and then get himself over to Doc Evans's place for tending.

If it had been his right leg that had been wounded, he doubted he would have been able to get mounted, especially with the horse curveting as though to rid himself of the stranger who smelled like fresh blood. But Leon managed to toe the left stirrup and, with a shrill sigh he swung his wounded right leg over the horse's rump and got the toe of that boot in its corresponding stirrup.

He whistled raspily, neck-reined the jittery horse around, and pulled it out onto the wagon trail, directing it northeast, in the direction of town. The horse broke into a trot, ears and tail up, muscles bunching tensely beneath the saddle.

The horse's jouncing felt like a twisting knife in the wound, so he slowed the horse to a walk, and took another couple of pulls from his flask, draining it. He tossed it away with a wince of regret. It would take longer, walking instead of trotting, but at least he'd arrive in town with a pint or two of blood left in his veins.

Fatigue lay heavy on the deputy's shoulders. Before he realized what was happening, his eyes were closing and he was leaning forward to snug his cheek down taut against the roan's mane, letting his arms dangle both sides of the pole.

He became aware that the horse was no longer moving.

Leon jerked his head up.

The sun was high and warm.

He looked around, blinking his eyes. A sledgehammer of shock smashed into his forehead, and his belly filled with the hot tar of dread when he realized that the horse had not taken him back to town but right into the Triple H Connected compound!

The horse stood near one of several corrals, nose to nose with a horse inside the corral. Smoke issued from the main house's broad stone hearth only fifty, sixty yards away. A chaise with its top down stood near the front porch, a black horse in its traces.

Anxiety ripped through the deputy. He looked around for his horse's reins. They were on the ground, cracked and broken. The horse had apparently dragged them and stepped on them.

"Oh, shit," Leon said, glancing at the house once more. He thought he saw a curtain move in an upper-story window. Someone had seen him.

His head swam. His heart pounded. He had to get the reins.

He swung awkwardly, painfully down from the saddle, looking around for the gall-blasted dog he'd seen before, when he'd come with the dead girl in the wagon, and who'd barked at him no end. As he reached for the reins, everything went black and silent. He was only vaguely aware of his knees and then his head hitting the ground.

And then he was out like a blown lamp, sound asleep in the middle of the Triple H. Connected headquarters.

CHAPTER 13

Nash Hollister held up his right hand and drew back on his horse's reins with the left one.

As his gelding slowed to a walk, the dozen or so riders—every man who'd been left in the Triple H Connected bunkhouse—slowed their own horses behind him. Nash studied the Appaloosa tethered to the blowdown pine ten yards off the side of the trail.

The Appy belonged to Joseph Triejo. Nash glanced around for Blaze Westin's mount, saw nothing but breeze-jostled grass and shrubs and pine-clad slopes rising around him. The eldest Hollister son had no idea why both men wouldn't have either been mounted or on foot, but he'd likely find out soon enough.

He touched spurs to his zebra dun's flanks and galloped around the base of the pine-stippled ridge and into the clearing, seeing the deputy's wagon on the right, about fifty feet from the fire ring and strewn gear. The stream chuckled over rocks beyond the fire and the gear. Blood stained the ground to the right of the fire, at the base of the southwestern slope.

His brother Zeb's blood. Blood from his youngest brother's ruined knee. Nash vaguely wondered if the kid was still alive. If he lived, he'd be a cripple for the rest of his life. Nash wasn't sure the kid wouldn't be better off dead.

"Head on up the ridge," he ordered the men around him, their breath as well as their horses' breath pluming in the chill, sunny air, aspen leaves tumbling around them to scrape along the rocks lining the streambed. "Spread out. That's where Westin and Triejo would have gone, lookin' for sign. They likely marked where they picked up the deputy's trail with a neckerchief tied to a branch, so keep your eyes open."

The men spurred their horses on around the cold campfire and across the stream, water droplets sparkling like diamonds. They glanced down at where Morgan still lay on the rocks in the creek, arms and legs spread and being nudged by the current. He stared sadly up at the blue sky arching over him.

Hooves clattered over rocks, and then the men's horses grunted and snorted as they lunged on up the ridge, weaving among the piñons, aspens, firs and occasional boulders. They rode abreast, spread out away from each other, looking around for that trail marker. A couple of men gestured to the other three dead Triple H Connected men and conversed among themselves.

Nash remained mounted near the fire ring mounded with gray ashes. There was no point in him climbing the ridge. That's why he had men working for him. There was little doubt in his mind that the grisly little opera that had played out here had come to an end earlier this morning.

Nash's only reason for riding out here was to make sure that all the loose ends were tied. He had to make sure the deputy did not get back to Clantick. If that happened—well, Nash didn't even want to think about what would happen, then. It *couldn't* happen, that's all.

What a goddamned mess.

And he'd been a part of it.

He should have stopped it before it had even begun, refusing the old man's orders to hunt the deputy down. But Nash had been drunk on the same emotion old Watt had been drunk on, learning that the Negro deputy had killed Orlean.

A black man killing Nash's sister, his family's pride and joy . . .

It had been a misdirected fury, but fury just the same. Now, he was filled with a vague but noxious sense of dread and menace. It had a tight hold on him, and it had put him in one hell of a bad mood. He didn't wonder consciously about what this all would lead to, but somewhere deep in the bowels of his consciousness, he was working on it, all right. The unoiled gears were grinding away, squawking and clattering.

He hadn't slept a wink since the botched ambush.

Now, hearing his men calling back and forth to each other as they climbed the slope on the far side of the stream, Nash hooked his right leg over his saddle horn, hauled out his makings sack, and built a cigarette while he brooded. He scratched a match to life on the wooden head of his saddle horn frame, which was protruding through a torn seam in the leather—winter was the time for such chores as tack repair—and touched the match to the end of his quirley.

"Boss!"

Blowing smoke into the cool air, Nash lifted his gaze to the ridge. He could see only one man sitting his white-socked black horse at the top of the bluff, waving to him broadly with one arm.

Nash lowered his right boot to its stirrup, and, casually puffing the quirley, touched spurs to his dun. He rode across the stream, not glancing at Morgan still wallowing there, and began climbing the ridge, letting the horse pick its own course through the trees and brush snags. When he'd gained the ridge crest, he saw several men sitting their horses just down the bluff's steep back side.

They all looked grim; none seemed eager to make eye contact with him.

"You find Triejo's trail?"

"Nah, boss," said Luther Simonson, the man who'd waved. "We found Triejo."

"Westin's over here," said a man standing atop the ridge beyond Simonson, flanked by a clump of tall fir trees and shaggy piñons. He glanced over his left shoulder to indicate something in the trees behind him, and stretched a bitter grin. "Bullet in the neck."

A cold anvil dropped in Nash's belly. The hair along the back of his neck pricked.

He looked down the slope where three men were standing in a ragged circle, holding their horses' reins and gazing grimly up the steep slope toward Nash. Rather than ride his own horse down the steep declivity, the elder Hollister son swung heavily, dreadfully down from his saddle, dropped his reins, and tramped down the slope. He almost fell on a patch of slippery grass, almost swallowed the quirley in his teeth, and cursed as he threw out his arms to catch himself.

The three men sat their horses outside another patch of scraggly cedars and piñons. Two backed their horses away from each other in the bowl-shaped depression, making way for Nash. He pushed through the branches, nervously puffing the quirley clamped between his jaws, and felt that anvil in his belly flop onto its side when he stared down at the broad back and the back of the head of Joseph Triejo.

Nash clenched his fists at his sides.

He turned and walked back out of the trees and shrubs, and looked around. His heart was hammering as he started climbing the slope toward his dun.

"What about the lawman?" asked one of the mounted men behind Nash.

"He's headed for town," Nash bit out, nostrils swelling, anxiety causing his heart to beat faster. He threw his arm violently forward. "Come on, goddamnit! We gotta find him before he gets to town!"

"Gotta get you up, Deputy. Hey, can you hear me? Gotta get you up or you'll be dead right quick!"

Leon had heard the high, Southern-accented, female voice as though she were calling softly to him from the top of a deep well that he lay at the bottom of. He had to be dreaming. But when someone began tugging on his arm, rolling him onto his side, he opened his eyes.

Nothing but a lemon-gray blur. But then the face of a pretty young woman—brown-haired, hazel-eyed, snub-nosed—clarified before him. She wore a man's tan felt hat, and tight braids draped down her chest, over an open, buckskin jacket showing a vest and a man's hickory shirt. She wore gray knit gloves with one torn finger, women's scuffed brown half boots, and a gray skirt.

She was tugging on his arms with both hands, glancing over and beyond him. "If you don't want to die out here, you'd best do as I say! Ole Barney's bound to come back from one of his rabbit-huntin' trips, and kick up a ruckus!"

McMannigle sat up and looked in the direction she was looking. The Hollister cabin sat large and formidable at the other end of the yard. A buggy with its top down sat in front of the porch. He just then remembered where he was, and as he began trying to heave himself to his feet, the girl crouched under his left arm and, grunting, helped him up and over to the side of a log shed that was likely a blacksmith shop or tack shed.

Here, he was out of sight of both the bunkhouse and the yard.

He leaned back against the shed and then fatigue caused him to sag down onto the lumber that had been piled there and around which brome grass and lamb's ear had grown tall. The girl ran back and, canting her pretty, hazel eyes toward the house again, grabbed the reins of Leon's appropriated horse and led the mount, clucking, out of the main yard and over toward Leon.

Clamping a hand over his wound, gritting his teeth, he looked up at the girl whom he judged to be not much over twenty. "Who're . . . you . . . and . . . why . . . ?"

"Hush!"

Holding the horse's reins, she began pulling on his arm again. He heaved himself to his feet, the ground and the horse pitching around him, the roan whickering anxiously.

"Can you get back up there?" the girl asked, glancing at the saddle.

McMannigle said halfheartedly that he thought he could. She turned the horse around, so that its left side faced him and the horse itself was facing back toward the yard. The deputy stepped up onto the lumber pile and from there to the stirrup, and from the stirrup—with an agonized groan—onto the saddle.

"Hold on, now," the girl admonished him, and, leading the horse by its reins, turned it around.

Leon grabbed the saddle horn as the girl led him and the horse off behind the shed, away from the yard and the corrals. The deputy's head hung heavily, and he realized that he was lapsing in and out of semiconsciousness, only vaguely aware that he and the horse were being led down a hill through sometimes-thick brush. They crossed what must have been a coulee or a creek bed at the bottom of the hill—he could hear and smell running water, mud, and the musk of verdant growth—and then she admonished him to hold on again, and he was pushed back in the saddle as they climbed a steep slope.

He hunkered low over the horse's mane.

He must have lapsed even deeper into semiconsciousness, for, while he sporadically heard and saw things and smelled things around him—the chirping of birds, the passing of evergreen trees, the sweet fetor of some dead, rotting animal maybe lying in the brush near the trail the girl was leading him down—time slipped away from him. He was half aware of being helped down off the horse, and then he heard the clomping of his own dragging boots and raking spurs on what must have been a wooden floor. He smelled pent-up air and wood mold and then the sweaty stench of old wool.

For a time, he was aware of nothing except the pain in his leg. It was as though the world had died around him, leaving only his throbbing wound and a nebulous dream of running from Apaches while trying to pull an arrow from his leg, and they were getting closer and closer, whooping and hollering . . .

Suddenly, his right leg started burning.

He gave a loud, shrieking grunt, and lifted his head and opened his eyes to see the girl sitting beside him.

"Hold still! Hold still!"

Placing her bare hand on his chest, she pushed him back down onto the cot he was on. She'd cut his pants open, revealing the bloody wound, and now she was dabbing at it with a cloth.

Each time she dabbed, Leon felt as though a fire burning under his heart were being fanned. He sucked air through his teeth and stared at the herringbone pattern ceiling adorned with cobwebs in which old flies, dirt, soot, and even ancient brown leaves and a piece of yellowed newspaper hung suspended.

"Where am I?" he asked as the girl worked on his leg.

"This is Watt Hollister's original homestead cabin. He and Carlton Ramsay built it after Watt ran his first herd of cattle up from Texas."

Leon clenched the wool blanket beneath him in his fists as the girl continued to clean the wound. "Who're you?" he asked.

"I'm Nash's wife." She looked up at him and smiled as she wrung the bloody cloth out in the tin basin resting on a chair beside the cot. There was an open whiskey bottle there, as well.

"I'm Carrie Anne Hollister," she said, and winked. "Pleased to make your acquaintance, Deputy." She frowned then, queerly, dramatically. "Though I'm sure the pleasure is all mine."

CHAPTER 14

Stillman caressed his Henry's hammer as he put Sweets up the hill and under the portal straddling the trail leading into the Hollister ranch headquarters. Just beyond the portal, he stopped and looked around.

Horses milled in the three corrals to his left, tails in the air, dust flying as a couple ran in circles around the corral, scenting the newcomer. Sweets fidgeted, gave a deep-lunged whicker. One of the horses in the corral whinnied in reply and stopped to stare over the corral gate. Sweets pranced, showing off.

There was another corral to Stillman's left—a round breaking corral with a snubbing post worn nearly clean through by all the riatas that had been wrapped there over the thirty years since Watt Hollister had built the place. A large log barn and a slope-roofed side shed sat beyond the corral. The bunkhouse, an L-shaped log affair with a shake-shingled roof and sagging front gallery, was a little farther away on the sheriff's left, beyond the corrals and stable.

The bunkhouse's wooden shutters were closed over most of the windows. Over the two glass windows flanking the closed front door, flour sack curtains were pulled back. Nothing moved behind the windows. At least, nothing that Stillman could see. No smoke rose from the large, adobe brick hearth running up the bunkhouse's far wall; nor did any rise from the tin chimney pipe likely venting a cookstove.

Seeing no one in the yard, either, Stillman left his repeater at off-cock, the barrel resting across his saddle pommel, and booted Sweets on into the yard and around the large windmill and stone stock tank. A chaise with a black Morgan hitched to it sat in front of the main house's front veranda, the horse tied to the hitch rail.

As he drew up in front of the lodge, the front door latch clicked. Hinges squawked as the heavy door, constructed against possible Indian attacks, drew open. Old Watt Hollister came out and stepped onto the porch—a craggy-faced, gray-haired old man with a walrus mustache and a bleary look in his rheumy eyes. The way he seemed a little uncertain on his feet, swaying from side to side, Stillman thought he'd likely been drinking, which is what he'd heard he mainly did these days, leaving the running of the ranch to his sons and hired men, of which he had plenty.

Where were they now? Stillman had taken the fastest route out here from town, an old horse trail probably first blazed by Crow and Blackfeet hunting parties, not the wagon trail that Leon had probably taken with his rented wagon. The wagon trail was slower going, looping around hogbacks and bluffs. He'd doubted that he'd find his deputy on the trail, anyway. If he was anywhere, he was probably here—in one condition or another.

"Well, Sheriff Stillman . . . ," Hollister said, drawing the heavy door closed behind him, giving a cordial nod. There'd been a dark, fateful pitch to his voice.

"My deputy make it out here with your daughter, Hollister?"

The old man nodded grimly as he shambled over to stand above the steps at the edge of the veranda. "Why, yes, he did. Yes, he did. Orlean is upstairs now, bein' tended by her mother and"—he glanced at the chaise and the Morgan standing with one hip cocked—"and our dear neighbor, Mrs. Wolfram."

"My condolences for your loss," Stillman said. "I'm guessin' that Deputy McMannigle explained how it happened."

"Yes. Yes, he did. He said it was an accident. Happened quite by mistake." Hollister sighed and planted a large, gnarled hand on a porch post. "It wouldn't have happened at all if she'd stay home where she belonged . . . 'stead of runnin' around with long-loopin' desperadoes."

Stillman was a little confused by that. Her death had not been a mistake. She'd been trying to shoot him, Stillman, and his deputy had intervened. Anyway, the explanation didn't matter. What did matter was Leon.

"My deputy hasn't turned up back in Clantick, Mr. Hollister." Stillman had pitched his voice quite purposefully with accusation, lifting his head to glance at the lodge's upper story windows and then turning slightly to scrutinize the bunkhouse, which sat hunched and silent, the mid-afternoon's autumn sunlight bathing its shake roof in copper hues.

With his other hand, old Hollister twisted an end of his mustache. "Oh? That's odd."

"It is odd. What's odder is that his horse showed up without him and the wagon he was driving."

"Worrisome."

"He did *leave* here?"

"Oh, yes—he left here right after he dropped Orlean's body off. We're gettin' her ready for burial now. Probably bury her later today, maybe in the morning. Virginia is quite upset, as you can imagine."

Stillman looked at him curiously. Hollister met his gaze with a level, oblique one of his own. "How 'bout you? How are you holding up, Mr. Hollister?"

"About as well as you can imagine, Sheriff. I don't wear my emotions on my sleeve. But Orlean . . . well, she was my only daughter." Hollister glanced away, brushed a hand across his nose. "She was a good girl despite who she might have thrown in with. Certainly didn't deserve to die. She'd have come to her senses and come back to her family who loved her, but . . . well, that's not going to happen now."

He turned his sad, bitter gaze back to Stillman once more. "It's a bitter pill, Sheriff. But I'm workin' on swallowing it. It'll take time, but we'll move on without . . . without our daughter."

Stillman glanced around once more. "Where are your men, Mr. Hollister?"

Hollister glanced toward the bunkhouse and then shuttled his gaze to the corral where there were only a half dozen or so horses milling. "I don't know. My sons handle all that. Probably down in the breaks, brush-popping any stubborn beeves they missed during roundup." He glanced at the sky. "Snow'll fly soon, most like."

Stillman looked around again in frustration. He'd found the old man convincing, though doubt lingered. He supposed about the only thing he could do was take the wagon road to town and hope that he found Leon stalled somewhere with a broken axle, maybe. He might have unhitched the horse from the wagon, and the beast might have simply spooked and hightailed it to town, stranding McMannigle in the mountains somewhere.

That didn't seem likely. Again, dread pinched the sheriff.

He gazed at Hollister, who was studying him with a faintly foxy look. The man didn't seem bitter enough over his daughter. He was hiding something. Only Stillman couldn't bring himself to believe that such a well-to-do, longtime rancher would do anything to threaten his and his son's livelihoods, their sprawling, prosperous holdings out here in the Two-Bears.

That's exactly what he would have done if he'd murdered Leon. If that's what they'd done, they'd just incurred Stillman's wrath, and he'd by god burn their whole place to the ground so there wasn't enough left to haul away in a wheelbarrow.

Stillman narrowed an eye at the old rancher. "Hollister, I

want to clarify something that my deputy in his good grace apparently left cloudy for you."

"What's that?"

"McMannigle shot your daughter because she'd been about to shoot me in the back. She was with two men, and she was as naked as the day she was born. I was fool enough to believe her story that she'd been taken hostage, and turned my back on her. She pulled a gun on me, and she would have shot me if my deputy hadn't shot her first. That's how it happened, and I've written out an affidavit for the circuit judge, and signed it."

Hollister's dark face turned crimson, all the warts and liver spots standing starkly out against it, as did his thick gray hair and mustache. He slowly raised his right arm and pointed a long, crooked finger at Stillman. His eyes blazed with unbridled fury. *"That's a bald-faced lie!"*

"That's bond," Stillman said mildly, backing his horse away from the veranda.

When he was even with the windmill and stock tank, he turned Sweets around and galloped under the portal and down the slope toward the creek. Behind him, he heard Hollister's phlegmy voice peel like thunder. *"That's a bald-faced lie!"*

"What do you think, Doc?" Evelyn Vincent asked Evans as the doctor came down the steep stairs in his house. She'd been waiting in the parlor for him while he'd examined Tommy Dilloughboy in the room he used for overnight patients.

The stocky Evans, dressed in his usual shabby suit minus the jacket, removed his stethoscope from around his neck and ran a thick hand through his unruly mop of dark-red hair. His round-rimmed spectacles flashed in the light of the parlor windows.

"Oh, I think he'll be fine. Right fine. Not to worry, Evelyn." The doctor clutched her arm affectionately and planted a kiss on her forehead. "He has the best sawbones in the territory, don't ya know." He chuckled wryly and started for the kitchen. "He lost some blood, but he's a strapping young man. He'll get his strength back in no time. Probably be able to walk out of here tomorrow, in fact."

"Is there anything I can do for him, Doc?"

Evans stopped in the parlor doorway, wrinkling the skin above the bridge of his nose. "Evelyn, isn't this the young fella I saw you walking around town with last spring?"

Her cheeks warming, Evelyn glanced at her hands, which she'd nervously entwined before her belly. She'd dreaded this part of the conversation, which she'd anticipated.

The doctor continued, "And isn't he the same one who Ben ran out of town when he heard about the younker's plans to rob the Drover's Saloon?"

"One and the same, Doc," Evelyn said with a sigh, turning down her mouth corners. "It's true, he got into some trouble last summer, and Ben told him to leave and not return for a year, but . . . but, Doc, what was I supposed to do? He was out there in the cold night, *wounded* . . ."

"How was he wounded? Who shot him?"

"Apparently, someone was trying to steal his horse. Dry gulched him!"

Evans appeared to consider that skeptically. "Dry gulched him, huh?"

"Yep."

"Well . . ."

"Doc, you won't tell Ben he's here, will you? Before Tommy agreed to come and see you, he made me promise that you wouldn't tell Ben."

Evans raked a finger down his mustache and goatee, which were the same dark red as his hair and flecked with crumbs from a sandwich he'd apparently eaten earlier. Evelyn had just come over from Sam Wa's Café, taking a break after preparing for the supper crowd, to check on Tommy Dilloughboy. She hadn't lingered here last night, after she'd brought Tommy over and turned him over to the doc, because she hadn't wanted to answer the very questions the doctor had posed to her now.

"Well, now, that sounds a might suspicious to me, Evelyn."

"I reckon it does to me, as well," she said with another fateful sigh. But then she gave the sawbones another look of beseeching. "Doc, I really think that deep down Tommy's a good sort. I think, being half-Indian an' all, he's had a tough life. I know as well as anyone that having a tough life can lead you to make some bad decisions. But I think if he's treated kindly, and helped . . . and trusted—well, I just think it sure couldn't hurt. I can't blame Ben, but he's a lawman, Doc. And you know how lawmen are."

"Yes, I know. They can be quite intransigent sometimes."

"They can be right *what*?" Evelyn was always amused as well as mystified by the doctor's vocabulary. She admired him terribly, and she had to admit that she rather fancied him, but now, with Tommy having ridden back into her life, she realized that the gulf between her and the educated sawbones encompassed more than just years. He could never feel toward her, a simple working girl, anything close to how she felt toward him.

"Uh . . . sorry," the doc said, looking sheepish. "What I mean is they can be rather stubborn at times. Ben has done a good job of cleaning up this town in the two years since he's been here, and he takes pride in keeping it that way. Can't blame him."

"I certainly don't, but . . ." She looked at the doctor from under her brows.

"But your secret's safe with me. I figure what Ben doesn't know can't hurt him, though I don't think young Mr. Dilloughboy best linger in Clantick overlong unless he wants to wind up in the calaboose."

"No, I suppose not."

"Don't look so long-faced, Evelyn. I can see how a young lady might be attracted to my bright-eyed and bushy-tailed patient up there. But rest assured there are other, better fish in the sea."

Evelyn knew that was true. And she cursed herself for having gotten so entangled with Tommy. Especially since she doubted that he felt as strongly about her as she did about him. Wasn't that just her fate, though—to always be tumbling for the wrong men?

"I know you're right, Doc. In the meantime, is it all right if I go up and see him?"

"Sure. Why don't you swab his forehead a few times. I've left a bowl of water and a cloth up there. We're going to need to get his temperature down, though I think it's already on the wane."

"You got it, Doc."

"As for me," Evans said, cupping a hand to his ear. "I hear a brandy calling me from the kitchen."

"Awfully early, Doc," Evelyn gently admonished.

"You sound like Katherine," he grumbled and turned away.

"Doc?"

"Yay-up?"

"Thanks."

The stocky, handsome pill roller shrugged and crooked his mouth, then turned and strode off toward the kitchen and his brandy bottle and likely a fat cigar and the several piles of books he kept on his table and which he read all night long. Evelyn would have felt lonesome for him though his lonesomeness—if he *was* lonesome; he'd never mentioned it to her and she considered them fairly close friends and confidants—would soon end.

Soon, he and the Widow Kemmett would marry.

Evelyn sighed as she climbed the steep stairs to the doctor's creaky second story. It wouldn't be long before the whole world had paired up and gotten married.

The whole world, that was, except for Evelyn Vincent. She'd be the only one left alone.

"There she is," said Tommy Dilloughboy as Evelyn tapped once on his half-open door and poked her head into the room. "There's the prettiest girl in the whole, gall-blasted world!"

CHAPTER 15

"Wait a minute." Leon sat up on the cot and wrapped his left hand around the girl's right wrist before she could touch the wet cloth again to his leg. "You're Hollister's *wife?*"

Her eyes were strangely innocent. She looked up at him as though she didn't think there was anything even faintly ironic about the information she'd just given him.

"Yes."

McMannigle scowled at her, his lower jaw hanging.

The disbelief must have been plain in his eyes, because she smiled and said, "Oh, I know what you're thinkin'. You're thinkin' ain't it odd for Nash's wife to be dressin' your wound for you. Oh, I bet you didn't even know Nash was married." She laughed. "That's all right. Nash acts like he don't even know most of the time himself!"

She dabbed at the bloody hole again. "And I reckon you'd be right about it bein' odd, me helpin' you . . . if I was the sort of person who could sit around and watch an innocent man be killed, when I had a chance to help him. You see, I seen you from my bedroom window in the house. I spend a *lot* of time up there, you understand. I don't fit in all that well with the family, especially with Virginia Hollister. She don't like it that her boy married me. So I don't go down much. I'm just in the way, anyway, and the old man—well, he looks at me strange. I've caught him peekin' through the keyhole in the door to me and Nash's room when I've been takin' a bath. Ain't that the most disgusting thing you ever heard? Sinful old codger!"

She wrung the rag out in the pan again, and set the pan on the floor.

"No, I was just sittin' there in the window, thinkin' about goin' for a ride—ridin' my horse, Biscuit, is my favorite thing to do; that and writing poetry in my journal—when I seen you ride up on Blaze Westin's horse. Why in the world did you come back *here,* of all places?"

"I reckon Westin's horse was homesick."

"The old man and Carlton Ramsay are drinking toddies in the parlor, and Virginia's upstairs with Zeb and Mrs. Wolfram, so no one seen you. That was close, though, for sure. You're lucky Barney's off huntin' rabbits or some such!" She laughed darkly. "All the men are out—well, they're out lookin' for you, but I reckon you know that better than anybody."

"Yeah, I know that pretty well."

"I'm going to splash some whiskey on that wound so I can sew it closed. If I sew it closed without cleanin' it out real good, it's like to putrefy and you could lose your leg."

Leon was looking out the one window from which the shutter was drawn back. The light had faded considerably; it felt like afternoon. "What time is it, anyway?"

"I don't know—around three, maybe. I had to leave you for a while, after I got you in here. Had to fetch the whiskey and my sewing pouch from the cabin. Told old Watt I was takin' Biscuit for a ride. When I got here, you were so sound asleep, I just let you sleep. I knew you needed it, and I got time to kill."

"Are your husband and his men back yet?"

"They weren't when I went back. You ready?"

Leon looked at the bottle she was holding up as though threatening him with it.

"Ah, Jesus—yeah, go ahead."

She lowered the bottle, turned it, let the whiskey splash over the ragged, red hole that she'd done a fine job of cleaning. The bust head hit the deputy's leg like liquid fire. It drove a bayonet of agony into the wound, up through his groin and into his belly where it twisted around demonically, flaring even more vigorously.

McMannigle gritted his teeth, stiffened his neck, arched his back, and dug his heels—she'd removed his boots—into the log frame at the bottom of the cot.

"Ay, yi, yi . . . yi—that hurt pretty good, all right!"

"I'm sorry," she said, smiling sweetly, with genuine regret.

"No need. I do thank ya mighty kindly, Mrs. Hollister."

"Call me Carrie Anne. That's my name."

"Thank you mighty kindly, Carrie Anne." The pain subsided, and as she corked the bottle, he said, "Carrie Anne, why in the hell are you doin' this, anyway? Your husband tried to kill me and now here you are—hidin' me out on his ranch, doctorin' my wound . . ."

She stood and moved to a table that abutted the one-room cabin's front wall, and retrieved a small, burlap pouch. "What's wrong is wrong, Deputy. Deep down, Nash knows it. Deep down, even old Watt knows it. They did a devilish thing in tryin' to kill you." She'd stopped after she turned away from the table and looked down at the pouch in her hands. "I hope . . . well, I hope you can find a way to forgive them."

She looked at Leon, her eyes searching his. She was beautiful. Her waifish, round-faced, hazel-eyed innocence accentuated her beauty. She had a small mole on the otherwise smooth line of her jaw. Her face was lightly tanned, likely from riding in the open air. Her eyes were as deep and luminous as fresh spring water.

McMannigle had never heard about her before; he'd had no idea Nash Hollister was even married, let alone hitched to this innocent, frank-eyed, earthy country girl who loved to ride her horse and write poetry. And who was obviously an alien here.

"Do you think you can forgive him, Mr. McMannigle?"

"I don't know," Leon said as she continued walking toward him. "I reckon I can work on it."

Forgive them? Would they forgive him if they found him here? Would they forgive *her* for helping him?

The deputy wondered if she realized the danger in the game she was playing. If it wasn't for her, though, he'd be dead about now.

"Best take a sip of that," she said, handing him the bottle as she pulled the chair closer to the bed, and sat down on it.

"Just a sip?" McMannigle gave an ironic snort and took a long pull. When he had that one down and it was working on him, soothing him, dulling the throb in his thigh, he took another and then one more. He felt so much better that he set the bottle down beside him on the cot, cradling it proprietarily in his arm. "Don't mind if I hold onto it, do you?"

"No, you go ahead. You'll likely need more of it, but you'd best not drink too much on an empty stomach, or you'll get sick." She was holding a needle up to the fading window light, frowning as she threaded the needle with catgut.

"You know what I think?" she asked when she'd threaded the needle and had sat down in the chair angled toward the cot.

"What's that?"

"I think everything's gonna be just fine. Trouble passes. You know, I've always believed that, and believing in that one simple thing has gotten me through a lot of hard times. It's kept me here in that big house with old Watt and Miss Virginia and her Bible, though Nash keeps promisin' that he's going to build us our own cabin right over here next to this one. We'll use this little cabin for storage, though that'd sorta be a shame."

She glanced around, that dreamy smile still quirking her lips. "If these walls could talk." She chuckled, and her hazel eyes sparkled prettily. "This is where me and Nash started out. I met him out on the range. My pa's ranch was down in the Missouri River breaks. That was before he got sick and died. But I'd sneak up here to see Nash on the sly—you know, so Miss Virginia never found out—and we'd meet up here for some wild times."

Something caught her eye in the corner over Leon's right shoulder. "Ah . . . look there." She reached over him and removed from a small, corner shelf a brass ambrotype case. She wiped cobwebs from the case, flipped the tiny latch, and opened the cover. "Oh, my gosh."

Leon took another pull from the bottle. He wanted to be good and soused when she started suturing the bullet hole closed. "What is it?"

Carrie Anne sniffed, smeared a tear on her cheek with the back of her hand. "They sat for a photograph." She turned the open case toward Leon, revealing a hand-tinted oval photograph showing a dark-skinned young man with thick, wavy brown hair and a soot-smudge mustache sitting on a chair with a girl standing beside him in a simple cream taffeta dress with lace on the sleeves and collar, a cameo pin holding the collar closed at her throat.

She held a small bouquet of what appeared to be wildflowers in her hands. The girl had her head tilted to one side, smiling serenely. She wore her hair braided and wound atop her head and also flowing down her slender shoulders. She looked like a springtime maiden from a fairy tale. The young man looked deadly serious and a little uncomfortable in his shabby, ill-fitting suit, but there was still a wry light in his dark-brown eyes that were shiny from the photographer's flash powder.

Leon returned his gaze to the thin, pale, delicately featured girl, smiling so sweetly and hopefully. The smile was in such contrast from the expression Leon had seen on her face just before he'd shot her that his guts clenched.

There was a thickness in the deputy's throat. He cleared it and said, "Miss . . . Orlean?"

Carrie Anne turned the photograph back toward her. "And her fiancé, Tommy Dilloughboy." Lowering the ambrotype case, she glanced pensively around the shabby cabin. "They met here . . . just like me and Nash did. I seen 'em. A coupla times. I was out ridin' and I spied their horses here. I shouldn't have watched"—she smeared another couple of tears on her cheeks—"but I did. They were so in love, havin' so much fun, just like me an' Nash once did—years ago, now! Right down there on this very same cot . . . in this shabby old cabin."

Leon glanced over his shoulder at the shelf, saw several burned-down candles lined up there on the lids of airtight tins, and a box of stove matches. There was also a small, pale, oval-shaped object. A sheepskin pregnancy sheath, most likely. The deputy rolled his eyes to glance down at the cot, feeling a little self-conscious suddenly, as though he'd invaded an intimate place, which he reckoned he had.

"Tommy Dilloughboy," he said, frowning at Carrie Anne. "He . . ."

"Worked for Nash and old Watt. When Watt caught Orlean and Tommy moonin' around together, he got suspicious and ordered Tommy off the ranch. Miss Virginia went after poor Orlean with a wooden spoon right out in the yard for all to see. That night, Orlean left. I begged her not to. Me an' Orlean were like sisters . . . I loved her . . . so enjoyed her spirit brightening up that dingy old house . . . but she couldn't bear another minute. It was like prison to her . . . just like it is to me, I reckon. The only reason I can stand it is because I know Nash is gonna build us our own lodge right here in this hollow—away from old Watt's lusty peeks and Miss Virginia and that Bible's she's always walkin' around the house, recitin' . . ."

She let her voice trail off.

McMannigle's mind was in a complicated knot. Carrie Anne. Orlean. Tommy Dilloughboy. Nash and his men. He couldn't work through the mess because of the pain in his leg and the whiskey he'd been drinking.

Really, what he mostly wanted to do right now was sleep. His eyelids were getting heavy.

"There, that's good," Carrie Anne said. "You're gettin' sleepy. You just go to sleep, and I'll stitch that hole in your leg. Then I'll try to fetch you some food from the cabin."

"Don't do nothin' dangerous, Carrie Anne," Leon heard himself say from far away, the warm tendrils of sleep reaching up to take him. "Don't do nothin' to get yourself caught . . . helpin' the bastard who killed Orlean. Likely wouldn't go . . . too well for you."

"Don't you worry," the girl said, her voice sort of revolving distantly around him, as if she were calling down from the top of that well again. "Everything's gonna be just fine. I know it is. I'm a strong believer in certain things, and I just know everything's gonna turn out just fine. We're all gonna live happily ever after. Except for . . . Orlean, of course . . ."

Leon thought he heard the girl choke back a sob.

CHAPTER 16

Evelyn could feel her whole face light up, ears warming, as she walked into the small room with a dormer window and one small bed beside a marble-topped washbasin and with the handsome Tommy Dilloughboy lying under the bedcovers, grinning up at her from where his handsome, brown-haired head lay deep in a snowy white pillow.

"How're you doing, Tommy? The doc says you're on the mend."

"I feel like I'm on the mend." The young man's darkly tanned cheeks dimpled as he smiled, and his brown eyes flashed warmly. "Thanks to you."

He patted the bed beside him, urging her to sit.

"Thanks to Doc Evans, you mean," Evelyn said, happily obliging the boy by sitting down beside him on the edge of the bed. She leaned over him and placed her hand on his forehead. "You're warm, all right. Doc said you still have a temperature though he don't sound too worried about it."

"My thermometer just started climbin' when I seen you walk into the room." He grinned, showing that chipped front tooth that made him look like a precious though devilish young schoolboy.

Tommy placed his hands on her arms and drew her down to him, and kissed her gently, sweetly.

"Now, Tommy," Evelyn said with mock admonition, because she didn't think anything in the world tasted as good as

Tommy's lips, "you best not let yourself get all het up. You got a bullet hole in your side, young man!"

But she did not resist when he drew her head down to his once more, and placed his lips more firmly against hers. She returned the kiss, enjoying the warmth of his mouth, the masculine smell of him beneath the medicinal smell of the arnica and the poultice that the doctor had placed over his wound.

But when she tried to pull away, he tightened his grip on her arms, holding her against him.

"Tommy," she said.

"Why don't you climb on in here?"

"What?" She chuckled. "No!"

He kissed her again, placed his right hand on her left breast, massaged it through the muslin of her bodice. She had to admit that his hand felt good but this was neither the time nor the place.

She pulled her head away from his. "Tommy, no."

"Remember last summer?" he said, continuing to massage her breast. "Down in that old stable by the river?"

"How could I forget? But we're not down by the river, and we're not alone."

"Ah, hell, I bet the ole sawbones is three sheets to the wind by now. I've heard his reputation for drink . . . and ladies. He's right handsome, ain't he?"

"I don't know. I guess."

"I hear he's got credit down at Mrs. Lee's place." Mrs. Lee ran the most respectable brothel in Clantick.

"I wouldn't know about that." Now she thought she could smell—and taste—more than just medicine. She thought she could taste whiskey on the young man's breath. "Tommy, have you been drinking?"

"Sure. I have a lot of pain, Evelyn. The doc gave me a few

snorts. Said it's the same as laudanum." He canted his head slightly to one side, studying Evelyn dubiously. "You like that old sawbones, don't you?"

"What? Why would you—?"

"I don't know—just somethin' in the way you two was talkin' last night. I heard you talkin' downstairs earlier, too. Tell me, you ever . . . ?" He raised and lowered his brows lasciviously.

"Of course not! The doc's going to marry the Widow Kemmett soon!"

"Bet he'd rather have you than some dried-up old widow." Tommy squeezed her breast harder until it no longer felt so good. "You ever show him these?" He gritted his teeth, and there was a hard, cold light that she'd never seen before in his eyes. It was almost as though he'd suddenly donned a mask that looked much like him but with hard, cold devils' eyes.

Feeling the heat of anger now, Evelyn stiffened and pulled away from him. "Tommy, you let me go! I don't like what you just said. I don't like it one blame bit!"

He laughed suddenly. Just as suddenly, his eyes were the old Tommy's again, deep and dreamy and vaguely almond-shaped. "Ah, I'm sorry, Evelyn. I didn't mean no harm. I reckon I just been up here all day thinkin' about you and . . . well, *us* . . . and I just started gettin' a little jealous is all, wonderin' what you been up to . . . who you been seein' . . . since I pulled out of town. I'm sorry. That was just the doc's whiskey talkin'. I should know better than to . . ."

He let his voice trail off. His eyes grew opaque, as though he were staring right through her. He was listening to something outside. Evelyn heard it, too—the thudding of many horses. The thuds were growing quickly louder.

Evelyn said, "What on earth?" She crouched to look out the dormer window. With a painful grunt, Tommy turned himself around in bed to peer out the window, as well. The window faced southeast, in the direction of town. Several horseback riders were just then galloping up the trail that climbed the bluff that the doctor's sprawling, old house was perched on.

More than several.

As the line of riders grew as they rose up from over the side of the bluff and galloped toward the house, Evelyn estimated there must have been a good dozen or more.

"Oh, my gosh," Evelyn said. "Why do you suppose all those men are—?"

"Ah, Christ!" Tommy threw his covers back and, wincing and holding a hand over the poultice bandaged over the bullet wound, dropped his legs to the floor. He leaned closer to the window, staring down at the riders just now lining out in front of the doctor's house.

Evelyn stared at Tommy, befuddled. "Tommy, what . . . ?"

"Get back!" he ordered, grabbing her arm and pulling her back away from the window, letting the curtain drop back into place.

Evelyn heard the doctor's footsteps on the floor downstairs. He'd apparently heard the riders and was going to the front door.

Evelyn looked out the window again, saw that all the riders were holding rifles. They were all dressed in the rough trail garb, including chaps and buckskin jackets and buffeting scarves, of cow waddies. Ranchmen.

The lead rider was tall and dark, with a brushy mustache mantling his grim mouth. He wore a high-crowned, gray Stetson and a red scarf under the collar of his buckskin coat. As he swung down from the saddle of his large dun, he turned back toward the men and told them something that Evelyn couldn't hear above Tommy's heavy breathing and the pounding of the doctor's shoes on the first-story floor. Evelyn could only hear the deep, business-like rumble of the man's voice.

"Tommy, who is that?" Evelyn turned to see that the young man, wearing only his faded red longhandles and black wool socks, had gone to the chair sitting against the opposite wall from the bed. His clothes were draped over the chair, and his cartridge belt and holster hung from a spool of the chair's back.

He unsnapped the thong from over his gun's hammer and slid the gun from its holster.

"Tommy, what on earth is going on?" Evelyn demanded, tightening her jaws as well as her voice.

He turned to her, and his face was a mask of anxiety. Veins forked in his forehead, over his right eye. Both eyes were sharp, his sweaty cheeks crimson. "You stay here!" He motioned to her angrily. "Just stay here, Evelyn! Don't make a sound—understand?"

"Tommy, I want to—"

"Shut up and do as I tell you, goddamnit!"

The harsh tone of his voice rocked the girl back on her heels. She watched, stricken, as he opened the door and, moving on the balls of his stocking feet, walked into the hall, turned right, and dropped nearly soundlessly down the stairs. Evelyn could hear the steps creaking under his weight. At the same time, she heard the downstairs door open, and men's voices, including Doc Evans's.

Too curious to follow Tommy's orders, Evelyn hurried into the hall and looked down the stairs. Tommy was nowhere in sight.

Quietly, Evelyn slipped down the stairs, holding the rail with one hand and running her other palm across the opposite wall, trying to lighten her tread on the stairs. She moved into the parlor and stopped when she saw Tommy standing beside the parlor's open French doors. He had his cocked revolver in one hand, and he was standing tensely, canting his head to listen to Doc Evans saying, ". . . why are you all looking for him, anyway?

Say, what's all this about, Hollister?"

Nash Hollister. Evelyn thought she'd recognized the lead rider. She'd seen the Hollisters in town from time to time though they never dined at Sam Wa's humble café but at the Boston House Hotel and Restaurant. That's where most of the mucky-mucks dined.

"Just answer the question, Doc," the brusque oldest Hollister son demanded in a menacingly level tone. "Is he here or have you seen him?"

"No, he isn't here and I haven't seen him," Evans said, his voice more muffled because he was facing away from the house. "Now, kindly tell me why you're looking for him. What's this all—"

"You mind if we come in and take a look around?"

Tommy shook his head. Evelyn heard him suck air through his teeth. He hadn't seen her standing behind him, at the bottom of the stairs. He was too intent on what was happening at the front door.

Evelyn gave a silent gasp as the young man began raising his cocked revolver and extending it through the open French doors toward the doctor's dingy foyer from which the men's muffled voices echoed woodenly.

"Yes, I do mind. And I got a shotgun that minds, as well," Evans said. "Now, you got a good dozen men. I understand that. Which one or two do you want filled with twelve-gauge buckshot?"

Despite her nervousness and exasperation, Evelyn had to give a thin smile at the doc's pluck.

No one said anything for a while. Tommy was aiming his revolver straight through the open French doors and through a dim, little vestibule that the doctor used for a closet—a cluttered, musty closet, at that—toward the foyer opening beyond it. Every muscle in his back stood out in sharp relief beneath his tight longhandle shirt.

"All right, all right," Hollister said. "We'll take your word the deputy ain't here, Doc. Where do you suppose Stillman is? We went by the jailhouse and it was closed for business."

"I couldn't tell you where either of them are," Evans said.

"You're just real helpful today—ain't ya, Doc?" said a more distant voice than Hollister's. It probably belonged to one of the men sitting their horses in the doc's yard.

"Who is that—Sandy Wilkes?" Evans said, raising his voice. "Sandy, you'd better hope you don't dislocate your shoulder again like you did last fall, 'cause you'll be looking for some other sawbones to snap it back into place for you."

A couple of the other men chuckled.

"All right, Doc—we get the drift," Hollister said. "Go back to your bust head and your books. We'll be on our way. Oh, and, uh . . . pardon the interruption."

Evans said forthrightly and not without a touch of irony, "Nash, I just hope to god your intentions are honorable—whatever they are. I have no idea why you're looking for Stillman and McMannigle, but this town and county holds them both in high regard. You remember that."

Boots thumped on the porch and then Evelyn heard Nash descend the porch steps, his voice lower now as he said, "Thanks for the advice, Doc. I'll remember it, for sure. Just wanna have a little chat—that's all. Nothin' to get your back in a hump over."

There was another silence. Evelyn saw Tommy's shoulder blades smooth out against his back, behind his underwear top. From beyond him, she could hear tack squawking and then men clucking to their horses and the thudding of hooves as the Triple H Connected riders started riding away. Evans closed the door with a latching click, muttering to himself, "Little chat, my ass. With a dozen armed riders?"

Tommy turned away from the French doors and froze when

he saw Evelyn. "Hey," the young man whispered as Evans's shoes thumped in the foyer. "I thought I told you to stay upstairs."

"I don't take orders from you, Tommy Dilloughboy. What have you gotten yourself into? Why were you thinkin' those Triple H Connected riders were after you?"

Before Tommy could respond, Evans said from the foyer, "Evelyn—that you?"

Tommy cast an anxious gaze behind him and then rushed passed Evelyn, giving her the stink eye, and then hurried on up the stairs to his room. Evelyn had returned his look, and now she stood in the foyer, arms crossed on her chest, anger burning through her.

She'd trusted that boy. But he'd lied to her. She didn't know what the lie was exactly, but he'd gotten himself in trouble again. Possibly, trouble out at the Triple H Connected, where he'd worked until, according to him, he'd been routinely turned loose after the autumn gather.

Evans stopped in the door to the foyer, peering into the parlor beyond the vestibule. "Evelyn?"

"Yeah, I'm here, Doc."

He hooked his thumb toward the front door. "Did you hear that?"

"I heard."

"They were looking for Leon. And Ben, too, but it sounds like the trouble starts with Leon. You know where he and Ben are off to?" He frowned, cocked his head a little. "Are you all right, girl? You look a little peaked."

"I'm just a little perplexed, is all."

"About them?" Evans asked, turning his head toward the front door.

"About life in general, I reckon. Including them." She walked toward Evans, her concern now shifting from Tommy Dilloughboy to Ben and Leon. "Doc, Ben rode out of town this morning like a mule with tin cans tied to its tail. He said he was gonna look for Leon out at the Triple H Connected. He was in such a hurry, he didn't tell me much—only said I was deputized."

"You? *Deputized?*"

Evelyn slapped a hand over her mouth. "That reminds me—I best check on Ben's prisoners, build up the fire in the woodstove over there. I gotta go, Doc." She patted the sawbones' shoulder, saw the concerned look in his bespectacled eyes, and paused. "What do you suppose that's all about Doc? You think Ben and Leon have trouble with the Triple H Connected?"

"Sure as hell sounds like it."

"It does, doesn't it?" Evelyn cast her peeved, indignant gaze toward the ceiling. "Trouble. Seems to be a lot of it these days."

CHAPTER 17

Stillman kicked the big man's body onto its back and saw the two brown eyes staring up at him from a broad, savage face.

Long, straight brown hair curled against the man's scarred, pitted cheeks that, while naturally ruddy, were turning pasty with death. Blood stained the front of the man's shirt and vest. It was dusk and it was cool, but the day's last flies buzzed around the blood staining the ground as well as the dead man himself. A light breeze jostled his long mare's tail mustaches.

A big bastard. Probably Mexican. Stillman thought he'd seen the savage, pockmarked face on a wanted dodger or two hanging in his office. Hiring known killers with paper on their heads meant that old Watt Hollister wasn't as upstanding as Stillman had once thought.

The sheriff inspected the ground to the right of the dead man. Dirt and gravel was badly scuffed. The dirt and short, brown grass and dried-up wildflowers showed where someone had lain flat not all that long ago. At least, sometime in the past twenty-four hours. Not the big Mexican. Stillman could see where he'd fallen, and he'd pretty much lain right there, not moving around much, if any. Whoever had killed him had been lying here in wait. There was a smear of blood about the size of Stillman's palm beside where the second man had lain.

The second man had been wounded.

Leon?

Stillman took a deep draught of air that burned in his throat and lungs like a dragon's breath. He'd seen the wagon parked beside the clearing. He'd seen the remains of the campfire and his deputy's gear strewn beside it. There was a dead man in the creek, three more on the slope above the creek, another one— the Triple H Connected foreman, Blaze Westin—lying dead on the crest of the ridge.

And there was this man here.

As yet, Stillman had not found Leon.

The light was fading quickly. It would be good dark within the hour. He had to keep looking, hoping to pick up his deputy's trail.

On the other side of the ridge, Sweets whinnied long and shrilly—a warning whinny. Close on the heels of his bay's alarm, hooves thudded farther off in the distance. He could hear a man's distance-muffled shout.

Stillman hefted his Henry, pushed through the screen of pine branches, and began climbing the steep slope toward the bluff's crest. As his boots slipped on the sharp incline, he pushed off the ground with his free left hand, grunting and panting with the effort. More shouting rose from the other side of the ridge.

Again, Sweets whinnied his shrill warning. Breathless, Stillman gained the crest of the ridge and dropped to hands and knees, peering into the valley on the other side.

Sweets stood ground-reined near Leon's cold fire ring. The bay was fidgeting and tossing his head as he looked toward the dozen or so riders galloping toward him from the direction of the wagon trail. The riders were spread out in a long line.

Some were sliding carbines from rifle scabbards. Others already had their rifles in their hands. Some were pumping cartridges into firing chambers. Though the light was a yellowish-amber dusky murk, Stillman recognized the mustached rider astraddle a clean-lined dun at the prow of the bow-shaped group. The fast-fading light from the west touched Nash

Hollister's left cheek and the crown of his hat.

Suddenly feeling like a fox with a party of Englishmen and their blooded hounds honing in on him, Stillman bit off a glove, stuck two fingers between his lips, and whistled loudly. Sweets bucked eagerly, swung around, gave his rear hooves an angry kick, and galloped across the creek before lunging up the slope nearly directly below Stillman.

The fading light flashed lemon-gray on the anxious horse's eyes as, trailing his reins, which bounced and leaped around his scissoring legs, the horse pounded up the slope. Below and beyond him, the riders now closing on the camp started shouting louder. A few triggered their rifles, which flashed fire and expelled smoke, the slugs spanging off rocks or breaking branches behind and around Stillman's thundering bay.

Stillman shouted, "Hey, you shoot my horse, I'll blow you to Kingdom Come, you sons of bitches!"

At the same time, he racked a cartridge into his Henry's breech, aimed down the slope over Sweet's bouncing, curving bulk, and fired. He didn't have a clear shot through the darkening trees but he thought he saw several riders hesitate. And then Sweets was pounding within eight feet of the ridge crest, and Stillman leaped to his feet, grabbed the reins, and swung into the saddle.

"He-yahhh, boy!"

The horse galloped on across the top of the ridge and down the other side, Stillman holding the reins up high against his chest in one hand, extending his big Henry out for balance in his other hand. The bay plunged down the slope, hammering his front hooves into the steeply pitched ground with each lunge, Stillman leaning far back over his cantle to keep from being thrown over the bay's head.

Behind him he heard Nash Hollister shout, "Keep goin' boys! Get that son of a bitch!"

Stillman had little doubt the shooters knew who he was. They'd been hunting somebody, likely his deputy, McMannigle, but now their sights had swung toward him, and they hadn't hesitated before giving chase. Something told him that the fact he was wearing a badge wasn't going to deter them in the least.

If you've killed one lawman, you might as well kill two. A man can hang only once.

This was war.

Stillman stopped Sweets at the bottom of the hill, and leaped out of the saddle. He winced at a sharp ache in his back—the flare-up of the bullet lodged within a hair's breadth of his spine. An old injury. One he'd been told he'd have to deal with sooner rather than later but one that he'd been putting off, now, with Faith pregnant. As he dropped down behind a low hummock of ground, he hoped it didn't impede him here.

Holding Sweets's reins in his left hand, he shouldered the Henry and gazed up the darkening slope. The dozen or so riders had crested the bluff and were making it down toward him, still spread out in a long, ragged line through the pine trees stippling the bluff's steep shoulder. A couple were taking shots at him, their bullets landing several yards short and wide.

Stillman racked another round into the Henry's breech, slid the rifle to his right, tracking and aiming about seventy yards up the slope, and fired. The horse of his target screeched shrilly, dropped to its knees, and rolled. The rider's own scream was clipped by the horse's plunge on top of him.

As the horse gained its feet, saddle hanging askew, its wounded rider flopped around, writhing and groaning.

Stillman aimed again, fired again, and felt the satisfaction of watching his second target tumble straight back over his horse's arched tail and disappear from view as the horse, apparently not knowing its rider had met his demise, kept running nearly straight down the slope. Stillman aimed again, fired again, and curled his mouth corners as a shouted epithet hurled toward him. His third target dropped his rifle, grabbed his left shoulder, and sagged forward over his horse's pole.

Two seconds later, he tumbled off his mount's left stirrup, gone from Stillman's view though the sheriff could hear him thrashing and snapping brush.

Stillman had not fired the third shot before a voice he recognized as Nash Hollister's started shouting loudly, "Hold up! Hold up! *Retreat . . . or he'll pick us off with that damn Henry of his like turkeys on fence posts!*"

Most of the last light was gone and stars were shimmering in the velvet sky touched with lilac, but Stillman could see the silhouettes of the Triple H Connected men as they whipped their horses around and headed back up the side of the bluff, meandering around trees, the horses grunting like blacksmiths' bellows as they dug their hooves in and lunged.

Hooves thudded and tack squawked and men grunted angrily and cursed.

The riders disappeared into the darkness at the top of the bluff.

Stillman waited, caressing his Henry's cocked hammer.

He waited some more. Silence grew as the air chilled, the temperature dropping fast.

"Stillman!" called Nash Hollister, his voice sounding hollow and oddly close in the vast, starry night. "Stillman, that you down there?"

Stillman angrily brushed his forearm across his mustache and narrowed his eyes. "It ain't Santa Claus, Hollister, you son of a bitch! Where's my deputy? Where's McMannigle?"

"He's dead! Or just as good as. Same as you, Stillman!"

Stillman ground his back teeth. "Why don't you come down here and try to make good on your threat, you yellow-livered coward!"

He waited for Hollister's reply. It didn't come for nearly a minute, and when it did, the eldest Hollister son's voice lacked its previous bravado. It was conciliatory, even chagrined. "Look, goddamnit, Stillman—I ain't the one that brung it to this!"

"Who did?"

"I was followin' the old man's orders. That Negro deputy of yours killed my sister, so you can understand how we was all upset about it. All right, we didn't think it through. You try thinkin' it through in a similar situation."

Stillman scowled, not quite able to believe what he was hearing.

"I know we shouldn't have lit out after him, but we did. I know he's wounded and he's on foot somewhere out here. Likely dead. I wish things could be different, and I reckon they could be if you'd just agree to forget about it, but I reckon you wouldn't be game for that—would you?"

"Game for forgetting that you murdered my deputy in cold blood? No, I don't think I'd be game for that, Nash."

"That's what I figured. And I understand. Say, Stillman?"

"What?"

"We was just in town earlier. Smashed hell out of the telegraph key in the Wells Fargo office, in case you get it in mind to ride back to town and invite more lawmen to our little fandango out here. Also told the telegrapher, Mr. Mitchell, about what would happen if he sent any telegrams off to, say, the US marshal down in Helena. You know, with any mentions of the Triple H Connected in 'em. I do believe he got the drift. Yessir. Anyways, it don't really matter. I doubt he'll be able to get another key for at least two weeks. One would probably have to be shipped out from Chicago or Saint Paul, most like."

Stillman laughed darkly. "So, you're goin' all the way with this—eh, Nash?"

"What choice do I have?"

Stillman off-cocked his rifle, rose, and, wincing at the creak in his back, grabbed his horse's saddle horn. "You could choose a trial, risk a hangin'." He swung up into the leather, almost certain that the darkness concealed him down here.

"Or I could just kill you, make sure your deputy's dead. Pains me to say it, it genuinely does, though I know that's a little tough to believe. But it really does, Stillman. I'm not a born killer. It's just a tough situation, that's all."

"You have my sympathy." Stillman neck-reined Sweets away from the bluff and touched spurs to the horse's flanks. Glancing over his left shoulder, he yelled, "You just remember that before I pull a bullet through your no-account head, you chicken-hearted son of a bitch! Both you and old Watt! You remember that!"

Stillman turned his head forward and touched steel again to Sweets's flanks.

"After him, boys!" Hollister shouted from the top of the bluff. "Whoever drills him first gets double pay!"

At the risk of breaking both his and his horse's neck, Stillman put Sweets into a full gallop through a crease in the buttes, heading generally south. His plan was to lead them all into the southern Two-Bears and kill them one by one and two by two.

CHAPTER 18

Carrie Anne entered the Hollister lodge through the back door.

She paused in the summer kitchen, which was screened in during the warm summer months but whose windows were all shuttered now with the approach of winter, and listened. Straight ahead lay a dark corridor that ran into the main part of the house's first story.

She could hear old Watt and Carlton Ramsay talking wearily, probably sitting in front of the fire and drinking bourbon that old Watt had shipped in from down south somewhere and that she knew he paid a pretty penny for, because of Nash's frequent complaints about it. They were probably drinking and talking over the situation at hand.

Meanwhile, straight beyond the ceiling above her head, she could hear young Zebulon Hollister's sporadic moaning and the creaking of his bedsprings and the complaining of the floor-boards beneath the bed.

Two women were speaking in hushed tones up there. Miss Virginia and Mrs. Wolfram. Carrie Anne had seen the Wolfram chaise still parked in front of the lodge when she'd entered the yard from the direction of the old cabin in which she'd left the wounded deputy.

A handsome black man. She'd never been with a black man. She wondered what that would be like. Shame touched her ear tips and it was immediately tempered with a wry humor. She choked back a chuckle, and then, glancing down at her coat pocket to make sure her sewing pouch wasn't visible, she opened the door on her left, stepped through into the well of the staircase that rose to the rear of the second story, and drew the door quietly closed behind her, chewing her lips against the consarned squeaking of the unoiled hinges.

She climbed the stairs that were lit by only the strip of light under the door at the top. She climbed quietly, holding the rail, not wanting to make any noise. As far as she knew, no one had known about her leaving the house either the second or third time, when she'd smuggled the wounded deputy out some food and a bottle of Watt's whiskey. They probably all thought—if they thought about her at all, which she doubted they ever did—that she was where she usually was, in hers and Nash's room, reading or just sitting by the window, darning one of Nash's socks or just staring out the window, dreaming of better days ahead.

She moved through the door, closed it quietly, and glanced at the door to her right. Virginia was reading aloud from her Bible, which she had been doing off and on all day, while Mrs. Wolfram worked on the moaning and groaning Zebulon, for whom the pain in his wounded knee was excruciating. Carrie Anne moved ahead and glanced through the door that was cracked a couple of inches.

Miss Virginia was out of sight but the square-bodied, gray-headed, bespectacled Mrs. Wolfram, a cream shawl draped about her beefy shoulders, was placing a cloth on Zeb's forehead, the young man grabbing at it as if to throw it away.

He was out of his head with fever and misery.

Carrie Anne stepped quietly past the door, entered her own room, and clicked the door closed almost silently behind her. She'd just gotten a lamp lit against the dusky shadows, when she heard furtive footsteps in the hall. Her porcelain doorknob turned, the latch clicked, the door opened and Samuel slipped into the room, wincing as he closed the door even more quietly than she had.

"Sam!" she hissed. "What are you do—?"

But then she was in his arms, and he'd closed his mouth over hers, kissing her. She felt engulfed by the young man—by his arms and broad chest as well as by his big, tender spirit. He was so much more gentle and kind than Nash. He was like the old Nash whom Carrie Anne had first fallen in love with what seemed a hundred years ago now. Samuel's lips were warm and pliant against hers. Despite the joy she took in his attentions, she wriggled out of his arms.

Keeping her voice low, she said, "Sam, Virginia is in Zeb's room. Not only Virginia but Mrs. Wolfram, too!"

"I know, I know. I'm gettin' so tired of hearin' his moanin' and groanin' I feel like puttin' a bullet through his wildcat head."

"Sam!"

Samuel laughed, drew her to him again, kissed her again. As he did, he opened her coat and slid his hands across her belly and breasts. "Oh, Samuel, stop it, please," she urged without heat, continuing to kiss him while trying to pull away.

"Let's do it."

"No."

"Come on."

"Sam, for cryin' out loud—your mother . . . Oh, Sam . . . how come I can't deny you anything?"

"Because you're gone for me, Carrie Anne. Just like I'm gone for you."

"They'll hear us."

"We'll be quiet."

"No."

"Come on, Carrie Anne. I need you so much, I'm about burstin' at the seams."

He had her dress open now and he'd pushed her camisole up around her neck. Her breasts were in his hands—his large, puppyish hands, caressing gently, rolling the pebbling nipples between his thumbs and forefingers.

"Oh, Sam. God. If he ever found us. If anyone ever found us . . ."

"Wouldn't be so bad," Samuel said, nuzzling her neck while continuing to manipulate her breasts. "We'd leave."

"He'd kill us. You know he would. He hardly ever even looks at me, only takes me about once a week but he won't even look at me, doin' that."

"Shhh. Stop talkin' about him."

"Oh, hell, Sam, we can't . . ."

But then she drew her dress up around her waist and, sitting on the edge of the bed, she quickly shed her drawers. At the same time, Samuel unbuckled his belt and slid his patched denim trousers down to his boots. She grabbed his jutting staff with a lusty chuckle and then lay back on the bed, spreading her legs as he lowered himself between her knees.

They finished in one final, hot gasp of conjoined passion.

Then, as though they both suddenly realized how dangerous was this thing they'd just done, they quickly pulled and pushed and buckled their clothes back into place. While Carrie Anne was standing at the washstand, Samuel came up behind her, wrapped his arms around her, and chewed her left ear.

"Let's pull foot now. Tonight."

"What're you talkin' about?"

"All hell's gonna break loose, Carrie. This ranch is a god-damn powder keg and the fuse is lit, sizzling and sparkin' only about two inches away from the powder. You hear me? It's over. All Pa and us worked so hard for over the years—it's all dyin' with that deputy we killed." He nuzzled the other side of her neck. "Let's take it as a sign for us to run away together! Get away from old Watt and Nash and that Bible-spoutin' old woman! Hell, not a single one o' them is even gonna care!"

She finished washing and turned around to stare at his chest with a pensive cast to her gaze. "Samuel?"

"What is it?"

"He's not dead."

"Who's not dead?"

"The deputy. He's not dead."

His hands on her shoulders, Samuel searched her eyes. "What're you talkin' about, Carrie Anne?"

"He's out in the old cabin."

Stillman stopped Sweets at the base of a low, pine-studded ridge, and hipped around in his saddle, staring back in the direction from which he'd come. Muffled hoof thuds rose softly in the night's dense stillness, stars shimmering in the vast arc of velvet sky from which every scrap of sunlight had long since faded.

Hollister's men were no longer galloping their horses. Stillman had led them into rugged terrain on the back side of the Two-Bears, nearly straight south of the Triple H Connected headquarters. There were many canyons out here, each threaded by a creek that snaked farther south to feed into the Missouri River. There was no way to push a horse very fast through this country without killing it.

Stillman had slowed Sweets, as well. Now, he had to take his time, think carefully through his options. He was outnumbered nearly a dozen to one. One misstep, and he would not live to raise his child.

He turned to stare ahead of him. The trail he'd been following along the side of a creek diverged, the left tine snaking off through mixed conifers and deciduous trees, the right tine angling down into the creek. He could see its pale ribbon climbing out of the creek and into the pines. The trail was rocky. He doubted he'd left any noticeable sign—at least none noticeable in the darkness.

When his shadowers reached the fork, they'd likely separate to investigate each tine.

He clucked to Sweets, turning the horse onto the right tine of the fork, and dropped down into the creek bed. Only a thin trickle of water murmured and flashed as it angled down the middle of the bed. The bay's hooves clacked sharply on the rocks. On the bed's far side, Sweets sucked a sharp breath as its rider booted him up the steep bank. Soon, the ramrod straight trunks of lodgepole pines closed around them, the thick canopy shutting out the stars.

Stillman had been on this trail before—another old Indian hunting trail, he figured, and one now used by the Triple H Connected riders, as it was most likely on Hollister's range. As he climbed the side of the ridge at a slant, he looked up the dark, steeper incline on his right. It took him a while to spy what he was looking for, and when he saw the escarpment rising out of the slope's shoulder, like a small stone castle, he turned Sweets sharply and rode straight up the side of the ridge.

As he approached the escarpment, he could hear the thudding and blowing of the Hollister horses below him. They were probably approaching the forking trails by now. Stillman steered Sweets around to the back side of the dinosaur-like spine of jutting rock, shucked his Henry repeater from its scabbard, and stepped out of the saddle and into a niche among the rocks.

"Stay, boy," he said softly, and began climbing.

He reached the crest of the spiny ridge where a few piñons and cedars twisted from narrow cracks. He made his way across the gently curving top of the ridge to the front, where he had a good view of the valley, and dropped to a knee beside a gnarled cedar. He could see the trail, a dark-tan ribbon, meandering through the pines about forty yards back down the slope.

He could hear the hushed voices of the Hollister men conferring farther on down the slope and probably on the other side of the creek. He had a few minutes, so he sat down on his butt, leaning back against a shallow wall of rock, and dug his makings sack from his shirt pocket. His nerves were jangled, and his worry over his deputy wasn't helping.

Rage, more like, he thought.

There was a constant, even, burning throb in both temples, a nagging ache in the pit of his belly. He hadn't fully realized it, but when he'd come upon the three dead men above McMannigle's camp, he'd decided that Leon was likely dead, as well. He'd left there wounded and he'd likely died out here . . . somewhere.

Hollister would pay for that. He'd pay dearly.

Stillman paused in the building of his quirley to remove the badge from his shirt and slip it into his coat pocket. For nearly half of his life, he'd considered himself first and foremost a lawman. But out here where outlaws badly outnumbered lawmen, friendship trumped all that.

Leon had saved Stillman's life, and he'd likely died for it. Now, the men who'd killed him would reap their rewards without any tempering by the law. Not that they'd give themselves up if Stillman ordered them to—Nash Hollister had already indicated as much—but Stillman didn't not want to feel bound by any professional authority whatever.

The Hollister riders were going to die tonight, and that's all there was to it.

It was a personal war they'd waged when they'd gone after McMannigle.

The sheriff fired a match to life on his cartridge belt and lit the quirley. He was sitting there smoking, his temper flaring just behind his eyes, when the thudding of a half dozen horses grew louder. He took another drag from the cigarette, blew it straight out over the valley, knowing that there was a good chance his hunters might smell it, and then he mashed the quirley out with the heel of his hand.

He grabbed his Henry and lay prone atop the scarp, staring out over the valley. He doffed his hat, ran a hand through his sweat-damp hair, and quietly levered a live round into the action.

"Come on, fellas," Stillman muttered. "You called the dance, now step to it . . ."

Below him, a horse whinnied. Shod hooves clacked and clattered. Judging by the noise on the trail angling up toward him, he judged at least six of the near dozen men had taken the same fork that he had.

"Whoa," he heard a man say.

"What it is, boss?" asked another.

Hooves thumped. Horses snorted. Stillman saw shadows shifting around on the trail.

"You—J.T. Take the lead."

"Why should I take the lead?"

Stillman could tell that Nash Hollister was trying to keep his voice down, but he wasn't doing a very good job. He also thought he detected a thickness in the man's voice, as though he'd been drinking. Stillman didn't doubt that all the men had imbibed in some liquid courage this evening. Tracking a man in the dark was a dangerous bit of work.

"Because I'm *ordering* you to," Nash said. "And I'm *payin'* you to take *orders*. You don't wanna *take* my orders, you don't wanna *take* my money, then, neither, and you can ride the hell on outta here!"

"Jesus Christ," said a voice that Stillman assumed belonged to J.T. "I was just askin'. *Christ!*"

Stillman gave a wry snort as the line of shadows began jostling along the trail, heading on up the slope. They were coming up at a slant, angling from his left to his right. He waited until the lead rider, J.T., was at his closest point to the escarpment on which Stillman lay, and then he clicked back his Henry's hammer to full cock. He pressed his cheek up to the rear stock, sited down the barrel.

One of the riders back in the small pack a ways said, "Hey—I smell . . . I smell cigarette smoke!"

"I do, too!" another rider said while one of the silhouetted men jerked so quickly back on his horse's reins that the beast pitched up off its front hooves, loosing an angry whinny.

Stillman aimed at one of the silhouettes jostling near the front of the pack, hoping it was Hollister. In the heavy, cool stillness of the autumn night, the Henry roared like the gates of hell being blown off their hinges. A half second later, Sweets added his own terrified whinny to the echo of Stillman's repeater.

With a feeling like cold water pooling in his belly, Stillman realized his mistake.

The second group of riders hadn't taken the left trail. Knowing the country and anticipating his move, they'd flanked him. Behind him, a spur chinged softly and a stone rolled down the scarp to drop over the ledge before him.

CHAPTER 19

Stillman rolled onto his back, rose to a half-sitting position, and, seeing the hatted silhouettes of riflemen jostling behind him, opened up with the Henry, the rifle leaping and roaring, flames stabbing from its octagonal barrel.

Men screamed and cursed and performed bizarre death dances, dropping rifles and losing their hats.

When he'd triggered six quick rounds, the brass cartridge casings clattering onto the stone surface of the escarpment, he rolled twice to his right, breathing hard.

He turned onto his belly, and opened up on the riders still trying to control their mounts on the trail thirty, forty yards away. When five more empty casings were rolling around the escarpment over his right shoulder, he heaved himself to his feet. As rifles thundered and men shouted on the downslope, he moved at a crouch into a stone breezeway of sorts. It was a shallow trough in the dyke rich with the smell of several cedars twisting among deep fissures.

Rifles hammering from the slope clipped one of the cedar's branches, sent it flying, bark pelting Stillman's Stetson.

He moved out of the far side of the shallow corridor, and dropped to a knee. Two rifles were flashing in the darkness of the slope, their slugs spanging off the face of the stone corridor.

He aimed just above one of the lapping flashes, squeezed the Henry's trigger. As the rifle bucked against his shoulder, he heard a low grunt, saw a shadow jerk back from the last place he'd seen the rifle flash.

Flames from another rifle lapped toward Stillman. The slug screeched past his left ear. Stillman ran to his right and down the incline of the dyke. A rifle opened up behind him, and Stillman dropped behind a large, square boulder. Two slugs hammered the boulder.

Stillman snaked his Henry around the rock's far side, saw a man-shaped shadow running toward him, starlight winking off the rifle he was extending in his hands. The man stopped, pumped a fresh round into his rifle's chamber with a harsh metallic rasp.

Stillman planted a bead on the center of the shadow.

Boom!

The man cursed and fired his rifle at the scarp's stone surface. The bullet ricocheted off the stony ground between his boots and made a sick, crunching sound as it hammered into the shooter's forehead and blew his hat off. He dropped his rifle and sat down hard, throwing his arms up and out.

Seeing two more shadows moving toward him over the caprock, Stillman pumped a fresh round into his Henry's chamber. Both shadows stopped, dropped.

"Shit!" one raked out.

Both men swung around and retreated in the same direction from which they'd come, boots thudding, spurs ringing raucously. Stillman held fire, waited. A few minutes later, hoof thuds rose somewhere ahead and on his right, brush crunching under the hooves of the fleeing mounts.

Hollister shouted from downslope, "Where the hell you boys goin'?"

More retreating hoof thuds.

"We're done!" one of the riders shouted.

Stillman grinned.

A minute later, the rataplan of more retreating horses rose

from the downslope. "Where the hell do you suppose *you boys* are goin'?" Hollister shouted with even more exasperation, his voice cracking at the end of the question.

"We ain't gettin' paid to get killed by some old mossy-horn lawman with a chip on his shoulder!" A pause filled with fading hoof thuds. "Sorry, boss. Hey, we'll see ya in hell, all right?"

One of the fleeing men hooted loudly, and then they were gone.

Nash Hollister cursed loudly until his voice gave out.

Stillman filled the Henry's loading tube with fresh brass from his cartridge belt, shoved the tube back into place beneath the barrel, locked it, cocked the sixteen-shot repeater, and moved out from behind his boulder. "Sounds like it's just us, Hollister. Let's finish it!"

The reply from the downslope was one more set of horse hooves dwindling into the distance.

Samuel Hollister placed his hands around Carrie Anne's upper arms. "What did you say?"

"The deputy's alive." She glanced at the door to make sure no one was listening, and then dropped her voice another octave. "He's out in the cabin."

"H-how, Carrie Anne? How . . . ?"

"He rode into the yard earlier. Er . . . I mean, his horse carried him here. He was riding that big roan Blaze always rode." Blaze. She had to admit she'd sort of liked the way Westin looked at her sometimes, but of course she hadn't let on. Doing so might have gotten her horsewhipped.

But Blaze was probably dead now. No loss to the world, because most of the time he had flat, evil eyes, and he mistreated his horses and he was always throwing horse apples at Barney when none of the Hollister men were around, but still, Carrie Anne had to admit that she'd liked the glinting admiration in his eyes when he saw her walking out to the well or to the stable, say. He'd been smart enough to never speak to her, however.

"Holy shit!"

Carrie Anne rose onto her toes and pressed two fingers to her lips. *"Shhh!"*

Samuel winced and glanced at the door. "He's alive?"

"Of course, he's alive. I'm not housing a dead man out there. What would be the point?"

"How bad is he hurt?"

"Not real bad. Took a bullet in his leg. He got the bullet out himself, but it grieves him something awful. I sewed up the wound, brought him a bottle of Watt's whiskey." Carrie Anne forced her mouth into a straight line, suppressing a smile.

Samuel turned to the door. "I'm goin' out there."

Carrie Anne ran to him. "What for?"

Samuel stopped with one hand on the doorknob. "I gotta get him out of there. What if Nash finds him? He'll kill him. If I can get him to town, I might be able to save the ranch. Not that I really give a shit about it anymore. But I don't wanna be a part of killin' an innocent man, and I would be, because I was there when Nash ambushed him. Besides, I'd hate to see all we worked for get plowed under by the evil ways of Nash and that demented old man!"

Samuel stared at Carrie Anne, thoughtful. "Pack a bag. I'll pack one, too. Then we'll hitch a wagon, drive down to the cabin, pick up the deputy, and take him to town. Then we'll buy train tickets—I got some money saved up—and get the hell away from here. Just you and me, Carrie Anne!"

"Oh, my god! Samuel, I don't know!"

"What choice do we have? When Watt doesn't find that lawman out in the mountains, he might think to look in the cabin. Probably not tonight, but I won't be able to sleep, anyway, worryin' about it."

Samuel took the girl in his arms again and kissed her. "Do you love me Carrie Anne?"

Her eyes grew wide, serious. "Do you love me?"

"I think I do, sure. Yes, I think I do."

Carrie Anne swallowed, nodded. Her heart was racing. It seemed like she'd finally found a way to change her miserable life. "All right," she said. "I'll pack my bag. You pack yours, and we'll meet in the summer kitchen."

Samuel kissed her and slipped out the door and into the hall.

CHAPTER 20

McMannigle was torn from a deep and dreamless sleep by the squawk of door hinges and a chilly draft wafting over him. He snapped his head up, grabbing the pistol he'd placed beside his right leg on the cot.

"Don't shoot, Deputy!" Carrie Anne said, flinching.

Leon blinked. For a second he thought he was seeing double but then he saw that she wasn't alone. She'd come with one of the Hollister sons—the middle one, Samuel, who was dressed in a long, quilted deerskin coat and cream Stetson. His curly brown hair fell down to nearly his shoulders. His wide, blue eyes shone in the light of the candle lantern that the girl had left lit on the table beside the cot.

Leaving the door open, the young man placed his hands on the girl's shoulders, and gently pushed her aside. "It's all right," he said to McMannigle, holding his gloved hands up in supplication. "I'm here to help."

"Help?" Leon groused, skeptically.

"No one else is here. Just me and Carrie Anne. We aim to get you to town, to that sawbones, Evans. I don't want any more trouble, mister." Samuel glanced over his right shoulder, toward where a horse and buckboard wagon stood out in the breezy darkness beyond the cabin's dilapidated stoop. "We got a wagon, plenty of blankets in it to keep you warm on the way to town."

Leon glanced from the boy to Carrie Anne and back again. He canted his head to one side. "Why?"

" 'Cause it's the right thing to do," said Carrie Anne, striding forward.

As she approached Leon to place a hand across his forehead, he depressed his Smith & Wesson's hammer and slid the revolver into the holster hanging off the back of the chair beside him. "Still got a fever, I'm afraid. Not as bad as before, though. How do you feel? Do you think you can make it to town?"

"Hell, yes! Uh . . . pardon my French, Miss Carrie Anne." Leon chuckled as he slung the blankets back and dropped his stocking feet to the floor.

"That's all right," Carrie Anne said. "We don't hold too much with form out here at the Triple H Connected."

"That's for sure," said Samuel, moving toward Leon. "Let me help you."

Leon's blood froze in his veins when he saw a shadow move in the open doorway. A floorboard creaked beneath a heavy tread, and a deep voice said, "Well, now, ain't this cozy?"

Carrie Anne gasped and swung toward Nash Hollister standing in the doorway, a cocked revolver aimed toward her, Leon, and Samuel. Samuel swung around to face his brother. Leon reached for his holstered Smithy but froze when he realized he didn't have a chance.

Nash curled one side of his upper lip, as though daring him to pull the hog leg from the holster. Leon lowered his arm, rested his hand on his left thigh.

Shit.

Nash took two slope steps into the cabin, keeping his lip curled and flaring his nostrils as he studied his brother and his wife. "Seen you leave the barn in the wagon. I was just ridin' in." He took one more step, sliding his cocked Colt between Carrie Anne and Samuel. "What in the hell do you two cork-headed tinhorns think you're doin'?"

"Nash, please," Carrie Anne said.

"I asked you a question, *wife!*"

Carrie Anne stomped one foot and clenched her fists at her sides. "I ain't no wife to you! Any more than you been a husband to me after we found out I was barren!" She clamped a hand over her mouth as though in shock over what had spewed from it.

Nash stared at her for a time. He slid his shocked gaze to Samuel and then back to Carrie Anne.

"So, you took up with my little brother. My chickenhearted little brother. Ain't this prime? Ain't this prime? And you were both gonna save the Negro here and send your family to hell!" Nash laughed maniacally, aiming his pistol at his wife straight out from his shoulder. He seemed totally surprised, as though even with them all living under the same roof together, he hadn't had an inkling about what had been going on between his younger brother and his wife. "You lyin', cheatin' little *whore!*"

Samuel threw up his arms and stepped between Carrie Anne and his brother. "Stop it, Nash!"

Nash was gritting his teeth. His revolver thundered.

"No!" Carrie Anne screamed.

Samuel yelped and flew back against the girl. At the same time, Leon bounded off the cot, ignoring the ripping pain in his right thigh, and lunged for his pistol hanging off the chair back. He was sluggish from sleep and from the shock of the situation, so he wasn't moving as lithely as he'd wanted to.

Carrie Anne was screaming. Samuel was bellowing. Nash's pistol roared again, and the slug curled the air beside Leon's left ear and smashed into the wall behind him. He pulled his revolver from his holster, tripped over his own feet, and fell to the floor.

The fall probably prevented him from taking Hollister's next shot to the forehead. Instead, the slug hammered the chair, knocking it over. Sitting on the floor on his butt, Leon extended the Smith & Wesson toward Nash, who was glaring through the wafting powder smoke, trying to draw another bead on the deputy.

Leon's Smithy flashed and roared.

Nash yelped and stumbled backward, clutching his left shoulder. He spun around, dropped to a knee, and then, bellowing like a poleaxed bull, heaved himself to both feet and stumbled out the door and into the night.

"Sam!" Carrie Anne was screaming, crouched over the young man flopping around on the cabin floor. *"Samuel!"*

"Let me have a look at him." Leon dropped to his good knee beside Carrie Anne and pulled her up off the boy she'd been sprawled across, sandwiching his face in her hands. Blood spotted the young man's left shoulder. "Shove some cloth into that bullet wound. He'll be all right!"

Pushing himself to his feet with a wince, clutching his revolver in his right hand, Leon began dragging his right foot toward the open door.

Hearing the girl rip the hem of her camisole, the deputy headed on out the door and then pressed his back against the cabin's front wall in case Hollister was waiting for him out here. When no shot came, he pushed away from the wall and stumbled out into the yard behind the wagon and the whickering horse in the traces.

Groans and the sounds of crunching brush rose to his left and he turned to see a silhouetted figure stumbling along the trail that led toward the main Hollister house.

McMannigle raised his revolver. "Hollister!"

The shambling, grunting figure continued to jostle away from him.

Leon fired. He fired again, once more, and watched the uncertain figure stumble over the top of a rise and out of sight. At the same time, the horse whinnied sharply to the deputy's right, and galloped away, pulling the clattering wagon along behind it.

Leon cursed and started limping after Hollister, gritting his teeth and grunting with each painful, dragging step.

As he moved down the trail, he could occasionally see Nash Hollister's shamble-footed prints in the dirt, and the frequent glint of blood on fallen, yellow leaves. He continued dragging his bad right leg along the trail, down through a shallow valley and then up and over the next hill and into the ranch yard. As he passed between the blacksmith shop and the corral in which several horses milled in the darkness, whickering curiously, he turned toward the main house.

Hollister had just gained the steps and he was pulling himself up onto the porch by the rail, stumbling as though drunk. He lifted his head, and his agonized voice echoed around the otherwise silent ranch yard, "Open . . . *open the goddamn door!*" There was a loud bang, as though he kicked the door with his boot.

McMannigle continued toward the house, raising his pistol and clicking back the hammer. Hoof thuds rose to his right. A familiar voice yelled, "Hold it!"

Leon turned to see a large man sitting what appeared a bay horse just inside the ranch portal, aiming a pistol at him. The deputy recognized the high-crowned, tan Stetson and buckskin mackinaw of Ben Stillman.

"Ben!" Leon cried, lowering his own revolver.

"Christalmighty!"

Stillman kicked Sweets into an instant gallop toward Leon, who threw up his left arm toward the house. "Hollister!"

Stillman swung his bay toward the house as the door opened, showing dull umber light and a tall, jostling figure silhouetted against it. The door closed and then there was the hollow pop of a gun being triggered inside the lodge. A woman screamed shrilly. There was a heavy thud as though that of a body hitting the floor.

Stillman leaped down from his saddle in front of the house, dropped his reins, and took the veranda steps two at a time. He pulled the door open and stood just inside the doorway, crouching and aiming his cocked Colt into the broad, warm space before him filled with the tang of pine smoke from the crackling hearth and the range.

Nash Hollister lay twisted on one side about six feet away. His eyes were half open, his hat was off, and blood was trickling down both sides of his head, matting his hair. There was a puddle of it on the front of his coat. Old Watt Hollister stood to the right, inside the parlor area of the large, open first story of the lodge. He held a smoking Remington revolver in his right hand, which he was slowly lowering as he stared in wide-eyed shock and befuddlement at his dead eldest son.

Hollister's housekeeper, the old cowboy Carlton Ramsay, was down on one knee beside Nash. He, too, stared in shock at the deceased son. Meanwhile, Virginia stood atop the steps that ran up the right side of the kitchen, clamping her hands to her face, screaming. "No! Not Nash, too! Oh, noooo—not Nash, too!"

Stillman lowered his pistol and walked over and snatched Watt's smoking Schofield from the old man's arthritic hand. Hollister appeared numb. He sagged back into a rocking chair behind him, glancing at Stillman and muttering, "I . . . thought . . . he . . . was . . . you . . ."

Then he returned his stricken gaze to his dead son once more and said nothing more.

CHAPTER 21

Tommy Dilloughboy lifted his head from his pillow in Doc Evans's spare bedroom, and blinked his eyes. Bright sunlight shone in the dormer window over his right shoulder. Loud, happily chirping birds darted past the window, flicking shadows through the golden sunshine splashing onto the throw rug on the floor beside the bed.

"Holy shit," Tommy said, squinting as he glanced out the window. "What the hell time is it?"

He looked around but he saw no clock. He didn't own a watch. He'd wanted to get a jump on the day. A jump on the doc, that was. But, judging by the muffled snores resonating faintly through the floor, Doc Evans was still sawing logs.

No wonder. The man had sat up drinking until late last night. Tommy had heard him down there, from time to time clinking a bottle against a glass as he'd refreshed his brandy. The doctor had staggered up the stairs once to check on Tommy and to replace the poultice on the young man's bullet wound, which he also smeared with arnica. Tommy had been amazed at how handy the sawbones was, even three sheets to the wind.

The pill roller had done a good job on him. Tommy felt relatively strong, and the wound in his side only pained him a little. Not bad. He could probably ride.

Once he acquired a horse . . .

Tommy sat up and dropped his feet to the floor. He rose slowly, not wanting to rip the stitches open. He had to get out of here fast, before Stillman learned he was here. If Stillman got wind of his presence in Clantick, the sheriff would likely put two and two together and figure out that Tommy had been the one rustler who'd gotten away from Stillman and his deputy Friday night.

Gotten away with a bullet in his side, that was.

Tommy had to light a shuck out of Clantick or he'd likely be spending the next fifteen years in the state pen down in Deer Lodge. Slowly, carefully, he dressed, wrapped his gun and cartridge belt around his waist, and carried his boots downstairs. He found a pair of saddlebags hanging over a chair back in the doctor's kitchen, and, listening to the doctor snoring in his bedroom off the parlor, he quietly scrounged the kitchen for trail supplies.

When he'd stuffed as many airtight tins of canned fruits and vegetables, and as much coffee, flour, sugar, and biscuits as the saddlebags would hold, he donned his boots near the front door, and went out.

The morning was cool and an inch of feathery snow had fallen overnight. But the sun was high, and it would likely warm up to above freezing. It would be a good day for riding. He'd ride south, maybe hole up in Denver for the winter. Come spring, he'd continue on down to Mexico.

But first he needed a horse. And then he needed a stake.

He tramped out to Evans's stable, and saddled Evans's horse—a beefy, hammerheaded chestnut. The horse obviously had too much weight on him for a long ride, but Tommy would trade the mount for a better one farther on down the trail. The horse whickered several times as Tommy saddled him, obviously not too pleased about the stranger strapping the doctor's saddle on his back. The lazy beast had probably planned on spending the day right here in his little stable and connecting pen, close to his hay and oats.

Tommy worked tensely, hoping Evans would not awaken and look out his window and find him stealing his horse. He kept cooing and patting the horse, trying to soothe the obviously peeved beast's nerves, hoping the horse didn't loose a warning whinny that would awaken the sawbones. He'd hate to have to shoot the doctor after all Evans had done for him.

He puffed out his cheeks and blew a deep, relieved sigh as ten minutes later he rode the horse to the bottom of the bluff that the doctor's rambling house sat upon, and headed on into the edge of town. He'd been about to swing south to avoid the main street, so he wouldn't be seen by either Stillman or his deputy, but then he saw a familiar figure tramping toward the Drover's Saloon. At the same time, he remembered that the Triple H Connected riders had said Stillman wasn't in town, and that they'd been searching for his deputy.

Maybe neither one was back yet. Or maybe the Triple H Connected riders had caught up with them both, and they'd *never* be back . . .

Tommy quirked his right cheek in a speculative, fleeting grin.

Tommy's heart thumped anxiously as he watched Elmer Burke mount the broad veranda of the Drover's Saloon, and fish in his trouser pocket for the keys to the saloon's winter door. Burke wore a wool coat over his portly frame, and a deerskin cap with wool earflaps obscured his face. Tommy's heart increased its frenetic pace as he watched Burke unlock the saloon's door, stomp snow from his boots, and go on inside.

Today was Sunday, if Tommy hadn't lost all track. That meant that Burke had probably taken in a handsome amount of cash last night. That cash was probably tucked away in the safe that Burke had in his office. Tommy knew about the safe from having scouted the Drover's for a possible holdup last spring.

When the saloon owner had gotten his door open, Tommy touched his holstered gun through the skirt of his wool coat, and booted the big chestnut forward. He gazed at the sheriff's office and was relieved to see no prints in the snow fronting the place, and no smoke curling from either of the two tin chimney pipes sprouting from the shake-shingled roof.

He pulled the horse up to one of the hitch racks, dismounted, and slung the reins over the rack. He looked around, hitching up his pants and trying to look casual. It being Sunday morning, no one else appeared out this early except three mongrel dogs rummaging around between two buildings on the other side of the street, the smallest one nipping commandingly at the other two.

Smoke wafted from a few of the main street business buildings that also served as homes, and from houses flanking the main drag. Smoke also lifted from Sam Wa's just down the street. The old Chinaman, being a heathen, probably worked on Sunday. In fact, he and Evelyn were probably getting ready for the after-church crowd. Squeeze the Christians even on their Day of Rest. That was the Chinaman's way.

Tommy Dilloughboy snickered. He lifted the skirt of his coat and pulled his Schofield .44 from its holster. He held the pistol down low against his thigh as he mounted the veranda fronting the Drover's. As he turned the knob of the winter door set behind the bat wings, and pushed the door open, he raised the pistol and flicked the hammer back.

He stepped inside, squinting into the dingy shadows, and quickly, quietly closed the door behind him. The saloon was lit by only the golden light pushing through the windows. Where the bright light didn't reach was all thick, purple shadows. He looked toward the massive, ornate bar and back bar running down the room's right side, but did not see Burke.

Then a voice called from a half-open door at the back of the room. "Can't you read the sign? I'm closed. This is Sunday. Won't be open till noon!"

Tommy recognized the room from which Burke's irritated voice had emanated. It was Burke's office. He'd probably come in to get a jump on his books.

"I know that, Mr. Burke," Tommy called, walking slowly down the room along the bar, holding his cocked revolver straight out in front of him. "This is an emergency."

"Emergency?" Behind the half-open door, a swivel chair chirped and boots thumped. "What the hell you talkin' about—an emergen—?" The burly saloon owner cut himself off when he peered through the door and saw Tommy walking toward him. Burke scowled, nose reddening.

"What in the hell are *you* doin' here, Dilloughboy? Put that goddamn gun down!"

"I don't think so." Tommy quickened his pace. "Step back away from the door, Burke. You try to close it on me, I'll blast it open. Get them hands raised!"

Burke raised his hands and stepped back away from the door. Tommy moved inside the room, rife with the smell of cigar smoke, and closed the door behind him. Burke stood facing him. His broad, pale face framed by bushy, sandy-colored muttonchops was crimson with fury, wide eyes hesitant, apprehensive. Tommy looked the portly man over. When he was sure that Burke wasn't carrying a weapon, he looked at the safe sitting against the far wall, beyond Burke's rolltop desk cluttered with papers and an open ledger. A cigar rested in a wooden ashtray, unfurling a skein of smoke toward the room's grime-stained ceiling.

Tommy studied the safe, grinned. He'd thought he'd have to force Burke to open it, which would take time, but the door was open about seven inches.

Burke was reading Tommy's devious mind. "Forget it, kid."

"You forget it." Tommy waved the gun at Burke. "Step back or I'll blast ya." He gave a menacing wink. "You don't think I will, just try me. I'm flat broke and out of options."

Burke's broad nostrils flared. He glanced at the pistol aimed at his bulging belly behind a blue wool shirt, its tails untucked. He swallowed and, keeping his pudgy hands raised, sidestepped toward his desk.

Keeping his gun aimed at the saloon owner, Tommy backed to the safe, dropped to one knee, and shoved the door wide.

Bright sunlight from the two windows flanking the safe spilled into the safe's dark interior, revealing several good-sized stacks of unbanded greenbacks. There had to be several thousand dollars in there.

"I work for a livin', kid," Burke said. "Why don't you try it?"

"Shut up," Tommy said mildly, taking quick, darting looks inside the safe as he scooped the money out with his free left hand, keeping his Schofield aimed at Burke with his other hand.

"You bastard," Burke said through a snarl as, panting with excitement, eyes bright with greedy merriment, Tommy stuffed the money into his coat pockets.

"Yeah," Tommy laughed. "Yeah, you could say that. You wouldn't be wrong."

Having emptied the safe into his pockets, the leathery, inky smell of the bills filling his nose and making his mouth water, a pouch of coins weighing down his right coat pocket, Tommy straightened and walked over to where Burke scowled at him by his desk.

"Yeah, you could say that," Tommy said, raising his pistol high above his head. Bringing the butt of the revolver down at an arc, he grunted savagely, "But it wouldn't be one bit *polite*!"

The butt of the Schofield smacked down hard against Burke's left temple. The saloon owner grunted and fell back against his desk, flailing with his hands to stay upright, blinking his eyes. But then he lost consciousness, sagged sideways, and hit the floor with a heavy thud and a rattling sigh.

Tommy gave a whoop, swung around, opened the door, and ran into the saloon's main drinking hall.

"Hold it, Tommy!"

He stopped dead in his tracks.

"Evelyn!"

She stood a third of the way down the bar from the saloon's open front door. She was somewhat silhouetted against the bright windows and the door behind her, but he could see that it was Evelyn, sure enough. She wore a long, ratty wool coat, and her braided, blonde hair hung down past her shoulders. Her light-blue eyes shone in the sunlight angling across her face.

She was holding a double-barreled shotgun that must have weighed nearly as much as she did, straight out from her right shoulder. Her head was canted toward the breech, and she was aiming down the barrel.

"Drop your pistol, Tommy," she ordered firmly, clicking both rabbit-ear hammers back to full cock and scowling down the heavy weapon that she held with surprising steadiness.

Evelyn felt a knife twist in her guts, but she kept her hands wrapped tightly around the shotgun, her right index finger curled through the trigger guard.

"Nah, nah, nah, nah," Tommy said, that grin of his dimpling his cheeks as he started walking slowly along the bar. "You put that big ole barn blaster down. You don't wanna shoot me, Evelyn. It's Tommy, fer chrissakes!"

He chuckled and held his hands out from his sides, keeping his revolver in the right one.

"You're a miserable human being, Tommy. You're a horse thief and a common robber. If you don't stop right there, I'm going to put you out of everyone's misery."

"Ah, come, Evelyn. I got over a thousand dollars in my

178

pockets. Maybe several thousand. Just think how far we could get with all that money!"

"Stop walking, Tommy."

"Evelyn, be reasonable."

"Stop walking, Tommy."

He must have read the seriousness in her eyes. The gravity in her tone. He stopped about ten feet away from her. He continued to hold his arms half out from his sides, about chest high, the pistol in the right one. It was like he was just showing her the gun, not outright threatening her with it.

But the threat was there. Even in his smiling, deep-brown eyes, in his dimpled cheeks, the threat was there.

"Toss it away," Evelyn ordered softly, grimly. "I'm takin' you to the jailhouse, Tommy. I'm turnin' the key on you. See, I'm the temporary deputy sheriff. I was headin' over to the jailhouse to stoke the cell-block stove when I saw the doc's horse, Faustus, standing outside."

"You're a deputy sheriff?"

Evelyn smiled without mirth as she continued aiming down the shotgun's twin barrels. "Ain't that a laugh? Drop it, Tommy, or I'll blast you to hell."

He studied her. The smile left his lips as well as his eyes. He narrowed his lids and turned his head slightly to one side. "Evelyn, think about it. Think about what a good time we could have—you an' me."

"You're scum, Tommy."

"Evelyn . . ."

"You got one more second."

His face became a mask of cold evil. He swung the revolver toward Evelyn, but before he could click the hammer back, Elmer Burke, who'd crept up behind him, smashed a hide-wrapped bung starter down hard against the back of the young firebrand's head.

Tommy was out before he hit the floor at Evelyn's feet. Burke sagged against the bar, holding a blood-spotted handkerchief against his head.

Evelyn sighed as she lowered the shotgun, depressing the heavy hammers.

"You all right, Elmer?"

"Yeah, yeah. Thanks, Evelyn."

"I'll fetch the doc. You're gonna need a stitch or two there."

Elmer just leaned back against the bar, holding the handkerchief against his forehead and staring angrily down at the unconscious Tommy Dilloughboy.

Evelyn didn't give the young outlaw so much as another look. She set Sam Wa's shotgun atop the bar and headed outside.

She stopped on the stoop to see that a wagon had pulled up in front of the Drover's. Stillman's horse, Sweets, was tied to the wagon's tailgate. Three people were riding in the back, on a mound of skins and furs. Leon was one of them, staring toward Evelyn with a question in his eyes. The other two were a young, pretty, brown-haired woman and one of the Hollister boys. The middle one, with curly brown hair. The Hollister boy sat back against the wagon's front panel, a blanket pulled up to his neck. He was staring at her skeptically. The girl, whom Evelyn had never seen before, sat close beside him holding a comforting hand on his chest.

Ben Stillman had dismounted the wagon and was walking toward Evelyn from the wagon's far side and around Sweets, boots crunching in the light dusting of snow.

"Evelyn?"

"Oh, Ben!" she said, tears washing over her eyes. Tears of sorrow, tears of guilt, tears of relief at seeing that Ben and Leon were all right.

"I was headin' for the doc's place when I saw Faustus standin' out here. What in the . . . ?" Stillman paused, studying her incredulously from the bottom of the steps. "What happened, girl?"

"Oh, nothin' really." Evelyn ran down the steps, wrapped her arms around Stillman's waist, and pressed her cheek against his buckskin coat, squeezing him.

She convulsed with a sob.

She laughed through her tears. "I just took down an outlaw for you, that's all!"

★ ★ ★ ★ ★

Blood Trail of the Horsetooth Widow

A Yakima Henry Western by Frank Leslie

★ ★ ★ ★ ★

CHAPTER 1

The red-bearded bartender swung his freckled face toward the tall, dark man in a calico shirt and smoke-stained buckskin trousers just then pushing through the bat wings of the Horsetooth Saloon & Hotel, and said, "Pardon me all to hell, breed, but you'd best take two steps back the way you came and read the sign posted to the front wall there!"

Yakima Henry stared at the bartender. The man stared back at him, frowning belligerently, a cleaver in one hand, a chunk of bloody rabbit in the other. There were seven other men in the dim, dingy place—three at a table near the front of the room, two more at a table near the bar, two more near the cold potbelly stove. No fire was needed. The dry desert air was hot and oppressive, mixing the smells of the pent-up saloon—raw meat, hot bodies, coal oil, tobacco, and cheap liquor—until it smelled like a bear den. The three at the near table, all hard-bitten, pie-eyed men in cheap suits ensconced in billowing clouds of cigarette smoke, stared at Yakima with expressions that were a nasty hybrid of distaste and cruel delight.

A dog had just sauntered into their camp. They didn't like dogs.

"You hear me, breed?" the barman said. "Step back out there and read the cotton-pickin' sign. I put it up there for a *reason!*"

Yakima gave a sheepish smile. "I reckon you're gonna have to come on out and read it for me, mister."

The barman chuckled. "Can't read, huh?"

The three men in cheap suits, which marked them as sales-men of a sort, laughed and snickered, though Yakima doubted they could read half as well as he'd taught himself to from whatever books he'd been able to get his hands on over his long years on the remote western frontier.

He doubted the bartender could read as well as he could, either.

The barman sighed with strained tolerance, plopped the meat chunk into the pot, and set the cleaver down on the bar. As he walked out from behind the counter, he wiped his hands on his apron, though Yakima doubted anyone could actually clean his hands on such a badly stained scrap of tattered cloth.

The barman was several inches short of six feet, but he was built like two rain-barrel-sized slabs of suet sitting one atop the other. He smelled like sweat, raw meat, and whiskey. He gave his hands another scrub on the apron and strode past Yakima and out the bat wings, holding the left wing open as he pointed.

"There it is right there. Come on out here—I'll give you a little lesson in English."

He beckoned to Yakima. The half-breed shrugged, stepped halfway through the bat wings, and followed the man's pale, pudgy finger to the sign nailed to the front wall right of the doors. It was a rough pine board on which someone had hand painted blocky letters in dark green trimmed liberally with dried drips.

The portly barman pointed out each word in turn as he read, "If yur skin is any darker than these doors"—he paused and slapped the top of the sun-bleached bat wing he was holding open—"then you can kiss my ass and point your hat in the op-positt direction!"

The men inside the saloon laughed.

The barman opened his mouth to show his teeth and then he laughed, as well, thoroughly delighted with himself.

"Give me your hand," he told Yakima, as though he were speaking to a moron.

Yakima glanced at the other customers, gave another sheepish hike of his right shoulder, and then gave the man his right hand.

"That's it—there you go. You're catchin' on." The barman held Yakima's hand, which was nearly the color of an old penny—heavily callused, scarred, and weathered—up beside the bat-wing door.

The bartender clucked and shook his head as though the contrast saddened him. "No, no. Now, you see there—that skin of yours is about seven, eight shades darker than these here doors. That means you're about as welcome on these premises as a goddamn full-blood Apache. Why, you're no more welcome here than Geronimo himself. You see?"

He grinned at Yakima, who stood a whole half a head taller. Yakima stared down at the fat man from beneath the flat brim of his low-crowned, broad-brimmed, black Stetson.

Yakima pulled his hand from the bartender's grip and used it to indicate the words painted on the pine board. "The sign says I should 'kiss . . . your . . . ass', right?"

The man's smile faltered and a slight flush pinkened the nubs of his fat, freckled cheeks. "Say again?"

"The sign there says that if my skin is any darker than these doors, I should kiss your ass."

The barman gave a nervous chuckle, snorted, and glanced at the sign. "Well, now, that it does, that it does."

The men inside had fallen silent. They were all holding their drinks and cigarettes or cigars in their hands and staring with bright-eyed interest at the doings at the doors.

"Well, then," Yakima said. "Let's step inside so I can do the honors."

"What's that?"

"I said, let's go inside so I can kiss your ass like the sign says."

The barman stared up at him, but now his smile looked glued on and his cheeks were growing pinker. The men inside were snickering, one lightly slapping the back of his hand against his partner's shoulder. Yakima held the barman's gaze with a stony one of his own.

"What're you talkin' about?" the barman said.

"Isn't that what the sign says?"

From inside, one of the cardplayers said, "Come on in, Clancy. If the breed wants to kiss your ass, let him kiss your ass. We'll watch to make sure he does it proper."

The barman stared up at Yakima, his smile fading fast, though the flush was still building in his cheeks, darkening his freckles. He rolled his eyes around, and then sucked his lower lip and pooched out his cheeks and gave a fake laugh, as though the joke were still on the half-breed, and said, "Well, hell, yeah! That is what the sign says, all right!"

He laughed and walked inside the saloon and stopped and faced the bar. "Okay, there you go, Injun. Pucker up now!"

He looked at the cardplayers and the two men sitting closer to the bar—one of the two was dressed in a dusty blue cavalry uniform. They and the drummers were all watching with keen interest now. The barman winked at the grinning, blond soldier, and snorted another nervous laugh.

"I want a nice soft one there on my left cheek." He leaned forward and patted his ass.

"Best drop your trousers," Yakima said, standing in front of the bat wings, thumbs hooked behind his two cartridge belts. "So I can do it proper."

"Go ahead, Clancy," one of the cardplayers said, laughing with the others. "Drop your pants so the breed can kiss your ass proper!"

He whooped as the others laughed and yelled.

"Go ahead, Clancy," said the beefy gent in common trail garb, sitting with the soldier, drinking beer.

"Pull 'em down, Clancy—what're you waiting for?" said the soldier.

"Oh, this is plush," said one of the others. "This is pure-dee plush! Pull 'em down, Clancy. Give him your fat, white ass so's he can lay a kiss on it!"

Clancy looked over his shoulder at Yakima. His grin looked as though it had been chiseled in granite. "That's all right. You can just kiss my pants. Don't want them half-breed lips touchin' my delicate skin. I'll likely catch somethin' the local sawbones can't cure!"

"Oh, come on, Clancy!" yelled one of the cardplayers farther back in the room. "Drop your pants. Show the breed what a fat white ass looks like!"

"Yeah, come on, Clancy!"

The others whooped and hollered. One slapped the table with both hands. One of the cardplayers stuck his two little fingers in his mouth and whistled.

The fat man turned around and glared up at Yakima. He said only loudly enough for Yakima to hear beneath the din, "What do you think you're doin'?"

"I'm gonna kiss your ass—like the sign says."

"What—you a pervert or somethin'?"

"I didn't make the sign."

The barman curled his upper lip at the half-breed and then shaped a grin as he turned toward the others in the room, throwing up his arms and saying, "All right, all right! The Injun wants to kiss my ass, who'm I to refuse? Shit, it's on the sign, ain't it?" He glanced at Yakima. "Then you can haul your ass out of here!"

"You tell him, Clancy!" yelled the beefy gent at the near table.

Chuckling nervously, the bartender walked over to the bar, removed his apron, and tossed it onto the bar. He slipped his suspenders down his arms, unbuckled his baggy, bloodstained canvas pants, and let them drop down around his ankles. He wore no other shirt than his longhandle top. He unbuttoned the top and slid it down his arms and down his legs.

The others in the room had fallen quiet. They were like a crowd in an opera house when the curtain rises. A couple rose to get a better look. The others snickered as they shifted around in their chairs.

Laughing loudly, jeeringly, the barman leaned forward against the bar, slapped his right butt cheek, making the pale, hairy flesh quiver, and yelled, "You wanna kiss my ass, breed? Well, there ya go—pucker up and kiss away!"

Yakima thrust his left hand against the back of the man's stout neck, holding his head fast against the bar top. With his other hand, he slid his horn-handled Colt .44 from the holster positioned for the cross draw on his left hip, and clicked the hammer back.

"Hey, wha . . . what the hell you doin'?" the barman said, struggling against Yakima's iron grip. "Hey, now . . . *oh-eeeee-heeee!*"

The others in the room fell deathly quiet as the half-breed rammed the barrel of his cocked Colt against the barman's pink asshole. The man tried to lift his head but Yakima kept it pressed taut to the bar.

Yakima twisted the Colt a little and said in a low, menacing voice, "There you go, you fat son of a bitch—I'm kissin' your ass. How do you like it?"

The barman grunted and groaned, struggling against the half-breed's grip. Yakima shoved the barrel a little farther into the hole, and turned it, raking the rim of the barman's anus with the revolver's front site. The barman lifted his head and loosed a high wail.

None of the other men were saying anything. Aside from the barman's wailing, the room was as silent as a boneyard at midnight.

"You had enough of my kissin' your ass?" Yakima asked the barman, twisting his pistol barrel in the other direction.

"Yes!"

"Invite me to sit down and have a drink."

"Huh?"

"Invite me to sit down and have a drink, and you'd better be real polite about it, because—you know what? I find I kinda like kissin' this big, fat, white, ugly, smelly ass of yours!"

"Sit down and have a drink!" the barman wailed.

"On the house?"

"On the house! Oh, for chrissakes, I'll give you a whole fuckin' bottle! Whatever you like!"

Yakima pulled his pistol barrel out of the man's ass and wiped it with a bar rag. "That's right friendly of you, pard. Don't mind if I do. I'll take a bottle of tequila. A fresh one."

The barman was panting as though he'd run a long ways, his lungs raking like a smithy's bellows. He scowled at Yakima as he turned around to lean back against the bar, and then he wrinkled his nose at the laughing customers.

He leaned forward, pulled his longhandles and his canvas trousers up his thick, pasty legs, and looped his suspenders over his shoulders. He walked a little stiffly, wincing, sweat dribbling down his freckled cheeks, around behind the bar and set a clear bottle onto the planks. He set a shot glass down beside the bottle. He glowered at Yakima over the bottle.

"Thanks, pard," Yakima said. " 'Preciate it."

"Don't mention it."

Yakima took the bottle and the shot glass and moved through the tables of grinning, snickering men, to a vacant table along the saloon's far, adobe-brick wall, under an unlit bracket lamp. Rage still burned in him. This wasn't the first time he'd been harassed for the russet tones of his skin. He was part Cheyenne, part Yakima, and part German, though aside from his jade-green eyes, he looked more Indian than northern European.

Still, the prejudice chafed him. When he was riled, there was usually trouble, for he was bigger than most men. And he knew how to fight. He was pushing thirty after a long and varied career on the western frontier, but he still had not yet learned to turn the other cheek.

He doffed his broad-brimmed, low-crowned, black hat, ran a big, red paw through his long, coal-black hair that was still sweaty and dusty from the trail. He'd just come through the White Mountains headed for the border. Why, he didn't know. Mexico would be as good a place as any to look for work to see him and his horse, Wolf, through another couple of months.

It would be winter up north soon, and he liked to stay as far away from snow as possible. He'd had enough of snow. And of trouble up north, for that matter . . .

He grabbed the bottle. He shouldn't drink the tequila. The Mexican firewater, probably mostly mescal, would likely only add kerosene to the already hotly burning blaze inside him. He knew that from experience.

What the hell.

He popped the cork, splashed the colorless liquid into the shot glass, and tossed back the entire shot at once.

"Hey, Clancy, how's your ass feel after the half-breed's kiss?" asked one of the drummers. He was red-faced drunk as were the two other drummers sitting at his table. "Me an' the boys're thinkin' you rather liked it!"

Laughter all around.

Yakima splashed another round of tequila into his shot glass. Out the corner of his left eye, he saw the barman turn away from the range on which he'd set the stew pot. The man's face was crimson, his little pig eyes bright with rage, his long, stringy hair hanging down against his sooty cheeks.

"Yeah, really?" he barked, reaching under his plank bar that was as rough-hewn and humble as everything else in the earthen floored, smoky, smelly place. "Well, why don't I just show you how much I liked it!"

Yakima turned to see the man haul up a big, double-barreled shotgun from beneath the bar. The man had just ratcheted both heavy hammers back when, moving instinctively and automatically, Yakima whipped up his Peacemaker from his cross-draw holster, extended the Colt quickly but adeptly straight out from his right shoulder, and drilled a hole through the barman's forehead.

The slug threw the portly bastard straight back against his cookstove, sending the stew pot to the floor.

The barman didn't make a sound as he slid down the front of the hot stove, the smell of scorched flesh instantly filling the room, for he was already shaking hands with the red-eyed, yellow-toothed demons in hell long before he hit the floor.

CHAPTER 2

"What in the hell is that racket!" a woman's voice careened into the main drinking hall from the dilapidated saloon/hotel's second story. The voice was Spanish-accented. Yakima heard a light, feminine tread, and then the woman was leaning over the balcony rail, glaring down into the bar. "What is that shooting about?"

"The breed here shot your husband, Miss Paloma!" one of the drummers yelled, pointing an accusing finger toward Yakima. "That one there. He shot ole Clancy!"

Ah Christ, Yakima thought, his gut tightening.

The woman stared over the balcony rail into the area behind the bar where her husband lay dead. Yakima stared at her, waiting. He was surprised when she did not scream or sob or show any emotion at all but only slowly turned her head with its long tresses of thick, wavy hair so dark that it owned a bluish sheen, and regarded the half-breed with pursed lips.

Yakima's gut tightened again, for the woman he was staring at was spectacularly beautiful. At least, she appeared spectacular from this distance.

He couldn't see all of the details of her face, but it definitely appeared superb, and there was no doubting the richness of her body clad in a metallic green and gold floral print dress that hugged her narrow waist and pushed up her ample bust that was only partly concealed by a fringe of white lace. Silver hoops dangled from her ears. Her arms beneath the dress's four-inch sleeves were pale and fine, her hands long-fingered and feminine, with silver rings on both her middle fingers.

She was one well-set-up creature. About as well-proportioned as a man could find. No doubt about it. So well-made, in fact, that Yakima felt chagrined at the warm stirrings in his loins so close on the heels of his having killed the woman's man.

She studied Yakima through hard, dark-brown eyes, her fine jaws set in a firm, smooth line. Her nostrils swelled. She drew a deep breath, and her lovely bust rose up higher against her chest.

Her eyes turned even darker as she curled her plump, ruby-red upper lip and, shuttling her gaze to the seven other men in the room, said, "Well, what are you men going to do about it? My husband has been killed in his own establishment, and you all just sit there like hogs in a wallow? Are you men or *mice*?"

With that last, she slapped both her hands down on the creaky balcony rail, gripping the rail as though it were the neck of a chicken she was ringing.

Silence.

The other men in the room glanced back and forth at each other, owl-eyed.

Dread dropped like a cold wheel hub in the half-breed's belly. Yakima knew what was coming. When a creature like the one standing on the balcony issued a challenge like the one she had just issued, there was no man alive with *cojones* large enough to deny her.

If she'd been ugly, sure. But this woman leaning over the rail just far enough to give every man in the saloon a good shot at the deep, alluringly dark valley between her large, pale breasts was so far from ugly that she couldn't hit ugly with a mountain howitzer.

Yakima looked at the seven other men in the room. They were all looking back at him.

Very slowly, the two men nearest Yakima set the cards they'd been playing facedown on the table. They were both clad in rough trail gear, and they both sported pistols in tied-down holsters. None of the drummers appeared armed, though they were all probably carrying hideouts, little poppers tucked away in sleeves or jacket pockets for warding off robbers.

Yakima didn't think he had to worry about them.

The other two men who sat between the drummers and the cardplayers were hard to figure. One was a long-faced albino wearing the dark-blue attire of a cavalry soldier. The bar on his shoulders made him a first lieutenant. His eyes were a queer yellow beneath the broad brim of his sun-burnished Hardee hat. He was sunk back in his chair, chewing a stove match and staring toward Yakima with a cunning grin.

The beefy, broad-faced man sitting beside him was clad in denim trousers and a checked shirt under a brown leather vest, a salt-crusted tan Stetson on the table beside him. His thick body was turned away from Yakima, facing the bar, but he was looking over his stout left shoulder at the half-breed now, and he had much the same look as his albino friend. His eyes were pale brown and set too close together on either side of a fat, slightly crooked nose. He had about three days' worth of dark-brown stubble on his sunburned cheeks.

A brown bottle sat on the table between him and the albino lieutenant. The albino had a quirley between the long, pale, lightly freckled fingers of his left hand, beside a pair of cavalry gloves and gauntlets. His cold, dead eyes gave the lie to his smiling lips that flicked across Yakima, scrutinizing the half-breed thoroughly, mockingly.

It was those two and the two to Yakima's left he had to watch the most closely. Not the drummers, though drummers were known to be pistol savvy, as well. And no male of any stripe was immune to the cleavage hanging over the balcony rail.

"Well, what are you waiting for . . . gentlemen?" The woman, who, judging by the smoothness of her skin, was probably in her middle twenties, pitched her voice with a sultry disgust and condemnation.

Yakima held very still, sitting sideways to the wall but gazing into the room, his face implacable, his eyes moving, waiting.

One of the cardplayers, the one sitting sideways to Yakima, turned his head toward the woman. He turned his head slowly back, and his eyes were wide, his chest rising and falling heavily.

Don't, Yakima silently urged. *She's not worth dyin' for, amigo.*

But he was the one who jerked first, all right. And he was the first one to die as Yakima lurched to his feet, swiping his horn-gripped .44 from its holster and drilling the screaming carplayer between the flaps of his shabby wool vest and through the dead center of the hide tobacco pouch hanging there. He'd leaped to his feet, half turning toward Yakima, making a perfect target.

But now he was nothing but a blood-spewing, screaming bag of bones as he flew back, triggering his big Russian .44 into the ceiling and flying back against the cold potbelly stove. His partner hadn't wanted to join his friend's dance—his reluctance was evidence in his suddenly large, gray eyes that were opaque with cold fear—but he'd felt compelled by the fact that his friend had tried it.

And he probably thought that Yakima couldn't get a second shot off as fast as the half-breed did, blowing a quarter-sized hole through the second cardplayer's left eye and into the hand of his partner who was still slumped backward, arms spread, across the stove. Blood and brain matter from the second card-player's head splattered across that quivering hand, as well.

Yakima had spied movement out of his right eye.

As he turned, he was vaguely surprised to see that neither the albino cavalry lieutenant nor his beefy partner was making any offensive moves whatever. They merely sat their chairs, grinning shrewdly as before, as though they were watching nude dancers prance around in an opera house.

It was the foolish drummers who were squirming around, trying to haul out pocket pistols. The man in the orange checked suit had just pulled an ivory-gripped, over-and-under derringer from his vest pocket, and was wincing and stumbling backward, cocking one of the hammers, when Yakima punched his ticket with a .44-caliber round through his upper chest. He slid his smoking Colt toward the drummer standing to the orange-clad man's right, and that gent tossed his own little Smith & Wesson top-break .38, which he'd fished out of a shoulder holster beneath his torn tweed coat, onto the table as though it were a scorpion that had fallen onto his lap from the ceiling.

"No, no, no!" he cried, rubbing both hands through his thin, brown hair as he stepped back away from the table, squeezing his eyes closed and closing his hands over his face, as though to ward off a bullet.

Yakima held fire.

He slid the Colt toward the next drummer—a scrawny little man with a bizarrely cherubic face and yellow mutton-chop whiskers shaved into arrow points pointing toward his chapped, pink mouth. He just stood there holding a stubby, brass-framed pepperbox revolver pointing toward the floor beside his scuffed, manure-streaked, right half boot.

He, too, had closed his eyes and was shaking his head from side to side, muttering, "No. No. No. No . . ."

There was a soft thudding sound.

Yakima frowned, looking around. Then he saw the liquid dribbling down from inside the scrawny drummer's right, broadcloth pant leg onto the instep of his right half boot. The liquid beaded on top of the shoe, and each bead rolled down like a brown ball bearing onto the floor to form a dark pool that was growing on the scarred puncheons.

"No. No. No," he continued mechanically, keeping his eyes closed. "I want no part of this."

"Then you might drop the pepperbox," Yakima suggested.

The man's knobby, little hand opened, and the stubby pin-fire pistol dropped to the floor with a clanging thud.

Meanwhile, the first drummer looked down at the hole in his chest, and his eyes acquired a shocked, horrified cast. He placed a hand near the hole, smearing the oozing blood with his fingers.

Then he looked up at Yakima and said in a matter-of-fact tone devoid of accusing but pitched with mild bewilderment, "You killed me."

"Nope." Yakima shook his head and glanced up at the heavy-breasted Mexican woman staring down over the balcony rail. "She did."

"God damn you," the drummer said with a sob, though it was hard to say whom he was addressing, because he'd dropped his shocked gaze to the floor.

His knees buckled and hit the floor. His eyes rolled back into his head. He fell forward onto his face, sighed, shook, and lay still.

Yakima looked around. The albino and the beefy gent sat as before, as though they'd turned to wax about three minutes ago. The woman stared down from the balcony. She didn't look as angry anymore as perplexed.

"You two ain't playin'?" Yakima asked the other two customers.

"Nah." This from the albino, who slid his matchstick from one side of his mouth to the other, showing the ends of his yellow teeth. "MacElvy done told me about your reputation . . . Yakima Henry."

Yakima frowned at the beefy gent with little eyes set too close together. And then he recognized him. MacElvy hauled his big, beefy frame out of his chair, smiling affably and sweeping a hand through his thick, light-red hair that curled onto his sun-blistered forehead.

"Sergeant MacElvy," he said. "Remember?"

"Yeah," Yakima said, depressing his Colt's hammer but keeping the pistol aimed between the two men, not yet willing to let his guard down. "I remember."

MacElvy had been a line sergeant at Camp Hildebrandt over at Apache Pass, when Yakima had been a civilian scout and tracker at "Fort Hell," as the lonely outpost had been more informally dubbed by those unfortunate enough to have been stationed there, just after Lee had surrendered to Grant at Appomattox Courthouse. When he'd accrued more sins than even the frontier, Indian-fighting cavalry, hard pressed to find enough men to throw against Geronimo and the other Apache war chiefs in Arizona, had been able to swallow, MacElvy had been run out of the army in disgrace.

General drunkenness, insubordination, and the maiming of a whore at one of the hog pens near Fort Hell had been only a few of the noncommissioned officer's crimes, as Yakima remembered. It had been ten years since Yakima had worked at Hildebrandt, longer still since he'd last seen MacElvy, but he also remembered the man to be a general lout and no-account who'd actually seemed to have been working *toward* having his chevrons stripped from his uniform sleeves.

MacElvy stood facing Yakima. He was a big, burly gent, as tall as Yakima. He was grinning, narrowing his light-brown eyes, but the expression was hollow, his face a mask. He smelled as though beer and forty-rod were oozing from his pores on the tails of his sour sweat.

"Been a while since Camp Hell, Henry." MacElvy glanced around the bloody room. "You been busy." He narrowed an eye at the half-breed. "And your reputation precedes you. You've killed your share."

"Only those that needed it."

MacElvy glanced at his albino partner. "Bruno Hilger . . . uh . . . *Lieutenant* Bruno Hilger, that is . . . meet Yakima Henry. One of the best trackers, aside from the Aravaipa scouts, we had at Camp Hell back in them days. Him and his Southern pal, Seth Barksdale."

Hilger gave his chin a cordial dip. "Pleasure."

"All mine."

"Wonder where that old gray back, Barksdale, is now," said MacElvy.

"Probably dead," Yakima said, meaning it. He remembered that his dashing young partner, only a few years older than Yakima, and born and bred on a rich cotton plantation in Georgia, had trod a dangerous course between women, not all of whom had been unattached.

Yakima hadn't heard from Seth in six, seven years. If he wasn't dead, he'd probably gone back to his family's plantation to live the life of Southern-style luxury, fishing for catfish, a basket of fried chicken by his side, a tumbler of corn liquor in hand, a busty, beribboned Southern belle clad in crinoline sprawled on a blanket beneath a mossy oak.

MacElvy laughed. "What brings you to Horsetooth?"

Yakima shrugged. "Nothin' to speak of. What brings you to Horsetooth?"

MacElvy studied him with a faint, fleeting suspicion in his eyes. Then he laughed. "Same as you, I reckon. Nothin'!" He patted Yakima's stout right shoulder, hitched his denims higher on his broad hips. "Nice to see ya again, Henry. That was some right fancy shootin'. I reckon them stories I heard about you weren't stretchin' things much. Well . . . anyway . . ." He glanced at Hilger. "I reckon we'd best pull our picket pines, eh, Lieutenant? Get on back to the post?"

Still seated, Hilger was studying Yakima with much the same

look that MacElvy had worn, only Hilger's look wasn't nearly as fleeting as the former sergeant's.

"I said," MacElvy said, raising his voice and giving the lieutenant a commanding look, "we'd best get on back to the post—eh, Lieutenant?"

"Right," said Hilger, rising and adjusting the angle of his hat over his pale, washed-out eyes, his long, coarse, white hair hanging straight down past his collar.

He picked up his gloves and gauntlets, fished a pair of rectangular, rose-lensed sunglasses out of his tunic pocket, donned the spectacles, and walked to the saloon's bat wings. He was a tall man, Yakima saw now. Taller than either he or MacElvy, but he probably weighed only a hundred and fifty pounds still dripping wet from a bath.

MacElvy pinched his hat brim to Yakima, winked, and followed the lieutenant outside.

When they were gone, Yakima found himself staring at the saloon owner's wife, now a widow, standing at the bottom of the stairs. She was looking around at the devastation and pensively fingering a gold locket hanging from a gold chain around her long, pretty neck.

CHAPTER 3

"You're a hard man to kill," the barman's widow said, strolling toward Yakima while continuing to finger the locket hanging to just above her cleavage.

Yakima knew he should take his bottle, mount up, and ride into the desert. Trouble had a way of dogging him. It had dogged him here. He tried to keep one step ahead of it. But he couldn't take his eyes off the splendid creature walking toward him, letting her mud-brown eyes flick from his head to his boots and back again and then across the broad stretch of his power-ful shoulders straining the top buttons of his black-and-red calico shirt.

"My condolences," Yakima said.

She stopped before him, glanced down at the horn-gripped revolver angled across his left hip. "You are a *pistolero*."

"Sometimes."

She arched a brow. Her cheeks were perfectly sculpted, rounded, not at all severe, and her eyes were a deep, luminous brown. They glittered in the trapezoids of copper, mote-shot light angling through the windows and casting sharp-edged shadows onto the floor. Her wavy, raven hair was very long, and down here where he could see her better, it fairly glowed with a bluish undertone. Where the light did not reach, the room was all purple shadows swarming with flies that had already found the freshly spilled blood and dead meat.

Her lips were full. Bee-stung, some would call them. And

cherry red. Her skin was the off-white of almond butter. If it were any darker, she would not be allowed in her husband's saloon. She was not very tall, but she was curved in ways to make a man want to cut his own head off with a rusty saw. The faint smell of sandalwood and wild cherry blossoms that hovered around her freshly bathed body enhanced her primitive allure.

Behind the wild urges she evoked in him—would evoke in any man, young, old, or half dead—Yakima was trying to figure out what in hell she'd been doing, married to a pig like Clancy.

"An outlaw?" she asked, her gaze flicking once more across his chest.

"Only when necessary."

"The man mentioned you were an army scout at Fort Hildebrandt."

"A while back."

"And a tracker."

Yakima frowned. "What does that have to do with—?"

"Why don't we sit down and have a drink?" she said, cutting him off and dropping lithely into the extra chair at his table.

She crossed her legs beneath her skirt, the skirt drawing taut against them, outlining the curve of each knee and thigh in turn. He couldn't help imagining what they would look like without the skirt, wrapped around his back.

It had been a long ride down from Colorado . . .

There was only one glass. She filled it with tequila from his bottle, held the glass up to her lips, sniffed, ran the rim against the underside of her bottom lip, and then very slowly closed her upper lip over the rim, and sipped.

She swallowed, pressing her lips together. Her throat moved, and he heard the faint sound of the liquid dropping down her throat. There was a faint sheen of moisture on her mouth as she stared up at him through those brown eyes beneath her coal-black brows.

Yakima scowled down at her, baffled, "You always drink with men who shoot your husbands?"

"Clancy was my first," she said with an offhand air, glancing pensively over her shoulder to where her deceased husband could not be seen sprawled behind the bar. "I'd never intended to marry, but I guess there's just no stopping true love . . . once it gets a hold on you."

She gave a half smile, half slitting her eyes, and he couldn't make up his mind if she'd been serious or not. It was hard to imagine such a succulent creature as she falling in love with a pugnacious old dog like Clancy, who had to have been nearly twice her age.

"I'm Paloma," she said. "Paloma Collado. Formerly"—she glanced again toward the bar—"Brewer." She smiled. "Please, sit down."

Yakima kicked his chair to adjust it, and then sagged slowly into it, still studying her, scowling, wondering what Paloma Collado's game was. A voice in his head told him to take the bottle and ride. *Leave* the bottle and ride. But his feet would not comply.

Holding his gaze and smiling a little brighter, causing a hot knife of unfettered desire to twist in his heart, she slid her glass across the table to him. He could see the faint smudge where she'd pressed her lips to it.

The knife twisted.

Boots thumped above the sound of occasional horse and wagon traffic outside the saloon, along the main street of the little Arizona desert town of Horsetooth. Yakima slid his hand to the horn grips of his .44 but kept the revolver in its holster as a big, bull-legged man in a tattered canvas coat and equally tattered canvas hat ambled into the saloon, sweating. Brown-streaked pewter hair curled to his coat collar, and a walrus mustache of the same color framed his mouth.

He stopped just inside the bat wings, glowered down toward where the dead men lay before him, and then slid that glowering, confounded gaze toward Yakima and the young widow. Something else must have caught his eye, because now he stepped to his right and canted his head to stare down at the floor behind the bar.

"Ho-lee shit!" He doffed his hat and scratched the back of his head. "I *thought* I heard gunshots. I was takin' a nap back at my . . . Miss Paloma, do you realize that Clancy is layin' dead back here? At least . . ." He ambled back behind the bar and made a jerky, twisting movement that was followed by a soft thud, telling Yakima he'd kicked the barman's body over. "Yep, he's dead, all right. Dead as a post."

"Yes, it's a tragedy, Marshal Wade. Would you haul the bodies over to the undertaker's for me, please? There are two more over here." Paloma glanced toward the first two men—the card-players—whom Yakima had dispatched.

From behind the bar, and scratching the back of his head again, the marshal, who appeared to be pushing a hard-earned fifty, said, "Well, who done all this *killin'*?"

"They all shot each other," Paloma said, keeping her eyes on Yakima. "Those two there grabbed me in a most humiliating way, and Clancy, being the good, devoted husband he was, tried to intervene with his shotgun, and took a bullet for his trouble."

The cool beauty splashed more tequila into the glass and threw back half of it before sliding the glass back toward Yakima. "I'm having a drink to calm my nerves. This gentleman was kind enough to share his bottle."

The town marshal stared at Yakima suspiciously. "Ain't that nice of him . . ."

"Please, Marshal Wade," Paloma urged. "Just clear the place. I'm sure whatever these men have in their pockets will more than pay for their burial."

The marshal sighed, shook his head, and shrugged. "If you say so . . ."

The big, sloppy gent ambled out from behind the bar and pushed through the bat wings. He stopped on the front porch, stuck a finger of each hand in his mouth, and loosed a shrill whistle. "Albert, Johnny—get your worthless asses over here and clear these cadavers out of the saloon. Your pa's got business!"

Presently, the marshal moved back into the saloon with two thickset, rawboned, young, overall-clad men, both smelling like fresh horseshit, on his heels. Their clothes were liberally smeared with dung. The boys had the blank stares and awkward, halting gaits of half-wits. They both glanced with mute interest at Miss Paloma and the big half-breed sitting at the table against the far wall, both sipping tequila from the same glass.

"Well, I didn't call ya in here to mooncalf around," the marshal said, gesturing with his arm. "Haul them dead men outta here and over to your daddy's livery stable. There's another one, ole Clancy himself, behind the bar. Whatever you find in their pockets belongs to your pa. Tell him he owes me a beer and steak and a free shoein'."

The big, sloppy marshal, who'd likely been a cowpuncher at one time before getting too old for the strenuous work, leaned against the bar while the boys cleared the place of the bloody cadavers, one taking the legs, the other the arms and shoulders.

While the boys did the heavy lifting, the marshal leaned back against the bar, poked at his teeth with a shaved matchstick, and studied Yakima and Paloma with a skeptical, befuddled expression. The pretty widow and the man who'd widowed her said nothing until the place was cleared and the boys and the marshal had left, the marshal calling out his condolences over his shoulder as the bat wings clattered back into place behind him.

"I didn't think they'd ever leave," Paloma told Yakima.

His heart was thudding in his temples. His throat was dry. He cleared it, swallowed.

"Me, neither."

"Would you like to join me upstairs?"

"No."

She threw back the last half inch of tequila in the bottom of the shot glass, licked her lips, and smiled. "But you're going to."

"Hell, yes."

She placed one of her hands on his, leaning forward slightly, pressing her full bosom against the side of the table. Wrapping her hand around his, she rose.

He slid his chair back and rose, as well, and let her lead him across the room to the uncarpeted stairs. As they climbed the stairs, the staircase creaking beneath them, the sounds from the street dwindling as they rose toward the second story, that voice in Yakima's head was growing more fervid but it, too, was fading as though into the distance.

Desire sharpened by dread touched him like an ice pick to the loins. The girl's hand was soft and small in his own. She was flexing her fingers, and the slight pressure of her flesh against his enflamed him further.

"Nothing good will come of this," he told himself. "Not one damn bit of good, you stupid, good-for-nothin' half-breed. In fact, you'll be lucky to get out of here alive."

Still, he thought, looking down at the girl walking up the steps beside him, her bosom rising and falling behind the low-cut dress . . . what a way to go!

The muffled crack of a distant pistol woke him.

He jerked his head up from his pillow, and instinctively reached for the Colt hanging from a chair beside the woman's bed.

"No," she said, groaning as she too awoke from her postcoital slumber. "It's just . . . someone over at the Mexican cantina on the other side of town. It's crawling with *banditos* over there." Her voice was deep and raspy. She clawed at his back, trying to draw him back down to where she sprawled naked on the sheets still damp and hot from their ravenous coupling.

Yakima released the pistol. He looked at the two wooden balcony doors thrown open to catch a breeze in hopes of relieving the fierce desert heat. When he and the girl had finally separated and slumbered from exhaustion, the sun had not quite set.

Now, it was good dark. Stars shimmered in the sky above the village of Horsetooth. This side of town was quiet, but he could hear men's and women's voices raised in raucous revelry to the south—straight out from the hotel/saloon that now had only a single owner.

"The Mexican part of town," the girl said, nibbling his arm. He could feel her hot tongue and the dull ends of her teeth. "Let them all kill each other, give us some peace and quiet."

She was running one hand across his back while she nuzzled his arm. Her hair felt coarse as a mare's tail where it touched his skin, lifting chicken flesh.

Yakima blinked sleep from his eyes, cleared his throat, looked down at her where she was pressing her cheek against his bicep, staring up at him with dark, erotic eyes, her mussed hair framing her ivory face.

"How in the hell did you come to marry Clancy?"

"I told you."

"Bullshit. You couldn't love him any more than I could love the grizzly this necklace came from." He glanced at the claw necklace still hanging down from his stout, red neck and which he'd fashioned from the claws of a bear that had attacked him, nearly killed him, not all that long ago.

She looked down. "It was a marriage of . . . convenience. I was an orphan. I needed a man. Preferably, a wealthy man. So, judge me. I married Clancy because he had money. The saloon is successful, though I know it doesn't look like it. He never put much back into it. That was fine with me. More for myself when he kicked the bucket."

Yakima chuckled. "Now, you're talkin'."

She pressed her moist, silky lips to his bicep that bulged like a wheel hub. "Come back down here and make love to me again. I am twenty-three, and Clancy was the only man I ever had. Rest assured, you are the first man who has ever . . . come back here, damn you!"

Yakima had risen, running his hands through his long, sweat-damp hair. The room was as hot a desert jailhouse, and it smelled like sex and sweat. "Gotta get some air."

He didn't bother grabbing his underwear, just his makings sack. He stumbled out the open balcony doors and collapsed into a wicker chair that sat beside a small whicker table, against the wall to the left of the open doors.

"You're a bastard!" she yelled behind him.

"You're gonna kill me," he laughed, leaning forward, elbows on his knees.

"Wouldn't it be a sweet death?" she said in a pouting, little girl's voice.

"Leave me alone. Gotta catch my breath."

She threw a pillow. It landed just inside the doors and skidded out onto the balcony. Ignoring her, Yakima opened the hide pouch and withdrew chopped tobacco and wheat papers, and rolled a tight quirley. He removed a match from a box inside the pouch, struck it to life on the floor, and touched it to the cigarette.

He flipped the match over the balcony rail and into the street that was dark save one saloon across the street to his left.

Lantern light pushed out through the open windows, but it was fairly quiet over there. It was probably around ten, maybe eleven o'clock, and the whores were probably entertaining their customers in their rooms.

The hot, dry desert air was scented with the smell of mesquite smoke and frijoles remaining from supper fires.

Yakima leaned forward, elbows on his knees, smoking and staring over the rail and into the night. Her soft tread sounded behind him, and she stopped between the open, rough-hewn doors, naked, long hair hanging down her back and curling around her sides to her flat belly.

CHAPTER 4

"We need a breeze," she said, and slumped onto his lap, resting her head against his neck.

He hooked his right arm around her, liking the feel of her. It had been a long time since he'd had a woman. Not since Denver. There'd been no time for women on the trail, as he had a couple of law dogs after him. Turned out he'd killed a brother of one of the law dogs, and, though the dead man had been trying to steal Yakima's horse, the lawman, a local sheriff from Colorado Territory, had wanted to see the half-breed hang.

He looked at the girl slumped against him. His mouth quirked a wry smile as he ran his gaze down one of her slim arms to her crossed legs hanging down off his knee.

Out of the frying pan and into the fire . . .

What was her game?

She turned her face to him, kissed his cheek. When that got no reaction, she stuck her tongue in his ear. Then she dropped her hand between his legs, and she smiled at him shrewdly.

Yakima groaned.

"You are much *hombre*," she said, plying her magic.

He stiffened. The cigarette burned down to his fingers, and he dropped it. She cooed in his ear while her hand did its dance. Yakima leaned back, stretched his lips back from his teeth, groaned, and shuddered.

"It is nice, giving you pleasure," she whispered.

Yakima didn't say anything. He felt spent and dreamy.

"Do you like me?"

"What's not to like?"

"How much do you like me?"

"How much do I need to like you?"

She smiled. "A lot."

Time to leave, he thought. Go. *Now!*

Voices rose from the far side of the street. Shadows moved behind the bat-wing doors of the saloon, and Yakima glimpsed a blue Hardee hat and cavalry tunic. He also recognized the brawny frame of Edgar MacElvy just before he and Lieutenant Hilger pushed through the doors and stepped out into the inky darkness of the street.

They were laughing drunkenly, boots clomping off down the boardwalk, away from Yakima and Paloma. She'd sat up now, straddling the half-breed's knee, and was staring out over the balcony rail, turning her head slowly, tracking the drunken pair.

"What's wrong?" Yakima asked.

"Them. They've been snooping around here for days now. I wish they'd go back to their outpost like they said."

"Why do you suppose they've been snooping around?"

"Who knows?" Paloma hiked her bare shoulder. "They are snoops." She turned to him. "Anyway, they are gone now. Too drunk to cause any trouble tonight. Are you hungry?"

"Nah." Between bouts in her large, four-poster bed, she'd gone downstairs and brought up four beef burritos and beans and a fresh bottle of mescal. "Just tired."

"Me, too. You're the kind of man who wears a girl out." She slipped off his knee, leaving it hot and moist where she'd been sitting, and jerked his arm. "Come on—let's go to sleep."

Suddenly, he was even more tired than he'd thought he was. All the lovemaking, the good food, and forty-rod were tugging hard on his eyelids. The bed sounded good. He rose, wrapped his arms around her, and kissed her, liking the pliant way she kissed him back and ran her fingers lightly down his shoulder blades, causing chicken flesh to rise once more.

He'd sleep in her bed tonight, because he was too tired to find another even if he'd been strong enough to tear himself away from this Spanish succubus. He was curious about what she wanted from him. That she wanted something was obvious. He was a stranger who'd killed her husband, and she'd made love to him like the most gifted, best-paid whore in the toniest New Orleans brothel.

But he no longer wanted to know. Whatever it was, it was trouble, just as she was trouble.

The worst kind of trouble. Woman trouble.

He'd ride out first thing in the morning and cross the border into Mexico around noon.

He followed her inside and flopped down in the bed. She folded up with her smooth, warm butt pressed up against his groin, pulled his arm around her, taking his hand in both of hers and holding it very tightly to her breasts.

Sometime later he woke to see her dressing stealthily in the room's thick shadows, her jostling hair glinting dully in the cool, blue light of dawn. She was trying to make no noise, he could tell. He could hear her tight, little breaths. She was breathing hard, anxiously. She dropped a serape over her shoulders, plucked a brown sombrero off a wall peg, and carried her boots out the door and closed the door softly behind her. He heard her bare feet on the steps. She wasn't going to put her boots on until she was downstairs. That's how badly she wanted him to keep sleeping.

Yakima sighed and sat up, raked his hands through his hair.

What was she up to?

"Push on, fool," he grumbled aloud. "Saddle Wolf and ride for the border."

Knowing that what he *should* do and what he *would* do were polar opposites, he dressed and headed outside just as she rode out from behind the saloon and hotel on a short, rangy Mexican blue. She wore a striped serape, with a thin scarf wrapped around the lower part of her face, beneath the brown sombrero, as though she did not want to be recognized. Fortunately, she did not look toward the saloon's front porch but spurred the mount down the street in the opposite direction.

In seconds, she was hunkered low over the blue's neck, and she and the mustang were galloping toward the end of town like a bat out of hell. They followed a bend to the right, and the morning shadows consumed them, the thuds of the horse's galloping hooves dwindling quickly beneath the raucous chirping of the morning birds.

Yakima headed over to the livery barn and in less than five minutes he was saddled up and galloping on out of the morning-quiet town in the direction the woman had gone. He had no problem trailing her. Her hoofprints were the freshest ones on the wagon trail that curved through the desert, meandering around low bluffs and boulder snags, creosote shrubs stretching their long, bristly tendrils from both sides of the trail.

He hadn't been on the trail long before he spied movement ahead.

Paloma was galloping up a long, gentle incline ahead of Yakima and gradually curving to his right, which was south. She was merely a brown-and-black blur from this distance of a half a mile, but it had to be her.

She was angling up the shoulder of a sawtooth, sandstone ridge that was glowing copper now as the sun broke free of the horizon and began sliding its buttery light across the bristling chaparral, stretching long, slender shadows toward the west sides of shrubs and rocks. Larger, darker shadows stretched away from the walls of dykes and mesas.

When Yakima had gained the top of the sandstone ridge, he

saw the woman riding the blue up the side of another, low hill to the southwest. She'd slowed her mount considerably since she'd left town, but Yakima hadn't. She was only a hundred or so yards ahead of him.

She was pulling the blue up toward an ancient, brown adobe church that sat atop the broad, sandy crest of the hill and which was ringed with the remains of an old, mostly abandoned Mexican village. Yakima knew the place, for he'd taken this trail in and out of Mexico many times in the past, and stopped for water provided by the well of the congenial old *padre* who ran the church.

He touched spurs to Wolf's flanks and galloped on the down the ridge. At the bottom, he swung off the main trail and followed a slender game trail along the side of a bristling, boulder-choked wash that ran along the northwestern base of the bluff that the church and the village perched on.

As he rode, he scared up several cactus wrens and a couple of turkey buzzards that had been feeding on some dead thing in the wash, and he gnashed his teeth together, hoping the birds hadn't given his presence away to the woman.

He followed the game trail about three quarters of the way up the ridge and stopped his white-socked, black stallion in a shady place where mesquites and sycamores pushed up around a gravelly seep. Yakima threw Wolf's reins perfunctorily over a branch—the horse had been trained to stay wherever its reins hung—and clambered to the top of the bluff.

Crouching low behind a boulder, he saw Paloma just then riding into the barren yard of the church. Yakima was flanking the church's northeast corner, so she was sort of riding toward both him and the front of the church, the morning sunshine glistening beautifully in her coal-black hair that was still beguilingly mussed from their lovemaking.

The *padre*'s shack, constructed of adobe bricks and vertical mesquite rails, sat to the right of the church, which fronted several dilapidated outbuildings. One was a chicken coop. Chickens from the coop were out foraging in the yard, and they squawked and scattered now as the girl drew up to the well that sat in the middle of the yard.

The *padre* himself was just then stepping off the stoop of his humble shack. He was clad in a calico smock belted with rope around his bulging waist, and canvas trousers and rope-soled sandals. His coarse, gray-brown hair hung in a long braid down his back.

He donned his ratty, straw sombrero as he walked out toward where the woman was dismounting her horse, patting the blue's neck appreciatively. Yakima took advantage of the morning shadows and the tufts of brush and rocks for partial concealment as he ran, crouching, toward the *padre*'s cabin. As he did, he saw the *padre* spread his arms out, palms up, and by the sound of his voice, he was not happy about the woman's visit.

Yakima crouched behind a pile of rocks bristling with cactus off one corner of the priest's hovel. From here, he could see around the left side of the shack and into the yard, where the woman and the priest were talking while the blue drew water from a bucket she'd winched up from the well.

Yakima couldn't hear what they were saying, but the priest continued to throw his arms up and out, as though he were arguing. Finally, the woman stepped around him and began striding for the shack.

Yakima ducked down behind the pile of rocks, and when the woman and the priest were both out of sight in front of the cabin, the half-breed darted out away from the rocks and, running nearly silently on his moccasin-clad feet, dashed to the hovel's back wall.

He crept around the left-rear corner and now he could see, through a window of the tiny shack, the priest saying, ". . . well enough for a visit. I told you to wait at least a week, Paloma."

They were speaking Spanish, but Yakima understood enough to catch the jist of what they were saying.

"I want to see my one true love, *Padre* Joseph. Is that so hard to understand?" The woman's voice had a mocking, condescending tone.

"Your one true love. That's a crock, Paloma!"

"Out of the way, *Padre!* You wouldn't want me to inform your superiors in Durango that your brother is the notorious *bandito,* Octavio La Paz—would you?"

Yakima felt his jaw drop.

The name Octavio La Paz had been notorious both north and south of the border for a long time. The half-breed had heard off and on over the years that the man was dead only to hear again that he'd robbed a large mine or a gold shipment in the border country. Once it was said he'd killed several Chiricahuas in cold blood, fanning the flames of the Southwestern Apaches wars. The wars were a great way to divert attention from his savage outlawry.

"You are the devil's sister," the priest told the woman. "And to think that I warned you about getting mixed up with *mi hermano* back when you started . . . when you started stepping out on your husband. Now, I realize it was Octavio I should have warned against taking up with the likes of *you,* Senora Brewer."

"It's Collado once again, *Padre.*" Yakima couldn't see the woman, but he could tell from her tone that she was grinning. Sneering. "My beloved husband fell pretty to a big *mestizo* faster with a pistol than Clancy was with his shotgun. A tragedy. I will be in mourning for weeks!" She chuckled.

"The devil's sister," said the priest in a bewildered, crestfallen tone.

A third, weaker voice rose from the other side of the cabin and probably another room, judging by the muffled quality. "Joseph, I am awake. Send her in."

There was a slapping sound, as though the priest had let his arms drop to his sides in defeat. "You heard him," he told the girl. "He's awake. But he is very weak. He lost a lot of blood when the Apaches scalped him. He needs his sleep to fight the infection. Mind what I say. He might be a *bandito,* but he is still my brother and I will not let you . . ."

The priest let his voice trail off. Apparently, Paloma had left the room. Yakima had heard the clomping of her boots dwindling off to the opposite side of the shack. Yakima retraced his steps to the back of the cabin and followed the sound of voices to a window on the other side of the back door.

"There you are, *mi amor!*" the woman said. "How are you feeling?"

"How does it look like I am feeling?" came the sickly male voice. "You should try being scalped sometime. It is the most pleasant feeling in the world!"

The *bandito* sobbed miserably.

"And my eye. Oh, my poor eye. Those heathens stuck a hot poker in it and left me to suffer and die!"

Paloma made a hissing sound.

Yakima dropped to one knee beside the window, doffing his hat so the crown wouldn't be seen through the closed curtain buffeting slightly in the breeze, and heard her say, "I am so sorry, Octavio, you poor wretch!" A pause. "And . . . the money . . . ?"

The man gave a groaning sigh. "I won't be able to go back for it for quite some time, if ever. I'm miserable. I certainly can't sit a horse."

Octavio La Paz sobbed again, sucked a rattling breath.

There was a creaking sound. Yakima knew that Paloma had sat down on the bed beside her lover. The half-breed vaguely wondered how many she had, and felt foolish for feeling an annoying rake of jealousy.

But that's what a night like the one he'd just spent with a woman like Paloma Collado, formerly Brewer, would do to a man.

Turn him into a foolish mooncalf.

He snarled and closed his hand over the grips of his Colt.

CHAPTER 5

Get a grip on yourself, Yakima told himself. *You spent one night with the woman, and look what she's got you doing. Like a simpering idiot, you've followed her out to some other man's cabin. You're acting like a twelve-year-old boy with a schoolyard crush!*

He wanted to leave. Not only the alluring woman but the name of her legendary lover—Octavio La Paz—held him in place beneath the notorious *bandito*'s window.

She was saying just beyond the open window, "You have no choice but to tell me where the payroll money is, now, *mi amor.* I alone you can trust. The others were going to double-cross you; if you hadn't taken the loot from them, they would have taken it from you."

With an air of desperation, La Paz said, "You haven't seen any of them, have you? *Jorgenson?* In my condition, I'm a sitting duck out here!"

"No, no, no, *mi amor*—I have not seen Jorgenson or any of the others." Yakima wished she'd quit calling him her lover. "I assure you that if I do, you will be the first to know. I will come to you first. And I don't care what they threaten me with . . . or what they may promise me, if it comes to that . . . I will never tell them where you are!"

Yakima had to choke back a snicker. She was playing La Paz like a well-tuned mandolin.

"You wouldn't do that, would you?" begged the one-eyed

Octavio La Paz. "After all we've meant to each other this past year?"

"Shhhh," said Paloma. "Lie back down, now, *mi amor*. You're getting overwrought. Look there, sweat is breaking out on your forehead." There was the tinkle of water being wrung from a cloth into a washbowl. "There. Now, why don't you tell me where you buried the payroll money. I know someone I can trust to help me fetch it for you. For us. Once we have the money, we will go down to Mexico City. There, we will get you the very best doctors and find a master carver who will whittle you a new eye almost as good as the one the Apaches took from you."

Again, there was the sound of the cloth being wrung out.

"I am . . . I am not so sure. I want to, but . . ."

"Octavio, don't tell me that after this wonderful year we spent together, all the thrilling and joyous trysts, fooling around behind my pig of a husband's foolish back, you don't *trust* me!"

"It is not that, *mi amor*," La Paz said. "It is that I don't want to endanger your life, Paloma. You have no idea the savagery of the other men in my gang. Jorgenson and Cordoba alone are wildcats! If they followed you into the desert, you might never come back. Believe me, they're out there looking for the loot they would have taken from me if I hadn't taken it from them first!"

"Shh, shhh, *shhhhhh*! There you go again, my darling. You must rest easier, don't get your blood up. Like I said, I have found a man who can help me. One very capable of guiding me into the desert and protecting me from all that might be out there. And rest assured, you can trust him. He is big, somewhat savage, and, while good with a gun, a little dunderheaded. Such a man is good at taking orders . . . and respecting a girl's wishes."

With that last, Yakima could hear the grin in her voice. His cheeks burned with indignation. She'd played him for the same kind of fool she'd played La Paz for . . .

"How did you meet this man?" La Paz asked, his voice pitched with suspicion.

"He killed Clancy."

"What?"

"He did us both a favor. Now, we can be together . . . after I've retrieved the loot."

"How do I know you will not run off with this hombre? This big savage, as you call him."

Paloma laughed. "Dear heart, he is as ugly as a dog. In fact, he even has fangs. And he is cow-stupid, but he knows the desert. He was once a tracker and scout at Fort Hildebrandt. No, *mi amor*, I could never have feelings for such a big, dumb, ugly desert rat. He will help me retrieve the loot, nothing more. And when we have no more use for him . . ."

La Paz chuckled, but there was a skeptical tone to the laughter. "You must bring him to me. I must meet this man and make sure he knows who he is dealing with . . . and what will happen to him if he chooses to deceive me."

Yakima felt his lips raise a satisfied smile.

How was she going to meet this obstacle?

Head on, it turned out.

In a soft, sensual voice, she said, "*Mi amor*, there is no time for that. That white-haired cavalry lieutenant, the *albino*, and his friend, MacElvy, have been hanging around the saloon. I think they suspect something. I took a chance riding out here this morning. I meant to come earlier but . . . I guess I was more tired than I realized. Don't worry," she added quickly. "I made sure I was not followed."

Again, Yakima had to choke back a dry snicker. Paloma was good at many things, but making sure she wasn't followed wasn't one of them.

"Trust me, my darling," she said, in an even softer, more sensual voice. It sounded as though she was nuzzling the man's neck or perhaps a lower area. "Please, trust me. I want so much for us to be together." There was the quiet rustle of sheets being slid around. "The only way . . . for that to happen, however . . . as you well know . . . is if we have enough money for us to make our escape . . . together."

Throatily, La Paz said, "You expect me to believe that you could still love me now . . . ugly wretch that I am?"

Silence.

La Paz groaned throatily.

Yakima's ear tips warmed.

After a while, La Paz said, his voice slightly pinched, "Find me some paper. I will draw you a map."

"Padre!" Paloma shouted, shattering the intimate quiet. "A pad of paper. *Hurry!"*

Yakima waited, pressing his back against the adobe bricks of the priest's shack, a skeptical scowl on his face. There wasn't much more to hear for a while. He assumed that La Paz was sketching a map to where he'd hid the army payroll loot. The priest was stomping around in the front of the shack, grumbling, but finally stalked out the front door.

Yakima worried that La Paz's more devout brother might head this way, but was relieved when he didn't hear the slap and scuff of the older man's sandals.

"I think that's right," La Paz told Paloma in Spanish, sounding fatigued now from the woman's visit and her ministrations. There was a clink like a pencil being dropped on the floor, and the ripping of a leaf from a notepad. "The X there marks where I buried the money when the trackers from Fort Bryce were bearing down on me. Them on one side, Jorgenson to the other side, with the Apaches hovering over us all from the ridges."

He gave a ragged sigh and another liquid sob. "At least, the

Apaches massacred the trackers. If only they would have done the same to Jorgenson and his little friend, Cordoba."

The infamous *bandito* chuckled with devilish delight. He clipped the laughter with a groan. "They'd done their damage, though. I was hurt too bad to go back for the loot. You'll have to do it. I trust you, Paloma. See to it I can trust both you and this stupid savage you've signed up to guide you into the desert."

"Don't worry. He knows who he is working for, *mi amor*. He trembled at the sound of your name. He stopped trembling when I promised that you would pay him handsomely."

"Be very careful, my dear Paloma. Many hazards out there in the desert, the Chiricahuas not the least of them!"

"Please, do not worry about me, my love," Paloma said. "Here, have a drink of this. It will make you feel better."

"What is it?"

"Mescal. Fresh from Mexico. I bought a barrel of it from traders last week."

"Ahhh," La Paz said. "Paloma, you are as thoughtful as you are beautiful."

She giggled.

Yakima rolled his eyes.

There was the gurgling sound of La Paz drinking the mescal. The gurgling stopped. The outlaw smacked his lips, sighed. "Ah, that hits the spo—*awwwwwwwwchhht-t-t-chh!*"

Yakima frowned, glanced sidelong at the window from which violent strangling sounds emanated.

La Paz croaked out in Spanish, "Wha . . . what did. . . . *achhhhh-achhhhhh!* . . . did you put in . . . ? *Achhhhh-achhhh!*"

Paloma giggled. "Snakeroot. Boiled up and strained, it blends very well with the mescal, does it not?"

"My . . . eyeballs . . . *achhhhh-achhhhh-awwwwwwckkkkkkkkk* . . . are . . . exploding . . . *help!*" He wasn't able to raise his voice very loudly.

"So that's how it feels. I always wondered. I was going to give some to Clancy when he was no longer useful. My new man saved me the trouble." Paloma laughed. "Thanks for the map. I do hope it won't take you too long to die, *mi amor. Dios,* you do look awful. I swear your head has swollen to twice its size, and I didn't think an hombre's face could ever get *that* red!"

"Awckkkkkkkk-awcckkkkkkkkk-awckkkkkkkkkawhkkkkkkkk!"

"Good-bye, you fool," Paloma said. "Sleep well."

Yakima heard only the strident clomping of her boots on the shack's stone floor. They faded quickly beneath the violent strangling, choking, and retching sounds of the soon-to-be-expired Octavio La Paz.

Yakima moved away from the window and looked around the side of the shack toward the front yard. Paloma was strolling toward where she'd left her horse. The priest was trimming some transplanted and irrigated rose bushes growing up from a bed of rich, black dirt lined with rocks and which sheathed a shrine of some sort.

"Better see to your brother, *Padre,*" the woman said, stepping into the Mexican blue's saddle. "I think he might have caught something in his throat."

Laughing, she neck-reined the horse around and galloped out of the yard.

As the priest started running toward the shack, Yakima drew back behind the hovel's back wall. He stared off, in hang-jawed shock at the girl's vileness and pluck.

"That there is one evil little bitch!"

As Octavio La Paz continued to strangle even more violently than before, Yakima jogged back toward where he'd left his horse.

He no longer cared if the priest saw him, which was doubtful, anyway, as the priest was probably trying futilely to administer to his hard-dying brother. Yakima ran straight out from the corner of the shack, dropped down the back side of the bluff, and swung up onto his black stallion's back.

Wolf whickered curiously.

"I told you, partner," Yakima said as he booted the horse on down the slope, "there are wicked women in this world and then there are *wicked* women! Even more wicked than some men I've known." The horse lunged on down the slope, loosing rocks in his wake. "But that one back there—that one gets the ribbon!"

He only wished he could take his own advice.

But, against his own will, he could not. Especially, now, for some damned reason he wasn't entirely sure about.

Maybe it was due to the fact that Paloma Collado was just so insanely beautiful and . . . well, insane. There was something inexplicably intoxicating and compelling about a ravishing young woman who could make such sweet heavenly love to the man who'd killed her husband and then ride out at dawn of the next day to entice her notorious outlaw lover into drawing her a map to his stolen loot—*and then to poison the poor son of a bitch!*

Maybe Yakima was just curious about what exactly she was made of, and what she'd do next. What else did he have to do except head to Mexico to lie low from the American law and look for some menial job to see him through the winter?

This was a hell of a lot more exciting than that!

What he found himself intending was to intercept her where the game trail diverged from the main one, and see how she'd play it . . . him . . . if for no other reason than for entertainment, though he fully realized that playing with diamondbacks would likely be a whole lot healthier.

He swung Wolf onto the main trail, and stopped him.

Yakima stared toward the southeast, which was the direction from which Paloma should be heading toward him shortly.

The sun had climbed high. It hammered down on the trail.

Insects buzzed in the arroyos around him. That was the only sound until the woman's scream cleaved the heavy, mid-morning silence and set the half-breed's pulse to throbbing in his ears.

CHAPTER 6

The half-breed gave Wolf the steel, and the black stallion lunged into an instant gallop.

The black gained the top of the first hill to the east, and barreled down the other side. It ran to the top of another higher hill and blasted past the turn off to the large, brown church mounted atop the bluff on Yakima's left and where, if the *bandito* was lucky, Octavio La Paz had drifted on over the Divide.

When the desert leveled off, Yakima checked down the black, stopping him and turning him sideways to the trail. Ahead, three horses were galloping off in the opposite direction, heading off away from the main trail and angling through the chaparral, heading toward a range of dun mountains rising in the south. They were blurry streaks from this distance of two hundred yards or so, trailing plumes of adobe-colored dust.

Yakima reached back and pulled his spyglass from one of his saddlebag pouches. Telescoping the brass-plated piece, he raised it to his right eye and adjusted the focus until the three horses and three riders swam into clarified view.

The lead rider, on a bay horse, wore the blue uniform of the frontier cavalry. Bruno Hilger. The large man riding beside him wore rough, earth-toned range gear, and a high-crowned black hat. Paloma was mounted in front of Edgar MacElvy, whose bulk all but hid the woman, but Yakima could see her long, blue-black hair flying out behind both hers and MacElvy's right shoulders as they galloped hell-for-leather toward the dun line of craggy peaks ahead of them. Her sombrero blew out in the wind, as well, fixed to her neck by the chin thong.

Hilger was trailing Paloma's Mexican blue by the horse's bridle reins.

Yakima scowled after the retreating horses and riders. The woman had been right. The men had been snooping around for a reason. They must have suspected that Paloma had been in cahoots with the *banditos* who'd robbed the army payroll. They'd likely been keeping an even closer watch on her than she'd realized.

Now her goose was cooked.

She may have fooled La Paz into giving her the map to the stolen loot, but now the only two for whom it was doing any good was the albino cavalry lieutenant, Hilger, and the belligerent former sergeant who'd been kicked out of the cavalry in disgrace. Since they had the map, they probably had very little use for the woman. Oh, they maybe saw *some* use for her, all right.

But as soon as they'd had their fill—if you could ever have your fill of a woman like Paloma Collado—they'd likely shoot her and throw her into an arroyo as wolf bait.

Yeah, that's probably what would happen to her, and why in the hell did it matter to Yakima Henry? He had no dog in this fight. Oh, he'd spent a night with the woman. She'd given him a rollicking good time. One he'd likely remember for years to come. But she was every bit as much of an outlaw as the man she'd poisoned. Every bit as much of a thief.

Yakima didn't need the kind of trouble a stolen army payroll could bring.

So why did he find himself, fifteen minutes later, hard on the trail of Bruno Hilger and Edgar MacElvy?

Because he was as stupid as Paloma had told La Paz he was. That's why. And he couldn't get the bewitching memories of last night out of his head.

He didn't try to overtake the two kidnappers of Paloma Collado. That would be foolish by the light of day, when they could so easily spy him on their back trail and set up an ambush. Instead, he kept them at the far edge of his vision and followed their trail across the uneven floor of the hot, bristling, rocky desert.

Hell, he told himself by way of rationalizing his actions, they were headed south and, since he was headed south, he might as well trail them and once he caught up to them, he'd see about doing what he could for the girl. He suspected that Hilger and MacElvy were no better than she was, and, since she was a whole lot better-looking, he might as well spring her from the trap they'd set for her.

Then what he'd do, he had no idea. No point in thinking that far ahead. He sure as hell wanted nothing to do, however, with a stolen army payroll. He might be wanted by the law, but for unreasonable reasons. He was not an outlaw.

Steadily, doggedly, he followed his quarry across the desert. Up and over low hills, through shaggy, rocky arroyos littered with animal bones and, in one, the strewn half-rotted remains of a human—most likely an Apache, judging by the bits and pieces of calico and deerskin littering the area around the bones. Probably a warrior killed in a skirmish with another tribe or with a cavalry patrol.

The sun dropped behind the western ridges standing in near-black silhouette against the rage of bayoneting pastels. Yakima had slowed his progress when the shadows of dusk had grown long, wary of riding into an ambush, when the distance-muffled crack of a pistol echoed from somewhere ahead of him. Close on its heels came a woman's shrill scream.

Yakima jerked back on Wolf's reins, frowning into the

distance. The black whickered uneasily. The half-breed echoed his mount's sentiment with: "Now, what?"

Fifteen minutes earlier, the albino, Bruno Hilger, dropped his saddle on the ground near the fire ring that his beefy partner, Edgar MacElvy, had built after gathering wood, and stood threateningly over Paloma Collado. He glared down at her through his weird, colorless eyes set in shallow, pink sockets, brushed a hand across his blunt nose, which he'd smeared with salve against sun blisters, and held out his hand as if to shake hers.

He snapped his fingers.

"Let's have it."

"Have what?"

"What you got from La Paz!"

Paloma glared up at the strange-looking gringo with the long, colorless hair tumbling down over the collar of his blue wool uniform shirt. His pale, faintly freckled cheeks were gaunt and hollow, giving him a cadaverous appearance. His yellow neckerchief buffeted in the finally cooling breeze that made the flames in the fire ring flutter and smoke.

She removed her sombrero in disgust, tossed it down beside her. "How did you know . . . ?"

"That La Paz was with his brother?"

The big man with thick, wavy, light-red hair, a bull neck, and a broad unshaven face with angry eyes, was on one knee, snapping twigs and feeding them to the fire. "Hell, I've known for a long time the *padre* was a half brother of that old *bandito*. I always believed him when he told me he rarely saw hide or hair of his darker half. Didn't believe him so much that when the old *bandito* was known to be in the area . . . and was known to be gravely wounded . . . I didn't pay him a visit. Trouble was, when me an' my white-haired friend got to the *padre*'s shack,

La Paz was so out of it he couldn't remember his own name, much less where he'd buried the loot. The *bandito* was only about one quarter conscious and howlin' like a leg-trapped mountain lion. Likely would be for days . . . if he lived. Nasty mess, them 'Paches make, scalpin' a man, burnin' out one of his eyes with a hot coal."

MacElvy grimaced. "We were in Horsetooth, waitin' around for him to heal up enough to deal."

"To deal?"

"Yes, deal," said the albino. "The location of the loot for his life."

MacElvy said, "Found out it's rather common knowledge around Horsetooth you was meetin' up with the bandit in some old, abandoned *casa* just outside town." He chuckled. "Is that a blush? You thought it was your secret, huh? Look at that, Hilger, the chiquita's blushin'."

"Looks good on her." Hilger's weird eyes flicked down to her low-cut dress and held there. She'd removed her serape when the day had turned hot. "If only your husband knew what you was sharin' with someone else—a regionally notorious *bandito*, the very one who'd robbed the army payroll."

Embarrassment burned in Paloma's cheeks. She wondered who in Horsetooth had known about her and Octavio, and how they'd found out. For so long she'd been commending herself on her furtiveness.

She supposed someone, anyone, might have seen her stealing along that goat path to the abandoned casa. It would only take one man, perhaps a boy hunting rabbits in the arroyos, to spy the pretty, young wife of Clancy Brewer out walking alone, and to follow her to her proscribed destination, for the juicy tale to start spreading like wildfire.

Vaguely, Paloma wondered how much longer it would have taken for the indelicate news to have spread to Clancy, who would likely have stripped her naked and whipped her raw with a blacksnake.

"Come on," the albino said, sliding a lock of her black hair behind her ear. "We know he told you where he buried it. We know it's out here somewhere—somewhere in the Chiricahuas, because that's where he was last reported seen with the strongbox. Went into the mountains with it, was ambushed by the patrol sent out from Bryce, and rode out without his hair, his eye, and the strongbox. The one soldier who survived the Apache attack seen him, told about it back at Bryce."

"He didn't tell me about any strongbox," Paloma said, feigning incredulity. "I rode out to the *padre*'s shack merely to check on him."

"Bullshit."

"Seriously."

"Seriously, bullshit!" MacElvy laughed. "You know how we know? You was seen out back of Fred's Café in Horsetooth, diggin' up roots. Old Fred Meyer himself said it looked a might suspicious because about the only roots that grew out there was snakeroot . . . and he nor anyone else in town had known you to be such a forager." He winked. "Problem with bein' so damn fun to look at, Miss Paloma, is that most folks in town—at least, most of the *menfolk* in town—keep a pretty watchful eye on ya."

Hilger said, "We doubted we'd ever be able to get the location of the stolen army payroll from La Paz himself. Hell, an old border tough like that can take a lot of pain. We figured, however, that you could get it out of him, though. And then you'd give him a nice, long drink of that deadly snakeroot. We could tell from the priest's screams . . . and that big happy grin we saw on your face when we first spied you gallopin' along the trail back to Horsetooth . . . that you'd accomplished the nasty task."

Hilger smiled lustily and caressed Paloma's right cheek with the first two, long, pale fingers of his left hand. She jerked her head away from him, revolted, and spit at him. "Go lie with a javelina!" she screeched in Spanish. "A pig is the only one who would couple with such a pink-eyed, vile creature!"

"Oh, I doubt even a pig would lay with ol' Hilger here," laughed MacElvy.

Hilger jerked an indignant look at his partner. "You should talk!" He turned back to Paloma. "Hand it over!"

"Hand what over, fool?"

"He must have written out instructions for locating the strongbox. Or maybe he drew you a map. I know you got somethin'. You looked too happy—and you wouldn't have killed him—to not have got *somethin'*. Hand it over." Hilger stretched his lips back from his yellow teeth grimed with the tobacco he'd chewed and spat with disgusting, liquid plops all the time they'd been riding. "If not, I'd just love to go lookin' for it myself."

His seedy eyes flicked to her bosom.

Again, she recoiled, crossing her arms on her all-but-exposed breasts. "Keep your hands off me, you white-faced devil!"

"That tears it!" Hilger dropped to a knee and, bunching his lips in anger, pushed her back hard against the ground and held her there with one hand around her neck.

Paloma screamed and fought against him as he ran his left hand up the inside of her right leg. He grinned, apparently surprised to discover that she was wearing very little beneath her dress.

Back at the saloon, she'd dressed quickly and skimpily, merely throwing the dress over a pair of silk panties, for she'd wanted to make her trip out to La Paz as quickly as possible. She'd wanted to get back to town before her lover of last night, the handsome, mysterious, green-eyed *mestizo*—Yakima Henry—awakened and lit a shuck out of Horsetooth. She'd wanted to show him the map to the treasure by way of convincing him to help her look for it, as she'd known she'd need a man's help in this dangerous country.

She knew the half-breed to be a very capable hombre in more ways than one.

"Where is it?" Hilger yelled, running his hand brusquely over her writhing body.

"Unhand me, devil!" Paloma shouted, and kicked him hard in the groin.

Hilger yowled, and closed a hand over his crotch. "You little *bitch*!"

"Hilger, knock it off!" yelled MacElvy, who'd just set a pot of coffee on the fire.

Enraged by the assault on his groin, Hilger lunged at Paloma, who tried to skitter back away from him on her rump. He grabbed one of her legs and pulled her back toward him, the dress sliding up around her waist.

"I'm gonna strip you naked and whip the skin right off you, girl!"

MacElvy started to stride over toward his partner and Paloma. One of their horses whinnied shrilly. Both men froze. Hilger twisted around to stare off toward where they'd picketed the horses about thirty yards from the fire.

A gun cracked. Paloma saw the lapping flame in the darkness to the right of the shifting, dark shapes of the horses. She jerked with a start. So did Hilger. Only, the albino wasn't just startled. As he grunted and clapped his hands over his chest, Paloma saw dark, frothy blood geysering out from his breastbone.

"Oh . . . oh, *shit!*" the albino cried, and fell back across Paloma's bare legs.

She couldn't help but scream.

CHAPTER 7

There was more shooting and more screaming.

Despite his concern about what was happening in the darkness ahead, Yakima held Wolf down to a fast walk, heading in the direction from which the din of an obvious dustup was originating. There was a little faint green light left in the sky, but only enough to make travel even more treacherous than in solid darkness.

Shadows against faint light could hide dangerous obstacles.

A slope angled up on the half-breed's left. At the bottom of the slope, still to his left and ahead, was a curving wash. He could see no water at the bottom of the arroyo. The gravel paving it was pale in the darkness. Another slope angled up on Yakima's right. He pushed the nervous stallion ahead between the two slopes, but he was moving very slowly now, letting Wolf take only one step at a time.

The sounds of a deadly skirmish had stopped about ten minutes ago. The silence now was denser than before. Two coyotes howled somewhere to the north and there were the distant, infrequent hoots of an owl that seemed to have gotten over whatever anxiety it must have felt over the shooting and screaming.

Yakima had not.

He stopped Wolf among some large boulders, dropped the stallion's reins, ground-tying him, and slid his rifle from its scabbard. Pumping a round into the Yellowboy's chamber, he dropped quietly into the wash. He kept his ears attuned to the ratcheting hiss of a sidewinder that might be moving about with more vim and vinegar now that the sun had gone down and the air was cooling.

At the bottom of the wash, Yakima dropped to a knee and doffed his hat so there would be less of his shape to see in the murky, fast-fading twilight. A breeze rustled in the brush to his left, bringing to his nostrils the faint smell of wood smoke. But it was laced with the peppery tang of powder smoke, as well. It was issuing from somewhere ahead of him.

Yakima donned his hat as he straightened and started moving along the bottom of the wash, the five-foot-high banks shifting darkly around to each side of him. There was a sound to his left, and he stopped and dropped again to his knee, holding his breath and pricking his ears.

The sound came again—a man's raspy breath. A boot clipped a stone, sent it rattling.

"Shit!" the man rasped.

He seemed to be moving toward Yakima from down a southern offshoot of the wash that the half-breed was in. Yakima moved quickly forward and to his left, hugging that side of the wash until the mouth of the offshoot appeared only a few yards ahead. The man was still moving toward him, his footsteps growing louder—the thud and crunch of boots on gravel, the faint ching of spur rowels.

All the daylight had faded from the sky, but starlight revealed a man-shaped shadow moving out of the offshoot ahead of Yakima. The man wore a high-crowned black hat. Starlight winked off the barrel of the carbine in the man's hands, and off his spurs. He was a stocky, beefy hombre in a checked shirt, brown leather vest, and denim trousers.

Yakima raised his Yellowboy. "Stop but don't turn around, MacElvy."

The big man jerked with a start but did not turn around. "Drop that rifle."

MacElvy turned his head to one side. "That you, breed?"

"Drop the rifle."

"Christ!" MacElvy tossed the Winchester carbine into the brush to his left.

"Now the pistol belt."

Looking straight ahead, heavy shoulders rising and falling as he breathed, MacElvy said, "You got it wrong!"

"We'll discuss it when you're lighter by about four pounds, give or take an ounce."

With an air of frustration, cursing under his breath, Edgar MacElvy untied the holster thong from around his stout right thigh, unbuckled the cartridge belt, and tossed the rig into the brush.

"You got anything else?"

MacElvy sighed and lightened his load by a bowie knife and a .41-caliber pocket pistol, both of which he'd slipped out of boot sheaths and also tossed into the brush.

"Turn around," Yakima told him.

MacElvy did, canting his head to one side incredulously. "You just love givin' white men orders, don't ya? You gonna stick your gun up my ass?"

"I got a feelin' you'd enjoy it too much. What the hell was all the shootin' about? Where's the woman?"

"The shootin' was about an ambush I barely evaded. Fortunately, I'm a lot lighter on my feet than I'd appear to be, and I managed to run like hell before they could do to me what they did to Hilger."

"What happened to Hilger?"

"Gone to heaven . . . if he's lucky."

"The woman?"

"Probably wishin' she was with Hilger about now."

Yakima saw a dim umber glow up ahead a ways. "That your fire?"

"Yep."

"Move."

"Mind if I fetch my guns? I—"

"Yes."

Cursing, MacElvy walked on up the arroyo, boots crunching gravel. Yakima followed him up the shallow, left bank and over to where the remains of a fire glowed. A coffeepot hung from a steel tripod over the dull, red coals that were mostly black. The strong smell of scorched coffee tainted the air.

Yakima looked around. The blue-clad Bruno Hilger lay beyond the fire on his back, near a palo verde whose limbs overhung the arroyo. The albino had lost his hat. His ankles were crossed. Starlight shone in his pale, half-open eyes. His bloody hands lay palm open at his sides, and his lips were shaped with wonderment.

MacElvy was stumbling around in the brush on the other side of the fire. He cursed under his breath and came out of the brush, saying, "Horse is gone. Either they took him or run him off." He looked at the fire. "Coffee? Probably burned, but it's coffee just the same. You can have Bruno's share."

Yakima turned to face in the direction from which he'd come, and whistled loudly. MacElvy dropped to a knee beside the fire, lifted the pot with a hook, and swirled it. There was a faint sloshing sound, and seam hissed from the spout. "A little left. Probably strong enough to melt a banker's heart, but—"

"Yeah, it's coffee just the same."

MacElvy filled them each a cup and sat down on a rock near his strewn gear. Yakima sat on a log near the arroyo. He could hear Wolf coming at a fast walk.

He blew on the coffee, made a face at the burned leather smell of the scorched brew wafting up with the steam, and said,

"Let's start with you tellin' me why you grabbed the former Mrs. Clancy Brewer. Or should I save us time by answerin' my own question? You and Hilger are simply on the sniff for the stolen payroll money as, I assume, are whoever took Paloma out of your incapable hands?"

"Paloma, is it?" MacElvy grinned in the darkness. "Yeah, I suppose last night got you on a first-name basis with the *former* Mrs. Brewer. You sure worked that one fast. Shot her husband then diddled the poor grief-stricken widow seven ways from sundown. Shit, the whole town could hear you two goin' at it. Set the dogs to barkin' and the whores to lookin' all glum."

He laughed.

"Just answer the damn question before I shoot you in the foot, MacElvy."

"We figured after the way you two was makin' eyes at each other when me and Bruno left the saloon that she'd draw you into it. Yep, that's what she did, all right."

"How can you be so sure it wasn't love at first sight, you cynical bastard?"

"And, yeah, to answer your question, breed, we took her because we knew she knew where La Paz hid the stolen payroll money. But it ain't what you think."

Yakima sipped the coffee. It was strong, so bitter it made his tongue retreat to the back of his mouth, and bracing.

Wolf climbed the bank and came to a stop behind the half-breed, giving a snort as though to let his rider know he was there, as though his shod hooves couldn't have been heard on so quiet a night from a quarter mile away. "How ain't it? Were you two aimin' to spread the money around to the poor orphans of Old Mexico?"

"No, our intentions were not quite that noble," MacElvy said. "We were merely going to return it to its rightful owner, the United States government."

Yakima arched a brow. "For the reward?" He chuckled. "Don't try to make me believe you were going to do it simply because you're such good citizens."

"Hilger there's a lieutenant, just like his uniform says, in the US cavalry. Belongs to a special office that investigates payroll robberies out here on the wild frontier. He's a detective of sorts, I reckon. Or was, more like. Not only that, but he was married to the daughter of the territorial governor. Can you believe that?"

"Let me work on it."

"And I'm a deputy United States marshal. The head marshal made me throw in with poor dead Bruno there—before he was dead, of course—to investigate the robbery, locate and secure the stolen scrip and specie, return it to Fort Bryce, where it was headed when it was so rudely stolen on its way from Tucson, and bring to justice the dunderheads who stole it."

"I can believe almost anything. You bein' a marshal, MacElvy . . ." Yakima shook his head. "I can't believe that."

"Believe it. I'll show you my badge, if you promise not to shoot me while I'm reachin' into my back pocket."

"One-handed." Yakima aimed his rifle at MacElvy. "Anything else comes out of that pocket besides a badge, you'll be shovelin' coal in hell with Hilger."

MacElvy pulled out a flimsy, brown leather wallet with a badge of a deputy United States marshal pinned inside.

"You could have stolen that," Yakima said, narrowing a shrewd eye.

"Could have."

"All right, I believe you. These is sad times when the federal government is so hard up for badge toters that they let a fork-tongued, likkered-up old devil like you carry one. Kicked out of the army, no less."

"Takes a special sort to work out here in this dangerous

country, breed." MacElvy returned his wallet to his pocket and threw back the last of his coffee. "Now, you gonna let me retrieve my guns? Don't wanna be caught out here unarmed any longer than I have to be."

"How do I know you won't shoot me?"

"I'm a lawman!"

"You're gonna have to do better than that, MacElvy."

"All right—how's this? I know you were a scout out here for Fort Hell. A right good one, too. You were green back in them days, but you knew the lay of the land and how to track a man . . . even Apaches . . . across it. Like few others, save maybe the sergeant, old Gila River Joe." The sergeant had been Chief of Scouts back at Fort Hildebrandt, or Fort Hell as it was more commonly known, back when Yakima had been on the government payroll. "I need a tracker," MacElvy continued. "I'll pay you two dollars a day out of my own salary, and if we find the stolen payroll, I'll see to it that you're given a reward."

"How much?"

MacElvy spat to one side distastefully. "Five hundred dollars sound about right?"

"How much is in the payroll?"

"Damn near a hundred thousand. Silver certificates, gold and silver coins."

"I'd want at least a thousand for helpin' you retrieve a hundred thousand. Shit, that's only one percent."

MacElvy doffed his hat and ran a hand through his sweaty hair. "All right, goddamnit. Major Fitzgerald—he's the payroll master for the Arizona Division—he's a fair man. If I tell him I promised you one percent, he'll honor it. It is Apache country, after all."

Yakima knew he was giving the army a hell of a deal, but he didn't need any more than a thousand dollars. A thousand would get him through the winter all right, over in California, in a little village by the ocean. That's all he wanted. "Who took her?"

"I didn't see 'em. All I know is they were speakin' English without accents, so they weren't La Paz's bunch—the half of the gang he double-crossed after the robbery. Probably just fortune hunters. Plenty enough of 'em out here."

"And common thieves."

"Yay-up." MacElvy waited. "Will you do it?"

Yakima doffed his hat, ran his hand back through his long, black hair. Setting his hat back on his head, he turned to give the unlikely deputy US marshal a level stare. "Up north, I got law trouble."

"Federal or territorial?"

"County sheriff."

"I'll fix it."

Yakima didn't have to think about it. He needed the money, and it would be nice to have that sheriff off his trail. "All right."

"Ha!" MacElvy swiped his hat jubilantly across Yakima's shoulder, almost knocking him off the log he was sitting on. "Thanks, breed. You won't regret it."

"Yeah, right," Yakima said, dryly. It wasn't in his nature to not regret most of his actions. Or, maybe it was just that most of the actions he'd taken over the course of his nearly thirty years had just turned out to be so damned regrettable . . .

What would make him think things were going to change?

"I'm gonna fetch my shootin' irons," MacElvy said ebulliently, and stomped off away from the fire.

"You do that," Yakima grouched.

Behind the half-breed, Wolf reminded his rider of his presence by shoving his long, sleek snout up close to the back of Yakima's neck and giving a deep, uneasy whicker.

"Ah, shut up," Yakima said, and rose to unsaddle the beast. "When I want your advice, I'll ask for it—all right?" He draped a stirrup over his saddle and reached under the horse's belly for the latigo. "And I doubt that time's gonna be comin' any time soon."

CHAPTER 8

Yakima and MacElvy were up before dawn the next morning. They built a fire, and when they'd boiled coffee, the half-breed took a steaming cup of the brew as well as a handful of jerky, and walked a ways out from the camp.

By the gauzy, gray light of dawn, he cut the trail of Paloma's captors.

There were five horses. They'd ridden into Hilger's and MacElvy's camp from the southwest, and they'd left the same way, angling off to the south of the arroyo, in the brush of which quail and cactus wrens were piping.

There was nothing to distinguish any of the tracks—merely five shod horses moving fast across the flat stretch of gravelly, yucca- and greasewood-stippled desert south of the arroyo. Sometimes you'd see that one of the shoes was cracked or had some other flaw in it that would help you track the horse wearing it, but there was nothing like that here.

Judging by the age of some of the horse apples littering the area, the riders had been here a while before they'd attacked MacElvy and Hilger and taken the woman. They'd left the horses on a picket line, and five men in run-of-the-mill stockmen's boots had approached the camp on foot. They'd knelt in the dirt, concealed by brush and boulders, which meant they'd either been waiting for the right time to make their move, or they'd been eavesdropping on the trio's conversation.

They'd fired from a good distance away. Yakima found their

cartridge casings, over a dozen in all, scattered about thirty yards away from the fire.

MacElvy had said they'd just started shooting, and that's when he'd grabbed his rifle and run. The haphazard way they'd gone about their task told the half-breed they hadn't been professionals. Professionals would have gotten closer and shot surer.

Yakima just hoped no others riders obscured their trail. He wanted to catch up to Paloma. He knew it wasn't only because of the job or for the reward money that he wanted to catch up to her. He wanted to catch up to her for some other reason—some instinctive, primitive male reason. A hard, hot knot in the pit of his gut.

She was a killer—that was certain. She'd have killed Yakima for the same reason she'd killed La Paz. But she was a damned ravishing, hypnotic killer, and there was no denying his attraction to her. The frontier was hard on women. Damned hard. Who knew why she'd become what she'd become? He'd like to see that she wasn't tortured or raped, shot or stabbed, and dumped in an arroyo.

She was too much woman for that.

The sun was beginning to separate from the horizon when Yakima started back to the camp. He'd saddled Wolf, and the horse stood ground-tied near the fire that MacElvy had just kicked dirt on. MacElvy tossed away an airtight tin from which he'd been breakfasting, tucked his tin coffee cup into his saddlebags, and picked up his rifle.

"I cut their trail," Yakima said, approaching Wolf. "They're headed toward the mount . . ."

He let his voice trail off as the deputy US marshal loudly cocked his Winchester carbine and aimed the rifle at Yakima. "Sorry, breed. The deal's off. They must've taken my horse;

otherwise he'd be back by now. I'll be requiring the use of yours."

"Why, you double-crossin' son of a bitch," Yakima grated out, poking his hat brim back off his forehead.

MacElvy waved his rifle. "Step aside. Get over there by the tree."

"I knew I never should have trusted you."

"I'm truly sorry, breed. I meant to give you the job. Hell, I need a tracker. But I also need a horse. Ridin' double even on your stout stallion there, there's no way we'd get to that payroll strongbox ahead of the others lookin' for it. La Paz's former friends are likely combin' the whole western Chiricahuas about now."

Yakima was exasperated. "So you're just gonna take my horse. That's a hangin' offense—you realize that, don't you, MacElvy?"

"Not in this case. I'm confiscatin' this mount to fulfill my duty as a federal lawman. Like I said, I do apologize." Keeping the cocked carbine aimed at Yakima, MacElvy grabbed Wolf's reins. He winked at the half-breed. "Damn nice stallion, though. I'll be glad to have him."

The lawman stepped into the saddle. Wolf whickered, shook his head, whickered again.

"Come on, now, don't give me any trouble, black," the lawman warned.

Off-cocking his carbine's hammer, he rested the barrel across the pommel of Yakima's saddle, and neck-reined the wary horse around. "Good luck, breed!" he called, and ground his spurs into the stallion's flanks.

Wolf whinnied and loped off toward the west, following a well-worn path along the arroyo.

Yakima watched, grinning shrewdly. Then he stuck two fingers between his lips, and whistled. The black whinnied again, louder, stopped, dug his rear hooves into the ground, and lifted his head and front quarters high into the air, catching MacElvy completely by surprise.

The lawman gave an indignant cry as he dropped both his rifle as well as Wolf's reins, and tumbled backward off the mount's rear end. He turned a backward somersault over Wolf's tail and hit the ground with a dusty thud and the crunch and crackle of stiff, abused joints.

"*Oh . . . aah-ohhhh!*" the lawman cried, rolling around in agony while holding his left arm across his belly.

"Serves you right, ya damn fool. Wolf don't like to be ridden by no one else but me, and it don't take much for him to get shed of those he don't want on his back." Yakima grabbed Wolf's reins. "Besides, if you would have looked around, you would have seen your own horse wandered back some time ago."

He glanced to the north. A brown, bald-faced, blue-eyed gelding stood grazing on the far side of the arroyo, casually cropping wheatgrass. It wore only a hackamore from which its picket rope trailed.

"Shit." Sheepish, his joints crackling, MacElvy climbed to his feet.

Yakima didn't take it personally that the pugnacious MacElvy had tried to steal his horse. He knew the belligerent cuss would have done it to anybody. A thousand dollars was a thousand dollars, and he needed that county sheriff off his trail.

They rode together along the trail of the five bushwhackers. Yakima could tell which horse had been carrying both its first rider and Paloma by the slightly deeper indentation of its hooves in the desert sand. The riders had switched the girl to three different horses as they'd ridden between bluffs and mesas toward the southwest and the dark humps of the Chiricahuas.

They'd ridden through open desert, not letting the darkness of the previous night stop them. They'd probably figured that

MacElvy, having escaped their dry gulching, could be on their trail. Or maybe something else compelled them to ride so hard after dark. Yakima wondered if they'd learned the whereabouts of the loot from Paloma. They seemed to have been making a very purposeful, unwavering beeline for the Chiricahuas, and they'd stopped to rest their horses only twice before Yakima and the lawman nearly rode up on them.

The half-breed heard a sound on the breeze, and then he caught a whiff of wood smoke.

"Hold up," he told MacElvy, pulling back sharply on Wolf's reins.

MacElvy looked annoyed. "What the hell is it?"

"I think we found 'em."

MacElvy looked around, frowning. "I don't see nothin'."

"Tell you what," Yakima said, swinging down from his stallion's back. "If you learn to use *all* your senses instead of just your eyes, you might, just *might* live to retirement. And quit bein' in such a goddamn hurry. Life's short, MacElvy, and we're dead a long time."

The lawman dismounted with a grunt, the aches from his tumble from Wolf's back still grieving him as his indignation still plucked at him. "Christ, I'm trailin' with a dog-eatin' philosopher. Just my luck."

Yakima swung around, brought a haymaker up from his right hip, and watched the lawman drop like a hundred-pound crate falling from a freight wagon. Both horses sidestepped, whickering. Dust rose around the sprawled MacElvy, who groaned and winced against the dust, and cupped his left hand to his jaw. Blood oozed from an inch-long gash low on his left cheek.

"What the . . . what the *hell* . . . was *that* for?"

"You've eaten as many dogs as I have."

The lawman scowled up at him, working his jaw to check if it was broken. "Don't like bein' called a dog eater, huh?" He nodded, turning his mouth corners down. "All right. Fair enough."

Yakima slid his 1866 Winchester Yellowboy repeater from its saddle sheath and walked through a crease between high, steep bluffs. As he strode, holding the Winchester up high across his chest and looking around cautiously, sounds grew in the distance ahead of him. He frowned, trying to place them. It sounded like an Indian's war whoop. Or the imitation of one. A bad imitation, at that.

Ahead, the buttes leaned back away from him, the crease widening. Beyond lay a small, mud-brick cabin and a barn and two corrals of unpeeled pine poles. Smoke issued from the cabin's stone chimney. A low mesa with boulder-strewn slopes humped behind the place, casting its shadow over most of the yard from which the Apache-like war whoops were originating. Figures milled in the shade, obscured by it. One was moving more than the others.

An arroyo lay between the half-breed and what appeared to be a small ranch hunkered at the base of the mesa. There was plenty of brush lining both sides of the arroyo, offering cover, so Yakima dropped down into the ravine. As he crossed it, he heard footsteps and low grunts behind him.

He turned to see MacElvy dropping sideways into the wash behind him, boots sliding on the steep cutbank, his spurs rattling faintly. Anger burned between the half-breed's ears. He waved his arm, glaring, and pressed two fingers to his lips. MacElvy caught the look, and his face reddened sheepishly beneath the brim of his high-crowned, black hat.

The big, slope-shouldered lawman took pains to make his tread quieter as he followed Yakima across the arroyo. Wincing, MacElvy sort of hopped on the toes of his worn stockmen's boots. He and Yakima dropped to knees side by side, and stared through a thick screen of mesquites and over the beans and fine, slender leaves that had dropped from their branches, toward the small ranch yard.

The raucous howling was coming from a young man hopping Indian-style in a circle before the cabin. A short, lanky kid wearing only a beaded brown vest and black opera hat, with a necklace of what appeared animal teeth flopping across his chest, he was batting his hand against his mouth as he gave his Apache-like, ululating war cry, hopping from one foot to the other.

His schoolyard-style Indian dance rotated around a figure lying spread-eagle on the ground before him. The figure was Paloma Collado. Yakima recognized her without even a stitch of clothes on. In fact, he could probably recognize her better that way.

Her long black hair billowed on the ground around her head, which she lifted frequently to spat and growl and hurl Spanish epithets at the young man dancing around her. As she strained at the four stakes to which her wrists and ankles were tied, the round, cream globes of her breasts jostled against her chest. She shook her head back from her face, and called the kid the offspring of a promiscuous weasel.

The kid stopped suddenly and turned to one of the four other men sitting on the rough-hewn front porch of the cabin, and said, "Pa, can I diddle her? She's awfully purty! *Can I?*"

Chapter 9

"Damnit, no, you can't diddle that girl!" raked out a raspy-voiced man sitting back against the cabin's wall, farthest from the other three, all of whom were lounging with either a hip on the rail or sitting on the porch's front step.

They were all staring toward the kid and Paloma.

The man who'd spoken rose and moved to the top of the porch steps, where Yakima could get a better look at him. He was tall and lean, and he wore a suit vest over a hickory shirt, and baggy broadcloth trousers. He wore a bowler hat from beneath which curly gray hair tufted. His face appeared long, angular, and pale save for his nose, which was bright red.

He appeared to be in his late sixties, early seventies, and he was stooped slightly forward, as though his back had been broken and hadn't healed right.

"We didn't take her for no diddlin'!" he yelled. "She knows where that payroll money is, and I'll be damned if she won't tell us." The old man glanced at the sky. "Soon as the sun edges over her and starts burning down hot as a smithy's forge, she'll start yammerin' so's we won't be able to shut her up!"

The kid lowered his chin to stare longingly down at her. "I'll shut her up."

"Knute, you get away from there," the old man said, raising his voice until it cracked. "We aren't that kinda people! We don't ravage women!"

No, Yakima thought. *You just strip 'em and stake 'em out naked.*

"Rustlers," MacElvy said out the side of his mouth to Yakima. "Name's Vernon Nygaard and his boys. I been wonderin' where they hole up when they ain't rustlin' beef from the ranchers across the southern half of the territory, doctorin' the brands and sellin' it on the San Carlos Reservation. Vermin. But slippery vermin, for all that. They're killers, all five. That kid's worst of all. He's a cross-eyed little demon, and fast as greased lightnin' with them shootin' irons hangin' off his hips."

Yakima studied the other three sitting on the porch. The one sitting on the top step was whittling, one leg extended, the other leg curled beneath it. A yellow mutt was lying with its head between its paws on the bottom step. The other two men were sitting back against the cabin's adobe brick wall, arms crossed on their chests, staring hungrily toward the girl.

While he studied each man in turn, Yakima was thinking that they must have come upon MacElvy and Hilger's fire the night before, and thought maybe they'd gun the men for their horses and whatever else they had of value . . . including the woman. The old man might have seen himself above rape, but Yakima would have bet silver cartwheels to horse apples he wouldn't see himself above selling her to a top bidder. Out in the loneliest stretches of the territory or down in Mexico, many men would pay as much or even more for a woman than they would for a horse.

Especially as fine a woman as Paloma Collado.

The old man moved down off the porch, the dog getting up and moving away to sit in the yard, also staring toward the girl as though she were a meal it figured it might be indulging in later. Old Nygaard strolled in his bandy-legged way out to where the kid in the top hat stood staring down at Paloma like she was some wonderful toy in a store window.

Nygaard reached into his vest pocket, pulled out what appeared to be wedding cake tobacco and a knife. As he approached the woman, he sliced off a hunk of the wedding cake, and stuck it in his mouth.

"Honey, the sooner you tell us where that payroll money is, the sooner we'll let you go."

Paloma lifted her head, bent her knees, and spat up at the old man.

"That ain't no way for a purty young woman to act," said Nygaard. "You're only hurtin' yourself, see?"

The other three men—young men of various ages—were coming down off the porch now, grinning. The dog joined them to sniff around at Paloma's bare feet.

The old man dropped to a haunch beside the girl, holding his open knife over one of her breasts in casual threat.

"The sun's gonna be gettin' right hot. In fact, it's almost here, now." Nygaard glanced at the curved line of sunlight inching toward Paloma. "Save you a lotta time and trouble," he said, working the chaw around in his mouth, moistening it, "if you'd just tell us where it's at."

Paloma told him to go lie down with a horse.

The old man shook his head, scowling, and touched the point of the knife against her breast.

"Ahh!" Paloma said. *"Pig!"*

"How 'bout if I turn you over to my boys?"

"I thought you were not that kind of an hombre!"

"You got me thinking twice about that—surely, you have."

The tallest of the four young men said, "Let me whip her, Pa. I'll fetch a bullwhip from the barn, and whip her good. Then she'll tell us."

"Get on with ya, Luther," said the young man in the top hat, Knute. "Me . . . I'm gonna diddle the greaser bitch."

"How's that gonna make her do anything but laugh?" asked one of the young men wearing a billowy red neckerchief and holding a sawed-off, double-barreled shotgun in both hands, as though it were a security blanket.

The others laughed. They were standing in a semicircle around the girl, between her and the cabin. Knute was the only one with his back to the arroyo. Yakima thought that he and MacElvy could probably take them all down relatively quickly, standing as they were, but there was a good chance a bullet would hit Paloma.

Another, larger problem—the dog had stopped sniffing the girl's feet to stare toward where Yakima and the lawman were concealed in the mesquites at the arroyo's bank. The dog was sort of narrowing its eyes and working the black tip of its long, thick, white-mottled, yellow nose, as though it had scented the interlopers.

"Oh, shit . . . ," said MacElvy, taking the words out of Yakima's mouth.

"Come on, boys," the old man said, rising. "This girl here is just plain stubborn. Let's let her season out here in the sun for a while and then—"

The young man with the billowy red neckerchief said, "Pa—Rover sees somethin'." He took a long step to one side, tensing and raising his shotgun.

The others stared in the direction at which he was aiming his gut shredder and the dog was staring and sniffing, now whining deep in its throat. The old man had started walking back toward the cabin, but now he turned and shucked both of his Remington revolvers, clicking the hammers back.

"Shit," MacElvy said again.

The dog growled and started trotting toward the arroyo, holding its head down, its eyes dark and suspicious.

"Who's there?" the old man demanded as the rest of his brood stepped away from each other, all drawing at least one weapon. "Show yourselves!"

MacElvy jerked his carbine to his cheek and aimed down the barrel.

Yakima clamped his hand over the carbine's breech. "Hold on!"

MacElvy said, "Hold this!" and jerked his Winchester out of Yakima's grip, and the carbine roared. The dog, ten feet from the arroyo, yipped, wheeled, and ran away, its tail between its legs.

For five seconds, a funereal silence hung over the yard. Yakima turned to stare toward the four men spread out in a semicircle on the far side of the girl, and toward the kid standing between the arroyo and Paloma. All their eyes were on their father who stood statue-still, extending his pistols straight out in front of him.

Only, now those pistols began to sag. The old man's lips moved as he gasped and took a halting, stumbling step straight backward. He lowered his knobby chin to look down at the red stain growing on the front of his shirt, just left of his heart.

"Dirty bastards," Yakima heard him choke out. "Dirty, rotten bastards killed me, boys . . ."

"You stupid son of a bitch, MacElvy," Yakima said, aiming his Yellowboy repeater as the kid screamed, "Pa!" and the old man sat down as if he'd thought a chair had been behind him.

The others jerked their heads back to the arroyo, and the young man with the red neckerchief cut loose with his shotgun, spraying the ground a few feet in front of MacElvy with buckshot. Yakima drew a bead on the kid, and squeezed the Yellowboy's trigger. The shot sailed wide and thudded into a porch post as the kid, having obviously taken part in lead swaps before, threw himself to his left, and rolled, coming up onto his chest and cutting loose with the shotgun's second barrel.

The buckshot pelted the brush around Yakima and his lawman sidekick, snapping branches and shredding leaves. MacElvy cursed sharply and jerked his head back, wiping a hand across his face as though he'd been bee-stung. Yakima glimpsed smoke and flames lapping from the yard around the now loudly yelling Paloma, and pulled his head down beneath the bank as several bullets plumed dust from the bank's lip.

He crabbed several feet down the arroyo from where he'd been, snaked the Yellowboy up over the bank, picked out a target, and fired. This time he punched a bullet through the billowy red neckerchief, evoking a wild yowl from the kid with the shotgun, who'd tossed the gut shredder away and was hauling a Schofield out of a shoulder holster.

Yakima managed to drill the thigh of another Nygaard as the tall, lean kid in a striped shirt, suspenders, and armbands fanned a Colt Lightning toward the arroyo.

"*Ach!*" the kid screamed.

He fell, rolled several times, kicking up dust and cursing. He rolled onto his chest and lifted his head, firing another two rounds with his Lightning before Yakima took hasty aim and blew out the kid's right eye, turning the eyeball to instant paste. The kid's head jerked sharply back on his shoulders.

It jerked back again. As it slid forward, there was a hole in the forehead. The head fell abruptly onto its face and the kid lay quivering and rolling his head and shoulders from side to side, as if in vehement denial of his grisly fate.

Yakima glanced to his left. MacElvy had recovered from the barn blaster's pelting and was firing his carbine through the mesquite screen before him. He returned Yakima's glance, blood dripping from several pellet holes in his cheeks and chin and one in his forehead. He gave a sheepish hike of his left shoulder in acknowledgment of the unnecessary shot, and slid his gaze back toward the yard.

He held his fire.

Yakima did, as well.

The half-breed merely stared through his wafting powder smoke, looking for another target. Four of the five Nygaards were down. Only the shotgun kid was moving—writhing, cursing, and spitting blood while clutching his neck as though trying to strangle himself. Yakima drilled a bullet through the kid's forehead, putting him out of his misery, though the younker didn't deserve the favor.

Running footsteps and a shrill groan sounded, and Yakima saw the fifth Nygaard, who had long, red hair hanging down from a tan Sonora hat, run out from behind the cabin, limping and casting anxious gazes over his left shoulder. A pistol in his right hand, he ran up the gravelly, red slope at the base of the mesa, disappearing into the formation's shadow.

"There!" MacElvy said, triggering his carbine.

The bullet plumed red dust at the young hard case's heels as he disappeared into the mesa's dark-purple shadow.

"I got him."

Yakima scrambled up the wash, pushed through the brush, and paused to look down at Paloma, who was smiling up at him, showing all her fine, white teeth between wings of her blue-black hair. "Yakima," she said, brown eyes glinting ethereally in the morning sunshine that was now shining full on the ranch yard. "I knew you would come for me. Somehow, I knew . . ."

The half-breed sighed, dropped to a knee beside her, and couldn't help admiring her fine body, full in all the right places and jiggling to make a man's loins burn, as he slipped his Arkansas toothpick out of its sheath behind his neck and used the five inches of razor-edged Damascus steel to cut her loose.

Free, Paloma sat up and threw herself at him, trying to wrap her arms around his neck. Her breasts brushed against his calico shirt and bear-claw necklace before he shoved her aside, rose, stared down at her coldly, and said, "Best get some clothes on before the deputy United States marshal over there starts thinkin' you're a loose woman."

He glanced over at where MacElvy was just then pushing through the brush, growling like a wounded bear and dabbing at his blood-streaked face with a handkerchief. The half-breed didn't wait for Paloma's reaction to hearing the law was present, but jogged along the left side of the cabin and dropped to a knee at its rear corner, aiming his Yellowboy toward the mesa. There was a dark notch in what from a distance had looked like a solid sandstone wall. The fleeing Nygaard must have run into that notch. Yakima threw some lead at the gap, his slugs gouging chunks of sandstone from the wall on either side of it, and then sprinted up the steep, rock-strewn slope, keeping his eyes on the notch in case the kid poked a pistol out of it and started triggering lead.

At the top of the slope, Yakima pressed his right shoulder to the sandstone wall beside the gap, which was a good ten feet wide—a fissure that led into the mesa. He edged a look with one eye into the gap. The corridor between high, sandstone walls was empty. The sky over the corridor was cerulean blue, streaked with high, salmon and green clouds.

The empty corridor was edged in red shadows.

Yakima walked into it, holding his Yellowboy straight out from his right hip, taking one slow step at a time.

Ahead, the corridor curved slightly to the left.

A sound rose from up the notch. It sounded like a gurgling grunt. Then heels and spurs scuffed gravel.

Yakima took two quick steps forward and crouched, tightening his finger on the Winchester's trigger. He held fire. Down the red-shadowy corridor, a man was stumbling toward him. Yakima blinked. At least, it appeared to be a man. Hard to say for sure. It would have helped if the man had had a head on his shoulders. But this hombre had no such thing.

A headless man was stumbling, knock-kneed and heavy-footed, dragging the toes of his boots, toward Yakima. His bat-wing chaps buffeted around his legs, and the conchos trimming his belt winked in the sunlight angling into the shaft from above. Blood was oozing out the ragged neck, spurting and dripping and bubbling down the front of the man's collarless, pinstriped shirt and butterscotch leather vest.

Yakima crouched, staring, his wide eyes bulging in their sockets. As the headless man's knees buckled, something rose into the air from behind him. Something dark and round. Yakima jerked to the left, and the thing thumped onto the ground just ahead and to his right, between him and the head-less corpse that had just now fallen to its knees.

Yakima stared down at the young man's head capped in thick, wavy red hair curling down over the ears. Blood oozed out from the neck, where it had been dislodged from the corpse's shoulders. The face was pale and lightly freckled and there was a half-assed fringe of mustache mantling the upper lip and another fringe of goat beard drooping from the lightly freckled chin.

The pale blue eyes stared up at the half-breed in desperation, the large, black pupils slowly contracting as the eyes blinked once, twice, three, times and then lowered halfway and stopped. The eyes turned instantly to glass.

As the kid's body fell flat on its chest, jerking, an ear-rattling whoop rose behind it.

Yakima stared down the corridor to see the silhouette of an Apache backlit by a broader fissure into which sunlight spilled. Yakima could see the Chiricahua's long hair held back by a red flannel bandanna and the whang strings jostling down the sides of the brave's deerskin leggings. The young warrior jerked his right hand back behind his right ear, and another object came hurling toward Yakima, the wan, reddish light flickering off the wooden handle and feather-trimmed stone head of a war hatchet.

Yakima ducked.

The hatchet turned end over end in the air, whistling, and smashed into the sandstone wall behind the half-breed.

Warm blood had dripped from its head into Yakima's right eye, and he blinked to try to clear it, wincing, as he squeezed the Winchester's trigger. He brushed the blood from his eye with his sleeve, and pumped and fired the Yellowboy three more times, but only watched his bullets hammer dust from the wall where the Indian had been standing.

The brave's whoops and wicked yowls echoed shrilly as they dwindled off down the corridor and into the dense shadows beyond, the taps of his moccasin feet fading to silence.

Heart thudding, Yakima looked down at the headless corpse that was still moving its feet as though trying to run. The eyes in the severed head continued to stare up at Yakima with vague beseeching.

A voice was screaming inside the half-breed's head.

Apaches!

He brushed at the blood on his cheek, turned, and ran.

CHAPTER 10

When Yakima had gotten back to the yard, Paloma had pulled on her low-cut cambric dress printed with little yellow suns and moons, and donned her brown sombrero. She was on the ground, her wrists handcuffed behind her back. She was bellowing and throwing her head angrily to and fro as MacElvy sat on her legs, his back facing her, wrapping a rope around her ankles.

"Pig!" Paloma cried, trying to jerk her legs out from beneath the heavy man's weight. "Your mother was the puta pig of all puta pigs! You are feelthy and ugly and you smell *baaaaaddddd!*"

"No point in that!" Yakima said as he ran up to the pair, breathless.

"What do you mean there's no point?" MacElvy said, scowling up at the half-breed. "This little bitch knows where the payroll's at, and I'm not lettin' her out of my sight!" He looked down to knot the rope around Paloma's black, hand-tooled stockmen's boots, into the tops of which a bucking horse had been stitched in white thread. "You get that last Nygaard son of a bitch?"

"Nah, turned out I didn't have to."

MacElvy looked at Yakima again, who was glancing warily back in the direction from which he'd run. "Didn't *have* to?"

"An Apache did the dirty work for me. And believe me, it was dirty. Believe I'll be seein' those two eyes blinkin' up at me for a while, just as soon as I lay my head down on my saddle to go to sleep. We'd best pull our picket pins." Yakima stepped forward and, facing the arroyo, stuck two fingers in his mouth, and whistled for Wolf.

MacElvy had the southwesterner's understandably exaggerated reaction to the word "Apache."

He stood and faced Yakima, scowling, the nubs of his cheeks turning pale as though with frostbite though the sun was hammering down hot and hard on the dusty ranch yard. "What the *hell* are you talkin' about? You fall on your head?"

"Cut her loose," Yakima said, gesturing at Paloma's tied ankles. "She's gonna have to ride." He headed over to the corral in which the rustling family's horses were running in anxious circles, red dust rising thickly.

MacElvy didn't seem to understand—or to want to understand. "Cut her loose?"

"Cut her loose!"

By the time Yakima had roped and rigged a buckskin from the rustlers' string of no-doubt-stolen horses, and led it out into the yard by its bridle reins, Wolf was pushing up the arroyo bank and bulling through the brush, the lawman's horse hard on the black's heels, both mounts trailing their reins around the ground.

Yakima glanced toward the mesa, relieved to see no sign of Apaches heading toward them. Yet.

He'd only seen one. But Apaches were like rattlesnakes. When you saw one, you could bet the seed bull there was a whole nest of more somewhere close.

MacElvy had cut Paloma's ankles free and removed her cuffs. As he strode over to his horse, Yakima turned to Paloma, who stared up at him with a pouting look of grave injury. "Why did you have to go and bring a *lawman,* of all people? The treasure could be ours, Yakima!"

"Where is it?"

"Where is what?"

"The treasure!"

"You think I'll tell you now . . . after you brought *him*?"

Yakima glanced back toward the mesa. Still no Apaches. He had no doubt they'd be coming soon, however. Those who hadn't allowed themselves to be herded like cattle onto reservations were the wildest of the lot, and they tended to kill white men . . . and women . . . for sport.

There was no time to argue with the woman. He pulled her to her feet and lifted her onto the waiting buckskin. She cursed him and spit at him. Ignoring her, taking the buckskin's reins, he mounted Wolf. MacElvy rode up beside Yakima and grabbed the buckskin's reins out of his hand.

"I'll take those," he said, customarily belligerent. "Don't want you and her gettin' no ideas. You might decide to go dig that money up, just the two of you, and run off to Mexico and get hitched!"

"You smell bad, gringo lawman!" Paloma shouted, red-faced with fury.

"She's got you there, MacElvy," Yakima said with a wry chuckle and putting the steel to Wolf's flanks.

He and the horse bounded through brush and into the ravine. He wasn't sure which way to head, but as directly away from where he'd seen the Apache seemed the most sensible route, since he'd seen no sign of the others yet.

He followed the ravine on an angling course west for probably a mile, and then followed a game trail up out of the arroyo and headed south across the desert, the cholla, ocotillo, and occasional saguaros and palo verde trees standing tall around him, obscuring his view in every direction.

The Chiricahua Range stretched from left to right ahead of him, the left end closer than the right end. They were closer now, and their craggy peaks were velvety green with evergreen forests. The land before and around them was a rugged jumble of up-thrust rock, strewn boulders as large as cabins, and tabletop mesas large enough to hold a city the size of Denver.

Vast country. All Apache country. Chiricahua country. If he wasn't careful, he was liable to ride away from one group of broom-tailed, bronco warriors into another group. If he had any brains, he'd angle around the mountains and make a beeline for the border, leave MacElvy and Paloma to their own devices.

For some reason, he just couldn't do it. It wasn't just that he was woman-drunk. Seeing that Apache and the headless Nygaard boy had slapped him sober right quick. Now, he felt he was in too deep to just ride away. He'd started something, and he needed to ride it out—whatever *it* was.

He led MacElvy and Paloma to the top of a short, flat-topped bluff and halfway down the other side, to where a spring oozed water among rocks sheathed in sand grass and oak shrubs. They were climbing higher now, and the creosote brush was giving way to sagebrush, gooseberry, and wild rose. They weren't high enough to escape the stifling heat, however.

Yakima remembered this spring from the time, a couple of years ago, when he and his now-dead wife, Faith, had ridden here from their little ranch on the slopes of Mount Bailey to trap wild horses in the deep canyons flanking the Chiricahuas. Most southwesterners had a good memory for water, drawing clear maps in their minds.

Faith . . .

No, he wasn't going to start thinking about her now.

"I want some water!" Paloma said.

MacElvy glared at her. "Why don't you just talk a little louder so you'll bring them 'Paches right down on top of us?"

Paloma slipped down from her saddle and leaned far forward, flaring her nostrils at MacElvy. "You smeeellll baaaaad, lawman."

Yakima slipped his spyglass in its little hide pouch from his saddlebags, and walked back up the slope. Near the top of the bluff, he got down on his knees, doffed his hat, and raised the glass to his right eye, shielding the lens with his right hand to keep it from flashing in the sunlight.

He scanned the dun-colored corduroy country tufted with lime-green behind them, marked here and there with snaking, cream-colored watercourses, and interrupted by hulking sandstone or black volcanic dykes or mesa formations. He was looking for mare's tails of rising dust, but after he'd scanned the country for nearly five minutes, he saw nothing.

That didn't make him feel any better about their situation. When there was one Apache, there were always more, and he had to assume they were following him, because that was the only way you stayed on your toes and kept your head in *Apacheria*.

"Anything?" MacElvy said, just loudly enough for Yakima to hear. The lawman was sitting on a rock near the spring, keeping his rifle aimed at Paloma, who was sitting back and combing spring water through her hair with her fingers. Her sombrero was hooked over one upraised knee.

Yakima reduced the spyglass, donned his hat, and moved back down the slope. "Nothin'."

"You sure you saw an Apache?"

"Yeah, I've seen 'em before. I know what they look like."

"Don't get your dander up, breed. Uh . . ." MacElvy grinned sheepishly. His face was streaked with dried blood from the half dozen shotgun pellets he'd taken, and the little wounds were swelling. "I mean . . . Yakima. It's just that I ain't seen any on our trail since we left the rustlers' ranch, and, believe me, I been keepin' an eye out for 'em."

"They're back there, all right." Filling his hat at the spring, Yakima glanced at Paloma, who was cool toward him now, unwilling to meet his gaze. He said, "Enough screwin' around. Where's that payroll loot?"

She cursed him mildly in Spanish, smiling at him winningly.

Yakima set his water-filled hat down in front of Wolf. He scratched the back of his head, and said, "Wait a minute—he scribbled you a map. Yeah, I remember, he scribbled you out a map to the loot, La Paz did."

"No shit?" said MacElvy.

"You are both fools," Paloma said. "Do you think I have it on me?" She raised her hands. "I memorized it, tore it up, and tossed it to the wind."

"I don't think you had time to memorize it," Yakima said. "Where is it?"

"Hell, they had her staked out on the ground naked as a jaybird but a whole lot better lookin'," said MacElvy, narrowing a lusty eye at the woman. "If anyone would have found it, they would have found it."

"Did you like what you saw, old man?" Paloma asked him in that insouciant tone of hers.

"Yeah, I liked it just fine," MacElvy said. "I bet the breed here . . . uh, I mean *Yakima* here . . . liked it even better . . . back at your husband's hotel."

"I assure you he did," Paloma said.

Thumbs hooked in his pocket, one hip cocked, Yakima studied her comely figure barely concealed by the thin, dusty dress that hung low on her shoulders. "The Nygaards wouldn't have known to look for a map."

He stepped toward Paloma, who crossed her arms on her breasts. "Leave me alone. I told you—I don't have the map. I tore it up and . . ."

"I know, threw it to the wind." Yakima knelt beside her and lifted her skirt high up and away from her left leg. "I think you're a liar. I think you still got it on you . . . where?"

"Stop!" she insisted, tugging at the dress.

Yakima lifted her dress up her legs, inspecting the hem. He brusquely rolled her onto her belly, holding the skirt up high. She wasn't wearing a stitch of underwear except a thin pair of silk panties. The panties weren't large enough to house a map—they were so insubstantial, in fact, that he could have wadded them up in his mouth and still have had room to chew a full meal—but she might have an inside pocket in her dress . . .

Paloma cursed him and punched and kicked her black boots at Yakima, who, ignoring the pummeling, thoroughly inspected the dress and the woman's naked body underneath it. MacElvy howled. When he'd given the dress a good going-over, the half-breed left her cursing, belly-down on the ground, dust wafting around her, and grabbed her hat.

She reached for the sombrero. "Pig, give me that!"

Yakima pulled it away from her, and rose. He looked inside the low-crowned sombrero. Inside the brim was a thin, leather pocket. He slipped his index finger and thumb into the pocket and pulled out a neatly folded scrap of notepaper.

"You are the child of a whore!" Paloma spat out at him, rising, her dress hanging down off one arm and revealing nearly all of her beautiful left breast. "Give me that! It is no business of yours! It is between me and La Paz!"

MacElvy grabbed her around the waist and, laughing, spun her around. "You're a foxy little thing, Miss Paloma!"

While the lawman held the raging woman, Yakima inspected the map hastily drawn in pencil. It had been drawn for someone who knew the country, for it wasn't very detailed. There was one detail that caught the half-breed's eye, however. He didn't recognize it right away, but when he realized what the mark signified in relation to the other marks around it, he lowered the map and scowled off to the southwest.

Toward where a broad shoulder of the Chiricahuas humped

darkly, broodingly against the brassy sky, striped with cloud shadows.

"Ah, shit."

"What is it?" MacElvy said.

Paloma suddenly grew silent in defeat. She stared at Yakima, hard-eyed, jaws like stone, the hot breeze sliding her hair around her shoulders.

"Why?" Yakima said, staring into the southwestern distance. "Of all the goddamn places in the Chiricahuas he could have hid that loot, why in hell did he have to hide it *there*?"

CHAPTER 11

"So . . . where'd he hide it? What's on the damn map?"

MacElvy sounded a little reluctant to ask the question. Now it came, an hour after Yakima had voiced his dismay at the loot's location.

They'd ridden up into cooler, fresher country—pine country. Lodgepoles and firs towered around them, silhouetted against the bright sunlight pouring like liquid brass through the canopy in which squirrels chittered, blackbirds cawed, and nuthatches and chickadees peeped.

The tang of pine resin was so strong it nearly took the half-breed's breath away at times.

Yakima was riding at the head of the three-person line, Paloma riding behind him, MacElvy bringing up the rear, holding his carbine butt up on his right thigh.

"It's an old stone line shack beside a pretty creek bubbling down out of the higher reaches. A damn pretty place."

MacElvy said with gentle probing, "I take it you been there before?"

"Yep."

They continued riding along at a moderately slow, even pace, climbing a long, gentle grade through the pine forest, occasional basalt escarpments humping up around them. High overhead, a hawk was hunting, giving its ratcheting screech. Sometimes pinecones tumbled to the forest floor with quiet thuds, and the breeze rustled the boughs, the cool air drying the sweat on

Yakima's face.

"This ain't a place you care to go back to," MacElvy said after a while, with the same halting prodding as before.

Yakima pulled back on Wolf's reins, curveted the horse, and glared back at the broad-shouldered, round-bellied lawman riding up from about forty yards away, beyond Paloma on her buckskin. Both the other two riders stopped when they saw the hard look in the half-breed's eyes.

"Let's just leave it at that, MacElvy."

The lawman studied him for a time. So did Paloma.

Finally, MacElvy rolled a rounded shoulder, smiled, and said, "Okay. All right. Just curious, is all."

"Yakima." Paloma pulled the buckskin up to within ten feet of the half-breed. Her eyes were round and soft. She hadn't called him anything but a pig since he'd rescued her from the rustlers' ranch, so this was a change. "You know there is almost a hundred thousand dollars in gold, silver, and paper money in that box."

"That's what I hear."

"If you shoot this man, this so-called *lawman,* it can all be ours."

"Hey, now," MacElvy objected.

"He is not even a lawman," Paloma said, wrinkling her nose at him. "He calls himself one, but everyone knows he is an outlaw. He stole that badge from the deputy United States marshal he killed. Everyone knows that, too, but no one says anything because they are afraid of him. He runs with no gang, but he is a killer. A shootist. A regulator. If someone wants somebody dead, and they have enough money to hire it done, they hire him to do it."

"Well, now, listen to this," MacElvy said, laughing. "That's pretty damn good. You must've been concocting that story for a time now. That's why you been so damn quiet. Been runnin' your brain instead of your mouth for a change. That lie ran pure as rainwater off your devilish little tongue, senorita."

MacElvy caught Yakima studying him, and he opened and closed his gloved hand around the breech of his carbine.

"Don't make the mistake of falling for that, now, bre . . . uh, Yakima. She's pretty, and I'm sure you had a good time in the sack with the lyin' little trollop, but lyin' little trollop is just exactly what she is."

Paloma stared at Yakima, her wide, dark-brown eyes deep with desperation. "Once he gets his hands on that money, he's going to kill you. And then he'll kill me"—she turned to stare in repugnance at the beefy lawman—"after he's done what he's been imagining doing to me, that is." She shuddered. "The thought sickens me. I'd rather lie with *javelinas.*"

Yakima said, "That how it is, MacElvy? She's right—you could have taken that badge off any old dead lawman's corpse. There's probably more dead lawmen in these parts than livin' ones."

MacElvy pointed with the hand holding his reins. "Don't you fall for it, breed. She'd like nothin' more than to get you an' me crossways!"

"Maybe we're already crossways," Yakima said. "And I just don't know it."

MacElvy booted his horse up slowly toward the half-breed. He glowered at the girl and turned back to Yakima. "She's a liar. Plain and simple. Remember how she poisoned her beloved Octavio?"

"You are the liar," Paloma said in a hard, quiet voice. "You are a lying pig. Yakima, I swear on my mother's grave . . . on the grave of—"

"Octavio's grave?" said MacElvy, laughing.

"Shut up, pig! I swear on the grave of *mi padre.* He is lying. Sure as we are sitting here now, he will shoot us both as soon as he gets his hands on that strongbox."

MacElvy's face turned the red of Arizona sandstone as he jutted his jaws at Paloma. "You know what I'm going to do to you, you little—?"

"All right, all right," Yakima said. "This is gettin' us nowhere. Let's get on up to the shack before the sun goes down. We got another hour of easy ridin' left. MacElvy, I'd appreciate it if you rode up here next to me instead of behind me, like you been doin'."

"Ah, shit," the lawman complained, shaking his head and glaring at the woman.

Paloma curled one side of her upper lip, pleased with herself.

"All right, all right—we'll ride together," MacElvy said, putting his dun up beside Yakima. "But she rides ahead, then, where I can keep an eye on her. She's under arrest."

"For what?" Yakima asked. "She hasn't done anything yet except poison a known outlaw."

"I'll think of somethin'."

"You smell baaad, outlaw," Paloma said, leaning forward in her saddle and slitting her eyes maliciously.

"And that's enough out of you about how he smells," Yakima reprimanded her. "I think we can all agree he doesn't smell like no poppy field in May, but I'm tired of hearin' about it. In fact, I'm tired of this whole damn thing."

MacElvy extended his gloved hand. "Why don't you just give me the map and ride away, then? We're close enough now I can find it on my own. And if there were any Apaches on our trail, we'd have seen 'em by now."

"Ha!" Paloma said. "I'd be feeding the cougars by sunset!"

MacElvy slitted one eye at Yakima. "You know, if it makes you feel any better, I can't trust you any more than you can trust me. She's made you one right enticin' offer. Her and a hundred thousand dollars. Boy, you two could have a right wonderful time with all that loot! Why, you could move to San Francisco and buy you a big fancy house, lounge around in silk pajamas, and never have to work another day in your life."

"I know—it does sound good," Yakima said, rubbing his chin. "I've never had me no silk pajamas. Let's get movin'. Paloma, get up there. And, you, MacElvy, I'd just as soon you stowed that carbine in your saddle boot. If you haul it out for no good reason that I can see, you're gonna look mighty funny with it sticking out your hind end."

MacElvy slid the Winchester into the saddle boot. "You got a thing about stickin' firearms up men's asses."

Yakima winked. "I do, at that."

As the three started off once more, moving through the pine-fragrant, sun-dappled forest, the beefy lawman spat, sighed, and shook his head. "Now, this is a shame. You've gone and let this little Mexican trollop sour what I was startin' to think was a nice little partnership." He spat. "Damn shame."

Around an hour later, they rode up into a little clearing on the shoulder of a mountain that overlooked the vast, dun stretch of the desert from which they'd just come. It was rocky here, and the rocks seemed to sprout pine and fir trees. This was on the mountain's western edge, and the angling sun stretched long tree and escarpment shadows, so that the hovel was almost hidden in a niche in the rocks and trees.

An eagle was perched on the house's steeply pitched roof thatched with pine boughs. There were no shutters over the windows, and no door, and the cavities stared out on the clearing like the empty eye sockets of a bleached skull. The eagle watched the three riders draw near—the two men riding side by side, following the woman.

When the group was fifty yards from the shack, the eagle spread its large ungainly wings, launched itself with its blacktaloned feet, and made a creaking, whooshing sound as it flew up and over the interlopers. The wind ruffling its brown feathers, it gave an indignant screech as it topped the pines with a whoosh and disappeared against the dark green of the late afternoon sky arching like a vast bowl over the craggy peaks of the Chiricahuas.

Yakima reined Wolf up in front of the shack. He pushed away the memories that threatened to wrap themselves around him like slithering snakes, and instead inspected the shack objectively, making sure no one else was here.

Hearing and seeing nothing but blackbirds cawing in the pine boughs, he turned to MacElvy regarding him expectantly. The man said nothing. He stretched an eager half-smile, and arched a brow. Paloma dismounted and stood holding her buckskin's reins, an oblique look in her dark eyes.

Yakima swung down from Wolf's back, dropped the reins, and fished the hastily scrawled map out of his pocket, wrinkling his brows as he inspected it. He grimaced, gave the scrap of notepaper to the wind, which sent it sailing off across the gravelly, rocky ground toward the tan desert stretching off to the west.

"Map just indicates the cabin," he said, looking around. "Doesn't say exactly where La Paz stowed the loot." He doffed his hat, ran his elbow around the sweatband, soaking the sweat up with his shirtsleeve, then stuffed the hat back on his head. "Let's take a look around."

MacElvy and Paloma silently dogging his steps, he inspected the inside of the shack. Save for pine needles and cones and windblown leaves and a couple of pack-rat nests and spiderwebs, the three-room shack was as empty as a cave. He brushed past the lawman and Paloma and went out to stand just outside the shack's door, on the sunken, badly worn patch of ground fronting it.

He'd figured the place had been a line shack for some old *ha-ciendado* who'd run a *hacienda* in the area and maybe still did. When he and Faith had spent time up here, corralling wild horses to take back to their ranch on the slopes of Mount Bailey farther north, he'd imagined the old vaqueros who'd taken up residence here from time to time, and all the Mexican tobacco they'd no doubt smoked, wearing away the ground in front of the door.

Then he remembered . . .

His face brightening speculatively, he swung to his right.

"Hey, where you goin'?" MacElvy asked suspiciously behind him.

Yakima walked around the north side of the shack to the back. MacElvy and Paloma followed him, MacElvy striding quickly, scowling. Yakima dropped to a knee at the back wall of the shack, and studied the ground. Slowly, he smiled.

"It's here, all right."

"Where?"

Yakima used his gloved right hand to smooth away the thin skin of dirt and pine needles that had been tossed a little too carefully over the area, to reveal several halved pine logs.

"I left these exposed," he said, "last time I was here. Other pilgrims probably used this hole for the same thing we did."

"Root cellar?" asked MacElvy.

"Of sorts."

"Well, let's have a look at it."

The lawman jerked his trousers up his broad thighs, and knelt with a grunt on the opposite side of the halved logs from Yakima. The logs were about four feet long. Both men pried them up with their fingers, and tossed them aside. They stared down into the four-feet-deep hole that was roughly four feet square.

Neither said anything. They just stared down at the wooden

box banded with rusty steel and lightly dusted with dirt and pine needles. There was a padlock on the hasp but the lock was open. There were two ragged-edged bullet holes through the front of the lock.

Obviously, the box hadn't been in the hole for more than a few weeks.

"Well, it ain't gonna just come floatin' up out of there on its own," MacElvy said, grunting as he lowered his right arm into the hole. "Help me, here!"

"Hold on." Yakima was staring into the breeze-brushed pines and pale rocks and boulders beyond the shack's rear, up along a storybook stream that trickled down the mountain to jog a curving course along its base.

MacElvy turned to follow his gaze. "What is it?"

A fir bough moved. To the left of that bough, a pinecone dropped from another one, landed with a soft thud on the slight incline, and rolled several feet to plop into a small, dark bend in the stream.

"Thought I heard somethin'."

"What?"

Slowly, Yakima rose, staring into the trees and rocks near the trickling water, and unsnapped the keeper thong from over the hammer of his holstered Colt. He wished he had his Yellowboy, but he'd left it on his horse. He glanced at Paloma who stood just off the corner of the shack, staring into the forest, her eyes apprehensive, the breeze tussling her hair and nipping at her dress.

Yakima drew his Colt and walked over to the edge of the trees, staring up the incline amongst the trees and escarpments, the tang of pine and warm forest duff heavy in his nose. He saw nothing but the trees and the moving branches, a squirrel flicking its upraised tail as it scolded him from a juniper farther up the slope.

"I don't see nothin'," said MacElvy, who'd come up to stand beside him, the lawman holding his own Remington .44 down low by his right thigh. "But now you got me wonderin' about Apaches. Sure wouldn't want to get caught in this clearing with twenty, thirty of 'em movin' around us."

Yakima stared up the slope for another minute.

"Musta been my imagination," he said, returning the Colt to its holster.

"Seein' one Apache will make you see more even when there ain't more to be seen. Come on—let's get that box up outta that hole!"

"Yeah," Yakima said, reluctantly giving his back to the slope and following the lawman back toward the strongbox. "I reckon."

CHAPTER 12

Yakima took one end of the box and MacElvy took the other
end, and they pulled it up out of the hole, cursing and grunting
with the effort. The lawman turned the box toward him, his
eyes so wide that Yakima thought they'd pop out of their sockets,
and removed the padlock from the hasp. He opened the creaky
lid.

"Hol-leee . . . !"

Yakima glanced around the side of the box to see inside.
There were wads of greenbacks and canvas pouches that no
doubt contained gold and silver.

MacElvy laughed and pulled out one of the packets of scrip
with one hand, a coin pouch with the other hand. He hefted
both. The coins rattled. "Damn near one hundred thousand
dollars!"

"You could go a long way on that much money, Marshal."
Yakima glanced at Paloma who, inexplicably, had not reacted to
the finding of the strongbox or the money inside it. In fact, now
she merely turned and walked back around toward the front of
the shack.

Yakima turned back to MacElvy and said, "That is what you
are, right, MacElvy?" After all they'd been through to locate the
strongbox, he wanted the reward money he'd been promised.
He'd be damned if he was going to let the lawman—if that's
what he really was—abscond with the goods. He would let
himself be taken for no fool. When a woman did—that was one

thing. But he didn't want a man doing it.

MacElvy looked at Yakima from beneath his bushy brows, and pursed his lips. "Ah, that's a shame—you believin' that girl's lies. Just a shame. Of course I'm a lawman, and I'll be headin' out first thing in the mornin'—takin' it back to Fort Bryce."

"*We'll* be headin' back to Bryce," Yakima corrected him.

MacElvy was putting the money back into the strongbox. "Yeah, yeah—I meant 'we.' Of course, that's what I meant. Take an end, will ya?"

They carried the box back around to the front of the shack. They set the box down by the front door, the lawman saying, "I reckon here's a good a place to stow it as any. We'll bivouac right here in the front yard, where we can both keep an eye on it." He chuckled.

"Sounds right by me . . . Marshal," Yakima said, giving the man another suspicious look. MacElvy had seemed a little too pleased about finding all that *dinero*. *Outlaw*-pleased as opposed to *lawman*-pleased.

MacElvy looked at him, breathing hard from exertion, and mopped his neckerchief across his face pocked and swollen from the opera-hatted kid's buckshot. "Shame," he said, wagging his head sadly again. "Damn shame." He frowned as he looked out across the clearing. Paloma was walking out there, heading toward an escarpment at the edge of the mountain that offered a view of the desert below, out beyond the foothills. "Look there," he said. "Looks awful sad, don't she?"

She did look sad, Yakima thought. He supposed he'd feel sad, too, if he went to all the work she'd gone to for a hundred thousand dollars and gotten it swiped out from under her. He didn't feel too badly for her, though. She'd done nothing to give MacElvy cause to arrest her, so she was a free woman. A free *poor, widowed* woman, but a free woman, just the same.

A haunted feeling came over him again, and he moved to a corner of the shack, staring up the slope he'd felt compelled to investigate a few minutes ago. Hair bristled at the back of his neck—an old, cautionary sensation, one he'd done well to heed in the past. He had a feeling the Apaches had followed them, after all.

Why they didn't strike, he didn't know. Maybe they were waiting till sundown though most Apaches in general did not like to wage war at night.

But maybe they thought that taking down only two men and one woman wouldn't really be much of a war.

Damn funny, though, that they hadn't shown themselves by now.

Maybe MacElvy had been right. Maybe seeing that one Apache had caused the half-breed to have Apaches on the brain. He'd be damned, though, if he didn't feel someone watching from the forest.

He went back and stripped his gear off Wolf. He had an urge to get the hell out of that little clearing, but the sun would be down in an hour and the cabin, even without shutters over the windows, would probably offer as much protection as anyplace else.

He'd sleep outside where he could keep an eye on things.

He tossed his gear down in front of the cabin. He stripped the gear off Paloma's mount, as well, and tossed it down near his and MacElvy's. He fed and watered Wolf and then gave the horse a thorough rubdown with a scrap of burlap. MacElvy was doing the same to his brown gelding, looking mighty pleased with himself over the loot. That made the half-breed uneasy. The lawman just looked too damned pleased, as though he had every intention of keeping the money for himself.

When he'd inspected all of Wolf's hooves, pulling a couple of cactus thorns out of the frogs, Yakima picketed the mount on a rope line that MacElvy had strung between two gnarled cedars, near a pool in the stream that ran down the mountain.

Then he tramped off to join the lawman in collecting firewood.

As he did, he kept looking around for suspicious movement around the canyon that was growing darker and darker, and quieter and quieter. From time to time he looked off to where Paloma sat in the rocks overlooking the desert, which was pink and salmon now as the sun tumbled behind the Dragoons in the northwest, its long shadows growing.

She looked so glum about losing the strongbox that Yakima almost felt sorry for her. At the same time, he knew she'd just as easily have poisoned him as La Paz, if he'd been in La Paz's position. Drinking snakeroot was about the same as drinking lye—a hard way to die. Not that he felt much sympathy for La Paz, however.

When it was nearly dark, she came over to the camp and accepted a cup of coffee from Yakima. MacElvy was in a celebratory mood. While they boiled a pot of beans to which Yakima had added the jerky remaining in his food pouch, the lawman shared his whiskey with his campmates, adding a splash to the coffee of each.

Yakima ate a bowl of beans and sipped the coffee laced with bourbon and tried not to let the fire compromise his night vision, as he wanted to keep his eyes skinned for possible Apaches stealing down from the surrounding ridges. Or for whoever might be on the lurk up there.

"How 'bout a game of cards?" MacElvy asked after they'd all eaten and cleaned their plates at the stream, and Yakima had checked the horses.

Paloma shook her head and rolled up in her blankets, turning onto her side and resting her head against the underside of her saddle.

"Yakima?" MacElvy asked.

"Nah, think I'll get a little shut-eye," the half-breed said, pulling his hat brim down over his eyes as he too reclined against his saddle.

MacElvy chuckled as, lying on one hip on his blanket roll, he began laying out a game of solitaire. "Shit, you ain't gonna sleep a wink."

"How's that?"

"You got your neck up over me and 'Paches. Me—I ain't worried. If 'Paches were near, that horse of mine would be goin' wild. He'd pull them cedars he's tied to plum out of the ground!"

Yakima glanced at where both horses lay in black humps beyond the cabin and near the base of the ridge, where the little stream curved. MacElvy had a point. Wolf would be kicking up a Texas-sized twister, too, if he so much as whiffed an Apache, and he could wind an Apache from a quarter mile away.

"All right," Yakima said, pulling his hat brim down over his eyes for a second time. "Maybe I'll catch my forty winks, after all, MacElvy. Thanks for putting my mind to rest."

"Shit, you still ain't gonna sleep."

Yakima grunted in frustration, and poked his hat back up off his forehead again. "Somethin' on your mind?"

The lawman snapped a pasteboard down onto another card and grinned with one side of his mouth, the firelight playing over his broad, shot-pocked face in need of a shave. In the guttering firelight, the pores in his skin as well as the swollen pellet wounds looked large and dark, giving him a menacing aspect. The hollows of his eyes were also dark, though the eyes themselves were tiny red dots beneath his hat brim.

"You're gonna be worried I'll gun you in the night and run off with the loot." He chuckled and shook his head. "Shit, you ain't gonna sleep a wink."

Yakima turned up his left cheek with a burn of annoyance. The former-sergeant-turned-lawman hadn't changed one stripe over the years. He was still as much fun to have around as a hydrophobic boar hog. "Yeah, well, you're gonna be thinkin' the same thing about me, so don't get all high-hatted about it."

MacElvy's dark nostrils flared, the orange firelight playing over his big nose. "Yeah . . . well . . . keep in mind, even if I should nod off, I'm a light sleeper. And I can *smell* a man aimin' a gun at me!" He turned his head slightly toward where Paloma lay soundlessly beneath her blankets, her back to the fire. "Women."

MacElvy had been right. Yakima couldn't sleep despite being sleepy. He'd nod off and just begin to feel the warm, soothing arms of slumber wrap around him before an image floated up through that murky warmth. It was MacElvy's devil face, eyes flashing wickedly, grinning, as he raised his cocked Remington.

Then Yakima would jerk his head up with a grunt, reaching for his own pistol and shooting a fearful look across the umber coals of the near-dead fire toward where MacElvy lay mounded inside his own soogan.

MacElvy had been right about Yakima's sleepless night. But Yakima had been wrong about MacElvy's. The big, pugnacious lawman seemed to be sleeping just fine, his chin rising and falling as he snored luxuriously, making raspy whistling sounds with each exhalation.

"Son of a bitch," Yakima muttered, and tossed his blanket back.

He rose to his knees and cast a glance toward where both horses still lay as before, sound asleep. Obviously, there were no Apaches in the area.

That was good. But Yakima felt an almost undeniable urge to trigger his pistol into the air and give MacElvy something to think about. The only reason he didn't was because he didn't want to wake Paloma. No need for that.

He heaved himself to his feet, pulled on his moccasins, wrapped his Colt and shell belt around his waist, and stomped off into the clearing beyond the cabin. There was no moon, but there were so many stars that the clearing seemed to glow as though from a pearl light emanating from the ground. He could see every sage clump and hackberry shrub.

A lone owl hooted somewhere on the ridge to his right. Far off across the dark desert stretching away to the west, a couple of coyotes were holding a wild conversation though it was barely a murmur up here on this stony mountain shoulder.

He climbed to a perch in the rocks overlooking the desert that was a soft tan in the darkness below and beyond. When he'd waggled his big body into a comfortable position against the rough escarpment wall behind him, he dug his makings sack from his shirt pocket. He paused, weighing the sack in his hand. Might be foolish smoking out here, but if there were Apaches around, he'd likely know by now.

Damned stupid, him getting hooked on tobacco. He'd gotten started smoking as well as drinking back at Fort Hell, when he'd been a contract scout. It had been his way of trying to fit in with others, though he'd been a fool to think he could ever fit in anywhere. Now, he just had some bad habits. His habit of imbibing in strong spirits had left a swath of broken-up saloons and jail time in his wake.

He rolled the quirley tightly with his thick fingers, sealed it closed, returned the pouch to his shirt pocket, and thumbed a lucifer to life, holding the flame down behind a finger of rock jutting to his right. He inhaled deeply on the slightly stale Durham, which he'd been carrying since he'd left Cheyenne several months ago, and sat back against the stone wall.

He smelled her first.

The pleasant sweetness of nearly ripe chokecherries mixed with the primitive musk of woman. There was a footfall, and then her voice: "Yakima? It's me."

He remained sitting there, smoking, until he saw her shadow move in the starlit darkness to his left. She stood there for a time, looking down at him. At least, he thought she was looking at him. Her face was silhouetted against the starry sky above and behind her. The starlight flickered in her black hair.

"You couldn't sleep," she said.

"Restless, I reckon. That's all right. I thought I'd nod off a few times out here, after I had a smoke." He paused. When she didn't say anything, he said, "What about you? I thought you were asleep."

"With you waking up every ten minutes and reaching for your pistol? With that outlaw snoring like a bear in a cave?"

Yakima gave a wry chuff, blowing smoke into the darkness through his nostrils. "He really an outlaw?"

"Yes."

"Well, then I reckon I'd best keep an eye on him." Yakima narrowed an eye. "Or I reckon I could just shoot him. He's so sound asleep I doubt he even stirred when I left the camp."

"You could." She lifted her skirt and dropped to her knees beside him. "But why bother?"

She leaned toward him, and then she was in his arms, and her warm, moist lips were pressed against his.

CHAPTER 13

She kissed him hungrily, poking her tongue into his mouth, entangling it with his. He felt her breasts against his chest, the nipples pebbling behind the thin cambric. Despite the thundering in his loins, he placed his hands on both sides of her head, and pushed her back, holding her there.

He stared at her, not saying anything, wondering through the fog of his desire what game she was laying out now. Her dark eyes were indecipherable. He knew one thing—he'd never want to play poker with her.

He chuckled, ran his fingers down through her long, coarse, straight hair, and rested his hands on slender shoulders. "All right," he said. "Go ahead."

"Go ahead with what?" she said, and he could see her brows ridge in the starlight. She placed a warm hand on his thigh.

"With what you're doing out here."

She lifted her hands toward his face, and he jerked with a start, grabbing both her wrists. He raised them to where he could get a look at them. In neither hand was a weapon.

He frowned, surprised.

She smiled a little sheepishly, shrugged and then turned and lay back against him, drawing his right arm around her, holding his hand in both of hers against her belly, gently caressing it with the backs of her fingers. "No tricks tonight, amigo. I came out here because I couldn't go back to sleep after you left."

"No tricks . . . Well, I'll be damned." He liked how she felt, leaning back against him, her warmth sliding into him, relieving his apprehension. "And the money?"

"Oddly, I care nothing about it anymore. Let MacElvy, whoever and whatever he is, have it."

Yakima craned his head to look at her, skeptical. "Why the change of heart?"

"I don't know. Why do you suppose? Maybe my heart has changed because it has been taken."

"Forgive my skepticism, Paloma."

She turned around, her face only inches from his, and sandwiched his head in her hands. "Tell me about the woman who has so marked this place for you, *mi amor.*"

Very gently, she pressed her lips to his and then pulled her face back slightly. "Tell me."

"Faith," he said. But it was almost like he hadn't said it. It was as though her name was always on the tip of his tongue, ready to slide out with the slightest nudge on his next breath. "She was my wife. A former workin' girl. Former whore. We weren't together long. But I loved her. Still do. Always will."

Paloma's dark eyes, inches from his, waited for him to continue. Her breath was a soft, easy rasp. Her breath caressed his chin. She was warm and pliant against him.

Yakima looked around her toward the night-cloaked desert. "Met her up in Colorado, took her away from her pimp, Bill Thornton. Thornton was right proprietary. He didn't like that. Didn't like a man, especially a breed, makin' off with his property. His men chased us. Makin' a long story short, we fought 'em off, came down here, Faith and I. Built up a ranch. Trapped wild horses in a canyon near here. Gentled 'em, sold 'em to the cavalry. The next year, Thornton's bounty hunters sniffed us out. They took Faith back up to Colorado, so Thornton could have the satisfaction of killin' her himself. I chased 'em but couldn't catch up to 'em until there was only about two breaths of life left in Faith. She died in my arms. But only after she'd killed Thornton"—he ground his teeth in remembered rage—"and burned him up in his saloon."

Yakima drew a deep, rattling breath, feeling moisture in his eyes. "I brought her back down here, buried her on our ranch." He looked at Paloma. "She's dust now. Just dust. Still, she's as real to me as you are, sittin' here tonight."

"You must have many fond memories of your time here, in the little shack, eh?" Paloma curled her lip insinuatingly.

Yakima smiled, remembering. "Yeah."

Paloma pressed her lips to his once more, kissed him for a time, grinding her breasts against his chest. Finally, she placed both her hands against his chest, and pushed away from him, rising. Her dress had come down, exposing one entire breast and most of the other. They were rising and falling heavily as she breathed.

"Don't worry, big Indio," she said, breathless, "I will not intrude on your memories."

She rose and pulled the straps of her dress up over her shoulders. She gave him a cockeyed smile and then turned away, the dress drawn taut across her round rump.

Yakima reached out, caught her wrist, and turned her around. He pulled her back down to him, hot blood surging through his lower regions, desire pulsing in his temples. He felt a hard knot of yearning in his throat—a yearning for this alluring woman before him, a yearning to be free of the long, imprisoning tentacles of remembered love gone forever.

"Like I said," he said, sliding the straps of Paloma's dress down her arms until both nubile orbs jiggled free of their confines, and he took them both in his hands, "she's dust."

Their fervid coupling was short but passionate.

She slumped against him, recuperating, breathing hard, for

several minutes. She lifted her head and stared down at him, a celestial smile glittering in her eyes and pulling at her mouth. Her dress was bunched around her belly.

She waggled her hips against his, lowered her head to kiss him once more.

"I'm sorry, *mi amor*," she said in a throaty whisper.

He frowned. He was about to ask her what she meant, but then she raised her right hand above her head. He saw the rock too late. Before he could react, she'd smashed it against his right temple, laying him out cold.

Misery woke him.

He felt as though someone were smashing a sledgehammer against his head, over and over again. He opened his eyes, stretched his lips back from his teeth, and groaned. He closed his eyes again, for the sun was blasting down at him. He could see the broad, lemon ball still blossoming against the backs of his eyelids, adding to his agony.

He rolled onto his side, raised a hand to his right temple. Oily with blood. Blood had dribbled down his temple and across his cheek to his jaw. It was partly dried to the texture of jelly.

When he'd taken several deep breaths to begin to start to quell the painful barking in his head, he sat up, pulled his pants up, and buckled his cartridge belt. He was surprised to find that his Colt was still in its holster. As bad as his head ached, she might have thought she'd killed him and seen no reason to take the revolver.

Or maybe she'd been too eager to get to the payroll loot to worry about something so insignificant as a gun.

Yakima groaned, cursed, and gained his knees. That caused a bayonet of razor-edged agony to slide between his ears, and he lowered his head to his hands, grinding his forehead into his palms.

"Crazy bitch!"

But then he realized that she'd only been doing what he should have expected her to try, and he redirected his anger toward himself.

"Damn fool!"

But it wasn't the first time his pecker had nearly gotten him killed. If he didn't die from the head clubbing Paloma had given him, and which he felt was entirely likely, he'd vow to never trust another beautiful woman again.

He heaved himself to his feet, grinding his molars against the pain, and steadied himself against a boulder. The ground pitched and swayed. He squeezed his eyes closed, then slitted them, staring out across the desert. He thought he saw something move out there.

Shading his eyes with his hand, trying to ignore the sharp daggers the brassy sun stabbed at his eyes, he could see a dark shape far away on the butterscotch desert. The shape was little larger than a dust mote from this distance, but it was a horse and rider, all right.

It was her.

Had to be her.

Who else would be traveling alone out there?

She was riding southwest, likely heading for Mexico.

Yakima looked around, got his bearings, and then clamored down out of the rocks. When he turned at the bottom of the escarpment, Wolf was standing not twenty feet away from him, staring at him, the mount's molasses-colored eyes on either side of the white blaze on his snout vaguely incredulous, baldly condemning. The horse wore its halter, and the short length of rope the half-breed had used to tie him to the picket line dangled halfway to the ground. The stallion had been turned loose.

Yakima supposed he should have been grateful that his gun

and his horse were still with him, but he wasn't in the mood to feel grateful about anything. His neck was in far too big of a hump for that.

Little bitch wasn't going anywhere. Surely not with the payroll loot. And surely not until he'd whipped her backside so she wouldn't be able to sit down without bawling for a month of Sundays!

Wolf shook his head and came running, nearly knocking over Yakima, who had to sidestep and dodge, cursing. Wolf ran past him, turned and stopped, shaking his head again and loosing a long whinny. Obviously, the horse was happier to see his rider than his rider was to see his horse.

"Thanks, you stupid cuss!" Yakima bit out, pressing the heel of his hand against his bloody temple. "What that little bitch started you wanna finish, huh? Christ . . ."

Wolf whickered, came over, and extended his snout toward his rider, sniffing at Yakima's bloody forehead.

"Yeah, she got me good."

Yakima started walking back across the little clearing in the direction of the shack, Wolf following close on his heels. The half-breed wondered what condition he'd find MacElvy in. As he approached the shack and the fire ring piled with gray ashes, however, he slowed his pace, frowning curiously. Not only was Paloma's gear missing from around the fire, but MacElvy's was, as well.

"I'll be goddamned," Yakima muttered.

He cursed again when he saw that his saddle scabbard, which was bent over a rock near his overturned saddle, was empty. He moved around the fire ring and cast a look down along the side of the shack still swathed in morning shadows though its thatched roof was limned with golden sunlight. Both the other two horses—MacElvy's and Paloma's—were gone.

Not surprising in light of the fact that the lawman's gear was gone.

Yakima looked at the shack. The strongbox was still there. He walked over to it, dropped to a knee, and opened the lid.

Empty.

Not surprising, either. They would have stuffed the loot into their saddlebags for easier packing.

Yakima swung back toward where Wolf stood twitching his ears near Yakima's gear, and felt the burn of indignation as well as a deep, sharp-edged chagrin. They'd thrown in together. He'd only seen one rider down on the desert, but there must have been two. He just hadn't seen the other one because of the sun glare.

He wondered when they'd paired up—before or after she'd gone out to the escarpment to bash Yakima's head in with the rock?

"Damnit," he said.

Wolf was staring at him, switching his tail slowly, curiously from side to side, as though to say, "What in hell have you gotten yourself into now?"

"Wolf," Yakima said, again pressing the heel of his hand to his forehead. "You're lookin' at a damn fool. I know you already know that, but you're right. You oughta pull foot and find you one with a nickel's worth of sense."

The horse momentarily stopped switching his tail and twitching his ears, staring at his rider. Then he resumed switching his tail again, still staring.

Yakima walked back to the stream, dropped to a knee, and bathed his temple, washing out what felt like a six-inch gash. He removed his neckerchief, wrapped it round his head, and then set his hat down lightly on top of it. Wincing against the continuing throbbing, he gained his feet and walked back over to the camp.

MacElvy or Paloma had taken his Yellowboy repeater. That added to the rage already stoked inside the half-breed. He valued the Winchester almost as much as his horse. They were about the only two things of value he had.

At least they hadn't taken his horse or anything else, he saw, looking around at his gear. They'd wanted to travel lightly and leave as small a trail as possible. But even if they'd tried to take Wolf, the black wouldn't have gone, and there wasn't a mule alive more stubborn than the black.

Cursing and grunting, Yakima threw his saddle onto Wolf's back, and buckled the latigo. He stuffed his gear into his saddlebags, rolled his blankets up in his rain slicker and the four-point capote he wore in cold weather, and secured the bags and bedroll behind the saddle.

Right there was all he owned in the world. It was light by one Yellowboy repeater.

He swung heavily into the saddle and sat still for a moment, waiting for the hammering in his skull to abate. He remembered that soft, sensual look in her dark eyes—a half a second before she had smashed that rock against his head.

She'd left him for dead. MacElvy must've believed that she'd left the half-breed dead in the rocks. The lawman had probably been too distracted by other things—namely the money and the woman's supple body she'd no doubt promised him—to have investigated and finished the job she'd started.

"He'll live to regret that."

Yakima touched spurs to the stallion's flanks, and loped off across the clearing toward the forest and the way back down out of the mountains.

"They both will."

CHAPTER 14

Something was running through the creosote, coming fast on Yakima's left.

The half-breed jerked back on Wolf's reins and slipped his Colt from its holster, raising the barrel and clicking the hammer back. The padding grew louder. It was accompanied by rasping pants and the occasional scrape of a creosote branch, the grinding of gravel.

Suddenly, the oak shrubs moved ahead and left, between two barrel-sized boulders, and something gray and brown darted through them and into the trail. The coyote stopped suddenly, flicked its head with raised ears and close-set, fear-sharp eyes toward the half-breed, gave a startled yip, and then dashed into the brush on the trail's opposite side, tucking its bushy, gray-brown, white-tipped tail firmly between its hind legs.

Yakima looked around. Escarpment loomed around him, all turning dark now with the sun's westward plunge. He'd ridden hard all day, trying to ignore the hammering in his head until the hammering somewhat abated around noon, no thanks to the rough ride through the rocky, uneven terrain and the sun's relentless assault. It was a testament to his will that he'd folded up the pain and slid it into a partially hidden drawer.

His eyes and mouth were dry as parchment, and he wanted a drink but was trying to conserve water because he didn't know where there were any springs out this way. He'd given Wolf a few drops here and there, and swabbed the black's nostrils with a moistened handkerchief. He figured he was close to the Mexican line, traveling cross-country, avoiding trails, because that's what the two riders he was tracking were doing.

Normally, he'd have filled two or three canteens for a trip out here. Unfortunately, he hadn't had the benefit of knowing he'd be making such a trip ahead of time.

He peered off in the direction from which the coyote had run. Something had frightened the beast.

What?

Yakima booted Wolf ahead and turned him right through an opening in the chaparral. He kept his cocked Colt aimed straight out over his horse's head, and he shuttled his gaze from left to right. Finally, seeing nothing, he stopped the horse.

He'd felt Wolf's back expanding and contracting nervously beneath the saddle since he'd seen the coyote. Maybe it was only the coyote that had spooked him. But now the horse gave his tail a hard *swish!* and jerked his head up, whickering. He dug a front hoof at the ground. That set the hair bristling at the back of the half-breed's neck, his heartbeat quickening.

He looked around wildly, sweat sliding down the sides of his face from beneath his hat brim, carving runnels through the desert dirt coating him.

"Psssst!" came a voice somewhere to his right.

He jerked his gaze in that direction. All he could see were tufts of prickly pear and barrel cactus and clumps of catclaw and desert oak amid the taller creosote shrubs, ocotillo, and saguaro.

"Ya-ki-ma!" came the hissing voice, causing Wolf to whicker again and lurch.

Yakima continued to look around, his desperate gaze probing every mound of gravel and boulder and sandstone dyke thrusting itself up out of the red caliche. "Who . . . who . . . the hell . . . *where* the hell—?"

The hiss was louder this time: *"Look out!"*

Yakima turned to see an Apache diving at him from halfway up a sandstone scarp sheathed in Mormon tea and catclaw and behind which the warrior must have been hunkering. The brave gave a loud, coyote-like bark and then gritted his teeth as he swung the feathered war hatchet in his left fist. Yakima dropped his Colt and grabbed the Indian's left wrist as the brave slammed into him. He stopped the war hatchet's arc toward the opposite temple that Paloma had likely scarred for life, with about one cat's whisker of room to spare!

The Apache grunted and wheezed as he drove Yakima from his saddle, both going airborne, groaning and grunting, clinging to each other like two lovers after a long separation. The ground rose up fast to smack Yakima hard about the back of his head and his shoulders.

Despite the reignited fire in his right temple, he managed to keep his right hand wrapped around the Apache's left hand wielding the hatchet, and jab his left fist against the brave's jaw. That took some of the demonic delight out of the brave's dark eyes. The brave blinked and rolled half over. Yakima slammed his left fist into the brave's face twice more before the brave released the war hatchet.

The brave gave another loud yip, his long, coarse hair flying around his head, and he had just started to wrap both his hands around Yakima's neck when his eyes opened wide in shock. His eyes rolled down in their sockets to stare at the Arkansas toothpick that the half-breed had just slipped into his neck, just right of the warrior's Adam's apple. The brave's mouth opened, and, rising to his knees, a horrified expression scrunching up his sandstone-colored face, he flailed both hands at the hide-wrapped handle of the knife sticking out of his throat.

"Here, let me help you," Yakima said with a grunt, reaching up to pull the toothpick out of the brave's neck.

Blood geysered as the blade slipped free. More blood oozed out the brave's open mouth before Yakima gained his feet and kicked the brave over backward. Instantly, more war whoops rose shrilly, sounding as though Yakima were being surrounded by rabid coyotes. Rifles belched. Bullets plumed the dust and gravel around the half-breed's moccasins, chewing into cholla plants and snapping oak branches.

Crouching, Yakima looked around for Wolf. No sign of the beast. Normally loyal to a fault, the black wasted no time in fleeing Apaches. He was long gone. But then Yakima remembered that the horse wasn't carrying his Yellowboy, anyway.

He saw his still-cocked Colt lying under a greasewood. As the rifles continued to belch and the braves continued to whoop and bullets plunked into the ground around his moccasins, Yakima dove on the piece, and rolled. He pushed up on his butt, extending the revolver before him, and fired through ocotillo branches.

A brave yowled and fell.

He fired again and a brave yipped and flew backwards off an escarpment.

Yakima found another target, and fired, not sure if he'd his mark or not. There were too many figures dancing among the brush and cacti, too many dark-skinned, loincloth-clad braves running toward him from the chaparral, some flinging arrows, others shooting old-model army carbines.

He got up and ran, dropped when a bullet screeched past his head, and rolled. He came up firing from a knee until his hammer clicked on an empty chamber. He tossed away the Colt, grabbed the old Spencer carbine of one of the braves he'd killed, and dodged behind a boulder. He pressed his back to the boulder, pricking his ears, listening.

The firing had stopped. He gritted his teeth against the searing pain that was roaring like a wounded lion in his head, and tried to listen for the Apaches. As he did, he worked the carbine's trigger guard cocking mechanism—he'd used the same model back when he'd been a contract scout—and drew the heavy hammer back to full cock.

"Behind you!" a pinched voice called.

He turned to his right, edged a peek around the side of his covering boulder. A crouching brave stopped dead in his tracks, raised his Springfield trapdoor carbine, and fired. Yakima drew his head back behind the boulder as the .45-caliber bullet smashed loudly into the rock where his head had been. Yakima stepped out from behind the boulder and fired his seven-shot Spencer from his waist. The Apache dropped his own carbine, doubled over and kicked up dust as Yakima's bullet drove him five feet back. Yakima fired the Spencer again, the .52-caliber ball smashing into the black crown of the Apache's skull, where the hair had been parted into separate braids.

The brave crumpled into a bloody, quivering heap.

Yakima quickly cocked the Spencer once more and side-stepped, pivoting from the hips and looking around. Dust wafted, acrid with the smell of fresh blood and burnt powder. He heard nothing but distant birds until hoof thuds rose.

He ran around an escarpment and saw three braves galloping up a slight rise to the north, each leading several riderless mustangs behind them. One glanced over his shoulder, showing his white teeth through a grimace, and then turned his head forward and lowered it, batting his moccasin-clad heels against the ribs of his short-legged coyote-dun.

The braves topped the rise and disappeared down the other side, their tan dust sifting behind them.

Holding the cocked Spencer's butt against his hip, Yakima walked slowly back in the direction from which he'd come. He scowled into the brush, looking for the bearer of the voice who'd warned him both times. But nothing moved in the chaparral.

"Breed!" rose the voice again.

Yakima stopped, looked around. He could see nothing but rocks and shrubs. It was as though someone were toying with him.

"Yakima, over here, damnit!" said the voice he could not recognize nor pinpoint.

"Where?"

"Here. To your right. I mean, *left*!"

Yakima moved slowly to his left. He passed a droopy mesquite, moccasins crunching on the fallen beans, and stopped.

"Here I am!" the voice said as though from only a few feet away. "Right here."

"Still don't see you."

"Look down."

Yakima looked down. All he could see was a rock about the size of a man's head resting on a mound of soft desert sand. But then the rock moved—at least the lower half of it moved. Yakima jerked with a start, and tightened his grip on the carbine. But then he saw that the rock was not a rock at all. It was a head. A human head. And what had moved were the man's badly chapped, pink lips. They'd formed a smile.

"MacElvy?"

The lips formed another smile. The man's eyelids fell and rose. One eye was bloody. The man's short, brown hair was mashed flat against his skull, showing the indentation of his hat. "Give a fellow traveler a hand?"

Yakima glanced around once more and then off-cocked the carbine and lowered it. Anger flamed in him once more. "Why in the hell should I?"

"Well, because I'm buried to the neck and I do believe there might be fire ants down here around my privates." MacElvy blinked his good eye, and winced. The other, bloody eye remained closed.

"Where's your partner?"

"My . . . *who* . . . ?"

Again, Yakima looked around, scanning the chaparral now for the woman instead of Apaches. "Paloma. Where is she?"

"Hell, she was a good hour, maybe two hours ahead of me."

"Huh?"

"Yeah, she tried to shoot me while I was still in my blankets. Her bullet chewed off my earlobe but left me otherwise intact. But she ran my horse off. Ran both our horses off. Took me just north of forever to run mine down, after she high-tailed it with the loot. I thought you was dead! Didn't you hear the shootin' and then me *callin'*? I called for you several times before I lit out after her. Figured you was *dead,* like she tried to do to *me!*"

Yakima narrowed a skeptical eye. He was damned tired of being made a fool of, though he knew he'd had plenty to do with that himself. "You sure you and her didn't throw in together? Didn't decide you'd head down to Mexico with the loot and live high on the hog?"

"Hell, no! That's her in your head again! Look, could you dig me out of here before the fire ants start chompin' into my balls. We can palaver all you want after that, all right? Those damn Chiricahuas was just about to slice off my eyelids before they heard you comin'. Let the sun cook my eyeballs like poachin' oysters. Nasty devils! They'd just started slicin' on my right one, and my eye's so full of blood I can't see out of it. Christ! I am so goddamn unenthusiastic about this mission, I'm ready to pull my picket pin and ride back to Prescott and tell the chief marshal he can shove my badge so far up his ass that . . ."

He let his voice trail off as Yakima started to dig with the butt of his carbine.

"Oh, thank you. Thank you. There will surely be a place for you in heaven. I will see to that myself."

"Don't do me any favors, MacElvy. I've been lied to so many

times I still don't know what to think."

"Not by me you haven't!"

"Just shut up and let me dig."

"Hey, that forehead of yours looks nasty. Does it hurt?"

Yakima stopped and gave him a look of severely strained patience.

"Right," said MacElvy. "I'll shut up and let you dig."

CHAPTER 15

Just after sundown, Paloma stopped her buckskin on a rise from which she'd been hearing the patter of piano music for nearly the last mile or so. Now she saw where the music was coming from.

Below, a pale ribbon of wagon road—probably a freight road—curved through the desert that was spruce green and burnt orange now in the last light. On the far side of the wagon road from Paloma stood a sprawling structure composed of wood and mud bricks. It must have been three stories tall. The sun had gone down behind it, a bright splash of yellow behind the mountains that stood black against it.

Against the mountains stood this large structure, all of its windows lit against the coming night. On the broad front gallery, two hanging lanterns swung back and forth in the rising night breeze, squawking on their rusty chains. In the large yard fronting the place were a dozen wagons of every shape and size, some with mules or horses standing hipshot in the traces.

There was a small barn behind the place with an adjoining corral in which more stock milled. A burro was braying raucously as it hung its head over the corral rails, staring toward the large building from which the cacophony rose. It either didn't like the noise or it was calling its owner.

At the same time, a horse—probably a stallion—was rising up onto its back legs and whinnying loudly, aggressively, probably bedeviling another mount trying to get away from it. A mare, no doubt. The stallion looked black against the sunset, its glistening mane buffeting in the breeze. Pink dust rose around the stallion's hooves, disappearing like vapor against the heavy, growing shadows.

The stallion caused Paloma to think of the fine half-breed stallion she'd coupled with to such great satisfaction the night before. She glanced over her shoulder warily. For some reason, she'd sensed that he was trailing her though she'd been certain that she'd killed him with the rock. She'd smashed him hard enough to kill most men. Probably Yakima, as well.

But now, sensing him behind her, she had her doubts. She should have checked to make sure.

She turned her head back forward and shook her breeze-jostled hair back behind her ears. No, he was dead, all right. A shame for such a man to be dead, but now the money was hers, and no one would stand in her way of finally attaining the rich life she'd always yearned for, striven for.

She'd spent two years with that fetid javelina otherwise known as Clancy Brewer. For two years, she'd let him mewl around between her legs, taking his satisfaction in haste and giving her absolutely none in return. In fact, he'd given her absolutely *nothing* in return. Which was why she'd been so happy when the handsome outlaw rake, Octavio La Paz, had come along.

She sensed that now her luck was changing, though she had to admit she wished it had changed *with* Yakima instead of *against* him. Some men just wouldn't listen to reason. If he'd given Paloma half a chance, she could have made that half-breed drifter's life so much better . . . in more ways than one.

No point in thinking about what might have been. She needed to keep looking ahead. And that's what she did now as she considered the noisy building sitting below. It was likely a roadhouse. Probably a brothel, as well. She could probably get a warm meal and something to cut the trail dust down there.

And likely a hot bath, as well. She had enough money for just about anything she wanted.

The only problem was that anywhere there were men—especially drinking men—there would likely be danger, as well. Oh, well. Not taking a chance now and then never got a girl anywhere. Besides, Paloma was no shrinking violet. She swung down from her buckskin's back, reached into a saddlebag pouch, and pulled out a holstered pistol and cartridge belt. The gun had been in the saddlebags she'd acquired back at the rustlers' camp. A fortunate happenstance for Paloma. A beautiful girl on the run with a hundred thousand dollars had best arm herself against snakes.

Especially human *male* snakes.

She wrapped the belt around her lean waist. She had to notch the very last hole, and even then the gun dropped low on her hip. She unwrapped her striped serape from around her blanket roll, and dropped it over her head. Fortunately, the man-sized poncho fell to nearly her knees, hiding the gun and holster. It was also baggy enough that the gun didn't bulge to an overly obvious degree.

Now, most importantly, what was she going to do about the loot?

She couldn't very well waltz into the roadhouse with the saddlebags draped over her shoulder. No, that wouldn't do. Just herself alone—a *beautiful young woman alone*—would attract enough attention without dressing herself in a hundred thousand dollars of stolen army payroll money.

Quickly, she looked around. When she found what she was looking for, she led her horse over to a niche in a small pile of rocks along the trail's left side, just back from the brow of the hill and out of sight from the roadhouse. She pulled the saddlebags off the buckskin's back, hauled them around a palo verde and over to the niche sheathed in cactus.

She removed a packet of greenbacks from one of the pouches, buckled the flap, and then shoved the saddlebags deep into the niche. It was so dark that she couldn't see them now by night; she hoped that they would not be seen by day, either. Anyway, they were far enough off the trail that anyone spying them would have to be looking for them.

That task accomplished, she stuffed the packet of bills down her dress and into her cleavage. A lascivious thrill bit her, spread a warmth through her belly, and she smiled sensuously as she strode back over to the buckskin, and swung up into the saddle. Having that much money snuggling in her cleavage was even better than having a handsome man nuzzle her breasts.

She put the buckskin down the gradual slope and rode on into the roadhouse yard. The piano music grew louder as did the low roar and laughter of the customers whose silhouettes she could see swaying and jostling through the red-curtained windows. Now she could see in the lamplight shed by the window a large sign over the place's broad front veranda announcing KING'S FORK SALOON. Smaller letters below the larger ones read, "Kingston Ballantrae III, Prop."

There were several hitch racks on each side of the sprawling building, all festooned with saddled horses standing hang-headed and droopy tailed, saddle cinches dangling so the patient beasts could breathe freely while their riders drank and frolicked. Vaguely, as she turned the buckskin toward the lesser populated of the hitch racks on the building's left side, Paloma wondered where all these people hailed from. The land stretching away from the roadhouse in all directions was a vast, dry desert broken by ravines and canyons and lumpy with various mountain ranges—home, she'd always thought, to not much more than coyotes, mountain lions, and Apaches.

Mexico, she believed, lay just south. How far away, she wasn't sure. She hoped to inquire inside about that as well as about the distance to the Sea of Cortez, where she intended to buy a ticket for a steamship ride up the west coast to San Francisco. With the army payroll loot, she'd buy a home there in that beautiful city on the bay, which she'd heard much about, seen pictures of, and had dreamt of one day living in.

She'd start her own business and take up with a handsome, wealthy man.

Adjusting the holster hanging low on her right hip beneath the serape, she climbed the porch steps. There were three or four men lounging in the shadows outside the saloon's bat-wing doors, smoking. They'd been talking when she'd ridden up. Now they'd fallen quiet as they studied her over the glowing coals of their cigarettes and cigars.

Paloma pointedly ignored them as two stepped reluctantly aside for her, and she pushed through the heavy, scrolled, oak louver doors into the two front panels of which had been carved the shape of a king's crown. She stopped just inside the vast main drinking hall, and shoved her sombrero off her head, letting it hang by its hemp thong down her back.

She glanced quickly around the impressively appointed, rollicking place and then maneuvered her way through the crowd toward the large, ornate, horseshoe-shaped bar at the front of the room being tended by three bartenders in white shirts, sleeve garters, stylish brocade vests, and ribbon bow ties. Another bar ran along the right wall, manned by two more barmen.

The crowd was mostly male, of course—a colorful mix of gringos as well as Mexicans. Paloma spied a few Negroes, as well. Most appeared to be cattlemen or freighters. Five or six men in the blue uniforms of the US cavalry were playing poker at a large, round table in a smoky corner. Two of the soldiers had scantily, brightly clad girls lounging on their laps.

Seeing the soldiers, Paloma grew conscious of the money

snugged in the deep cleavage between her breasts, and she brushed a hand across the holstered revolver that hung heavily off her hip.

Men stepped aside for her, favoring her with their goatish gazes, eyes raking her up and down. She did not meet any of the gazes directly, for she'd learned when she'd first started acquiring the curves of a woman that doing so often attracted unwanted attention.

She wanted as little attention as possible here. Food, drink, a room, and a hot bath would do nicely, and she wanted to acquire them with no pomp or circumstance.

Two more men and a dove in a sheer pink dress, through which Paloma could see everything, stepped aside for her, and she bellied up to the bar. It took a few moments for her to catch the eye of one of the busy bartenders, but when she did the tall man with pomaded hair and a waxed mustache hustled right over.

"Evenin', senorita. What can I get for you, this fine evenin'?" Leaning forward on his elbows, he winked lasciviously.

"A double shot of tequila. I assume you rent rooms?"

"We sure do rent rooms."

"I would like a double shot of tequila, a quiet room, a plate of food delivered to my room as well as hot water for a bath."

The barman frowned as he glanced around her and then he raked her once more with his oily gaze, and said, "You all alone?" They both had to raise their voices to be heard above the low roar of the crowd and the continuing patter of the piano from somewhere to Paloma's left. Somewhere to her right, a woman kept cackling raucously as though at the funniest jokes she'd ever heard.

"I can get you the drink and the room," the barman said. "As for the bath—we're a little busy right . . ."

He let his voice trail off as Paloma reached down the wide

neck of the serape, and pulled the packet of bills out of her cleavage. She couldn't help flashing the money. She'd always wanted to be rich and now she was. While she knew it was dangerous for her to let anyone know how much money she was carrying, she acknowledged the admonition with only half of her brain. The other half, which enjoyed the surprised look on the barman's pockmarked face, overrode the less powerful, more prudent half.

Slowly, luxuriating in the man's admiring, incredulous stare, she peeled a ten-dollar note from the packet. As she did, she glanced to her right to see another man staring down at her from the balcony over the other bar. The man had thick, wavy blond hair that fell to his shoulders. He was maybe thirty-five or forty, well-built and handsome, with dark-blue eyes. He wore a flashy, burgundy suit with a double-breasted, gold-buttoned corduroy coat. A gold chain drooped from a watch pocket. The man was smoking a small cheroot tucked into the end of a long, wooden cigarette holder.

He stared down at Paloma with one eye narrowed, a faint smile tugging at one corner of his mouth. And then, drawing musingly on the cigarette holder, he turned away from the balcony rail and the several men he'd been standing with. Paloma returned her attention to the barman and set the ten-dollar note down on the bar.

"Will that cover it?" she asked, giving her nose a snooty tilt.

The barman leaned farther forward and laid his hand over the bill, covering it, and glanced sheepishly around. "For that much money, I'll run back to the kitchen and fetch the hot water myself. Say, uh, who are you anyway? Haven't seen you in this neck of the desert."

"Rest assured you never will again, *amigo*," Paloma said. "Now, if you don't mind—my drink and my room key. I will wait here while you prepare my bath. *Vamos, por favor.*" She gave a regal smile. She'd been wanting to give a smile like that—a rich woman's smile—for most of her life. While she'd had money a time or two, she'd never had even half as much as she had now, and as she returned the packet to its niche between her breasts, she felt the burn of the bills in her brain.

Eyeing her shrewdly, the barman grabbed a tumbler off a pyramid, filled it to the brim with tequila, winked at her, and set the short, heavy glass down on the mahogany. He turned away for a moment, and then turned back and set a small, gold key engraved with the number 23 down beside the tequila. He'd taken the ten-dollar note off the bar and slipped it into a pocket of his brocade vest. Now, he said, "Your room . . . and your bath . . . will be ready in twenty minutes. Shall I . . . hang around and wash your back?"

"I doubt that all these customers will allow you to spare that much time away from the bar, amigo," Paloma said, raising her shot glass to her mouth in a mocking salute.

His cheeks colored as he turned away, and, wiping his hands on his apron, hustled through swinging doors into what was probably the kitchen. As he did, several customers with empty glasses berated him and cast her angry glances. Trying not to smile her satisfaction, Paloma scooped the room key off the bar, closed her upper lip over the rim of the tumbler, and sipped the tequila.

It burned pleasantly in her throat and chest, behind the comforting weight of the bills. She was about to take another heady swallow when a man's soft, resonant voice said in her right ear, "Shame, shame, shame on you, senorita."

CHAPTER 16

Paloma jerked with a start.

She turned her head to see the handsome, burgundy-clad man from the balcony standing beside her. He was drawing on the cigarette holder from the corner of his mouth and arching a brow at her.

She drew a steady, calming breath and regarded him with faint disdain, as though he were intruding. "Shame on yourself. You're standing awfully close, you know?"

He chuckled, spewing smoke from his mouth as well as from his nostrils. Obviously, he hadn't been expecting such an impudent admonition, and he'd found it delightful, coming from such pretty lips. When he'd gathered himself he said, "You've distracted one of my very busy bartenders. May I ask why?"

Coolly, Paloma raised her tequila glass and then showed him the key in her hand. "And food and a bath to go with the room."

"Ah, you're renting a room," said the man in the burgundy suit, taking another puff from his cigarillo. "Then all is forgiven." He smiled and extended his right hand to her. "Allow me to introduce myself. I am Kingston Ballantrae, proprietor of this old watering hole." His smile broadened with pride, his dark-blue eyes flashing in the lantern light.

She allowed him to squeeze her hand. She continued to regard him with faint disdain, though he'd suddenly piqued her interest. Handsome, wealthy men didn't grow on trees. "Paloma

Collado," she said offhandedly, rolling her eyes around. "Some watering hole you have here, amigo."

"Why, thank you, Senorita Collado. It is Senorita, I take it?' Still clinging to her hand, Ballantrae glanced around as though her husband might be lurking behind him. "Or is there a Senor Collado?"

"There is no Senor Collado. What on earth would I want with a man?"

Ballantrae regarded her wistfully. "You aren't from around here, are you, senorita?"

"Do I look like I would be from around here?"

He appeared to take that as an invitation to look her up and down though he did so with customary male lasciviousness. He chuckled. "No, no—I'll say you don't look like you'd hail from this neck of the desert. At least, I've never seen you before. And I assure you I am not a man who forgets a pretty face."

"How lovely for you."

"Where might you be from . . . if I'm not being rudely inquisitive . . . ?"

"Most people tend not to stick their noses in other people's business," Paloma said again snootily, "but since it's been a long ride and I've spoken to no one for several days except my horse and the jackrabbits, what the hell? I am from a little village on the Yaqui River called Orozco."

"Mhmmm . . . never heard of it. But I'm afraid I don't travel often south of the border. My establishment here keeps me hopping, if you know what I mean."

"I'm sure it does."

He hesitated as though sheepish about continuing his inquiry. "And . . . what does such a beautiful young senorita do in this village of Orozco, and, furthermore, what is she doing so far away from home . . . *alone*? That's quite extraordinary, is it not—a beautiful young woman traveling alone through this *bandito-* and Apache-infested desert?"

She just realized that he had a faint English accent.

Paloma's mind was nimble. Without hesitation—automatically, in fact—the lie flowed like water over her lips. "My family was murdered recently by Apaches. Finding myself alone, I took the money my father made while working in a silver mine north of the border, and left Orozco. I am on my way to live with my grandmother in Tucson."

In fact, she had been born in Orozco, and she did indeed have a grandmother in Tucson, but she hadn't seen the old bat in years and had no intention of ever seeing her again.

"She is alone, as I am, and she is old and decrepit," Paloma continued. "I will live with her and care for her until she dies. I have enough money to make us both quite comfortable."

"What a sweet girl you are."

"Don't be silly. Any girl would do such a thing for her grandmother, Senor Ballantrae."

"The trails are dangerous, my sweet."

"Don't I know it! I had to run my horse hard to escape two separate sets of *banditos*. And I saw the smoke of Apache signal fires in the distance, two days in a row." Paloma sipped her tequila, swallowed, licked her upper lip and savored the look he gave her, watching her tongue. She shook her head. "I am not worried, though. My horse is fast. Speaking of him, I can stable him in your barn?"

"Certainly!" Ballantrae looked around the room and then, apparently finding who he was looking for, chomped down on his cigarette holder and clapped his hands twice loudly. A short, stocky young man in a cheap suit limped over to them. He was carrying two trays of empty glasses and bottles. Probably a swamper. There were several such men shambling about the room, cleaning tables, emptying spittoons, and hustling drinks from the bar.

Ballantrae asked Paloma to identify her horse, and when she did, the saloon owner ordered the swamper, David, to stable the buckskin in the barn and to tend him thoroughly, providing plenty of straw, water, hay, and a bait of oats.

When David had set the trays down atop the bar and limped away, Paloma said with an impressed arch of her right eyebrow, "That's two men I've now taken from their regular duties."

"I have plenty of help. Former desert rats, mostly. They work for cheap just to have a roof over their heads. Besides, a girl alone in the desert deserves all the comforts she can find. And I assure you, Miss Paloma, you will find all the comforts you require right here, under my humble roof." He favored her with a gentlemanly dip of his chin.

"Oh, I don't think it is so humble, senor." She stopped and turned her head slightly, casting him a saucily suspicious gaze. "And what will you be expecting in return for these comforts, Senor Ballantrae?"

The handsome saloon owner exhaled the last drag from his cigarillo, plucked the stub from the cigarette holder, and dropped it into the nearest brass spittoon. "Merely that you dine with me this evening, Paloma. I dare say I've never met a young woman as lovely, enchanting, and brave, and I would very much like to learn more about you."

Paloma sipped the tequila again, maneuvered her tongue again, enjoying the way his eyes sort of crossed and lit up as he watched her. She swallowed, shrugged. "If the grub's on you, how can I refuse?"

"Not only the grub, my dear."

"Oh?"

"It's a surprise. Why don't you go on up to your room and have that bath Chester is heating for you, and I'll send your surprise up shortly."

★ ★ ★ ★ ★

Paloma didn't know what to make of Ballantrae's "surprise," whatever it was. But she enjoyed surprises as much as the next girl. As long as they weren't a bucketful of rattlesnakes, that was. She had to admit that she was enjoying the handsome man's ministrations, not to mention the free room and board for her horse.

Sure, she had plenty of money. But why spend it when she didn't have to? The trail had been lonely; it would get lonelier. She'd enjoy a night in the saloon owner's company.

And she'd bet that the supper she'd be eating with him would be tastier than any plate that ole Chester would send up from the kitchen. The tequila would probably taste better than the glass she'd just drunk, too. If the man played his cards right, she might just sleep with him.

Why not?

Ever since her time with Yakima Henry, she'd felt a needling desire in the pit of her belly though she doubted any man could live up to the high expectations the half-breed had left her with.

She did not need to unlock the door to room 23. As she strode down the red-carpeted hall of the building's second story, the first-story crowd's racket muffled now behind and below her, she saw that her door was standing half open. She nudged the door wide and stepped into the room.

Chester was just turning away from a long, deep, ornately painted copper tub up from which tentacles of steam unfurled against the ceiling that was mostly in shadow. More steam lifted from the now-empty wooden buck he was just now lowering to his side.

"You make friends right quick," Chester said, tugging on one of his bushy side whiskers. "The boss—he fancies you."

"Don't feel too badly, Chester," Paloma said, giving a teasing smile as she tossed her hat on a brocade-upholstered chair to her left. "You never had a chance, anyway."

Chester gave a dry snort and brushed past her toward the door. "I'll be back with another couple of buckets." He glanced over his shoulder, giving a leering smile. "And I'll help you out of those duds. Don't worry—it comes with the room!" He laughed and left.

"Thank you, Chester!" Paloma yelled as his footsteps retreated down the hall.

She crouched to dip a hand into the half-filled tub. Good and hot. She was eager to climb in, but she'd wait until Chester had finished filling it. She didn't want to get him overwrought by the sight of her beautiful body.

Strolling around the room, admiring the humble but comfortable furnishings, she found herself humming. She was in a good mood, and why shouldn't she be?

She was a beautiful, wealthy young woman about to take a luxurious bath in a pretty tub in this unexpected saloon and hotel out here in this vast desert. She had a rich, handsome man to wine and dine her this evening, and a large, comfortable bed to sleep in—if she didn't find herself sleeping in his, that was.

She gave a devilish chuckle at that as she ran her fingertips around the globe of a lit Tiffany lamp on a table by the small balcony door. What's more, she was bound to become even wealthier than she was now, because just as it took corn to grow more corn, it took money to grow even more money.

And what better place than San Francisco to plant her seeds?

The steam was making the room overly warm and humid. Deciding to let some air into the room, she drew the heavy drape back from the glass balcony door. As she did, a shrill scream exploded from her throat and, gazing in horror at the tall, pale, sombrero-clad figure staring in at her through the door's black glass, she stumbled backward, caught her boots on the rug, and fell to her ass.

"Holy shit!" Chester cried behind her, his shoes tapping on the rug. "You all right?"

He set his buckets down and crouched beside her. Paloma turned to him and grabbed his arm as though it were a life raft, and then she turned back to the balcony door again. As she did, she jerked up the skirt of her serape and shucked her revolver from its holster.

"Oh, god—it's him!" she cried, lifting the heavy gun in her hand and fumbling with the hammer. "It's him! *Mierda!*"

"It's *who?*"

"La Paz!" She stared at the black glass glinting with the reflected light of the Tiffany lamp, and her brows ridged with a scowl. The face of Octavio La Paz was no longer there. There was only the darkness of the night pushing toward her, and the glass reflecting the umber lamplight.

But she'd been sure he was there!

His eyes had been bulging—one had been eggshell white—and his unusually pale face had been pocked with oozing sores . . .

Or . . . maybe she'd just imagined him . . . ?

"I could have sworn I saw him there," she muttered in Spanish.

"Say again," Chester said. "No *sabe.*"

Slowly, she lowered the pistol. "La Paz," she whispered to herself.

Chester glowered at her suspiciously. "*Octavio* La Paz? The old border bandit? That Mexican *killer?*"

Getting hold of herself, Paloma turned to Chester. She swung the pistol toward him, as well, and clicked back the hammer. "Shut up. Not one word about this or I'll gut shoot you!"

Chester raised his hands, palms out, and slowly straightened.

"Pour the water into my tub and get out!" Paloma ordered, rising.

Quickly, the barman picked up one of the buckets and poured it into the tub, staring at the gun she kept aimed at him. "Careful now," he urged. "That's a mighty big gun for such a delicate little hand."

"You be careful, you bastard. Remember—one word of this and I will gut shoot you and leave you to die slowly, bellowing for your mother!"

When he'd emptied the second bucket into the tub, Chester backed away to the door. Turning, he grumbled, "Boss has got his hands full tonight," and he went out and pulled the door closed behind him.

Paloma went over to the door and locked it. Keeping the cocked pistol in her hand, she walked back over to the balcony door. Holding her free hand up to shield the glare from the lamp, she stared out. Finally, she opened the door, which squawked on its hinges, and stepped slowly out onto the narrow balcony.

She could hear the roar of the crowd and the raucous hammering of the piano coming up from below. Several burly men dressed in the jackboots, buckskins, and the broad-brimmed leather or canvas hats of freighters were milling in the yard among the big freight wagons, smoking, drinking, and laughing. They were mostly in silhouette though the light from the first-floor windows limned an occasional swatch of bearded cheek or a man's buckskin-clad shoulder or glinted in a laughing eye.

There were the intermittent red glows of cigarettes or cigars or pipe bowls. Tobacco smoke wafted on the nearly still, fresh night air that also owned the tang of the desert.

Paloma wanted to call down there to ask if anyone had seen a man climbing around up here, but nixed the idea. She didn't want to attract any more attention to herself than she already had. Besides, they would likely think her crazy. And maybe she *was* crazy. Maybe the long ride in the hot desert sun had boiled her brains, and she had only imagined that Octavio had come back from the dead to take his revenge.

She'd been dreaming.

Of course, she'd been imagining Octavio. She'd left him dying from snakeroot poison. And she'd given him a liberal jigger of the stuff, too. No man could survive that!

Depressing the pistol's hammer, she dropped it into its holster. She gave a caustic chuff, mocking herself, and turned back toward her room. Something caught her eye, and she stopped, turned back toward the balcony, and dropped to a knee. She lowered her hand and touched a finger to the small, dark stain on the balcony's wooden floor.

She raised the finger to her nose, and sniffed the odor of fresh horse dung.

The fine hairs at the back of her neck bristled.

Chicken flesh rippled across breasts.

Slowly, she rose and turned to the yard. "Octavio?" she whispered.

She stood staring into the night for another full minute.

"No, silly girl," she said. "Octavio is dead. Someone else soiled the balcony. You've had too much sun, is all."

Trying to ignore the consternation causing her heart to quicken, she went back inside, closed the balcony door, and drew the heavy drapes closed.

CHAPTER 17

"Did you like my surprise?" Ballantrae asked when Paloma had answered his knock on her door. "I know I do." His eyes nearly crossed again, glinting, as he stared down at the low-necked, silk-and-taffeta frock edged in gold that clung to her body like a second skin. "I see it definitely likes you, too, my dear."

"It is a beautiful dress," Paloma said, holding the wine-red, gold-edged shawl about her naked shoulders. "*Por favor.* It makes me feel much more like a woman than I did in my dusty trail clothes."

The dress had been brought to her room by one of Ballantrae's lovely ladies of the evening. The whore, whose name was Candace, had helped Paloma into the tight affair, and buttoned the back for her. She'd also brought a bottle of fine Mexican tequila, and the two young women had enjoyed a glass while Candace had fixed Paloma's hair, adorning it with a ribbon the same wine-red as the frock and the shawl.

"Radiant," the saloon owner cooed, gravely shaking his head and furrowing his brows. "Absolutely radiant. I am still trying to imagine how such beauty could just walk in out of the desert."

He turned and crooked his arm for her. "Shall we stroll down to the dining room? I've given our order to the cook. I hope you like steak with all the trimmings. I thought we'd start with a bottle of French wine."

"Lovely."

Paloma took his arm and let him lead her along the hall.

They dropped slowly down the stairs, and the piano's raucous hammering faded as the player caught sight of the handsome couple. All eyes followed his to the stairs, and the roared died gradually. The crowd stared in rapt attention, men elbowing other men and jerking their chins toward the stairs.

Paloma felt her cheeks warm under the scrutiny. It was not a bad feeling. She no longer cared if she was noticed. She welcomed it, in fact. She could imagine herself thrilling to a life filled with such fawning.

Only she wanted the fawning to occur in a place like San Francisco, not a saloon brothel in the middle of the Sonoran Desert. The smelly desert rats and scantily clad, over-painted percentage girls would probably gawk at a girl even half as beautiful wearing the wine-red frock.

Still, Paloma felt quite elegant, and her belly trembled at the thought of the bountiful life awaiting her. All made possible by those saddlebags she'd tucked away in the niche atop the northeastern ridge.

"Now, if that ain't a purty couple!" yelled a tall man standing at the bar. Obviously drunk, he turned full around to point at Ballantrae and Paloma with a half-empty whiskey bottle. "Yessir, that there is one damn purty couple. In fact, you two make damn near as handsome a pair as Miss Paloma and Octavio La Paz once did!"

Paloma jerked to a stop at the bottom of the stairs, releasing Ballantrae's arm. Gazing in shock and horror at the tall, horse-faced, bearded American at the bar, she slapped a hand to her cleavage, her heart hiccupping beneath her heaving breasts. The man who'd spoken—a tall gringo dressed in a flashy Mexican-style calico shirt and deerskin vest and deerskin leggings, and wearing a low-crowned, black-and-red sombrero—was none other than Octavio's former American partner, Kris Jorgenson.

Jorgenson was one of the several men whom La Paz had

double-crossed when he'd killed several others in his gang and absconded with the stolen payroll money, keeping it all for himself.

"Hah! Hah! Hah!" the American border bandit roared, stomping one high-heeled, spurred boot down on the strip of bare floor running along the bar. He tapped the shoulder of a much shorter Mexican standing beside him, facing him, his back to Paloma. "Look there, Miguel! Don't ole Paloma look like she's seen a ghost?"

The short Mexican in a brown leather charro jacket turned his black-haired head toward Paloma, and spread his lips back from his large white teeth in a heavy-lidded, drunken smile.

"Miguel Cordoba," a voice whispered in Paloma's head.

And then she saw the rest of them—three others, one more gringo and two more Mexicans lined up to either side of Jorgenson and Miguel Cordoba. The rest of the gang whom La Paz had double-crossed when they'd split up to evade the soldiers.

They were all in dusty, smoke-stained trail garb. They were dirty and sweaty and sunburned. They wore beards or mustaches and bright neckerchiefs, and they all had at least two pistols and a knife or two hanging from their shell belts. She'd seen them all several times before back in Horsetooth with Octavio though she remembered only the names of Jorgenson and Cordoba.

"What on earth is he talking about?" Ballantrae asked beneath Jorgenson's continuing guffaws, regarding Paloma dubiously. "Octavio La Paz? The *Mexican killer?*"

All the onlookers had been silent. Now, a quiet, collective noise of muttered exclamations rose, sounding like a wind playing in a near canyon. Paloma barely heard. She'd just become aware that Jorgenson had a pair of saddlebags thrown over his left shoulder. The saddlebags appeared terrifyingly familiar. The butterscotch-colored bag hanging down the tall man's chest had a torn flap, just as hers did. It was also bulging.

But those couldn't be *her* bags. She'd placed them in the niche out of sight from the trail. And no one had been around. No one could have possibly seen her . . .

But the glow in Jorgenson's pale blue eyes set deep beneath shaggy, pewter brows told her that *he* had seen. He and his men must have been shadowing her.

"No!" Paloma heard herself scream. *"No!"* She stumbled forward, broke into a run. "No, you bastard! Those are *mine*!"

Jorgenson laughed and dropped his hand to the long-barreled .45-hanging low on his right thigh. One of the swampers had been standing near the bar, a filled tray ready to be delivered to a table resting heavily in a hand raised above his head. He stepped forward into Paloma's path, as though to forestall the imminent skirmish, but got a bullet in the small of his back for his efforts.

The crash of Jorgenson's .45 caused every person in the room to jump.

Facing Paloma, the beefy, lazy-eyed swamper made a horrified expression. Stumbling forward, he dropped the tray, which went crashing to the floor.

Paloma screamed and threw her arms out as though to hug the swamper, and he fell into her, knocking her off her feet and falling on top of her as her back and the back of her head hit the floor with a loud thud despite the carpet.

Staring over the shoulder of the quivering swamper, Paloma screamed again as Jorgenson stepped toward her, cursing and clicking his .45's hammer back once more. At the same time, Chester pulled a sawed-off, double-barreled shotgun from beneath the bar, and shouted, "Hold it right there, you son of a—!"

The last word either died stillborn on his lips or was drowned by the thunder of Jorgenson's revolver, which the tall, gringo outlaw had swung toward Chester and fired.

Chester had not quite gotten his shotgun leveled before Jorgenson's bullet plowed through the dead center of his pretty brocade vest, just down from his bow tie. Chester screamed and, pivoting to his left, tripped one of the shotgun's two triggers, spewing buckshot into the crowd but not before shredding Miguel Cordoba's left ear and cheek and turning that eye the color of a ripe tomato.

Shrieking, Cordoba grabbed that side of his face while several innocent bystanders also bellowed furious complaints as the rest of Chester's buckshot found more flesh to tear.

Insane with pain and rage, Cordoba stumbled forward, screaming, clutching his bloody face, and grabbing a silver-chased revolver from its holster. Continuing to stumble forward, he began cutting loose with the Spanish epithets as well as the gun, firing willy-nilly into the crowd. Behind him, Jorgenson laughed and followed suit with his own Colt while the other three *banditos* unleashed their own hog legs and followed the lead of the first two men.

Beneath the ear-rattling cacophony of thundering six-shooters and screaming men and women, Paloma could hear whom she believed to be Ballantrae shouting, "No! No! Stop shooting you fools!"

To no avail.

The shooting and screaming continued, the floor fairly leaping like a living thing being kicked beneath Paloma.

She grunted as she shoved the dying swamper off of her and rolled onto her belly, keeping her head low and holding her hands over her ears or surely the loud, booming reports would have shredded her eardrums. Bullets screeched and warmed the air around her as they plunked and slammed into tables and chairs and glasses and bottles, sending wood, glass, ashtrays, and playing cards spraying in all directions.

Paloma saw the piano and crawled for it, keeping one hand pressed to an ear. The piano player was slumped forward against the keys, his derby hat tipped forward against the open music book before him. Blood dribbled down the arm hanging straight down toward the floor at his side and forming a soggy pool on the rug near a leg of the bench.

Paloma made a face at the blood then crawled beneath the bench and hunkered there on her knees, clamping both hands over her ears, pressing her forehead hard against the rug.

Judging by the loudness of the varied din, every man in the room—every man still living, that was—was opening up with his own revolver. Amid the cacophony, Paloma could hear a throaty-voiced woman bellowing, "Oh, you dirty bastards! Oh, you lousy, filthy, dirty bastards!"

Time slowed to a cold molasses drip. The gunfire seemed to continue as though it would never die. The musky odor of coal oil reached Paloma's nose, and she heard herself mutter against the floor, "Uh-oh."

Her dread was proven well founded. A moment later she smelled smoke. A lit lamp or lamps had been shattered, and a fire had started somewhere not far away from her.

She could feel the ominous heat of the flames. A man's shouts turned to agonized screams. Paloma glanced up. Through the webbing smoke from the fire and the gunpowder, she saw a murky figure jostle violently. Flames were crawling quickly up both of the man's legs as he tried in vain to stomp them out.

Screaming even louder amid the flashing and the roars of pistols, he started running but seemed to trip over something. He fell hard, his screams dying as the flames grew brighter, consuming him and spreading along the floor around his slumped figure.

They were growing even brighter, which meant they were probably heading in Paloma's direction.

The gunfire was dwindling as those men still living were running outside as were, judging by the female screams, the working girls. Paloma crawled out from under the bench and tried to stand, but the heavy fumes of the coal oil and the thickening smoke gushed down her throat like thick tufts of warm wool soaked in kerosene, cutting off her wind. She coughed, choked, nearly passed out. Forcing herself to remain conscious, she started making her way toward where she thought the front door was located.

Many dead men impeded her way. She crawled over and around them, around tables and overturned chairs. She could hear the working girls sobbing and crying, could feel cool, fresh air threading through the thickening smoke. Coughing, trying to draw air down her badly constricted throat, she followed the sounds and the fresh air to the front door.

Rising to a crouch, she stumbled across the porch, down the steps, and into the yard that was nearly as smoky as the inside of the burning place. She ran, stumbling on the hem of her delicate dress, toward fresher and fresher air. Around her were other women either down on hands and knees or slumped forward, hands on their thighs, sobbing and coughing. In the distance, she heard men's yells and victorious shouts and the drumming of horse hooves.

Glancing to her right, she could see several horseback riders galloping out of the smoky yard lit by the fire's dancing flames, and into the darkness to the south of the roadhouse.

As they rode, they triggered pistols into the air.

She couldn't be sure because of the smoke and jostling shadows, but she thought Jorgenson, identifiable by his large black-and-red sombrero, was at the head of the pack, the saddlebags draped over his left shoulder.

"Bastardo," Paloma choked out, grabbing at the coping

around a large stock tank.

And then fatigue washed over her, and she collapsed.

CHAPTER 18

Paloma woke to squawking sounds. The squawking was growing gradually louder.

She opened her eyes and immediately grimaced at the sun beating down on her. She raised a hand to shield it from her face, and when she got her vision to focus, she saw a wagon heading toward her.

It was a large, long, leather-seated wagon with a makeshift canopy made of what appeared to be gold-tasseled red drapes stretched over support posts. Two horses were pulling the strange contraption around from behind what remained of the burned-down saloon—a pile of gray ashes and half-burned ceiling beams, a few scorched chimneys standing here and there amid the rubble.

Smoke still rose from the massive ruin, some columns thicker than others. The yard around Paloma was littered with ashes. Her dress was charred and showed where cinders had landed on her. She was lucky she, too, hadn't caught fire while she lay out here in the yard, unconscious.

The wagon made a wide arc around the front of the saloon, avoiding boards and shingles and beams from the burned building that had fallen into the yard. The wagon, Paloma now saw as it drew near, was being driven by a dour-looking Kingston Ballantrae. He was wearing the same burgundy suit he'd been wearing last night, only today it didn't look half as sharp.

The man himself didn't look a third as striking. He was so

dark with soot that he looked like a miner fresh from toiling in the earth's bowels. He wasn't wearing a hat, and his blond hair was sticking up in spikes around his head. Its ends appeared charred, as were his eyebrows.

Behind him, sitting sullenly in the wagon's four leather seats beneath the canopy, were at least a dozen soiled doves—all half-dressed in mostly underwear of all colors of the rainbow. They'd probably fled the burning building with what little they could hold in their arms, which hadn't been much. One girl wore merely a thin yellow wrapper and white pantaloons and black socks.

Ballantrae drew the wagon to a stop beside Paloma. He and the doves, including Candace, stared dully down at her. One was smoking a loosely rolled cigarette, curling her lips disdainfully at Paloma as she blew the smoke out from between her lips that were a mess of smeared pink lipstick.

Paloma had pushed up onto her elbows, staring sheepishly back at the group. Ballantrae continued to stare at her dully until finally he lifted his gaze above and beyond her, toward his once-grand, now-ruined hotel, and his lips formed a bitter expression. He shook the reins over the horses' backs, and the wagon lurched forward, ungreased wheel hubs squawking loudly. The girls turned their heads to stare back at Paloma as the wagon rolled on out of the yard, turned left onto the freight trail, and jounced off to the north, toward Tucson.

Paloma watched until the chaparral had absorbed her view of the wagon. Then she looked around once more. She was alone out here. There was only the massive ruin and the breeze ruffling the smoke and lifting dust and ash and throwing it at her.

She was alone. Her horse was gone. There were no horses anywhere around. All the corrals flanking the saloon had been emptied out, the gates thrown wide. A couple of tumbleweeds rolled in out of the desert, bouncing, and more dust lifted, and the wind caused the ruins to glow red in places, lifting cinders.

Paloma was alone and even poorer now than when Clancy Brewer was alive. Poorer than she'd ever been. Poorer by far than when she'd acquired the army payroll loot.

A sob exploded from deep within her chest. She rolled onto her belly, buried her head in her arms, and let the dam break. She bawled and bawled, tears dripping down her cheeks to form mud beneath her.

Muddy ash.

She bawled and bawled and bawled, occasionally kicking her black leather, side-button shoes that Ballantrae and Candace had outfitted her in, into the dust and ashes.

After a time, she realized that beneath her own wretched cries, she'd heard hoof clomps and felt the ground tremble slightly. Now a shadow slid over her. Apaches!

She whipped over onto her back.

No. Not Apaches. Yakima Henry was hunkered down beside her, staring dubiously down at her.

He was holding the reins of his black stallion, who stood behind him, also staring skeptically down at Paloma. Standing behind Yakima was MacElvy, a white, blood-spotted bandage over his left ear, a calico bandanna angled across his forehead to cover his right eye. He had his thumbs hooked behind his cartridge belt as he stared beyond Paloma at the burned-down saloon. His white-faced brown horse flanked him.

The lawman looked down at Paloma over Yakima's left shoulder. "Girl," MacElvy said, chuckling dryly, "you leave a bloody trail and carve one hell of a wide swath!"

Another sob boiled up from Paloma's chest, and she twisted around and buried her head in her arms once more.

Later, when they'd set up camp in an arroyo south of the burned-out saloon, where several sycamores and scrub oaks offered shade, Yakima stared down at the sullen-eyed, scantily-clad Paloma Collado and asked, "What're you gonna do with her?"

"What do you mean—what am I gonna do with her?" MacElvy asked, tossing his saddle down near their small coffee fire with a grunt. "She shot my damn ear off. And because of her I damn near lost both eyelids!"

He glowered down at Paloma through his one good eye. She sat back against a scrub oak, her handcuffed wrists resting on her breasts that were all but exposed by the wine-red, gold-edged dress. She'd torn the skirt of the delicate dress, exposing nearly all of one fine-turned, olive-colored leg.

"That's a federal damn offense," the lawman said, "and she's goin' back to Prescott with me to answer for it. In irons!"

Yakima winced as he fingered the still-painful cut on his forehead, which was still occasionally probing the area between his ears with a dull knife of agony. "Well, can't say as she don't deserve that or worse." He tossed the dregs of his coffee onto the fire, and heaved himself to his feet. "Me, though . . . well, I reckon I'll be ridin' on."

"Wait—where you goin'?" MacElvy asked, lifting the coffeepot away from the cup he'd been filling.

Yakima walked over to where Wolf stood ground-tied, latigo hanging beneath his belly, a feed sack draped over his ears. His Yellowboy was back in its sheath. Yakima had found it on one of the Chiricahuas he'd killed back near where they'd buried the lawman.

As he scrubbed out his cup with a gloved hand, the half-breed looked off, pensive. "Not sure yet. Maybe I'll try San Diego for the winter. By spring, the law up north'll likely have forgotten about my little doin's. They got bigger fish to fry now with the West openin' up the way it is, railroads layin' track all over, and gangs like the James boys runnin' off their leashes."

He dropped the cup into his left saddlebag pouch.

"Hold on, now, breed . . . I mean, Yakima." MacElvy scowled over at him, his half-filled coffee cup smoking in his hand. "You can't just pull out on me. We have an agreement, damnit!"

"Hell, the money's gone. You heard her—Kris Jorgenson and the rest of his and La Paz's gang has it. Hell, they're probably well into Mexico by now, and they probably already got half the loot spent on mescal and senoritas."

"They can't be that far along. They rode out from the roadhouse last night. They're only a few hours ahead of us. You got to figure they probably didn't ride all night, neither. Not out here in this scrub country with no moon to light their way."

Yakima was stripping the feed sack from over Wolf's ears, the stallion still trying to nibble every oat from the bottom of the bag. "The Old Mexican Road is a good trail. An old freight trail, leads all the way down to Mexico City."

"Hell, that bunch doesn't stick to the trails. With their reputations and haulin' that much dinero, they'll want to avoid the rurales and bounty hunters. Nah, they won't stick to the stage road. I'm guessin' they left the road by now and are headin' cross-country through the desert where they can't be tracked. There's a little village down by the Yaqui River they're likely headin' for. Isolated little place in rough country. It's where they hole up between jobs. They all got senoritas down there."

He gave Paloma a snide glance. "Includin' La Paz. Leastways, he did have . . . until someone gave him a drink that cored him like a damn apple!" He chuckled. "Had him one north of the border . . . and south of the border."

"Your mother laid with stinking mountain lions. She moaned for them. That's how you came to be, MacElvy." Paloma looked at Yakima. "Shoot him and take me with you. I will make it worth your while." She drew up her long, right leg, which was exposed by the tear in her skirt. She glanced down at it and gave him a seductive wink.

Yakima gave a caustic snort as he stuffed the feed sack into the saddlebag pouch. "You've given me enough misery, senorita. Time to fork paths with you for good."

MacElvy straightened, tossed his half-filled cup away in frustration, and walked over to where the half-breed was reaching under Wolf's belly for the latigo. "Yakima, you can't abandon me out here. I got a job to do. I gotta get that money back from them outlaws, and there's too many for me to take on alone."

As he cinched the latigo, Yakima said, "You'd best ride to Fort Bryce and tell them soldiers your sob story. I'm through. Finished." He glanced at Paloma sitting there in her dirty, sooty, torn dress, her hair hanging wild about her face. It too was sooty and dusty. She looked as though she'd rolled in the stuff. "I'm done with both of you."

"That your final word?"

"That's my final word."

"Even though I could make sure you're granted amnesty for that killin' up north? I could do it, you know. I got pull with the local sheriffs up that way. Sheriffs *and* judges."

"Yeah," Yakima said, taking his reins and toeing a stirrup. "Even though." He heaved himself into the leather. "My advice to you, MacElvy, is to—"

"I don't need your goddamn advice, breed!" the lawman spat out through gritted teeth. "I don't need nothin' from you. Not a damn thing. You been nothin' but a thorn in my side ever since I first laid eyes on you in the Horsetooth Saloon!"

He swung around, stumbled over a rock, cursed, and then picked up his coffee cup. Yakima watched him pick up the cup and use a leather swatch to remove the pot from the tripod over the fire, and fill the cup. Paloma stared back at Yakima through strands of hair hanging in her face. Her eyes were dark, glum.

She was too crestfallen to even bother pleading with him anymore.

As Yakima swung Wolf away from the camp, Paloma slowly turned her gaze back to the fire and stared down at it, the very picture of dejection. Yakima touched spurs to the stallion's flanks and rode on down the arroyo. He glanced back over his shoulder toward the fire. MacElvy sat there on the opposite side of the small flames from Paloma, tenderly touching the bandage over the ear she'd shredded.

A sorrier-looking pair he'd rarely seen. With one eye covered, one ear shredded, his face swollen from the buckshot pellets, MacElvy was in no condition to fight a small gang of border *banditos*. He had about as much chance of getting the stolen payroll money back by himself, with the handcuffed woman in tow, as he had of flying to the moon.

But he was too damned stubborn to give up.

Which meant he was going to get his fat ass killed, and Paloma right along with him. Why that mattered on iota to him, after all she'd done to him, he had no idea. Some-foolish-how, it did.

"Goddamnit!"

Yakima swung Wolf around, cursed again, and booted the horse back into the camp and stopped him. MacElvy and Paloma turned to him, hopefully.

Yakima snarled, "If you're that bound and determined to get yourself killed, we'd best at least get her a horse, because she sure as hell ain't ridin' double with me!"

CHAPTER 19

Three days later, Yakima held Wolf's reins as he dropped to a knee on the steep, rocky slope they were on. He plucked a horse apple out from a small slice of shade beside a rock, and sniffed. He pinched the apple. It did not come apart but merely compressed like semi-wet clay.

He looked up the slope toward several large sandstone knobs capping the mountain, beneath a Mexican sky the color of blue porcelain and just as flawless. The copper-colored knobs were marked by many caves semi-hidden by boulders that had tumbled down over the centuries from the top of the caprock.

The area had been home to some ancient people. Yakima had seen the petroglyphs they'd left behind, and broken clay pottery marking where they'd camped at one time, or where they'd built their homes. He'd also found discarded horns they'd apparently used as utensils of one kind or another, preserved by the dry air.

He shuttled his gaze across the caves, most sitting low against the knob, and felt a cool spider of menace scuttle up his spine, beneath his sweat-soaked calico shirt. "They've been through here, all right," he said. "Not long ago. Maybe two, three hours ago."

MacElvy was leading his horse toward Yakima from about thirty yards downslope. Paloma was ahead of him and to his left a bit, also walking her horse, a steel-dust gelding with three black socks which they'd run down in the desert. It was saddled and bridled, so it had likely belonged to one of the men who'd burned up in the saloon fire.

MacElvy doffed his hat and scrubbed his pale forehead with a grimy shirtsleeve. "I told you they'd cut through these mountains. Shortcut to the Yaqui River and that village they hole up in."

Yakima grimaced and said, "Keep your voice down."

MacElvy stopped suddenly and stared up the slope toward the caprock. "You think they're up there? Kinda early to camp."

"If we're as close as I think we are, they might have spied us on their back trail." Yakima leveled a warning look at the dim-witted lawman.

"Oh," MacElvy said, narrowing one eye, sheepish. "Yeah . . ." Slowly, with an air of caution and keeping his gaze on the caprock, he pulled his hat down on his sweaty head.

"My feet are sore," Paloma said. "I am not walking anymore. I am riding. That's what the horse is for, no?" She led the steel-dust over to a rock. She wasn't wearing the lawman's manacles now, as doing so would have slowed her up. MacElvy had only cuffed her and shackled her ankles at night—for good reason, as far as Yakima was concerned.

His head still ached from time to time.

MacElvy glanced at her. "Yeah, go ahead. It ain't so steep and rocky here, like before. Think I will, too."

Yakima shuttled his anxious gaze up the slope again. He thought it would be best if they stayed as low as possible, and a few seconds later he wanted to kick himself for not saying so. Because only a second after he had the thought, a bullet screeched through the air to his left.

A half second after that, MacElvy's horse gave a fierce whinny, and a rifle's flat report echoed down from the knobs.

MacElvy was caught half in and half out of his saddle. He did not have a good grip on the horn or on the reins. When the big brown curveted and rose high on its hind legs, scissoring its front hooves toward the azure sky, MacElvy went flying with a shrill scream.

Yakima lost sight of him, his view blocked by the massive, pirouetting horse, but he heard the man give a yelp following a dull thud, as though his head had hit a rock.

"Shit!" Yakima said, glancing at Paloma. "Get down! Get down!"

Those last two words were drowned by the belches of two more rifles and the sharp smacks of bullets against rock or thudding into the ground and spewing gravel. Yakima quickly shucked his Winchester from his saddle scabbard and then laid the rifle sharply down against Wolf's ass, shouting, "Get out of here, boy! Go!"

Wolf needed little urging. As more rifles hammered away near the knob, sending lead sizzling down the slope and smashing into brush or rock or snapping branches of low, gnarled pines, the black neighed his disdain at the commotion, wheeled, and galloped back down the long slope in the direction from which they'd all come.

Paloma's horse was doing the same thing, but she hadn't dismounted fast enough. She lay in a heap near a wagon-sized boulder and a shrub oak, her dress pulled up around her waist. Her bare legs were curled beneath her.

She sat there frozen, staring at something on her left. For a second, Yakima thought she was addlepated, but then he saw the rattler coiled in the shade beside the boulder, not three feet away from the woman.

The viper was sticking its flat, diamond-shaped head out into the sunlight, its forked tongue testing the woman's scent. Its button tail was curled and quivering and beneath the continuing rifle fire, Yakima heard the spine-splintering whine of an imminent strike.

Crouching behind a boulder of his own, which the slugs hurled from above were hammering, Yakima raised the Yellowboy to his cheek, and fired.

The snake had just started to thrust its head and open jaws toward Paloma when the half-breed's bullet sliced it in two, about seven inches back from the head. The head still flew forward but landed in the dirt and gravel by the girl's bare right knee.

Paloma screamed and jerked backward, kicking at the snake's striking head. Bullets triggered from the knob plumed the dust around her, one striking the snake's head and turning it to dirty jelly. Yakima bounded out away from his boulder and, taking his rifle in his left hand, grabbed Paloma with his right. He jerked her to her feet and half dragged her into some brush and mounded rocks.

He threw her down and turned to MacElvy. He cursed. The lawman lay in a small open area, head still propped against the low slab of rock he'd smashed it against. He lay on his back, arms and legs thrown wide. His eyes were closed. He was out like a blown lamp, but the slight rising and falling of his chest meant he wasn't dead.

Yet.

The bullets chewing into the sand and gravel around him weren't a good indication he'd still be alive in the next several seconds. He was so out in the open, the bushwhackers could use him for target practice, though it appeared they might have thought he was no longer worth wasting lead on. Most of the shots were now directed at the snag that Yakima and Paloma were in, the bullets spanging off rocks and snapping branches.

Keeping his head down, Yakima turned to the woman. "Can you shoot a rifle?"

She turned toward him, strands of hair pasted to her fear-flushed cheeks. "Of course."

Yakima cocked the Yellowboy and handed it to her. "Keep your head down, but try to send a few rounds up toward the knob. Don't worry about aiming; just throw some lead back at 'em, give me time to haul MacElvy's worthless carcass in here."

Paloma took the rifle in her hands, ran a hand erotically down the barrel, offering a crooked grin. "How do you know I won't shoot you with it?"

"I wish you would." Crouching, he turned toward MacElvy and said to Paloma, "Start shootin'!"

As Paloma snaked the Yellowboy's barrel over the top of the natural barricade, and started shooting, Yakima dashed out into the open, grabbed one of MacElvy's feet, and pulled. Two bullets kicked up gravel just behind him.

"Keep firing!" he shouted at Paloma.

"I'm doing all I can do, you bastard!" was the woman's sharp retort as she ejected a spent cartridge and pumped another one into the action.

"Now, no need for name-callin'," Yakima gritted out as he dragged the big lawman into the makeshift bunker.

"All right," Yakima told Paloma.

As she swung toward him a little too quickly for his taste, he grabbed the rifle out of her hands, and off-cocked the hammer. "Thanks."

She grinned through the dirt on her beautiful face, sliding a lock of hair back from her cheek with one hand. "Anytime." She frowned, pouting. "Now, how in the hell are we going to get out of this? You've led us right into their trap!"

Ignoring her, Yakima dropped to a knee beside MacElvy. The man was breathing, but he was full out. Yakima reached a hand around to the back of the lawman's head, felt the blood from a gash.

The half-breed sighed, grumbled, "You stupid son of a . . ." He saw no point in wasting his breath. The man was deep out and about as much use as the woman.

"Answer me!" Paloma said tautly.

Yakima whipped his head to her, pointed a gloved finger at her. "One more word out of you, I'm gonna beat you blue with a short stick."

She opened her mouth to retort, but snapped it shut. She glared at him, and then sat back against a rock, drawing her raised knees toward her belly and crossing her arms over her breasts.

The ambushers continued their fusillade, their lead spanging off the rocks along the top of the natural barricade, a few hammering the boulder and the bole of a large oak on the other side of it.

Yakima shucked MacElvy's Remington from the lawman's holster and thrust it at Paloma. "Take this and use it if you have to."

"What are you going to do?"

"The only thing I can do under the circumstances."

"Which is what?"

"I'm gonna go up there and kill all your friends."

She studied him as he pulled the Yellowboy's loading tube out from beneath the octagonal barrel, and began punching fresh cartridges from one of his shell belts down the slide. She sidled over to him, placed a warm hand on his thigh.

"Yakima," she said. "If you find the money, don't forget about the other night. There can be plenty more where that one came from, amigo." She canted her head slightly, smiled sweetly, her dark eyes flashing.

Yakima rammed the loading tube home and locked it. "The only thing I remember about the other night is one hell of a headache. Now keep your goddamn head down." He turned away, began crawling toward the far end of the barricade. He paused and glanced over his shoulder at her. "Or don't. I don't care what you do!"

Then he rose, crouching, glanced over the barricade toward the knob against which smoke puffed from rifle barrels, and bounded off his heels.

"Darling, don't say that!" Paloma cried behind him, her voice all but drowned by the reinvigorated rifle fire.

Yakima ran a zigzagging course across a twenty-yard stretch of open ground. He vaulted a low hummock of sandy turf and hunkered down behind a flat-topped boulder roughly the size of a Denver hansom cab while the men from above blasted away at it. When the shooting dwindled, he bounded out from behind it and ran straight up the slope between shelving escarpments.

The shooters opened up again, lead spanging shrilly off the scarps, splattering Yakima's hat with pebbles and stone shards. There was good cover most of the way up the slope. They could shoot all they wanted. Let them use up their cartridges. What he wanted to do was start bringing them, one by one, into efficient shooting range of his Yellowboy.

There were five of them. Long odds, but he'd seen longer.

Yakima stopped and dropped to his butt, leaned back against a stone wall. He stared up the slope. The knob was turning apricot. Craning his head to look west, he saw that the sun was starting its drop behind the western ridges.

Dark soon. That was all right. The darker the better. He had good night vision. Besides, he was the hunter now. Jorgenson and the other outlaws were his quarry. Of course, that could change at any time, if they located him and surrounded him, but right now he held the better hand. The dark was better for the hunter than his prey.

Staying low behind boulders and jutting dykes and tufts of pines and cactus, he moved to his right along the shoulder of the slope. There was only sporadic shooting now as Jorgenson's men tried to draw his fire. They'd lost his position and were trying to relocate him. He was only about seventy yards or so from the knob at the crest of the slope, so it was time to slow down and be patient.

Patiently, he'd disorient them and take them down one at a time, the way he'd often taken down Apaches in the canyon lands farther north, back when he was a scout at Fort Hell. He'd learned the Apache way of fighting and used it against them. He'd use that tactic here.

Moving slowly, often crawling, he worked his way up the slope through the stone formations, letting the terrain itself be his guide. A couple of the outlaws were shouting back and forth, but the breeze had come up and he couldn't hear what they were saying. Judging by the tones of their voices, he had them both puzzled and worried.

Suddenly, he stopped, dropped down behind a small, cracked boulder, and quickly doffed his hat.

Ahead and above him, about forty yards up the steep slope, a man in a black sombrero was moving toward him, striding cautiously between two large boulders turning the color of old pennies now as the sun continued to sink. The man was moving down a steep part of the slope between the boulders, holding his carbine in one hand, running his other, gloved hand along the boulder to his left for support.

Occasionally, Yakima could hear his spurs jingle faintly.

His face was round, eyes protruding from their sockets. His mouth was capped with a thick, black mustache. The ends of his mustache and his lime-green neckerchief ruffled in the breeze that was moaning among the rocks now and lifting occasional screens of tan dust.

Yakima raised his Yellowboy to his cheek, hoping that the fading rays of the sunlight angling over him from the west wouldn't glint off the barrel. But they must have. His quarry stopped suddenly and jerked his head up. He began to take his carbine in both hands.

Yakima squeezed the Yellowboy's trigger. As he did, one of his quarry's boots slipped on the steep slope and he lurched slightly to one side and fell to his butt. He screamed, dropping his carbine and clutching at the right side of his neck.

"He's here!" the Mexican shouted in English. "Here!"

Yakima pumped a fresh cartridge into the Yellowboy's breech. The Mexican turned onto his belly, pushed to his hands and knees, and began half-crawling, half-running up the slope between the boulders, spurs chiming raucously. He loosed red sand and gravel down the slope behind him.

Yakima fired the Yellowboy again, evoking another scream from the Mexican who grabbed the back of his right thigh. He screamed again. As Yakima fired again, the Mexican dragged himself to the mouth of the little canyon he was in, and darted behind the right boulder, falling.

Yakima's slug hammered a divot of stone from the side of the boulder where the Mexican's head had been a quarter second before, the screech resounding off the face of the knob.

The bandit was out of sight, shouting in Spanish now, telling the others he was badly hit. He needed help.

Yakima doffed his hat, retreated thirty yards back down the slope, turned to his right, and ran in the opposite direction as before across the shoulder of the slope. He dropped down behind a low hummock of gravelly ground tufted with prickly pear and a lone cedar, and pressed his chest and belly flat. He removed his hat and held it flat against the ground, as well.

Pricking his ears to listen above his heart's drumming in his ears, he could hear the other bandits shouting to each other anxiously. At the same time, the man Yakima had wounded was screaming and begging for help in Spanish. He was losing a lot of blood, he was saying. He cursed them and continued to beg for help.

His screams dwindled, became sporadic.

The breeze picked up and moaned.

Gradually, the light faded across the broken slope, and the knob at the top of it became silhouetted against a darkening sky. When the orange ball of the sun had disappeared behind the toothy, black, western ridges, Yakima rose and began to make his way up the slope again, where the riflemen had fallen ominously silent.

The whining and moaning of the breeze sounded like a stalking mountain lion.

Had the bandits abandoned the knob, fallen back in retreat despite the fact they were being hunted by only one man?

Yakima received his answer a minute later. As he continued to crawl, sniffing the breeze like a coyote or an Apache, he scented the sour sweat and leather smell of a man . . .

Chapter 20

In the darkness behind the natural stone barricade, Paloma crouched, listening, waiting.

Up the slope, a rifle cracked.

The rifle cracked again and there was one more report so close on its heels that it had to have come from another gun.

Silence rained down like lead from the direction of the knob. A new moon was rising, turning the sky behind the knob a dark purple. In the moon's wan light, the knob itself loomed the brown of old cowhide, against the dim stars.

The silence grew heavier as Paloma waited for more gunfire. Or, perhaps, there wouldn't be any more. Maybe Yakima had finished Jorgenson's bunch, as he'd promise. Or maybe Jorgenson's bunch had killed Yakima.

Her heart thudding tensely in her ears, wondering about the money, Paloma waited.

Her palms resting against her thighs were clammy. To her left, MacElvy groaned. The lawman moved his head slightly. In the faint, pearl light being shed by the thumbnail moon rising in the east, she could see the lawman's pale eyelids flutter. He groaned again, drew a deep breath, exhaled, and lay still.

Paloma turned toward the top of the barricade and the brown knob rising beyond it. Was the fight over? If so, who had won? Where were the saddlebags bulging with her money? That's how she saw the money now—as hers. Not stolen payroll loot but as money that belonged to her and that had been stolen from her.

She was almost relieved when a man shouted from the direction of the knob, and more rifles cracked. She lifted her head to see over the barricade, and saw an orange flash followed by the rocketing report of the rifle. She saw another flash a little left of the first one. More rifles spoke, though she couldn't see the flashes of those.

The fight was still on. Yakima was still alive. That meant that the fate of the saddlebags had not yet been decided.

Paloma swallowed, blinked, ran her bare arm across her sweat-moist forehead. Since their fate had not yet been decided, why shouldn't she herself decide it while the men were busy shooting each other?

Her heart hammered so anxiously, hopefully at the thought that she thought it would crack her breastbone.

Biting down on her lower lip, she picked up MacElvy's pistol. She cast another look up toward the knob. A breeze had risen, moaning and rustling, and beneath it she could hear a man yelling somewhere up there in the darkness. Quickly, she slipped out of her bloody shoes. Barefoot, she'd be quieter, and it would be easier for her to climb the gravelly slope.

Holding the pistol in both hands, she rose to a crouch and cautiously stole out from behind the barricade. Her skin prickled with the anticipation of bullets being hurled at her, but she suppressed the anxiety and forced herself to move slowly, deliberately up the slope.

She angled left as she climbed the mountain, intending to skirt the area where she'd seen the rifle flashes. If she could make her way to the knob and discover Jorgenson's camp, she'd also find the saddlebags. Since he and his men were hunting Yakima, they'd probably left the saddlebags in their camp. Near their horses. If she could lay her hands on both the saddlebags and a horse . . .

The anticipation caused her body to shudder, and her heart to hiccup. Inadvertently, she increased her pace and caught herself, set one bare foot deliberately down in front of the other.

"Slowly," she whispered. "Slowly, slowly . . ."

Suddenly, she stopped and wheeled to peer behind her. She'd thought she heard the crunch of gravel under a furtive foot.

She gasped, raised the pistol in both hands, expecting to see someone running toward her from the downslope. There was nothing behind her except an up-thrust thumb of tortured rock and a cedar to its left.

She dropped to a knee, trying to hold the heavy pistol out in front of her. Another sound, the same as before, to her right. She gasped and swung the pistol in that direction.

Still, nothing.

The moon was stretching eerie shadows but none seemed to be moving. The rocks and boulders were brown in the pearl-limned darkness, the brush and cactus purple.

The breeze lifted dust in front of her. The fine particles peppered her eyes, caused her to blink.

"Who's there?" she whispered. "Yakima?" She paused. "MacElvy, is that you?"

Up the slope, a rifle thundered. As she gave another startled gasp and turned in that direction, more rifles crackled, slugs spanging shrilly.

A shadow moved to her right, glowing long and angling up the slope in front of her from behind. Before she could wheel again, arms were wrapped around her and one gloved hand closed tightly over her mouth while the other slashed forward to jerk the pistol from her hand. The glove was over her nose as well as her mouth, tasting and smelling like smoky buckskin, cutting off her wind.

She tried to fight, but the man was tall and strong and he

had her in what felt like a death grip. He leaned back. She heard him grunt softly. Her bare feet came off the ground and she was dangling in midair, her toes several inches above the slope. She tried to kick and flail her arms but his hand over her mouth and nose instantly fatigued her, thrust her quickly toward unconsciousness.

A voice said into her right ear in Spanish, "Dearest Paloma, I will set you down and remove my hand from your mouth if you promise to not make a sound." The voice was eerily familiar. So familiar, in fact, that she shuddered at the sound of it. His smell was familiar, was well.

The man squeezed her harder, shaking her. "Do you promise?"

Quickly, her lungs constricting and her heart banging loudly at the lack of oxygen, she nodded.

He set her down. He removed his hand from her mouth.

Paloma continued to stare up the slope, seeing nothing, shuddering. She felt the man behind her. She did not want to turn around.

Finally, she turned her head to gaze back over her shoulder.

The face beneath the sombrero was the same one she'd seen through the balcony door at Ballantrae's saloon. Though one eye was eggshell white in the moonlight, and little black sores pocked his face, the face belonged to none other than Octavio La Paz.

He smiled, slitting his one good eye, the one the Apaches hadn't ruined with the end of a burning stick.

Paloma felt as though a black cloth had been thrown over the world.

Suddenly her knees were buckling and everything was quickly going dark.

★ ★ ★ ★ ★

Water splashed on her face. It was like a cold slap, and instantly she was awake, lifting her head from a hard stone floor and blinking the water out of her eyes.

"Oh, my god!" she cried, staring into the face again of Octavio La Paz now lit by the shunting light and shadows of small, orange flames. "It is you. But it can't be you. For the love of all the saints in Heaven, Octavio, I killed you!"

She wanted to flee but she was hog-tied, wrists tied to her ankles behind her, and lying on her side, one strap of her dress dangling to the stone floor.

"Keep your voice down," he said, scowling over his shoulder at the opening of what apparently was a cave they were in. "You want to wake the dead?" He turned back to her, chuckling. There was an insane look in his good eye.

She just stared at him, not quite sure she could believe she was actually staring at Octavio La Paz. Waves of terror rippled through her.

He smiled, touched the oozing ulcers on his cheeks. "Ahh . . . you wonder why I'm not dead. I came close. But fortunately my brother had an antidote to snakeroot. And old Apache remedy. The same one they used to cure the clap. A tincture of rattlesnake venom, a paste of crow's liver, and various herbs including shagbark brewed into a foul-smelling tea. It's not supposed to work without an Apache witch blessing it after hanging a coyote skull over a bowl of the stuff for twenty-four hours, during a full moon. Such a witch gave it to my brother as an offering, when she acquired religion. Apparently, it's rather common around Horsetooth for wives to poison their husbands in such a way. Evil bitches!"

La Paz chuckled.

He touched an ulcer just above his blind white eye, beneath the bandanna he wore over his hairless scalp. "Just what the doctor ordered, as they say. Still, your toxic poison fried my guts and caused these eruptions on my face. I may never be a man again," he snarled, taking her face in his hand and pinching her mouth into a small O. But at least I will have the satisfaction of having run you down, you little *puta* bitch."

He released her face and sat back on his rear, drawing his knees up and wrapping his arms around them.

The fire played across his skull-like, once-handsome face with its oozing ulcers and hollow jaws. "I'd stopped convulsing by the next morning. My anger fueled the healing, you see. I felt on top of the world by noon . . . despite a little weakness and nausea . . . so I saddled a fast horse and led another fast horse behind me, so I could switch off and catch up to you all the faster. Tracked you down, followed you and your friends from a distance, biding my time. I was still a little weak, and, blinded in one eye, I decided to wait until I could get you alone . . . and get close enough to do the killing most *efficiently.* Now, here we are at last."

"I don't understand," Paloma said, looking around at the small cavern and the crackling fire. Tack was strewn everywhere—saddles, blankets, bridles, saddlebags, cooking utensils. Outside, occasional rifle shots told her the battle for the money—*her* money—was still being waged on the slope below the knob. "Where are we?"

"This is Jorgenson's camp."

Paloma's jaw hinges loosened as she stared at La Paz's ghostly, silhouetted visage in shock.

"I came upon it just after the shooting started. Jorgenson and his men were distracted, so I thought I'd loot their lair here for the money. My money. Don't worry—it's not here," he said, when Paloma began casting her wide-eyed gaze around. "I went through all the gear. Jorgenson probably has the saddlebags with him. He, too, sniffed out your trail about half a day before you reached the saloon. As for me, I would have caught up to you, but I got waylaid by Apaches, same as your half-breed friend and the lawman, but I managed to run their gauntlet with far fewer injuries than before. I guess I learned from previous miseries. My friend Jorgenson must have been scouring the mountains for me when he saw you, recognized the pretty Mexican flower riding alone, and followed you to Ballantrae's saloon. Tell me, chiquita, how did he manage to get his hands on the money?"

Paloma sighed and stared at the floor, crestfallen. "Let's just say I was foolish."

"Oh, we can say that, all right. You were foolish from the start, my flower. It is well known by the old people that it's bad luck to poison a man. Especially one who loves you . . . as I did."

His gaze was fleetingly pensive, his good eye turning soft. Just as quickly it hardened, and his cheeks dimpled over his jaw joints. "And now, as soon as those men are done killing each other out there, and I have the money once again, I'm going to kill you slow."

He jerked a knife up from somewhere on his person and held it up over the fire, the light flashing off the long, wide blade. He laid the flat of the blade against the back of her naked right thigh—she gasped at the chill—and slid it slowly up to her exposed right buttock. "I'm going to savor every second of it."

He angled the point down between her thighs.

Chapter 21

Yakima hunkered Indian-style in a cleft beneath a cabin-sized boulder, the right-rear corner of which angled sharply back upon itself. The ground also sloped sharply back toward the corner of the rock. In this depression Yakima sat, as he'd been sitting for most of the night, waiting and listening.

He stared almost straight east. The eastern horizon had turned light green and salmon above a long, straight line of smoky white.

Dawn.

The moon had long since set.

Birds were chirping in the brush around him, flitting here and there, their wings flashing silver. A kangaroo rat sat a few feet away from him, in the purple shadow of another boulder, watching the half-breed suspiciously as it munched on the grass stem he held between his two front paws.

Suddenly, the rat dropped the grass and scuttled back behind the boulder, giving a little indignant screech and disappearing.

Yakima's back tightened.

He closed his hands around his Yellowboy's stock. Something had spooked the rat.

He'd killed three of the five outlaws so far, their bodies strewn a good distance apart across the slope. He wasn't sure the other two were still around but he'd decided to wait till daylight to find out. Many a scout had saddled a cloud because he hadn't been as patient as an Apache.

So he waited, ears pricked, hands slowly tightening around the breech and stock of the Yellowboy he held across the buckles of his shell belts. Several minutes later, he heard what the rat must have heard, the very quiet crackle of boots on gravel.

His heart quickened. The other two outlaws were still here. He was glad. He'd have hated to be wasting his time out here and to still have to track the last two even deeper into Mexico. He'd come this far, he wasn't giving up on retrieving the money for the bounty that MacElvy had promised.

If the lawman was still alive, that was. Or if his unceremonious meeting with that rock hadn't turned him into a blubbering idiot. Anyway, Yakima was getting the money back one way or another. He'd been through too much to let it go now.

Breathing slowly, calmly through his mouth, he waited.

Gradually, the soft crunch of boots on gravel grew louder.

Then one of those boots appeared in Yakima's field of vision. It was a badly scuffed, brown leather boot almost white with scuffmarks and dust, and soft as a moccasin. It had a high, undershot, Mexican-style heel. It bore the dark strap marks of a spur, which had wisely been removed so the jingle wouldn't give its wearer away.

The heel of the boot lifted and then the other boot appeared slightly ahead of the first one as well as a good six inches of a deerskin legging. This second, left boot was nearly identical to the right one—right down to the strap marks from the missing spur.

Both boots remained frozen in place for nearly a minute. Then the right boot moved slowly ahead of the left one as their owner moved from Yakima's left to his right, down the incline that was less steep here than elsewhere.

The left boot came slowly, gingerly down, followed by the right and then the left one again.

Yakima turned his rifle butt-out and slammed the butt as

hard as he could against the left boot. There was a clipped shriek as both feet were rammed out from beneath the man wearing the boots, and a sharp smack sounded as the boot owner's head struck the side of the boulder beneath which Yakima sat. The man dropped his rifle and fell on the ground— writhing and clutching at his left ankle.

Yakima hustled out from his hiding place and stood over the short, skinny Mexican, and frowned. The whole left side of the man's face looked like old rotting hamburger. It was swollen and pocked with little holes, and that ear was entirely gone. Not just shredded like MacElvy's ear, but entirely gone. In its place was what looked like semi-dry cherry jam.

The little Mexican looked up at Yakima, and stopped writhing. He looked so badly abused that Yakima hesitated to abuse him further.

He shouldn't have hesitated. A voice in his head told him so a half second before a man's voice outside of his head—behind him, in fact—also admonished him with: "Stop, big man, or I'll drill you right between the shoulders!"

Yakima swung around to see a tall American with a long, horsey face sheathed in pewter sideburns and dressed in gaudy Mexican garb holding a Winchester carbine on him, lifting his mouth corners in a delighted grin. He wore a large black-and-red sombrero, the thong drawn taut against his chin.

Saddlebags were draped over his left shoulder. Not just any saddlebags, but *the* saddlebags bulging with the army payroll loot. They were hard not to recognize.

"Drop the Yellowboy," the American said in a menacingly affable voice.

Yakima crouched and set the Yellowboy down on the ground by his right boot.

"Kick it away."

Yakima kicked it away. Then the American told him to shuck

his Colt with two fingers of his left hand, and toss that away, as well. Yakima didn't see that he had much choice. The American had him dead to rights from six feet away. He was most likely going to die, but he saw no reason to rush a likely awkward encounter with Saint Peter.

He tossed away the Colt.

"Miguel, stop moaning like a whipped dog and get up!" the American scolded the little Mexican.

Miguel did as he was told. Limping on his bad ankle and giving Yakima the hairy eyeball, he picked up his own rifle and strode daintily back to stand beside the tall American in the fancily stitched garb of a Mexican vaquero.

Yakima said, "Jorgenson?"

"That's right. You?"

"Yakima Henry."

The morning light grew, reflected in Jorgenson's pale blue eyes beneath the broad brim of his fancy sombrero, as those eyes raked Yakima up and down. "Half-breed."

Yakima didn't say anything.

"I've heard the name. You carry a reputation, Henry." Jorgenson rolled his eyes around as though to take in the entire slope on which they'd all spent the night exchanging lead. "I see why."

"Shoot him," said little Miguel, standing daintily on his no-doubt-broken ankle, stretching his lips back from his large, white teeth as he snarled up at Yakima, who towered over him. "Shoot him now! Why all the talk?"

"Don't be so hasty, Miguel. This man did us a favor."

Miguel scowled incredulously up at the tall American. "What favor?"

"He whittled our herd down considerably." Jorgenson smiled down at the saddlebags. "That makes more for us. Or . . . more for me, I should say."

Miguel frowned.

Keeping his smiling eyes on Yakima, Jorgenson swung his rifle across his belly toward Miguel.

Miguel had just opened his mouth to yell, when Jorgenson's rifle spoke. Miguel stumbled backward, dropping his rifle and clutching his belly with both hands. He fell and lay writhing, drawing both knees to his ruined middle, gasping through gritted teeth. Jorgenson put him out of his misery with a bullet to his left temple.

Yakima lunged for Jorgenson but the American was ready for that. He quickly jerked his rifle back toward the half-breed, stepping slowly backward, that maddeningly affable smile on his face.

"Make a deal with ya," Jorgenson said.

"Oh, yeah?"

"You throw in with me, I'll give you a third."

Yakima scowled at him, curious.

Jorgenson shrugged. "A man needs a partner. Me? I'm fresh out."

"That's what greed will do to a man," Yakima opined. "And you wouldn't be able to trust me any more than you trusted them"—he glanced at little Miguel—"or they trusted you."

A rifle belched somewhere behind Jorgenson.

The American's eyes snapped wide and he lurched sideways with a gasp. He swung heavily around, his rifle sagging in his arms, and then another shot rang out.

Jorgenson stumbled backward across little Miguel and fell to his butt, cursing like a gut-shot coyote, clamping both hands over the hole in his upper-left chest, from which frothy blood spurted.

Another man appeared on the slope above him. A Mexican in black leather leggings and with a red bandanna showing beneath the brim of his green, steeple-crowned sombrero. He wore a green sash above his pistol belt, and a long, black leather duster hung to the heels of his silver-tipped, black boots. He laughed as he moved down the slope, holding his rifle butt against his hip, aiming the barrel at Yakima. As he drew near, Yakima saw the sores on his face, and the one blind eye.

"Welcome to the party!" Yakima said, beckoning to the man with exaggerated vehemence. "The more the merrier!"

"Gracias, amigo," the newcomer said. "I don't mind if I do. Kindly keep away from your weapons or I will kill you now rather than later." He stood over the writhing form of Jorgenson, who glared up at him, his sombrero smashed flat against the ground behind him. "You devil! I thought she killed you!"

Yakima scowled at the newcomer with the diseased-looking face, and then he laughed. "Well, I'll be damned," he said in exasperation. "Here we've all been blamin' the innocent Miss Paloma for your demise, La Paz. But she didn't kill you at all, did she?"

Yakima laughed insanely. He truly thought he was going mad. Everything just seemed funny to him now. Like it was all such a big, insanely funny joke that he didn't even really mind that a big part of it was on him.

Including when Jorgenson glared up at Octavio La Paz and said, "A devil is what you are, La Paz. A double-crossing devil!"

"Don't call me that," La Paz said, glowering, his pale cheeks reddening with anger. "I don't like to be called a devil. It casts doubt on a man's character and brings bad luck to his family!"

He calmly drilled a rifle round through Jorgenson's forehead. Jorgenson's legs twitched across the slumped body of little Miguel and then the American outlaw rolled onto his side, and died.

Keeping his rifle aimed at Yakima, Octavio La Paz walked over to Jorgenson and crouched to pick up the saddlebags, which he brushed off and draped over his left shoulder.

"Now," he said to Yakima. "What to do about you . . ."

As if in reply to his question, another rifle blasted.

It blew La Paz's sombrero off his head, revealing the red, blood-stained bandanna stretched across the top of his scalped head. La Paz screamed and wheeled to his left, and the rifle barked twice more. Both slugs slammed into the outlaw's chest, throwing him straight backwards off little Miguel and Jorgenson.

He shook a boot once, gave a long, ragged sigh, blinking his good eye, and then lay still.

Behind the boulder on Yakima's left, hooves clomped. The sun was up now, and it shone salmon on the dust that rose as the brown horse came into view along the base of the copper-colored knob. MacElvy rode lazily in the saddle, extending his rifle out one-handed, aiming the barrel at the three bodies clumped to Yakima's right.

"Good morning," the lawman said, grinning and swinging heavily down from his saddle.

He moved down the slope, kicking up dust with every heavy step. He looked pale and haggard, his face and ear the same mess as before, but otherwise no worse for the wear. He still wore the bandanna like a patch across his cut eye.

"Damn," Yakima said, unable to keep from loosing a few more bars of skeptical laughter. "I didn't think I'd ever say this, MacElvy, but I sure am glad to see you."

The half-breed moved to retrieve his rifle.

"Not so fast, Yakima."

CHAPTER 22

Yakima stopped, looked at MacElvy. The lawman had his Winchester aimed at Yakima's belly. MacElvy's eyes were hard and cold.

Yakima chuckled giddily. "You ain't a lawman at all, are you?"

"Of course I am. The girl was lyin' through her pretty teeth, as usual. Just now, though, I decided to quit." MacElvy walked over to the pile of bloody dead men. Keeping his rifle trained on Yakima, he crouched and picked up the saddlebags. "I been through too damn much to give this loot up now."

Yakima chuckled.

MacElvy draped the saddlebags over his shoulder. "What's so funny?"

"You are. All of it is."

"All of what?"

"All of this, you damn fool."

MacElvy's broad face reddened. "You ain't gonna be thinkin' it's so funny after I kill you."

Yakima laughed again. "You ain't gonna kill me."

"Oh, no?" It was the outlaw lawman's turn to laugh. "Why not?"

"Because she's gonna kill you first!"

MacElvy's eyes widened. He stared blankly past Yakima. The outlaw turned slowly, tensely around in time to see Paloma just before she shot him.

The woman strode down the slope from the base of the knob.

She was holding a pistol in both hands—MacElvy's own Remington. Smoke licked up out of the barrel. Her long, black hair blew around her pretty head in the rising, hot, dry, morning wind.

Dust lifted around her bare feet and the leg exposed by the long tear in her skirt. One strap of the dress dangled down her arm. The filthy dress looked as though it was about to fall right off her voluptuous figure.

She said nothing but only kept her cool, dark eyes as well as the cocked Remington's barrel on Yakima. She crouched and picked up the blood-splattered saddlebags, slung them over her shoulder.

She regarded Yakima blankly for a time, and then canted her head to one side and arched her left brow. "Join me?"

Yakima looked at the cocked gun in her hand.

"We could have a good time together," she said. "This is a lot of money. We could go into business together."

"The confidence-game business?"

"Why not? I'm good at it. I've had a lot of practice over the years. A girl needs some way of making a living, and I never was much in to doing it on my back."

"Sure had me fooled."

She hardened her voice with frustration and urgency. "Join me!"

"Nah. I don't think so, Paloma."

She pursed her lips, nodded slowly, regretfully. Yakima watched the pistol in her hands, felt his belly tighten in anticipation of the bullet. She held the gun on him for close to another minute, and then she raised the barrel and depressed the hammer.

Yakima loosed a slow, relieved breath.

"Good-bye, Yakima," she said, backing away up the slope,

toward where MacElvy's horse stood, watching them both warily.

He pinched his hat brim to her.

She continued on up the slope. She grabbed the brown's reins, slung the saddlebags over her back, and climbed into the saddle.

She tossed her head at Yakima, and rode off along the base of the knob, heading east and then most likely south toward the Gulf of California. She stopped the horse suddenly, and smiled over her shoulder at the half-breed. "You know what?"

"No, I don't know much of anything."

"Well, I know something. I know that we will meet up again someday, my big, handsome half-breed friend. And I think we will have more fun than before."

Yakima watched her put the horse into a rocking-chair canter and dwindle to a brown blur pulling a soft, tan dust cloud along the base of the knob.

He sighed and said, "I sure hope not."

Then he gathered his weapons and headed on down the mountain in search of his horse and a trail. Any trail. To anywhere.

It didn't much matter.

ABOUT THE AUTHOR

Bestselling western novelist **Peter Brandvold** has penned over seventy fast-action westerns under his own name and his penname, **Frank Leslie.** He is the author of the ever-popular .45-Caliber books featuring Cuno Massey as well as the Lou Prophet and Yakima Henry novels. Recently, under the Frank Leslie name, he started the Revenger series featuring Mike Sartain. Head honcho at Mean Pete Publishing, publisher of lightning-fast western ebooks, he lives in western Minnesota with his dog. Visit his website at www.peterbrandvold.com. Follow his blog at www.peterbrandvold.blogspot.com.